Three Tales of Magic and Mischief

SOME OTHER BOOKS
BY ROALD DAHL

James and the Giant Peach
Charlie and the Chocolate Factory
The Magic Finger
Fantastic Mr Fox
Charlie and the Great Glass Elevator
Danny the Champion of the World
The Enormous Crocodile
The Twits
Revolting Rhymes
The BFG
Dirty Beasts
Boy
The Giraffe and the Pelly and Me
Going Solo
Rhyme Stew
Esio Trot
The Minpins
My Year
Revolting Recipes
Even More Revolting Recipes
Completely Revolting Recipes

Roald Dahl

illustrated by Quentin Blake

Three Tales of Magic and Mischief

JONATHAN CAPE
LONDON

ROALD DAHL: THREE TALES OF MAGIC AND MISCHIEF
A JONATHAN CAPE BOOK 978 0 857 55073 6

Published in Great Britain by Jonathan Cape,
an imprint of Random House Children's Publishers UK
A Random House Group Company

GEORGE'S MARVELLOUS MEDICINE first published by Jonathan Cape in 1981
MATILDA first published by Jonathan Cape in 1988
THE WITCHES first published by Jonathan Cape in 1983

This combined edition published 2012

1 3 5 7 9 10 8 6 4 2

The author and publishers are grateful to the Trustees for the Estate of Dylan Thomas for permission to quote lines from "In Country Sleep", from The Poems by Dylan Thomas, published by J.M Dent & Sons.

Set in Bembo

RANDOM HOUSE CHILDREN'S PUBLISHERS UK
61–63 Uxbridge Road, London W5 5SA

www.**randomhousechildrens**.co.uk
www.**randomhouse**.co.uk

Addresses for companies within The Random House Group Limited can be found at:
www.randomhouse.co.uk/offices.htm

THE RANDOM HOUSE GROUP Limited Reg. No. 954009

A CIP catalogue record for this book is available from the British Library.

Printed and bound in Great Britain by Clays Ltd, St Ives plc

George's Marvellous Medicine

This book is for doctors everywhere

Contents

Grandma	9
The Marvellous Plan	20
George Begins to Make the Medicine	25
Animal Pills	35
The Cook-up	42
Brown Paint	45
Grandma Gets the Medicine	48
The Brown Hen	60
The Pig, the Bullocks, the Sheep, the Pony and the Nanny-goat	69
A Crane for Grandma	80
Mr Kranky's Great Idea	85
Marvellous Medicine Number Two	91
Marvellous Medicine Number Three	97
Marvellous Medicine Number Four	101
Goodbye Grandma	104

WARNING TO READERS: Do not try to make George's Marvellous Medicine yourselves at home. It could be dangerous.

Grandma

"I'm going shopping in the village," George's mother said to George on Saturday morning. "So be a good boy and don't get up to mischief."

This was a silly thing to say to a small boy at any time. It immediately made him wonder what sort of mischief he might get up to.

"And don't forget to give Grandma her medicine at eleven o'clock," the mother said. Then out she went, closing the back door behind her.

Grandma, who was dozing in her chair by the window, opened one wicked little eye and said, "Now you heard what your mother said, George. Don't forget my medicine."

"No, Grandma," George said.

"And just try to behave yourself for once while she's away."

"Yes, Grandma," George said.

George was bored to tears. He didn't have a brother or a sister. His father was a farmer and the farm they lived on was miles away from anywhere, so there were never any children to play with. He was tired of staring at pigs and hens and cows and sheep. He was especially tired of having to live in the same house as that grizzly old grunion of a Grandma. Looking after her all by himself was hardly the most exciting way to spend a Saturday morning.

"You can make me a nice cup of tea for a start," Grandma said to George. "That'll keep you out of mischief for a few minutes."

"Yes, Grandma," George said.

George couldn't help disliking Grandma. She was a selfish grumpy old woman. She had pale brown teeth and a small puckered up mouth like a dog's bottom.

"How much sugar in your tea today, Grandma?" George asked her.

"One spoon," she said. "And no milk."

Most grandmothers are lovely, kind, helpful old ladies, but not this one. She spent all day and every day sitting in her chair by the window, and she was always complaining, grousing, grouching, grumbling, griping about something or other. Never once, even on her best days, had she smiled at George and said, "Well, how are you this morning, George?" or "Why don't you and I have a game of Snakes and Ladders?" or "How was school today?" She didn't seem to care about other people, only about herself. She was a miserable old grouch.

George went into the kitchen and made Grandma a cup of tea with a teabag. He put one spoon of sugar in it and no milk. He stirred the sugar well and carried the cup into the living-room.

Grandma sipped the tea. "It's not sweet enough," she said. "Put more sugar in."

George took the cup back to the kitchen and added another spoonful of sugar. He stirred it again and carried it carefully in to Grandma.

"Where's the saucer?" she said. "I won't have a cup without a saucer."

George fetched her a saucer.

"And what about a teaspoon, if you please?"

"I've stirred it for you, Grandma. I stirred it well."

"I'll stir my own tea, thank you very much," she said. "Fetch me a teaspoon."

George fetched her a teaspoon.

When George's mother or father were home, Grandma never ordered George about like this. It was only when she had him on her own that she began treating him badly.

"You know what's the matter with you?" the old woman said, staring at George over the rim of the teacup with those bright wicked little eyes. "You're *growing* too fast. Boys who grow too fast become stupid and lazy."

"But I can't help it if I'm growing fast, Grandma," George said.

"Of course you can," she snapped. "Growing's a nasty childish habit."

"But we *have* to grow, Grandma. If we didn't grow, we'd never be grown-ups."

"Rubbish, boy, rubbish," she said. "Look at me. Am I growing? Certainly not."

"But you did once, Grandma."

"Only *very little*," the old woman answered. "I gave up growing when I was extremely small, along with all the other nasty childish habits like laziness and disobedience and greed and sloppiness and untidiness and stupidity. You haven't given up any of these things, have you?"

"I'm still only a little boy, Grandma."

"You're eight years old," she snorted. "That's old enough to know better. If you don't stop growing soon, it'll be too late."

"Too late for what, Grandma?"

"It's ridiculous," she went on. "You're nearly as tall as me already."

George took a good look at Grandma. She certainly was a *very tiny* person. Her legs were so short she had to have a footstool to put her feet on, and her head only came half-way up the back of the armchair.

"Daddy says it's fine for a man to be tall," George said.

"Don't listen to your daddy," Grandma said. "Listen to me."

"But how do I stop myself growing?" George asked her.

"Eat less chocolate," Grandma said.

"Does chocolate make you grow?"

"It makes you grow the *wrong way*," she

snapped. "Up instead of down."

Grandma sipped some tea but never took her eyes from the little boy who stood before her. "Never grow up," she said. "Always down."

"Yes, Grandma."

"And stop eating chocolate. Eat cabbage instead."

"Cabbage! Oh no, I don't like cabbage," George said.

"It's not what you like or what you don't like," Grandma snapped. "It's what's good for you that counts. From now on, you must eat cabbage three times a day. Mountains of cabbage! And if it's got caterpillars in it, so much the better!"

"Owch," George said.

"Caterpillars give you brains," the old woman said.

"Mummy washes them down the sink," George said.

"Mummy's as stupid as you are," Grandma said.

"Cabbage doesn't taste of anything without a few boiled caterpillars in it. Slugs, too."

"Not *slugs*!" George cried out. "I couldn't eat slugs!"

"Whenever I see a live slug on a piece of lettuce," Grandma said, "I gobble it up quick before it crawls away. Delicious." She squeezed her lips together tight so that her mouth became a tiny wrinkled hole. "Delicious," she said again. "Worms and slugs and beetley bugs. You don't know what's good for you."

"You're joking, Grandma."

"I never joke," she said. "Beetles are perhaps best of all. They go *crunch*!"

"Grandma! That's beastly!"

The old hag grinned, showing those pale brown teeth. "Sometimes, if you're lucky," she said, "you get a beetle inside the stem of a stick of celery. That's what I like."

"Grandma! How *could* you?"

"You find all sorts of nice things in sticks of raw celery," the old woman went on. "Sometimes it's earwigs."

"I don't want to hear about it!" cried George.

"A big fat earwig is very tasty," Grandma said, licking her lips. "But you've got to be very quick, my dear, when you put one of those in your mouth. It has a pair of sharp nippers on its back end and if it grabs your tongue with those, it never lets go. So you've got to bite the earwig first, *chop chop*, before it bites you."

George started edging towards the door. He wanted to get as far away as possible from this filthy old woman.

"You're trying to get away from me, aren't you," she said, pointing a finger straight at George's face. "You're trying to get away from Grandma."

Little George stood by the door staring at the old hag in the chair. She stared back at him.

Could it be, George wondered, that she was a witch? He had always thought witches were only in fairy tales, but now he was not so sure.

"Come closer to me, little boy," she said, beckoning to him with a horny finger. "Come closer to me and I will tell you *secrets*."

George didn't move.

Grandma didn't move either.

"I know a great many secrets," she said, and suddenly she smiled. It was a thin icy smile, the kind a snake might make just before it bites you. "Come over here to Grandma and she'll whisper secrets to you."

George took a step backwards, edging closer to the door.

"You mustn't be frightened of your old Grandma," she said, smiling that icy smile.

George took another step backwards.

"Some of us," she said, and all at once she was leaning forward in her chair and whispering in a throaty sort of voice George had never heard her use before. "Some of us," she said, "have magic powers that can twist the creatures of this earth into wondrous shapes . . . "

A tingle of electricity flashed down the length of George's spine. He began to feel frightened.

"Some of us," the old woman went on, "have fire on our tongues and sparks in our bellies and wizardry in the tips of our fingers . . .

"Some of us know secrets that would make your hair stand straight up on end and your eyes pop out of their sockets . . . " George wanted to run away, but his feet seemed stuck to the floor.

"We know how to make your nails drop off and teeth grow out of your fingers instead."

George began to tremble. It was her face that frightened him most of all, the frosty smile, the brilliant unblinking eyes.

"We know how to have you wake up in the morning with a long tail coming out from behind you."

"Grandma!" he cried out. "Stop!"

"We know secrets, my dear, about dark places where dark things live and squirm and slither all over each other . . ."

George made a dive for the door.

"It doesn't matter how far you run," he heard her saying, "you won't ever get away . . ."

George ran into the kitchen, slamming the door behind him.

The Marvellous Plan

George sat himself down at the table in the kitchen. He was shaking a little. Oh, how he hated Grandma! He really *hated* that horrid old witchy woman. And all of a sudden he had a tremendous urge to *do something* about her. Something *whopping*. Something *absolutely terrific*. A *real shocker*. A sort of explosion. He wanted to blow away the witchy smell that hung about her in the next room. He may have been only eight years old but he was a brave little boy. He was ready to take this old woman on.

"I'm not going to be frightened by *her*," he said softly to himself. But he *was* frightened. And that's why he wanted suddenly to explode her away.

Well . . . not quite away. But he did want to shake the old woman up a bit.

Very well, then. What should it be, this whopping terrific exploding shocker for Grandma?

He would have liked to put a firework banger under her chair but he didn't have one.

He would have liked to put a long green snake down the back of her dress but he didn't have a long green snake.

He would have liked to put six big black rats in the room with her and lock the door but he didn't have six big black rats.

As George sat there pondering this interesting problem, his eye fell upon the bottle of Grandma's brown medicine standing on the sideboard. Rotten stuff it seemed to be. Four times a day a large spoonful of it was shovelled into her mouth and it didn't do her the slightest bit of good. She was always just as horrid after she'd had it as she'd been before. The whole point of medicine, surely, was to make a person better. If it didn't do that, then it was quite useless.

So-ho! Thought George suddenly. *Ah-ha! Ho-hum!* I know exactly what I'll do. I shall make her a new medicine, one that is so strong and so fierce and so fantastic it will either cure her completely or blow off the top of her head. I'll make her a *magic medicine*, a medicine no doctor in the world has ever made before.

George looked at the kitchen clock. It said five past ten. There was nearly an hour left before Grandma's next dose was due at eleven.

"Here we go, then!" cried George,

jumping up from the table. "A magic medicine it shall be!"

"So give me a bug and a jumping flea,
Give me two snails and lizards three,
And a slimy squiggler from the sea,
And the poisonous sting of a bumblebee,
And the juice from the fruit of the ju-jube tree,
And the powdered bone of a wombat's knee.
And one hundred other things as well
Each with a rather nasty smell.
I'll stir them up, I'll boil them long,
A mixture tough, a mixture strong.
And then, heigh-ho, and down it goes,

A nice big spoonful (hold your nose)
Just gulp it down and have no fear.
'How do you like it, Granny dear?'
Will she go pop? Will she explode?
Will she go flying down the road?
Will she go poof in a puff of smoke?
Start fizzing like a can of Coke?
Who knows? Not I. Let's wait and see.
(I'm glad it's neither you nor me.)
Oh Grandma, if you only knew
What I have got in store for you!"

George Begins to Make the Medicine

George took an enormous saucepan out of the cupboard and placed it on the kitchen table.

"George!" came the shrill voice from the next room. "What are you doing?"

"Nothing, Grandma," he called out.

"You needn't think I can't hear you just because you closed the door! You're rattling the saucepans!"

"I'm just tidying the kitchen, Grandma."

Then there was silence.

George had absolutely no doubts whatsoever about how he was going to make his famous medicine. He wasn't going to fool about wondering whether to put in a little bit of this or a little bit of that. Quite simply, he was going to put in EVERYTHING he could find. There would be no messing about, no hesitating, no wondering whether a particular thing would knock the old girl sideways or not. The rule would be this: whatever he saw, if it was runny or powdery or gooey, in it went.

Nobody had ever made a medicine like that before. If it didn't actually cure Grandma, then it would anyway cause some exciting results. It would be worth watching.

George decided to work his way round the various rooms one at a time and see what they had to offer.

He would go first to the bathroom. There are always lots of funny things in a bathroom. So upstairs he went, carrying the enormous two-handled saucepan before him.

In the bathroom, he gazed longingly at the famous and dreaded medicine cupboard. But

he didn't go near it. It was the only thing in the entire house he was forbidden to touch. He had made solemn promises to his parents about this and he wasn't going to break them. There were things in there, they had told him, that could actually kill a person, and although he was out to give Grandma a pretty fiery mouthful, he didn't really want a dead body on his hands. George put the saucepan on the floor and went to work.

Number one was a bottle labelled

GOLDENGLOSS HAIR SHAMPOO. He emptied it into the pan. "That ought to wash her tummy nice and clean," he said.

He took a full tube of TOOTHPASTE and squeezed out the whole lot of it in one long worm. "Maybe that will brighten up those horrid brown teeth of hers," he said.

There was an aerosol can of SUPERFOAM SHAVING SOAP belonging to his father. George loved playing with aerosols. He pressed the button and kept his finger on it until there was nothing left. A wonderful mountain of white foam built up in the giant saucepan.

With his fingers, he scooped out the contents of a jar of VITAMIN ENRICHED

FACE CREAM.

In went a small bottle of scarlet NAIL VARNISH. "If the toothpaste doesn't clean her teeth," George said, "then this will paint them as red as roses."

He found another jar of creamy stuff labelled HAIR REMOVER. SMEAR IT ON YOUR LEGS, it said, AND ALLOW TO REMAIN FOR FIVE MINUTES. George tipped it all into the saucepan.

There was a bottle with yellow stuff inside it called DISHWORTH'S FAMOUS DANDRUFF CURE. In it went.

There was something called BRILLIDENT FOR CLEANING FALSE TEETH. It was a white powder. In that went, too.

He found another aerosol can, NEVERMORE PONKING DEODORANT SPRAY, GUARANTEED, it said, TO KEEP AWAY UNPLEASANT BODY SMELLS FOR A WHOLE DAY. "She could use plenty of that," George said as he sprayed the entire canful into the saucepan.

LIQUID PARAFFIN, the next one was called. It was a big bottle. He hadn't the faintest idea what it did to you, but he poured it in anyway.

That, he thought, looking around him was

about all from the bathroom.

On his mother's dressing-table in the bedroom, George found yet another lovely aerosol can. It was called HELGA'S HAIRSET. HOLD TWELVE INCHES AWAY FROM THE HAIR AND SPRAY LIGHTLY. He squirted the whole lot into the saucepan. He did enjoy squirting these aerosols.

There was a bottle of perfume called FLOWERS OF TURNIPS. It smelled of old cheese. In it went.

And in, too, went a large round box of POWDER. It was called PINK PLASTER. There was a powder-puff on top and he threw that in as well for luck.

He found a couple of LIPSTICKS. He pulled the greasy red things out of their little cases and added them to the mixture.

The bedroom had nothing more to offer, so George carried the enormous saucepan downstairs again and trotted into the laundry-room where the shelves were full of all kinds of household items.

The first one he took down was a large box of SUPERWHITE FOR AUTOMATIC WASHING-MACHINES. DIRT, it said, WILL DISAPPEAR LIKE MAGIC. George

didn't know whether Grandma was automatic or not, but she was certainly a dirty old woman. "So she'd better have it all," he said, tipping in the whole boxful.

Then there was a big tin of WAXWELL FLOOR POLISH. IT REMOVES FILTH AND FOUL MESSES FROM YOUR

FLOOR AND LEAVES EVERYTHING SHINY BRIGHT, it said. George scooped the orange-coloured waxy stuff out of the tin and plonked it into the pan.

There was a round cardboard carton labelled FLEA POWDER FOR DOGS. KEEP WELL AWAY FROM THE DOG'S FOOD, it said, BECAUSE THIS POWDER, IF EATEN, WILL MAKE THE DOG EXPLODE. "Good," said George, pouring it all into the saucepan.

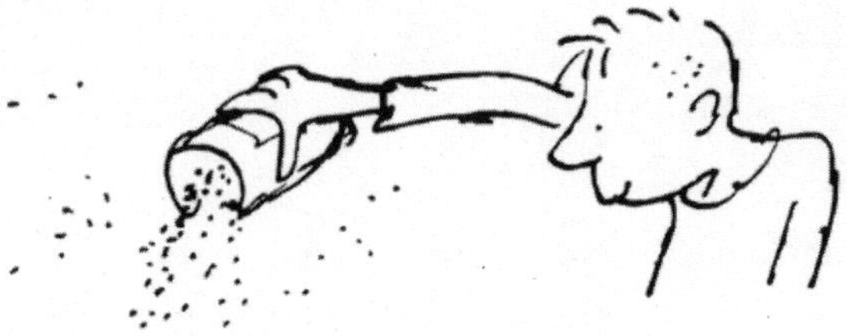

He found a box of CANARY SEED on the shelf. "Perhaps it'll make the old bird sing," he said, and in it went.

Next, George explored the box with shoe-cleaning materials – brushes and tins and dusters. Well now, he thought, Grandma's medicine is brown, so my medicine must also be brown or she'll smell a rat. The way to colour it, he decided, would be with BROWN SHOE POLISH. The large tin he chose was labelled DARK TAN. Splendid. He scooped it all out with an old spoon and plopped it into the pan. He would stir it up later.

On his way back to the kitchen, George saw a bottle of GIN standing on the sideboard. Grandma was very fond of gin. She was allowed to have a small nip of it every evening. Now he would give her a treat. He would pour in the whole bottle. He did.

Back in the kitchen, George put the huge saucepan on the table and went over to the cupboard that served as a larder. The shelves were bulging with bottles and jars of every sort. He chose the following and emptied them one by one into the saucepan:

A TIN OF CURRY POWDER
A TIN OF MUSTARD POWDER
A BOTTLE OF "EXTRA HOT"
CHILLI SAUCE
A TIN OF BLACK PEPPERCORNS

A BOTTLE OF HORSERADISH SAUCE

"There!" he said aloud. "That should do it!"

"George!" came the screechy voice from the next room. "Who are you talking to in there? What are you up to?"

"Nothing, Grandma, absolutely nothing," he called back.

"Is it time for my medicine yet?"

"No, Grandma, not for about half an hour."

"Well, just see you don't forget it."

"I won't, Grandma," George answered. "I promise I won't."

Animal Pills

At this point, George suddenly had an extra good wheeze. Although the medicine cupboard in the house was forbidden ground, what about the medicines his father kept on the shelf in the shed next to the henhouse? The animal medicines?

What about those?

Nobody had ever told him he mustn't touch them.

Let's face it, George said to himself, hairspray and shaving-cream and shoe-polish are all very well and they will no doubt cause some splendid explosions inside the old geezer, but what the magic mixture now needs is a touch of the real stuff, real pills and real tonics, to give it punch and muscle.

George picked up the heavy three-quarters full saucepan and carried it out of the back door. He crossed the farmyard and headed straight for the shed alongside the henhouse. He knew his father wouldn't be there. He was out haymaking in one of the meadows.

George entered the dusty old shed and put the saucepan on the bench. Then he looked up at the medicine shelf. There were five big bottles there. Two were full of pills, two were full of runny stuff and one was full of powder.

"I'll use them all," George said. "Grandma needs them. Boy, does she need them!"

The first bottle he took down contained an orange-coloured powder. The label said, FOR CHICKENS WITH FOUL PEST, HEN GRIPE, SORE BEAKS, GAMMY LEGS, COCKERELITIS, EGG TROUBLE, BROODINESS OR LOSS OF FEATHERS. MIX ONE SPOONFUL ONLY WITH EACH BUCKET OF FEED.

"Well," George said aloud to himself as he tipped in the whole bottleful, "the old bird won't be losing any feathers after she's had a dose of this."

The next bottle he took down had about five hundred gigantic purple pills in it. FOR HORSES WITH HOARSE THROATS, it said on the label. THE HOARSE-THROATED HORSE SHOULD SUCK ONE PILL TWICE A DAY.

"Grandma may not have a hoarse throat," George said, "but she's certainly got a sharp tongue. Maybe they'll cure that instead." Into the saucepan went the five hundred gigantic purple pills.

Then there was a bottle of thick yellowish liquid. FOR COWS, BULLS AND BULLOCKS, the label said. WILL CURE COW POX, COW MANGE, CRUMPLED HORNS, BAD BREATH IN BULLS, EARACHE, TOOTHACHE, HEADACHE, HOOFACHE, TAILACHE AND SORE UDDERS.

"That grumpy old cow in the living-room has every one of those rotten illnesses," George said. "She'll need it all." With a sop and a gurgle, the yellow liquid splashed into the now nearly full saucepan.

The next bottle contained a brilliant red liquid. SHEEPDIP, it said on the label. FOR SHEEP WITH SHEEP ROT AND FOR GETTING RID OF TICKS AND FLEAS. MIX ONE SPOONFUL IN ONE GALLON OF WATER AND SLOSH IT OVER THE SHEEP. CAUTION, DO NOT MAKE THE MIXTURE ANY STRONGER OR THE WOOL WILL FALL OUT AND THE

ANIMAL WILL BE NAKED.

"By gum," said George, "how I'd love to walk in and slosh it all over old Grandma and watch the ticks and fleas go jumping off her. But I can't. I mustn't. So she'll have to drink it instead." He poured the bright red medicine into the saucepan.

The last bottle on the shelf was full of pale green pills. PIG PILLS, the label announced. FOR PIGS WITH PORK PRICKLES, TENDER TROTTERS, BRISTLE BLIGHT AND SWINE SICKNESS. GIVE ONE PILL PER DAY. IN SEVERE CASES TWO PILLS MAY BE GIVEN, BUT MORE THAN THAT WILL MAKE THE PIG ROCK AND ROLL.

"Just the stuff," said George, "for that miserable old pig back there in the house. She'll need a very big dose." He tipped all the green pills, hundreds and hundreds of them, into the saucepan.

There was an old stick lying on the bench that had been used for stirring paint. George picked it up and started to stir his marvellous concoction. The mixture was as thick as cream, and as he stirred and stirred, many wonderful colours rose up from the depths and blended together, pinks, blues, greens, yellows and browns.

George went on stirring until it was all well mixed, but even so there were still hundreds of pills lying on the bottom that hadn't melted. And there was his mother's splendid powder-puff floating on the surface. "I shall have to boil it all up," George said. "One good quick boil on the stove is all it needs." And with that he staggered back towards the house with the enormous heavy saucepan.

On the way, he passed the garage, so he went in to see if he could find any other interesting things. He added the following:

Half a pint of ENGINE OIL – to keep Grandma's engine going smoothly.

Some ANTI-FREEZE – to keep her radiator from freezing up in the winter.

A handful of GREASE – to grease her creaking joints.

Then back to the kitchen.

The Cook-up

In the kitchen, George put the saucepan on the stove and turned up the gas flame underneath it as high as it would go.

"George!" came the awful voice from the next room. "It's time for my medicine!"

"Not yet, Grandma," George called back. "There's still twenty minutes before eleven o'clock."

"What mischief are you up to in there now?" Granny screeched. "I hear noises."

George thought it best not to answer this one. He found a long wooden spoon in a kitchen drawer and began stirring hard. The stuff in the pot got hotter and hotter.

Soon the marvellous mixture began to froth and foam. A rich blue smoke, the colour of peacocks, rose from the surface of the liquid, and fiery fearsome smell filled the kitchen. It made George choke and splutter. It was a smell unlike any he had smelled before. It was a brutal and bewitching smell, spicy and staggering, fierce and frenzied, full of wizardry and magic. Whenever he got a whiff of it up his nose, firecrackers went off in his skull and electric prickles ran along the backs of his legs. It was wonderful to stand there stirring this amazing mixture and to watch it smoking blue and bubbling and frothing and foaming as though it were alive. At one point, he could have sworn he saw bright sparks flashing in the swirling foam.

And suddenly, George found himself dancing around the steaming pot, chanting strange words that came into his head out of nowhere:

"Fiery broth and witch's brew
Foamy froth and riches blue
Fume and spume and spoondrift spray
Fizzle swizzle shout hooray

Watch it sloshing, swashing, sploshing
Hear it hissing, squishing, spissing
Grandma better start to pray."

Brown Paint

George turned off the heat under the saucepan. He must leave plenty of time for it to cool down.

When all the steam and froth had gone away, he peered into the giant pan to see what colour the great medicine now was. It was a deep and brilliant blue.

"It needs more brown in it." George said. "It simply must be brown or she'll get suspicious."

George ran outside and dashed into his father's toolshed where all the paints were kept. There was a row of cans on the shelf, all colours, black, green, red, pink, white and brown. He reached for the can of brown. The label said simply DARK BROWN GLOSS PAINT ONE QUART. He took a screwdriver and prised off the lid. The can was three-quarters full. He rushed it back to the kitchen. He poured the whole lot into the saucepan. The saucepan was now full to the brim. Very gently, George stirred the paint into the mixture with the long wooden spoon. Ah-ha! It was all turning brown! A lovely rich creamy brown!

"Where's that medicine of mine, boy?!" came the voice from the living-room. "You're forgetting me! You're doing it on purpose! I shall tell your mother!"

"I'm not forgetting you, Grandma," George called back. "I'm thinking of you all the time. But there are still ten minutes to go."

"You're a nasty little maggot!" the voice screeched back. "You're a lazy and disobedient little worm, and you're growing too fast."

George fetched the bottle of Grandma's real medicine from the sideboard. He took out the cork and tipped it all down the sink. He then filled the bottle with his own magic mixture by

dipping a small jug into the saucepan and using it as a pourer. He replaced the cork.

Had it cooled down enough yet? Not quite.

He held the bottle under the cold tap for a couple of minutes. The label came off in the wet but that didn't matter. He dried the bottle with a dishcloth.

All was now ready!

This was it!

The great moment had arrived!

"Medicine time, Grandma!" he called out.

"I should hope so, too," came the grumpy reply.

The silver tablespoon in which the medicine was always given lay ready on the kitchen sideboard. George picked it up.

Holding the spoon in one hand and the bottle in the other, he advanced into the living-room.

Grandma Gets the Medicine

Grandma sat hunched in her chair by the window. The wicked little eyes followed George closely as he crossed the room towards her.

"You're late," she snapped.

"I don't think I am, Grandma."

"Don't interrupt me in the middle of a sentence!" she shouted.

"But you'd finished your sentence, Grandma."

"There you go again!" she cried. "Always interrupting and arguing. You really are a tiresome little boy. What's the time?"

"It's exactly eleven o'clock, Grandma."

"You're lying as usual. Stop talking so much and give me my medicine. Shake the bottle first. Then pour it into the spoon and make sure it's a whole spoonful."

"Are you going to gulp it all down in one go?" George asked her. "Or will you sip it?"

"What I do is none of your business," the old woman said. "Fill the spoon."

As George removed the cork and began very slowly to pour the thick brown stuff into the spoon, he couldn't help thinking back upon all the mad and marvellous things that had gone into the making of this crazy stuff – the shaving soap, the hair remover, the dandruff cure, the automatic washing-machine powder, the flea powder for dogs, the shoe polish, the black pepper, the horseradish sauce and all the rest of them, not to mention the powerful animal pills and powders and liquids . . . and the brown paint.

"Open your mouth wide, Grandma," he said, "and I'll pop it in."

The old hag opened her small wrinkled mouth, showing disgusting pale brown teeth.

"Here we go!" George cried out. "Swallow it down!" He pushed the spoon well into her mouth and tipped the mixture down her throat. Then he stepped back to watch the result.

It was worth watching.

Grandma yelled "Oweeee!" and her whole body shot up whoosh into the air. It was exactly as though someone had pushed an electric wire through the underneath of her chair and switched on the current. Up she went like a jack-on-the-box . . . and she didn't come down . . . she stayed there . . . suspended in mid air . . . about two feet up . . . still in the sitting position . . . but rigid now . . . frozen . . . quivering . . . the eyes bulging . . . the hair standing straight up on end.

"Is something wrong, Grandma?" George asked her politely. "Are you all right?"

Suspended up there in space, the old girl was beyond speaking.

The shock that George's marvellous mixture had given her must have been tremendous.

You'd have thought she'd swallowed a red-hot poker the way she took off from the chair.

Then down she came again with a plop, back into her seat.

"Call the fire brigade!" she shouted suddenly. "My stomach's on fire!"

"It's just the medicine, Grandma," George said. "It's good strong stuff."

"Fire!" the old woman yelled. "Fire in the basement! Get a bucket! Man the hoses! Do something quick!"

"Cool it, Grandma," George said. But he got a bit of a shock when he saw the smoke coming out of her mouth and out of her nostrils. Clouds of black smoke were coming out of her nose and blowing around the room.

"By golly, you really are on fire," George said.

"Of course I'm on fire!" she yelled. "I'll be burned to a crisp! I'll be fried to a frizzle! I'll be boiled like a beetroot!"

George ran into the kitchen and came back with a jug of water. "Open your mouth, Grandma!" he cried. He could hardly see her for the smoke, but he managed to pour half a jugful down her throat. A sizzling sound, the kind you get if you hold a hot frying-pan under a cold tap, came up from deep down in Grandma's stomach. The old hag bucked and shied and snorted. She gasped and gurgled. Spouts of water came shooting out of her. And the smoke cleared away.

"The fire's out," George announced proudly. "You'll be all right now, Grandma."

"All right?" she yelled. "Who's all right? There's jacky-jumpers in my tummy! There's squigglers in my belly! There's bangers in my bottom!" She began bouncing up and down in the chair. Quite obviously she was not very comfortable.

"You'll find it's doing you a lot of good, that medicine, Grandma," George said.

"Good?" she screamed. "Doing me good? It's killing me!"

Then she began to bulge.

She was swelling!

She was puffing up all over!

Someone was pumping her up, that's how it looked!

Was she going to explode?

Her face was turning from purple to green!

But wait! She had a puncture somewhere!

George could hear the hiss of escaping air. She stopped swelling. She was going down. She was slowly getting thinner again, shrinking back and back slowly to her shrivelly old self.

"How's things, Grandma?" George said.

No answer.

Then a funny thing happened. Grandma's body gave a sudden sharp twist and a sudden sharp jerk and she flipped herself clear out of the chair and landed neatly on her two feet on the carpet.

"That's terrific, Grandma!" George cried. "You haven't stood up like that for years! Look at you! You're standing up all on your own and you're not even using a stick!"

Grandma didn't even hear him. The frozen

pop-eyed look was back with her again now. She was miles away in another world.

Marvellous medicine, George told himself. He found it fascinating to stand there watching what it was doing to the old hag. What next? He wondered.

He soon found out.

Suddenly she began to grow.

It was quite slow at first . . . just a very gradual inching upwards . . . up, up, up . . . inch by inch . . . getting taller and taller . . . about an inch every few seconds . . . and in the beginning George didn't notice it.

But when she had passed the five foot six mark and was going on up towards being six feet tall, George gave a jump and shouted, "Hey, Grandma! You're growing! You're going up! Hang on, Grandma! You'd better stop now or you'll be hitting the ceiling!"

But Grandma didn't stop.

It was a truly fantastic sight, this ancient scrawny old woman getting taller and taller, longer and longer, thinner and thinner, as though she were a piece of elastic being pulled upwards by invisible hands.

When the top of her head actually touched the ceiling, George thought she was bound to stop.

But she didn't.

There was a sort of scrunching noise, and bits of plaster and cement came raining down.

"Hadn't you better stop now, Grandma?" George said. "Daddy's just had this whole room repainted."

But there was no stopping her now.

Soon, her head and shoulders had completely disappeared through the ceiling and she was still going.

George dashed upstairs to his own bedroom and there she was coming up through the floor

like a mushroom.

"Whoopee!" she shouted, finding her voice at last. "Hallelujah, here I come!"

"Steady on, Grandma." George said.

"With a heigh-nonny-no and up we go!" she shouted. "Just watch me grow!"

"This is my room," George said. "Look at the mess you're making."

"Terrific medicine!" she cried. "Give me some more!"

She's dotty as a doughnut, George thought.

"Come on, boy! Give me some more!" she yelled. "Dish it out! I'm slowing down!"

George was still clutching the medicine bottle in one hand and the spoon in the other. Oh well, he thought, why not? He poured out a second dose and popped it into her mouth.

"Oweee!" she screamed and up she went again. Her feet were still on the floor downstairs in the living-room but her head was moving quickly towards the ceiling of the bedroom.

"I'm on my way now, boy!" she called down to George. "Just watch me go!"

"That's the attic above you, Grandma!" George called out. "I'd keep out of there ! It's full of bugs and bogles!"

Crash! The old girl's head went through the ceiling as though it were butter.

George stood in his bedroom gazing at the shambles. There was a big hole in the floor and another in the ceiling, and sticking up like a post between the two was the middle part of Grandma. Her legs were in the room below, her head in the attic.

"I'm still going!" came the old screechy voice from up above. "Give me another dose, my boy, and let's go through the roof!"

"No, Grandma, no!" George called back. "You're busting up the whole house!"

"To heck with the house!" she shouted. "I want some fresh air! I haven't been outside for twenty years!"

"By golly, she is going through the roof!" George told himself. He ran downstairs. He rushed out of the back door into the yard. It would be simply awful, he thought, if she bashed up the roof as well. His father would be furious. And he, George, would get the blame. He had made the medicine. He had given her too much. "Don't come through the roof, Grandma," he prayed. "Please don't."

The Brown Hen

George stood in the farmyard looking up at the roof. The old farmhouse had a fine roof of pale red tiles and tall chimneys.

There was no sign of Grandma. There was only a song-thrush sitting on one of the chimney-pots, singing a song. The old wurzel's got stuck in the attic, George thought. Thank goodness for that.

Suddenly a tile came clattering down from the roof and fell into the yard. The song-thrush took off fast and flew away.

Then another tile came down.

Then half a dozen more.

And then, very slowly, like some weird monster rising up from the deep, Grandma's head came through the roof . . .

Then her scrawny neck . . .

And the tops of her shoulders . . .

"How'm I doing, boy!" she shouted. "How's that for a bash up?"

"Don't you think you'd better stop now, Grandma?" George called out . . .

"I have stopped!" she answered. "I feel terrific! Didn't I tell you I had magic powers!

Didn't I warn you I had wizardry in the tips of my fingers! But you wouldn't listen to me, would you? You wouldn't listen to your old Grandma!"

"You didn't do it, Grandma," George shouted back to her. "I did it! I made you a new medicine!"

"A new medicine? You? What rubbish!" she yelled.

"I did! I did! George shouted.

"You're lying as usual!" Grandma yelled. "You're always lying!"

"I'm not lying, Grandma. I swear I'm not."

The wrinkled old ace high up on the roof stared down suspiciously at George. "Are you telling me you actually made a new medicine all by yourself?" she shouted.

"Yes, Grandma, all by myself."

"I don't believe you," she answered. "But I'm very comfortable up here. Fetch me a cup of tea."

A brown hen was pecking about in the yard close to where George was standing. The hen gave him an idea. Quickly, he uncorked the

medicine bottle and poured some of the brown stuff into the spoon. "Watch this, Grandma!" he shouted. He crouched down, holding out the spoon to the hen.

"Chicken," he said. "Chick-chick-chicken. Come here. Have some of this."

Chickens are stupid birds, and very greedy. They think everything is food. This one thought the spoon was full of corn. It hopped over. It put its head on one side and looked at the spoon. "Come on, chicken," George said. "Good chicken. Chick-chick-chick."

The brown hen stretched out its neck towards the spoon and went peck. It got a beakful of medicine. The effect was electric.

"Oweee!" Shrieked the hen and it shot straight up into the air like a rocket. It went as high as the house.

Then down it came again into the yard, splosh. And there it sat with its feathers all sticking straight out from its body. There was a look of amazement on its silly face.

George stood watching it. Grandma up on the roof was watching it, too.

The hen got to its feet. It was rather shaky. It was making funny gurgling noises in its throat. Its beak was opening and shutting. It seemed like a pretty sick hen. "You've done it in, you stupid boy!" Grandma shouted. "That hen's going to die! Your father'll be after you now!

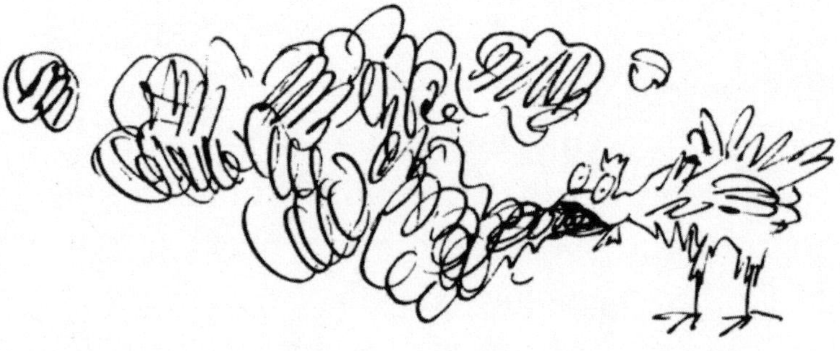

He'll give you socks and serve you right!"

All of a sudden, black smoke started pouring out of the hen's beak.

"It's on fire!" Grandma yelled. "The hen's on fire!"

George ran to the water-trough to get a bucket of water.

"That hen'll be roasted and ready for eating any moment!" Grandma shouted.

George sloshed the bucket of water over the hen. There was a sizzling sound and the smoke

went away.

"Old hen's laid its last egg!" Grandma shouted. "Hens don't do any laying after they've been on fire!"

Now that the fire was out, the hen seemed better. It stood up properly. It flapped its wings. Then it crouched down low to the ground, as though getting ready to jump. It did jump. It jumped high in the air and turned a complete somersault, then landed back on its feet.

"It's a circus hen!" Grandma shouted from the rooftop. "It's a flipping acrobat!"

Now the hen began to grow.

George had been waiting for this to happen. "It's growing!" he yelled. "It's growing, Grandma! Look, it's growing!"

Bigger and bigger . . . taller and taller it grew. Soon the hen was four or five times its normal size.

"Can you see it, Grandma?!" George shouted.

"I can see it, boy!" the old girl shouted back. "I'm watching it!"

George was hopping about from one foot to the other with excitement, pointing at the enormous hen and shouting, "It's had the magic medicine, Grandma, and it's growing just like you did!"

But there was a difference between the way the hen was growing and the way Grandma grew. When Grandma grew taller and taller, she got thinner and thinner. The hen didn't. It stayed nice and plump all along.

Soon it was taller than George, but it didn't stop there. It went right on growing until it was about as big as a horse. Then it stopped.

"Doesn't it look marvellous, Grandma!" George shouted.

"It's not as tall as me!" Grandma sang out. "Compared with me, that hen is titchy small! I am the tallest of them all!"

The Pig, the Bullocks, the Sheep, and Pony and the Nanny-goat

At that moment, George's mother came back from shopping in the village. She drove her car into the yard and got out. She was carrying a bottle of milk in one hand and a bag of groceries in the other.

The first thing she saw was the gigantic brown hen towering over little George. She dropped the bottle of milk.

Then Grandma started shouting at her from the rooftop, and when she looked up and saw Grandma's head sticking up through the tiles, she dropped the bag of groceries.

"How about that then, eh Mary?" Grandma shouted. "I'll bet you've never seen a hen as big as that! That's George's giant hen, that is!"

"But . . . but . . . but . . ." stammered George's mother.

"It's George's magic medicine!" Grandma shouted. "We've both of us had it, the hen and I!"

"But how in the world did you get up on the roof?" cried the mother.

"I didn't!" cackled the old woman. "My feet

are still standing on the floor in the living-room!"

This was too much for George's mother to understand. She just goggled and gaped. She looked as though she was going to faint.

A second later, George's father appeared. His name was Mr Killy Kranky. Mr Kranky was a small man with bandy legs and a huge head. He was a kind father to George, but he was not an easy person to live with because even the

smallest things got him all worked up and excited. The hen standing in the yard was certainly not a small thing, and when Mr Kranky saw it he started jumping about as though something was burning his feet. "Great heavens!" he cried, waving his arms, "What's this? What's happened? Where did it come from? It's a giant hen! Who did it?"

"I did," George said.

"Look at me!" Grandma shouted from the rooftop. "Never mind about the hen! What about me?"

Mr Kranky looked up and saw Grandma. "Shut up, Grandma," he said. It didn't seem to surprise him that the old girl was sticking up through the roof. It was the hen that excited him. He had never seen anything like it. But then who had?

"It's fantastic!" Mr Kranky shouted, dancing round and round. "It's colossal! It's gigantic! It's tremendous! It's a miracle! How did you do it, George?"

George started telling his father about the magic medicine. While he was doing this, the big brown hen sat down in the middle of the yard and went *cluck-cluck-cluck . . . cluck-cluck-cluck-cluck-cluck*.

Everyone stared at it.

When it stood up again, there was a brown egg lying there. The egg was the size of a football.

"That egg would make scrambled eggs for twenty people!" Mrs Kranky said.

"George!" Mr Kranky shouted. "How much of this medicine have you got?"

"Lots," George said. "There's a big saucepanful in the kitchen, and this bottle here's nearly full."

"Come with me!" Mr Kranky yelled, grabbing George by the arm. "Bring the medicine! For years and years I've been trying to breed bigger and bigger animals. Bigger bulls for beef. Bigger pigs for pork. Bigger sheep for mutton . . . "

They went to the pigsty first.

George gave a spoonful of medicine to the pig.

The pig blew smoke from its nose and jumped about all over the place. Then it grew and grew.

In the end, it looked like this . . .

They went to the herd of fine black bullocks that Mr Kranky was trying to fatten for the market.

George gave each of them some medicine, and this is what happened.

Then the sheep . . .

He gave some to his grey pony, Jack Frost . . .

And finally, just for fun, he gave some to Alma, the nanny-goat . . .

A Crane for Grandma

Grandma, from high up on the rooftop, could see everything that was going on and she didn't like what she saw. She wanted to be the centre of attention and nobody was taking the slightest notice of her. George and Mr Kranky were running round and getting excited about the enormous animals. Mrs Kranky was washing up in the kitchen, and Grandma was all alone on the rooftop.

"Hey you!" she yelled. "George! Get me a cup of tea this minute, you idle little beast!"

"Don't listen to the old goat," Mr Kranky said. "She's stuck where she is and a good thing, too."

"But we can't leave her up there, dad," George said. "What if it rains?"

"George!" Grandma yelled. "Oh, you horrible little boy! You disgusting little worm! Fetch me a cup of tea at once and a slice of currant cake!"

"We'll have to get her out, dad," George said. "She won't give us any peace if we don't."

Mrs Kranky came outside and she agreed with George. "She's my own mother," she said.

"She's a pain in the neck," Mr Kranky said.

"I don't care," Mrs Kranky said. "I'm not leaving my own mother sticking up through the roof for the rest of her life."

So in the end, Mr Kranky telephoned the Crane Company and asked them to send their biggest crane out to the house at once.

The crane arrived one hour later. It was on wheels and there were two men inside it. The

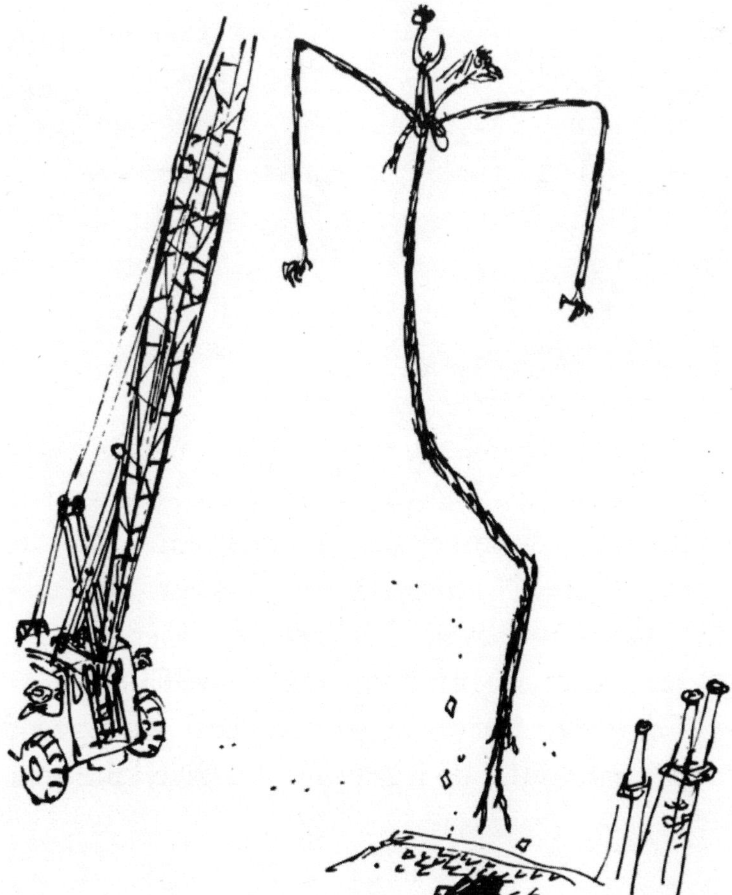

crane men climbed up on to the roof and put ropes under Grandma's arms. Then she was lifted right up through the roof . . .

In a way, the medicine had done Grandma good. It had not made her any less grumpy or bad-tempered, but it seemed to have cured all

her aches and pains, and she was suddenly as frisky as a ferret. As soon as the crane had lowered her to the ground, she ran over to George's huge pony, Jack Frost, and jumped on to his back. This ancient old hag, who was now as tall as a house, then galloped about the farm on the gigantic pony, jumping over trees and sheds and shouting, "Out of my way! Clear the decks! Stand back all you miserable midgets or I'll trample you to death!" and other silly things like that.

But because Grandma was now much too tall to get back into the house, she had to sleep that night in the hay-barn with the mice and the rats.

Mr Kranky's Great Idea

The next day, George's father came down to breakfast in a state of greater excitement than ever. "I've been awake all night thinking about it!" he cried.

"About what, dad?" George asked him.

"About your marvellous medicine, of course! We can't stop now, my boy! We must start making more of it at once! More and more and more!"

The giant saucepan had been completely emptied the day before because there had been so many sheep and pigs and cows and bullocks to be dosed.

"But why do we need more, dad?" George asked. "We've done all our own animals and we've made Grandma feel as frisky as a ferret even though she does have to sleep in the barn."

"My dear boy," cried Mr Killy Kranky, "we need barrels and barrels of it! Tons and tons! Then we well sell it to every farmer in the world so that all of them can have giant animals! We will build a Marvellous Medicine Factory and sell the stuff in bottles at five pounds a time. We will become rich and you will become famous!"

"But wait a minute, dad," George said.

"There's no waiting!" cried Mr Kranky, working himself up so much that he put butter in his coffee and milk on his toast. "Don't you understand what this tremendous invention of yours is going to do to the world! Nobody will ever go hungry again!"

"Why won't they?" asked George.

"Because one giant cow will give fifty buckets of milk a day!" cried Mr Kanky, waving his arms. "One giant chicken will make a hundred fried chicken dinners, and one giant pig will give you a thousand pork chops! It's tremendous, my dear boy! It's fantastic! It'll change the world!

"But wait a minute, dad," George said again.

"Don't keep saying wait a minute!" shouted Mr Kranky. "There isn't a minute to wait! We must get cracking at once!"

"Do calm down, my dear," Mrs Kranky said from the other end of the table. "And stop putting marmalade on your cornflakes."

"The heck with my cornflakes!" cried Mr Kranky, leaping up from his chair. "Come on, George! Let's get going! And the first thing we'll do is to make one more saucepanful as a tester."

"But dad," said little George. "The trouble is . . ."

"There won't be any trouble, my boy!" cried Mr Kranky. "How can there possibly be any trouble? All you've got to do is put the same stuff into the saucepan as you did yesterday. And while you're doing it, I'll write down each and every item. That's how we'll get the magic recipe!"

"But dad," George said. "Please listen to me."

"Why don't you listen to him," Mrs Kranky said. "The boy's trying to tell you something."

But Mr Kranky was too excited to listen to anyone except himself. "And then," he cried, "when the new mixture is ready, we'll test it out on an old hen just to make absolutely sure we've got it right, and after that we'll all shout hooray and build the giant factory!"

"But dad . . . "

"Come on then, what is it you want to say?"

"I can't possibly remember all the hundreds of things I put into the saucepan to make the medicine," George said.

"Of course you can, my dear boy," cried Mr Kranky. "I'll help you! I'll jog your memory! You'll get it in the end, you see if you don't! Now then, what was the very first thing you put in?"

"I went up to the bathroom first," George said. "I used a lot of things in the bathroom and on mummy's dressing-table."

"Come on then!" cried Mr Killy Kranky. "Up we go to the bathroom!"

When they got there, they found, of course, a whole lot of empty tubes and empty aerosols and empty bottles. "That's great," said Mr Kranky. "That tells us exactly what you used. If anything is empty, it means you used it."

So Mr Kranky started making a list of everything that was empty in the bathroom. Then they went to Mrs Kranky's dressing-table. "A box of powder," said Mr Kranky, writing it down. "Helga's Hairset. Flowers of

Turnips perfume. Terrific. This is going to be easy. Where did you go next?"

"To the laundry-room," George said. "But are you sure you haven't missed anything out up here, dad?"

"That's up to you my boy," Mr Kranky said. "Have I?"

"I don't think so," George said. So down they went to the laundry-room and once again Mr Kranky wrote down the names of all the empty bottles and cans. "My goodness me, what a mass of stuff you used!" he cried. "No wonder it did magic things! Is that the lot?"

"No, dad, it's not," George said, and he led his father out to the shed where the animal medicines were kept and showed him the five big empty bottles up on the shelf. Mr Kranky wrote down all their names.

"Anything else?" Mr Kranky asked.

Little George scratched his head and thought and thought but he couldn't remember having put anything else in.

Mr Killy Kranky leapt into his car and drove down to the village and bought new bottles and tubes and cans of everything on his list. He then went to the vet and got a fresh supply of all the animal medicines George had used.

"Now show me how you did it, George, he said. "Come along. Show me exactly how you mixed them all together."

Marvellous Medicine Number Two

They were in the kitchen now and the big saucepan was on the stove. All the things Mr Kranky had bought were lined up near the sink.

"Come along, my boy!" cried Mr Killy Kranky. "Which one did you put in first?"

"This one," George said. "Goldengloss Hair Shampoo." He emptied the bottle into the pan.

"Now the toothpaste," George went on . . . "And the shaving soap . . . and the face cream . . . and the nail varnish . . . "

"Keep at it, my boy!" cried Mr Kranky, dancing round the kitchen. "Keep putting them in! Don't stop! Don't pause! Don't hesitate! It's a pleasure, my dear fellow, to watch you work!"

One by one, George poured and squeezed the things into the saucepan. With everything so close at hand, the whole job didn't take him more than ten minutes. But when it was all done, the saucepan didn't somehow seem to be quite as full as it had been the first time.

"Now what did you do?" cried Mr Kranky.

"Did you stir it?"

"I boiled it," George said. "But not for long. And I stirred it as well."

So Mr Kranky lit the gas under the saucepan and George stirred the mixture with the same long wooden spoon he had used before. "It's not brown enough," George said. "Wait a minute! I know what I've forgotten!"

"What?" cried Mr Kranky. "Tell me, quick! Because if we've forgotten even one tiny thing, then it won't work! At least not in the same way."

"A quart of brown gloss paint," George said. "That's what I've forgotten."

Mr Killy Kranky shot out of the house and into his car like a rocket. He sped down to the village and bought the paint and rushed back again. He opened the can in the kitchen and handed it to George. George poured the paint into the saucepan.

"Ah-ha, that's better," George said. "That's more like the right colour."

"It's boiling!" cried Mr Kranky. "It's boiling and bubbling, George! Is it ready yet?"

"It's ready." George said. "At least I hope it is."

"Right!" shouted Mr Kranky, hopping

about. "Let's test it! Let's give some to a chicken!"

"My heavens alive, why don't you calm down a bit?" Mrs Kranky said, coming into the kitchen.

"Calm down?" cried Mr Kranky. "You expect me to calm down and here we are mixing up the greatest medicine ever discovered in the history of the world! Come along, George! Dip a cupful out of the saucepan and get a spoon and we'll give some to a chicken just to make absolutely certain we've got the correct mixture."

Outside in the yard, there were several chickens that hadn't had any of George's Marvellous Medicine Number One. They were pecking about in the dirt in that silly way chickens do.

George crouched down, holding out a spoonful of Marvellous Medicine Number Two.

"Come on, chicken," he said. "Good chicken. Chick-chick-chick."

A white chicken with black specks on its feathers looked up at George. It walked over to the spoon and went peck.

The effect that Medicine Number Two had on this chicken was not quite the same as the effect produced by Medicine Number One, but it was very interesting. "Whooosh!" shrieked the chicken and it shot six feet up in the air and came down again. Then sparks came flying out of its beak, bright yellow sparks of fire, as though someone was sharpening a knife on a grindstone inside its tummy. Then its legs began to grow longer. Its body stayed the same size but the two thin yellow legs got longer and longer and longer . . . and longer still . . .

"What's happening to it?" cried Mr Killy Kranky.

"Something's wrong," George said.

The legs went on growing and the more they grew, the higher up into the air went the chicken's body. When the legs were about fifteen feet long, they stopped growing. The chicken looked perfectly absurd with its long long legs and its ordinary little body perched high up on top. It was like a chicken on stilts.

"Oh my sainted aunts!" cried Mr Killy Kranky. "We've got it wrong! This chicken's no good to anybody! It's all legs! No one wants chickens' legs!"

"I must have left something out," George said.

"I know you left something out!" cried Mr Kranky. "Think, boy, think! What was it you left out?"

"I've got it!" said George.

"What was it, quick?"

"Flea powder for dogs," George said.

"You mean you put flea powder in the first one?"

"Yes, dad, I did. A whole carton of it."

"Then that's the answer!"

"Wait a minute," said George. "Did we have brown shoe polish on our list?"

"We did not," said Mr Kranky.

"I used that, too," said George.

"Well, no wonder it went wrong," said Mr Kranky. He was already running to his car, and soon he was heading down the village to buy more flea powder and more shoe polish.

Marvellous Medicine Number Three

"Here it is!" cried Mr Killy Kranky, rushing into the kitchen. "One carton of flea powder for dogs and one tin of brown shoe-polish!"

George poured the flea powder into the giant saucepan. Then he scooped the shoe-polish out of its tin and added that as well.

"Stir it up, George!" shouted Mr Kranky. "Give it another boil! We've got it this time! I'll bet we've got it!"

After Marvellous Medicine Number Three had been boiled and stirred, George took a cupful of it out into the yard to try it on another chicken. Mr Kranky ran after him, flapping his arms and hopping with excitement. "Come and watch this one!" he called out to Mrs Kranky. "Come and watch us turning an ordinary chicken into a lovely great big one that lays eggs as large as footballs!"

"I hope you do better than last time," said Mrs Kranky, following them out.

"Come on, chicken," said George, holding out a spoonful of Medicine Number Three. "Good chicken. Chick-chick-chick-chick-chick.

Have some of this lovely medicine."

A magnificent black cockerel with a scarlet comb came stepping over. The cockerel looked at the spoon and it went peck.

"Cock-a-doodle-do!" squawked the cockerel, shooting up into the air and coming down again.

"Watch him now!" cried Mr Kranky. "Watch him grow! Any moment he's going to start getting bigger and bigger!"

Mr Killy Kranky, Mrs Kranky and little George stood in the yard staring at the black cockerel. The cockerel stood quite still. It looked as though it had a headache.

"What's happening to its neck?" Mrs Kranky said.

"It's getting longer," George said.

"I'll say it's getting longer," Mrs Kranky said. Mr Kranky, for once, said nothing.

"Last time it was the legs," Mrs Kranky said.

"Now it's the neck. Who wants a chicken with a long neck? You can't eat a chicken's neck."

It was an extraordinary sight. The cockerel's body hadn't grown at all. But the neck was now about six feet long.

"All right, George," Mr Kranky said. "What else have you forgotten?"

"I don't know," George said.

"Oh yes you do," Mr Kranky said. "Come along, boy, think. There's probably just one vital thing missing and you've got to remember it."

"I put in some engine oil from the garage," George said. "Did you have that on your list?"

"Eureka!" cried Mr Kranky. "That's the answer! How much did you put in?"

"Half a pint," George said.

Mr Kranky ran to the garage and found another half pint of oil. "And some anti-freeze," George called after him. "I sloshed in a bit of anti-freeze."

Marvellous Medicine Number Four

Back in the kitchen once again, George, with Mr Kranky watching him anxiously, tipped half a pint of engine oil and some anti-freeze into the giant saucepan.

"Boil it up again!" cried Mr Kranky. "Boil it and stir it!"

George boiled it and stirred it.

"You'll never get it right," said Mrs Kranky. "Don't forget you don't just have to have the same things but you've got to have exactly the same amounts of those things. And how can you possibly do that?"

"You keep out of this!" cried Mr Kranky. "We're doing fine! We've got it this time, you see if we haven't!"

This was George's Marvellous Medicine Number Four, and when it had boiled for a couple of minutes, George once again carried a cupful of it out into the yard. Mr Kranky ran after him. Mrs Kranky followed more slowly. "You're going to have some mighty queer chickens around here if you go on like this," she said.

"Dish it out, George!" cried Mr Kranky. "Give a spoonful to that one over there!" He pointed to a brown hen.

George knelt down and held out the spoon with the new medicine in it. "Chick-chick," he said. "Try some of this."

The brown hen walked over and looked at the spoon. Then it went peck.

"Owch!" it said. Then a funny whistling noise came out of its beak.

"Watch it grow!" shouted Mr Kranky.

"Don't be too sure," said Mrs Kranky. "Why is it whistling like that?"

"Keep quiet, woman!" cried Mr Kranky. "Give it a chance!"

They stood there staring at the brown hen.

"It's getting smaller," George said. "Look at it, dad. It's shrinking."

And indeed it was. In less than a minute, the hen had shrunk so much it was no bigger than a new-hatched chick. It looked ridiculous.

Goodbye Grandma

"There's still something you've left out," Mr Kranky said.

"I can't think what it could be," George said.

"Give it up," Mrs Kranky said. "Pack it in. You'll never get it right."

Mr Kranky looked very forlorn.

George looked pretty fed up, too. He was still kneeling on the ground with the spoon in one hand and the cup full of medicine in the other. The ridiculous tiny brown hen was walking slowly away.

At that point, Grandma came striding into the yard. From her enormous height, she glared down at the three people below her and she shouted, "What's going on around here? Why hasn't anyone brought me my morning cup of tea? It's bad enough having to sleep in the yard with the rats and mice but I'll be blowed if I'm going to starve as well! No tea! No eggs and bacon! No buttered toast!"

"I'm sorry, mother," Mrs Kranky said. "We've been terribly busy. I'll get you something right away."

"Let George get it, the lazy little brute!"

Grandma shouted.

Just then, the old woman spotted the cup in George's hand. She bent down and peered into it. She saw that it was full of brown liquid.

It looked very much like tea. "Ho-ho!" she cried. "Ha-ha! So that's your little game, is it! You look after yourself all right, don't you! You make quite sure you've got a nice cup of morning tea! But you didn't think to bring one to your poor old Grandma! I always knew you were a selfish pig!"

"No, Grandma," George said. "This isn't . . . "

"Don't lie to me, boy!" the enormous old hag shouted. "Pass it up here this minute!"

"No!" cried Mrs Kranky. "No, mother, don't! That's not for you!"

"Now you're against me, too!" shouted Grandma. "My own daughter trying to stop me having my breakfast! Trying to starve me out!"

Mr Kranky looked up at the horrid old woman and he smiled sweetly. "Of course it's for you, Grandma," he said. "You take it and drink it while it's nice and hot."

"Don't think I won't," Grandma said, bending down from her great height and reaching out a huge horny hand for the cup. "Hand it over, George."

"No, no, Grandma!" George cried out, pulling the cup away. "You mustn't! You're not to have it!"

"Give it to me, boy!" yelled Grandma.

"Don't!" cried Mrs Kranky. "That's George's

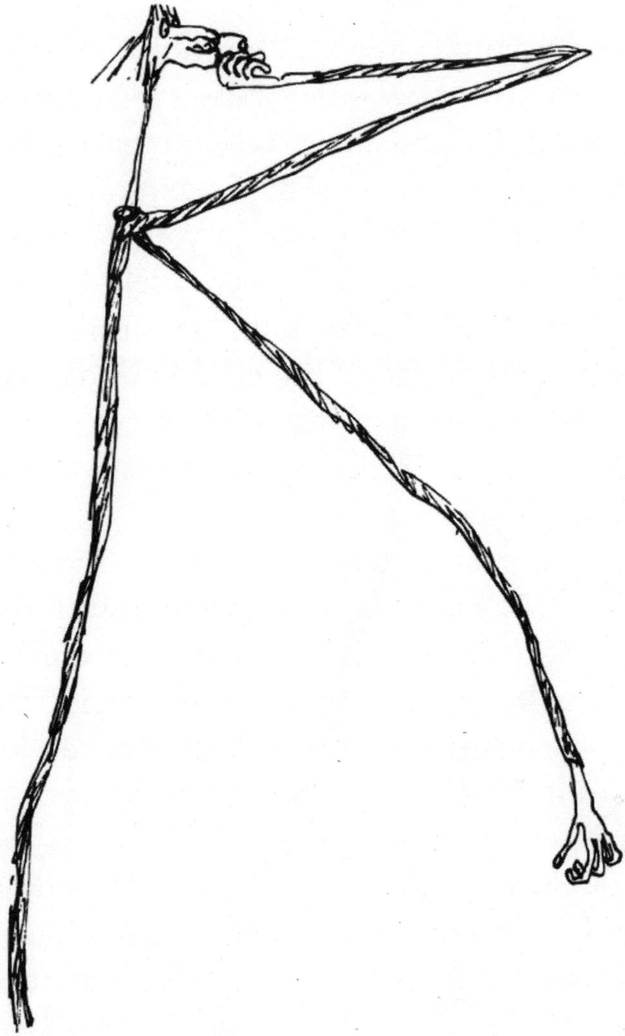

Marvellous . . ."

"Everything's George's round here!" shouted Grandma. "George's this, George's that! I'm fed

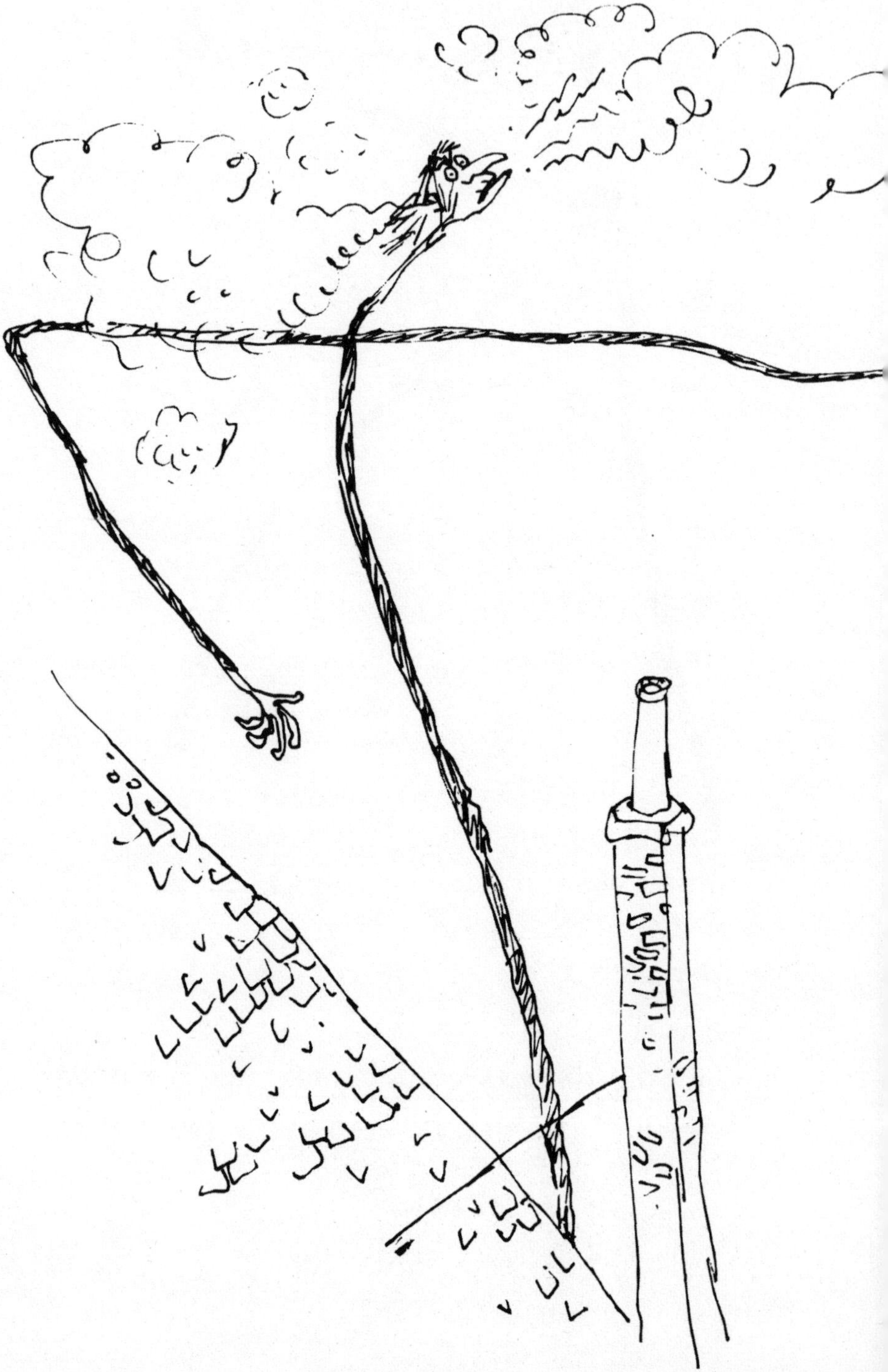

up with it!" She snatched the cup out of little George's hand and carried it high up out of reach.

"Drink it up, Grandma," Mr Kranky said, grinning hugely. "Lovely tea."

"No!" the other two cried. "No, no, no!"

But it was too late. The ancient beanpole had already put the cup to her lips, and in one gulp she swallowed everything that was in it.

"Mother!" wailed Mrs Kranky. "You've just drunk fifty doses of George's Marvellous Medicine Number Four and look what one tiny spoonful did to that little old brown hen!"

But Grandma didn't even hear her. Great clouds of steam were already pouring out of her mouth and she was beginning to whistle.

"This is going to be interesting," Mr Kranky said, still grinning.

"Now you've done it!" cries Mrs Kranky, glaring at her husband. "You've cooked the old girl's goose!"

"I didn't do anything," Mr Kranky said.

"Oh, yes you did! You told her to drink it!"

A tremendous hissing sound was coming from above their heads. Steam was shooting out of Grandma's mouth and nose and ears and whistling as it came.

"She'll feel better after she's let off a bit of steam," Mr Kranky said.

"She's going to blow up!" Mrs Kranky wailed. "Her boiler's going to burst!"

"Stand clear," Mr Kranky said.

George was quite alarmed. He stood up and ran back a few paces. The jets of white steam kept squirting out of the skinny old hag's head, and the whistling was so high and shrill it hurt the ears.

"Call the fire-brigade!" cried Mrs Kranky, "Call the police! Man the hose-pipes!"

"Too late," said Mr Kranky, looking pleased.

"Grandma!" shrieked Mrs Kranky. "Mother! Run to the drinking-trough and put your head under the water!"

But even as she spoke, the whistling suddenly stopped and the steam disappeared. That was when Grandma began to get smaller. She had started off with her head as high as the roof of the house, but now she was coming down fast.

"Watch this, George!" Mr Kranky shouted, hopping around the yard and flapping his arms. "Watch what happens when someone's had fifty spoonfuls instead of one!"

Very soon, Grandma was back to normal height.

"Stop!" cried Mrs Kranky. "That's just right."

But she didn't stop. Smaller and smaller she got . . . down and down she went. In another

half minute she was no bigger than a bottle of lemonade.

"How d'you feel, mother?" asked Mrs Kranky anxiously.

Grandma's tiny face still bore the same foul and furious expression it had always had. Her eyes, no bigger now than little keyholes, were blazing with anger. "How do I feel?" she yelled. "How d'you think I feel? How would you feel if you'd been a glorious giant a minute ago and suddenly you're a miserable midget?"

"She's still going!" shouted Mr Kranky gleefully. "She's still getting smaller!"

And by golly, she was.

When she was no bigger than a cigarette, Mrs Kranky made a grab for her. She held her in her hands and she cried, "How do I stop her getting smaller still?"

"You can't," said Mr Kranky. "She's had fifty times the right amount."

"I must stop her!" Mrs Kranky wailed. "I can hardly see her as it is!"

"Catch hold of each end and pull," Mr Kranky said.

By then, Grandma was the size of a matchstick and still shrinking fast.

A moment later, she was no bigger than a pin . . .

Then a pumpkin seed . . .

Then . . .

Then . . .

"Where is she?" cried Mrs Kranky. "I've lost her!"

"Hooray," said Mr Kranky.

"She's gone! She's disappeared completely!" cried Mrs Kranky.

"That's what happens to you if you're grumpy and bad-tempered," said Mr Kranky. "Great medicine of yours, George."

George didn't know what to think.

For a few minutes, Mrs Kranky kept wandering round with a puzzled look on her face, saying, "Mother, where are you? Where've you gone? Where've you got to? How can I

find you?" But she calmed down quite quickly. And by lunchtime, she was saying, "Ah well, I suppose it's all for the best, really. She was a bit of a nuisance around the house, wasn't she?"

"Yes," Mr Kranky said. "She most certainly was."

George didn't say a word. He felt quite trembly. He knew something tremendous had taken place that morning. For a few brief moments he had touched with the very tips of his fingers the edge of a magic world.

Matilda

Contents

The Reader of Books	121
Mr Wormwood, the Great Car Dealer	139
The Hat and the Superglue	149
The Ghost	158
Arithmetic	171
The Platinum-Blond Man	180
Miss Honey	192
The Trunchbull	212
The Parents	222
Throwing the Hammer	235
Bruce Bogtrotter and the Cake	255
Lavender	275
The Weekly Test	284
The First Miracle	306
The Second Miracle	320
Miss Honey's Cottage	329
Miss Honey's Story	349
The Names	365
The Practice	370
The Third Miracle	376
A New Home	390

The Reader of Books

It's a funny thing about mothers and fathers. Even when their own child is the most disgusting little blister you could ever imagine, they still think that he or she is wonderful.

Some parents go further. They become so blinded by adoration they manage to convince themselves their child has qualities of genius.

Well, there is nothing very wrong with all this. It's the way of the world. It is only when the parents begin telling *us* about the brilliance of their own revolting offspring, that we start shouting, "Bring us a basin! We're going to be sick!"

School teachers suffer a good deal from having to listen to this sort of twaddle from proud parents, but they usually get their own back when the time comes to write the end-of-term reports. If I were a teacher I would cook up some real scorchers for the children of doting parents. "Your son Maximilian", I would write, "is a total wash-out. I hope you have a family business you can push him into when he leaves school because he sure as heck won't get a job anywhere else." Or if I were feeling lyrical that day, I might write, "It is a curious truth that grasshoppers have their

hearing-organs in the sides of the abdomen. Your daughter Vanessa, judging by what she's learnt this term, has no hearing-organs at all."

I might even delve deeper into natural history and say, "The periodical cicada spends six years as a grub underground, and no more than six *days* as a free creature of sunlight and air. Your son Wilfred has spent six years as a grub in this school and we are still waiting for him to emerge from the chrysalis." A particularly poisonous little girl might sting me into saying, "Fiona has the same glacial beauty as an iceberg, but unlike the iceberg she has

absolutely nothing below the surface." I think I might enjoy writing end-of-term reports for the stinkers in my class. But enough of that. We have to get on.

Occasionally one comes across parents who take the opposite line, who show no interest at all in their children, and these of course are far worse than the doting ones. Mr and Mrs Wormwood were two such parents. They had a son called Michael and a daughter called Matilda, and the parents looked upon Matilda in particular as nothing more than a scab. A scab is something you have to put up with until the time comes when you can pick it off and flick it away. Mr and Mrs Wormwood looked forward enormously to the time when they could k their little daughter off l flick her away, preferably to the next county or even urther than that.

It is bad enough when parents treat *ordinary* children as though they were scabs and bunions, but it becomes somehow a lot worse when the child in question is *extra*-ordinary, and by that I mean sensitive and brilliant. Matilda was both of these things, but above all she was brilliant. Her mind was so nimble and she was so quick to learn that her ability should have been obvious even to the most half-witted of parents. But Mr and Mrs Wormwood were both so gormless and so wrapped up in their own silly little lives that they failed to notice anything unusual about their daughter. To tell the truth, I doubt they would have noticed had she crawled into the house with a broken leg.

Matilda's brother Michael was a perfectly normal boy, but the sister, as I said, was something to make your eyes pop. By the age of *one and a half* her speech was perfect and she knew as many words as most grown-ups. The parents, instead of applauding her, called her a noisy chatterbox and told her sharply that small girls should be seen and not heard.

By the time she was *three*, Matilda had taught herself to read by studying newspapers, and magazines that lay around the house. At the age of *four*, she could read fast and well and she naturally began hankering after books. The only book in the whole of this enlightened household was something called *Easy Cooking* belonging to her mother, and when she had read this from cover to cover and had learnt all the recipes by heart, she decided she wanted something more interesting.

"Daddy," she said, "do you think you could buy me a book?"

"A *book*?" he said. "What d'you want a flaming book for?"

"To read, Daddy."

"What's wrong with the telly, for heaven's sake? We've got a lovely telly with a twelve-inch screen and now you come asking for a book! You're getting spoiled, my girl!"

Nearly every weekday afternoon Matilda was left alone in the house. Her brother (five years older than her) went to school. Her father went to work and her mother went out playing bingo in a town eight miles away. Mrs Wormwood was hooked on bingo and played it five afternoons a week. On the afternoon of the day when her father had refused to buy her a book, Matilda set out all by herself to walk to the public library in the village. When she arrived, she introduced herself to the librarian, Mrs Phelps. She asked if she might sit awhile and read a book. Mrs Phelps, slightly taken aback at the arrival of such a tiny girl unaccompanied by a parent, nevertheless told her she was very welcome.

"Where are the children's books please?" Matilda asked.

"They're over there on those lower shelves," Mrs Phelps told her. "Would you like me to help you find a nice one with lots of pictures in it?"

"No, thank you," Matilda said. "I'm sure I can manage."

From then on, every afternoon, as soon as her mother had left for bingo, Matilda would toddle down to the library. The walk took only ten minutes and this allowed her two glorious hours sitting quietly by herself in a cosy corner devouring one book after another. When she had read every single children's book in the place, she started wandering round in search of something else.

Mrs Phelps, who had been watching her with fascination for the past few weeks, now got up from her desk and went over to her. "Can I help you, Matilda?" she asked.

"I'm wondering what to read next," Matilda said. "I've finished all the children's books."

"You mean you've looked at the pictures?"

"Yes, but I've read the books as well."

Mrs Phelps looked down at Matilda from her great height and Matilda looked right back up at her.

"I thought some were very poor," Matilda said, "but others were lovely. I liked *The Secret Garden* best of all. It was full of mystery. The mystery of the room behind the closed door and the mystery of the garden behind the big wall."

Mrs Phelps was stunned. "Exactly how old are you, Matilda?" she asked.

"Four years and three months," Matilda said.

Mrs Phelps was more stunned than ever, but she had the sense not to show it. "What sort of a book would you like to read next?" she asked.

Matilda said, "I would like a really good one that grown-ups read. A famous one. I don't know any names."

Mrs Phelps looked along the shelves, taking her time. She didn't quite know what to bring out. How, she asked herself, does one choose a famous grown-up book for a four-year-old girl? Her first thought was to pick a young teenager's romance of the kind that is written

for fifteen-year-old school-girls, but for some reason she found herself instinctively walking past that particular shelf.

"Try this," she said at last. "It's very famous and very good. If it's too long for you, just let me know and I'll find something shorter and a bit easier."

"*Great Expectations*," Matilda read, "by Charles Dickens. I'd love to try it."

I must be mad, Mrs Phelps told herself, but to Matilda she said, "Of course you may try it."

Over the next few afternoons Mrs Phelps could hardly take her eyes from the small girl sitting for hour after hour in the big armchair at the far end of the room with the book on her lap. It was necessary to rest it on the lap because it was too heavy for her to hold up, which meant she had to sit leaning forward in order to read. And a strange sight it was, this tiny dark-haired person sitting there with her feet nowhere near touching the floor, totally absorbed in the wonderful adventures of Pip and old Miss Havisham and her cobwebbed house and by the spell of magic that Dickens the great story-teller had woven with his words. The only movement from the reader was the lifting of the hand every now and then to turn over a page, and Mrs Phelps always felt sad when the time came for her to cross the floor and say, "It's ten to five, Matilda."

During the first week of Matilda's visits Mrs Phelps had said to her, "Does your mother walk you down here every day and then take you home?"

"My mother goes to Aylesbury every afternoon to play bingo," Matilda had said. "She doesn't know I come here."

"But that's surely not right," Mrs Phelps said. "I think you'd better ask her."

"I'd rather not," Matilda said. "She doesn't encourage reading books. Nor does my father."

"But what do they expect you to do every afternoon in an empty house?"

"Just mooch around and watch the telly."

"I see."

"She doesn't really care what I do," Matilda said a little sadly.

Mrs Phelps was concerned about the child's safety on the walk through the fairly busy village High Street and the crossing of the road, but she decided not to interfere.

Within a week, Matilda had finished *Great Expectations* which in that edition contained four hundred and eleven pages. "I loved it," she said to Mrs Phelps. "Has Mr Dickens written any others?"

"A great number," said the astounded Mrs Phelps. "Shall I choose you another?"

Over the next six months, under Mrs Phelps's watchful and compassionate eye, Matilda read the following books:

Nicholas Nickleby by Charles Dickens
Oliver Twist by Charles Dickens
Jane Eyre by Charlotte Brontë
Pride and Prejudice by Jane Austen
Tess of the D'Urbervilles by Thomas Hardy
Gone to Earth by Mary Webb
Kim by Rudyard Kipling
The Invisible Man by H. G. Wells
The Old Man and the Sea by Ernest Hemingway
The Sound and the Fury by William Faulkner
The Grapes of Wrath by John Steinbeck
The Good Companions by J. B. Priestley
Brighton Rock by Graham Greene
Animal Farm by George Orwell

It was a formidable list and by now Mrs Phelps was filled with wonder and excitement, but it was probably a good thing that she did not allow herself to be completely carried away by it all. Almost anyone else witnessing the achievements of this small child would have been tempted to make a great fuss and shout the news all over the village and beyond, but not so Mrs Phelps. She was someone who minded her own business and had long since discovered it was seldom worth while to interfere with other people's children.

"Mr Hemingway says a lot of things I don't understand," Matilda said to her. "Especially about men and women. But I loved it all the same. The way he tells it I feel I am right there on the spot watching it all happen."

"A fine writer will always make you feel that," Mrs Phelps said. "And don't worry about the bits you can't understand. Sit back and allow the words to wash around you, like music."

"I will, I will."

"Did you know," Mrs Phelps said, "that public libraries like this allow you to borrow books and take them home?"

"I didn't know that," Matilda said. "Could *I* do it?"

"Of course," Mrs Phelps said. "When you have chosen the book you want, bring it to me so I can make a note of it and it's yours for two weeks. You can take more than one if you wish."

From then on, Matilda would visit the

library only once a week in order to take out new books and return the old ones. Her own small bedroom now became her reading-room and there she would sit and read most afternoons, often with a mug of hot chocolate beside her. She was not quite tall enough to reach things around the kitchen, but she kept a small box in the outhouse which she brought in and stood on in order to get whatever she wanted. Mostly it was hot chocolate she made, warming the milk in a saucepan on the stove

before mixing it. Occasionally she made Bovril or Ovaltine. It was pleasant to take a hot drink up to her room and have it beside her as she sat in her silent room reading in the empty house in the afternoons. The books transported her into new worlds and introduced her to amazing people who lived exciting lives. She went on olden-day sailing ships with Joseph Conrad. She went to Africa with Ernest Hemingway and to India with Rudyard Kipling. She travelled all over the world while sitting in her little room in an English village.

Mr Wormwood, the Great Car Dealer

Matilda's parents owned quite a nice house with three bedrooms upstairs, while on the ground floor there was a dining-room and a living-room and a kitchen. Her father was a dealer in second-hand cars and it seemed he did pretty well at it.

"Sawdust," he would say proudly, "is one of the great secrets of my success. And it costs me nothing. I get it free from the sawmill."

"What do you use it for?" Matilda asked him.

"Ha!" the father said. "Wouldn't you like to know."

"I don't see how sawdust can help you to sell second-hand cars, daddy."

"That's because you're an ignorant little twit," the father said. His speech was never very delicate but Matilda was used to it. She also knew that he liked to boast and she would egg him on shamelessly.

"You must be very clever to find a use for something that costs nothing," she said. "I wish

I could do it."

"You couldn't," the father said. "You're too stupid. But I don't mind telling young Mike here about it seeing he'll be joining me in the business one day." Ignoring Matilda, he turned to his son and said, "I'm always glad to buy a car when some fool has been crashing the gears so badly they're all worn out and rattle like mad. I get it cheap. Then all I do is mix a lot of sawdust with the oil in the gear-box and it runs as sweet as a nut."

"How long will it run like that before it starts rattling again?" Matilda asked him.

"Long enough for the buyer to get a good distance away," the father said, grinning. "About a hundred miles."

"But that's dishonest, daddy," Matilda said. "It's cheating."

"No one ever got rich being honest," the father said. "Customers are there to be diddled."

Mr Wormwood was a small ratty-looking man whose front teeth stuck out underneath a thin ratty moustache. He liked to wear jackets with large brightly-coloured checks and he sported ties that were usually yellow or pale green. "Now take mileage for instance," he went on. "Anyone who's buying a second-hand car, the first thing he wants to know is how many miles it's done. Right?"

"Right," the son said.

"So I buy an old dump that's got about a hundred and fifty thousand miles on the clock. I get it cheap. But no one's going to buy it with a mileage like that, are they? And these days you can't just take the speedometer out and fiddle the numbers back like you used to ten years ago. They've fixed it so it's impossible to tamper with it unless you're a ruddy watchmaker or something. So what do I do? I use my brains, laddie, that's what I do."

"How?" young Michael asked, fascinated. He seemed to have inherited his father's love of crookery.

"I sit down and say to myself, how can I convert a mileage reading of one hundred and fifty thousand into only ten thousand without taking the speedometer to pieces? Well, if I were to run the car backwards for long enough then obviously that would do it. The numbers would click backwards, wouldn't they? But who's going to drive a flaming car in reverse for thousands and thousands of miles? You couldn't do it!"

"Of course you couldn't," young Michael said.

"So I scratch my head," the father said. "I use my brains. When you've been given a fine brain like I have, you've got to use it. And all of a sudden, the answer hits me. I tell you, I felt exactly like that other brilliant fellow must have felt when he discovered penicillin. 'Eureka!' I cried. 'I've got it!' "

"What did you do, dad?" the son asked him.

"The speedometer," Mr Wormwood said, "is run off a cable that is coupled up to one of the front wheels. So first I disconnect the cable where it joins the front wheel. Next, I get one of those high-speed electric drills and I couple that up to the end of the cable in such a way that when the drill turns, it turns the cable *backwards*. You got me so far? You following me?"

"Yes, daddy," young Michael said.

"These drills run at a tremendous speed," the father said, "so when I switch on the drill the mileage numbers on the speedo spin backwards at a fantastic rate. I can knock fifty thousand miles off the clock in a few minutes with my high-speed electric drill. And by the time I've finished, the car's only done ten thousand and it's ready for sale. 'She's almost new,' I say to the customer. 'She's hardly done ten thou. Belonged to an old lady who only used it once a week for shopping.' "

"Can you really turn the mileage back with an electric drill?" young Michael asked.

"I'm telling you trade secrets," the father said. "So don't you go talking about this to anyone else. You don't want me put in jug, do you?"

"I won't tell a soul," the boy said. "Do you do this to many cars, dad?"

"Every single car that comes through my hands gets the treatment," the father said. "They all have their mileage cut to under ten thou before they're offered for sale. And to think I invented that all by myself," he added proudly. "It's made me a mint."

Matilda, who had been listening closely, said, "But daddy, that's even more dishonest than the sawdust. It's disgusting. You're cheating people who trust you."

"If you don't like it then don't eat the food in this house," the father said. "It's bought with the profits."

"It's dirty money," Matilda said. "I hate it."

Two red spots appeared on the father's cheeks. "Who the heck do you think you are," he shouted, "The Archbishop of Canterbury or something, preaching to me about honesty? You're just an ignorant little squirt who hasn't the foggiest idea what you're talking about!"

"Quite right, Harry," the mother said. And to Matilda she said, "You've got a nerve talking to your father like that. Now keep your nasty mouth shut so we can all watch this programme in peace."

They were in the living-room eating their suppers on their knees in front of the telly.

The suppers were TV dinners in floppy aluminium containers with separate compartments for the stewed meat, the boiled potatoes and the peas. Mrs Wormwood sat munching her meal with her eyes glued to the American soap-opera on the screen. She was a large woman whose hair was dyed platinum blonde except where you could see the mousy-brown bits growing out from the roots. She wore heavy make-up and she had one of those unfortunate bulging figures where the flesh appears to be strapped in all around the body to prevent it from falling out.

"Mummy," Matilda said, "would you mind if I ate my supper in the dining-room so I could read my book?"

The father glanced up sharply. "*I* would mind!" he snapped. "Supper is a family gathering and no one leaves the table till it's over!"

"But we're not at the table," Matilda said. "We never are. We're always eating off our knees and watching the telly."

"What's wrong with watching the telly, may I ask?" the father said. His voice had suddenly become soft and dangerous.

Matilda didn't trust herself to answer him, so she kept quiet. She could feel the anger boiling up inside her. She knew it was wrong to hate her parents like this, but she was finding it very hard not to do so. All the reading she had done had given her a view of life that they had never seen. If only they would read a little Dickens or Kipling they would soon discover there was more to life than cheating people and watching television.

Another thing. She resented being told constantly that she was ignorant and stupid when she knew she wasn't. The anger inside her went on boiling and boiling, and as she lay in bed that night she made a decision. She decided that every time her father or her mother was beastly to her, she would get her own back in some way or another. A small victory or two would help her to tolerate their

idiocies and would stop her from going crazy. You must remember that she was still hardly five years old and it is not easy for somebody as small as that to score points against an all-powerful grown-up. Even so, she was determined to have a go. Her father, after what had happened in front of the telly that evening, was first on her list.

The Hat and the Superglue

The following morning, just before the father left for his beastly second-hand car garage, Matilda slipped into the cloakroom and got hold of the hat he wore each day to work. She had to stand on her toes and reach up as high as she could with a walking-stick in order to hook the hat off the peg, and even then she only just made it. The hat itself was one of those flat-topped pork-pie jobs with a jay's feather stuck in the hat-band and Mr Wormwood was very proud of it. He thought it gave him a rakish daring look, especially when he wore it at an angle with his loud checked jacket and green tie.

Matilda, holding the hat in one hand and a thin tube of Superglue in the other, proceeded to squeeze a line of glue very neatly all round the inside rim of the hat. Then she carefully hooked the hat back on to the peg with the walking-stick. She timed this operation very carefully, applying the glue just as her father was getting up from the breakfast table.

Mr Wormwood didn't notice anything when he put the hat on, but when he arrived

at the garage he couldn't get it off. Superglue is very powerful stuff, so powerful it will take your skin off if you pull too hard. Mr Wormwood didn't want to be scalped so he had to keep the hat on his head the whole day long, even when putting sawdust in gear boxes and fiddling the mileages of cars with his electric drill. In an effort to save face, he adopted a casual attitude hoping that his staff would think that he actually *meant* to keep his hat on all day long just for the heck of it, like gangsters do in the films.

When he got home that evening he still couldn't get the hat off. "Don't be silly," his wife said. "Come here. I'll take it off for you."

She gave the hat a sharp yank. Mr Wormwood let out a yell that rattled the window-panes. "Ow-w-w!" he screamed. "Don't do that! Let go! You'll take half the skin off my forehead!"

Matilda, nestling in her usual chair, was watching this performance over the rim of her book with some interest.

"What's the matter, daddy?" she said. "Has your head suddenly swollen or something?"

The father glared at his daughter with deep suspicion, but said nothing. How could he? Mrs Wormwood said to him, "It *must* be Superglue. It couldn't be anything else. That'll teach you to go playing round with nasty stuff like that. I expect you were trying to stick another feather in your hat."

"I haven't touched the flaming stuff!" Mr Wormwood shouted. He turned and looked again at Matilda who looked back at him with large innocent brown eyes.

Mrs Wormwood said to him, "You should read the label on the tube before you start messing with dangerous products. Always follow the instructions on the label."

"What in heaven's name are you talking about, you stupid witch?" Mr Wormwood shouted, clutching the brim of his hat to stop anyone trying to pull it off again. "D'you think I'm so stupid I'd glue this thing to my head on purpose?"

Matilda said, "There's a boy down the road who got some Superglue on his finger without knowing it and then he put his finger to his nose."

Mr Wormwood jumped. "What happened to him?" he spluttered.

"The finger got stuck inside his nose," Matilda said, "and he had to go around like that for a week. People kept saying to him, 'Stop picking your nose,' and he couldn't do anything about it. He looked an awful fool."

"Serve him right," Mrs Wormwood said. "He shouldn't have put his finger up there in the first place. It's a nasty habit. If all children had Superglue put on their fingers they'd soon stop doing it."

Matilda said, "Grown-ups do it too, mummy. I saw you doing it yesterday in the kitchen."

"That's quite enough from you," Mrs Wormwood said, turning pink.

Mr Wormwood had to keep his hat on all through supper in front of the television. He looked ridiculous and he stayed very silent.

When he went up to bed he tried again to get the thing off, and so did his wife, but it wouldn't budge. "How am I going to have my shower?" he demanded.

"You'll just have to do without it, won't you," his wife told him. And later on, as she watched her skinny little husband skulking around the bedroom in his purple-striped pyjamas with a pork-pie hat on his head, she thought how stupid he looked. Hardly the kind of man a wife dreams about, she told herself.

Mr Wormwood discovered that the worst thing about having a permanent hat on his head was having to sleep in it. It was impossible to lie comfortably on the pillow. "Now do stop fussing around," his wife said to him after he had been tossing and turning for about an hour. "I expect it will be loose by the morning and then it'll slip off easily."

But it wasn't loose by the morning and it wouldn't slip off. So Mrs Wormwood took a pair of scissors and cut the thing off his head, bit by bit, first the top and then the brim. Where the inner band had stuck to the hair all around the sides and back, she had to chop the hair off right to the skin so that he finished up with a bald white ring round his head, like some sort of a monk. And in the front, where the band had stuck directly to the bare skin,

there remained a whole lot of small patches of brown leathery stuff that no amount of washing would get off.

At breakfast Matilda said to him, "You *must* try to get those bits off your forehead, daddy. It looks as though you've got little brown insects crawling about all over you. People will think you've got lice."

"Be quiet!" the father snapped. "Just keep your nasty mouth shut, will you!"

All in all it was a most satisfactory exercise. But it was surely too much to hope that it had taught the father a permanent lesson.

The Ghost

There was comparative calm in the Wormwood household for about a week after the Superglue episode. The experience had clearly chastened Mr Wormwood and he seemed temporarily to have lost his taste for boasting and bullying.

Then suddenly he struck again. Perhaps he had had a bad day at the garage and had not sold enough crummy second-hand cars. There are many things that make a man irritable when he arrives home from work in the evening and a sensible wife will usually notice the storm-signals and will leave him alone until he simmers down.

When Mr Wormwood arrived back from the garage that evening his face was as dark as a thundercloud and somebody was clearly for the high-jump pretty soon. His wife recognised the signs immediately and made herself scarce. He then strode into the living-room. Matilda happened to be curled up in an arm-chair in the corner, totally absorbed in a book. Mr Wormwood switched on the television. The screen lit up. The programme blared. Mr Wormwood glared at Matilda. She hadn't moved. She had somehow trained herself by now to block her ears to the ghastly sound of the dreaded box. She kept right on reading, and for some reason this infuriated the father. Perhaps his anger was intensified because he saw her getting pleasure from something that was beyond his reach.

"Don't you *ever* stop reading?" he snapped at her.

"Oh, hello daddy," she said pleasantly. "Did you have a good day?"

"What is this trash?" he said, snatching the book from her hands.

"It isn't trash, daddy, it's lovely. It's called *The Red Pony*. It's by John Steinbeck, an American writer. Why don't you try it? You'll love it."

"Filth," Mr Wormwood said. "If it's by an American it's certain to be filth. That's all they write about."

"No daddy, it's beautiful, honestly it is. It's about . . ."

"I don't want to know what it's about," Mr Wormwood barked. "I'm fed up with your reading anyway. Go and find yourself something useful to do." With frightening suddenness he now began ripping the pages out of the book in handfuls and throwing them in the waste-paper basket.

Matilda froze in horror. The father kept going. There seemed little doubt that the man felt some kind of jealousy. How dare she, he seemed to be saying with each rip of a page, how dare she enjoy reading books when he couldn't? How dare she?

"That's a *library* book!" Matilda cried. "It doesn't belong to me! I have to return it to Mrs Phelps!"

"Then you'll have to buy another one, won't you?" the father said, still tearing out pages. "You'll have to save your pocket-money until there's enough in the kitty to buy a new one for your precious Mrs Phelps, won't you?" With that he dropped the now empty covers of the book into the basket and marched out of the room, leaving the telly blaring.

Most children in Matilda's place would have

burst into tears. She didn't do this. She sat there very still and white and thoughtful. She seemed to know that neither crying nor sulking ever got anyone anywhere. The only sensible thing to do when you are attacked is, as Napoleon once said, to counter-attack. Matilda's wonderfully subtle mind was already at work devising yet another suitable punishment for the poisonous parent. The plan that was now beginning to hatch in her mind depended, however, upon whether or not Fred's parrot was really as good a talker as Fred made out.

Fred was a friend of Matilda's. He was a small boy of six who lived just around the corner from her, and for days he had been going on about this great talking parrot his father had given him.

So the following afternoon, as soon as Mrs Wormwood had departed in her car for another session of bingo, Matilda set out for Fred's house to investigate. She knocked on his door and asked if he would be kind enough to show her the famous bird. Fred was delighted and led her up to his bedroom where a truly magnificent blue and yellow parrot sat in a tall cage.

"There it is," Fred said. "Its name is Chopper."

"Make it talk," Matilda said.

"You can't *make* it talk," Fred said. "You have to be patient. It'll talk when it feels like it."

They hung around, waiting. Suddenly the parrot said, "Hullo, hullo, hullo." It was exactly like a human voice. Matilda said, "That's amazing! What else can it say?"

"Rattle my bones!" the parrot said, giving a wonderful imitation of a spooky voice. "Rattle my bones!"

"He's always saying that," Fred told her.

"What else can he say?" Matilda asked.

"That's about it," Fred said. "But it is pretty marvellous don't you think?"

"It's fabulous," Matilda said. "Will you lend him to me just for one night?"

"No," Fred said. "Certainly not."

"I'll give you all my next week's pocket-money," Matilda said.

That was different. Fred thought about it for a few seconds. "All right, then," he said, "If you promise to return him tomorrow."

Matilda staggered back to her own empty house carrying the tall cage in both hands. There was a large fireplace in the dining-room and she now set about wedging the cage up the chimney and out of sight. This wasn't so easy, but she managed it in the end.

"Hullo, hullo, hullo!" the bird called down to her. "Hullo, hullo!"

"Shut up, you nut!" Matilda said, and she went out to wash the soot off her hands.

That evening while the mother, the father, the brother and Matilda were having supper as usual in the living-room in front of the television, a voice came loud and clear from the dining-room across the hall. "Hullo, hullo,

hullo," it said.

"Harry!" cried the mother, turning white. "There's someone in the house! I heard a voice!"

"So did I!" the brother said. Matilda jumped up and switched off the telly. "Ssshh!" she said. "Listen!"

They all stopped eating and sat there very tense, listening.

"Hullo, hullo, hullo!" came the voice again.

"There it is!" cried the brother.

"It's burglars!" hissed the mother. "They're in the dining-room!"

"I think they are," the father said, sitting tight.

"Then go and catch them, Harry!" hissed the mother. "Go out and collar them red-handed!"

The father didn't move. He seemed in no hurry to dash off and be a hero. His face had turned grey.

"Get on with it!" hissed the mother. "They're probably after the silver!"

The husband wiped his lips nervously with his napkin. "Why don't we all go and look together?" he said.

"Come on, then," the brother said. "Come

on, mum."

"They're definitely in the dining-room," Matilda whispered. "I'm sure they are."

The mother grabbed a poker from the fireplace. The father took a golf-club that was standing in the corner. The brother seized a table-lamp, ripping the plug out of its socket. Matilda took the knife she had been eating with, and all four of them crept towards the dining-room door, the father keeping well behind the others.

"Hullo, hullo, hullo," came the voice again.

"Come on!" Matilda cried and she burst into the room, brandishing her knife. "Stick 'em up!" she yelled. "We've caught you!" The others followed her, waving their weapons. Then they stopped. They stared around the room. There was no one there.

"There's no one here," the father said, greatly relieved.

"I heard him, Harry!" the mother shrieked, still quaking. "I distinctly heard his voice! So did you!"

"I'm certain I heard him!" Matilda cried. "He's in here somewhere!" She began searching behind the sofa and behind the curtains.

Then came the voice once again, soft and spooky this time, "Rattle my bones," it said. "Rattle my bones."

They all jumped, including Matilda who was a pretty good actress. They stared round the room. There was still no one there.

"It's a ghost," Matilda said.

"Heaven help us!" cried the mother, clutching her husband round the neck.

"I know it's a ghost!" Matilda said. "I've heard it here before! This room is haunted! I thought you knew that."

"Save us!" the mother screamed, almost throttling her husband.

"I'm getting out of here," the father said, greyer than ever now. They all fled, slamming the door behind them.

The next afternoon, Matilda managed to get

a rather sooty and grumpy parrot down from the chimney and out of the house without being seen. She carried it through the back-door and ran with it all the way to Fred's house.

"Did it behave itself?" Fred asked her.

"We had a lovely time with it," Matilda said. "My parents adored it."

Arithmetic

Matilda longed for her parents to be good and loving and understanding and honourable and intelligent. The fact that they were none of these things was something she had to put up with. It was not easy to do so. But the new game she had invented of punishing one or both of them each time they were beastly to her made her life more or less bearable.

Being very small and very young, the only power Matilda had over anyone in her family was brainpower. For sheer cleverness she could run rings around them all. But the fact remained that any five-year-old girl in any family was always obliged to do as she was told, however asinine the orders might be. Thus she was always forced to eat her evening meals out of TV-dinner-trays in front of the dreaded box. She always had to stay alone on weekday afternoons, and whenever she was told to shut up, she had to shut up.

Her safety-valve, the thing that prevented her from going round the bend, was the fun of devising and dishing out these splendid punishments, and the lovely thing was that they seemed to work, at any rate for short periods. The father in particular became less cocky and unbearable for several days after receiving a dose of Matilda's magic medicine.

The parrot-in-the-chimney affair quite definitely cooled both parents down a lot and for over a week they were comparatively civil to their small daughter. But alas, this couldn't last. The next flare-up came one evening in the sitting-room. Mr Wormwood had just returned from work. Matilda and her brother were sitting quietly on the sofa waiting for their mother to bring in the TV dinners on a tray. The television had not yet been switched on.

In came Mr Wormwood in a loud check suit and a yellow tie. The appalling broad orange-and-green check of the jacket and trousers almost blinded the onlooker. He looked like a low-grade bookmaker dressed up for his daughter's wedding, and he was clearly very pleased with himself this evening. He sat down in an armchair and rubbed his hands together and addressed his son in a loud voice. "Well, my boy," he said, "your father's had a most successful day. He is a lot richer tonight than he was this morning. He has sold no less than five cars, each one at a tidy profit. Sawdust in the gear-boxes, the electric-drill on the speedometer cables, a splash of paint here and there and a few other clever little tricks and the idiots were all falling over themselves to buy."

He fished a bit of paper from his pocket and studied it. "Listen boy," he said, addressing the son and ignoring Matilda, "seeing as you'll be going into this business with me one day, you've got to know how to add up the profits you make at the end of each day. Go and get yourself a pad and a pencil and let's see how clever you are."

The son obediently left the room and returned with the writing materials.

"Write down these figures," the father said, reading from his bit of paper. "Car number one was bought by me for two hundred and seventy-eight pounds and sold for one thousand four hundred and twenty-five. Got that?"

The ten-year-old boy wrote the two separate amounts down slowly and carefully.

"Car number two," the father went on, "cost me one hundred and eighteen pounds and sold for seven hundred and sixty. Got it?"

"Yes, dad," the son said. "I've got that."

"Car number three cost one hundred and

eleven pounds and sold for nine hundred and ninety-nine pounds and fifty pence."

"Say that again," the son said. "How much did it sell for?"

"Nine hundred and ninety-nine pounds and fifty pence," the father said. "And that, by the way, is another of my nifty little tricks to diddle the customer. Never ask for a big round figure.

Always go just below it. Never say one thousand pounds. Always say nine hundred and ninety-nine fifty. It sounds much less but it isn't. Clever, isn't it?"

"Very," the son said. "You're brilliant, dad."

"Car number four cost eighty-six pounds – a real wreck that was – and sold for six hundred and ninety-nine pounds fifty."

"Not too fast," the son said, writing the numbers down. "Right. I've got it."

"Car number five cost six hundred and thirty-seven pounds and sold for sixteen hundred and forty-nine fifty. You got all those figures written down, son?"

"Yes, daddy," the boy said, crouching over

his pad and carefully writing.

"Very well," the father said. "Now work out the profit I made on each of the five cars and add up the total. Then you'll be able to tell me how much money your rather brilliant father made altogether today."

"That's a lot of sums," the boy said.

"Of course it's a lot of sums," the father answered. "But when you're in big business like I am, you've got to be hot stuff at arithmetic. I've practically got a computer inside my head. It took me less than ten minutes to work the whole thing out."

"You mean you did it in your head, dad?" the son asked, goggling.

"Well, not exactly," the father said. "Nobody could do that. But it didn't take me long. When you're finished, tell me what you think my profit was for the day. I've got the final total written down here and I'll tell you if you're right."

Matilda sat quietly, "Dad, you made exactly four thousand three hundred and three pounds and fifty pence altogether."

"Don't butt in," the father said. "Your brother and I are busy with high finance."

"But dad . . ."

"Shut up," the father said. "Stop guessing and trying to be clever."

"Look at your answer, dad," Matilda said gently. "If you've done it right it ought to be four thousand three hundred and three pounds and fifty pence. Is that what you've got, dad?"

The father glanced down at the paper in his hand. He seemed to stiffen. He became very quiet. There was a silence. Then he said, "Say that again."

"Four thousand three hundred and three pounds fifty," Matilda said.

There was another silence. The father's face was beginning to go dark red.

"I'm sure it's right," Matilda said.

"You . . . you little cheat!" the father suddenly shouted, pointing at her with his finger. "You looked at my bit of paper! You read it off from what I've got written here!"

"Daddy, I'm the other side of the room," Matilda said. "How could I possibly see it?"

"Don't give me that rubbish!" the father shouted. "Of course you looked! You must have looked! No one in the world could give the right answer just like that, especially a girl! You're a little cheat, madam, that's what you are! A cheat and a liar!"

At that point, the mother came in carrying a large tray on which were the four suppers. This time it was fish and chips which Mrs

Wormwood had picked up in the fish and chip shop on her way home from bingo. It seemed that bingo afternoons left her so exhausted both physically and emotionally that she never had enough energy left to cook an evening meal. So if it wasn't TV dinners it had to be fish and chips. "What are you looking so red in the face about, Harry?" she said as she put the tray down on the coffee-table.

"Your daughter's a cheat and a liar," the father said, taking his plate of fish and placing it on his knees. "Turn the telly on and let's not have any more talk."

The Platinum-Blond Man

There was no doubt in Matilda's mind that this latest display of foulness by her father deserved severe punishment, and as she sat eating her awful fried fish and fried chips and ignoring the television, her brain went to work on various possibilities. By the time she went up to bed her mind was made up.

The next morning she got up early and went into the bathroom and locked the door. As we already know, Mrs Wormwood's hair was dyed a brilliant platinum blonde, very much the same glistening silvery colour as a female tightrope-walker's tights in a circus. The big dyeing job was done twice a year at the hairdresser's, but every month or so in between, Mrs Wormwood used to freshen it up by giving it a rinse in the washbasin with something called PLATINUM BLONDE HAIR-DYE EXTRA STRONG. This also served to dye the nasty brown hairs that kept growing from the roots underneath. The bottle of PLATINUM BLONDE HAIR-DYE EXTRA STRONG was kept in the cupboard in the bathroom, and underneath the title on the label were written the words *Caution, this is peroxide. Keep away from children*. Matilda had read it many times with fascination.

Matilda's father had a fine crop of black hair which he parted in the middle and of which he was exceedingly proud. "Good strong hair," he was fond of saying, "means there's a good strong brain underneath."

"Like Shakespeare," Matilda had once said to him.

"Like who?"

"Shakespeare, daddy."

"Was he brainy?"

"Very, daddy."

"He had masses of hair, did he?"

"He was bald, daddy."

To which the father had snapped, "If you can't talk sense then shut up."

Anyway, Mr Wormwood kept his hair looking bright and strong, or so he thought, by

rubbing into it every morning large quantities of a lotion called OIL OF VIOLETS HAIR TONIC. A bottle of this smelly purple mixture always stood on the shelf above the sink in the bathroom alongside all the toothbrushes, and a very vigorous scalp massage with OIL OF VIOLETS took place daily after shaving was completed. This hair and scalp massage was always accompanied by loud masculine grunts and heavy breathing and gasps of "Ahhh, that's better! That's the stuff! Rub it right into the roots!" which could be clearly heard by Matilda in her bedroom across the corridor.

Now, in the early morning privacy of the bathroom, Matilda unscrewed the cap of her father's OIL OF VIOLETS and tipped three-quarters of the contents down the drain. Then she filled the bottle up with her mother's PLATINUM BLONDE HAIR-DYE EXTRA STRONG. She carefully left enough of her father's original hair tonic in the bottle so that when she gave it a good shake the whole thing still looked reasonably purple. She then replaced the bottle on the shelf above the sink, taking care to put her mother's bottle back in the cupboard. So far so good.

At breakfast time Matilda sat quietly at the dining-room table eating her cornflakes. Her brother sat opposite her with his back to the door devouring hunks of bread smothered with a mixture of peanut-butter and strawberry jam. The mother was just out of sight around the corner in the kitchen making Mr Wormwood's breakfast which always had to be two fried eggs on fried bread with three pork sausages and three strips of bacon and some fried tomatoes.

At this point Mr Wormwood came noisily into the room. He was incapable of entering any room quietly, especially at breakfast time. He always had to make his appearance felt immediately by creating a lot of noise and clatter. One could almost hear him saying, "It's me! Here I come, the great man himself, the master of the house, the wage-earner, the one who makes it possible for all the rest of you to live so well! Notice me and pay your respects!"

On this occasion he strode in and slapped his son on the back and shouted, "Well my boy, your father feels he's in for another great money-making day today at the garage! I've got a few little beauties I'm going to flog to the idiots this morning. Where's my breakfast?"

"It's coming, treasure," Mrs Wormwood called from the kitchen.

Matilda kept her face bent low over her cornflakes. She didn't dare look up. In the first place she wasn't at all sure what she was going to see. And secondly, if she did see what she thought she was going to see, she wouldn't trust herself to keep a straight face. The son was looking directly ahead out of the window stuffing himself with bread and peanut-butter and strawberry jam.

The father was just moving round to sit at the head of the table when the mother came sweeping out from the kitchen carrying a huge plate piled high with eggs and sausages and bacon and tomatoes. She looked up. She caught sight of her husband. She stopped dead. Then she let out a scream that seemed to lift her right up into the air and she dropped the plate with a crash and a splash on to the floor. Everyone jumped, including Mr Wormwood.

"What the heck's the matter with you, woman?" he shouted. "Look at the mess you've made on the carpet!"

"Your *hair*!" the mother was shrieking, pointing a quivering finger at her husband. "Look at your *hair*! What've you done to

your *hair*?"

"What's wrong with my hair for heaven's sake?" he said.

"Oh my gawd dad, what've you done to your hair?" the son shouted.

A splendid noisy scene was building up nicely in the breakfast room.

Matilda said nothing. She simply sat there admiring the wonderful effect of her own handiwork. Mr Wormwood's fine crop of black hair was now a dirty silver, the colour this time of a tightrope-walker's tights that had not been washed for the entire circus season.

"You've . . . you've . . . you've *dyed* it!" shrieked the mother. "Why did you do it, you fool! It looks absolutely frightful! It looks horrendous! You look like a freak!"

"What the blazes are you all talking about?" the father yelled, putting both hands to his hair. "I most certainly have not dyed it! What d'you mean I've dyed it? What's happened to it? Or is this some sort of stupid joke?" His face was turning pale green, the colour of sour apples.

"You *must* have dyed it, dad," the son said. "It's the same colour as mum's only much dirtier looking."

"Of course he's dyed it!" the mother cried. "It can't change colour all by itself! What on earth were you trying to do, make yourself look handsome or something? You look like someone's grandmother gone wrong!"

"Get me a mirror!" the father yelled. "Don't just stand there shrieking at me! Get me a mirror!"

The mother's handbag lay on a chair at the

other end of the table. She opened the bag and got out a powder compact that had a small round mirror on the inside of the lid. She opened the compact and handed it to her husband. He grabbed it and held it before his face and in doing so spilled most of the powder all over the front of his fancy tweed jacket.

"Be *careful*!" shrieked the mother. "Now look what you've done! That's my best Elizabeth Arden face powder!"

"Oh my gawd!" yelled the father, staring into the little mirror. "What's happened to me!

I look terrible! I look just like *you* gone wrong! I can't go down to the garage and sell cars like this! How did this happen?" He stared round the room, first at the mother, then at the son, then at Matilda. "How *could* it have happened?" he yelled.

"I imagine, daddy," Matilda said quietly, "that you weren't looking very hard and you simply took mummy's bottle of hair stuff off the shelf instead of your own."

"*Of course* that's what happened!" the mother cried. "Well really Harry, how stupid can you get? Why didn't you read the label before you started splashing the stuff all over you! Mine's *terribly* strong. I'm only meant to use one tablespoon of it in a whole basin of water and you've gone and put it all over your head neat! It'll probably take all your hair off in the end! Is your scalp beginning to burn, dear?"

"You mean I'm going to lose all my hair?" the husband yelled.

"I think you will," the mother said. "Peroxide is a very powerful chemical. It's what they put down the lavatory to disinfect the pan only they give it another name."

"What are you saying!" the husband cried.

"I'm not a lavatory pan! I don't want to be disinfected!"

"Even diluted like I use it," the mother told him, "it makes a good deal of *my* hair fall out, so goodness knows what's going to happen to you. I'm surprised it didn't take the whole of the top of your head off!"

"What shall I do?" wailed the father. "Tell me quick what to do before it starts falling out!"

Matilda said, "I'd give it a good wash, dad, if I were you, with soap and water. But you'll have to hurry."

"Will that change the colour back?" the father asked anxiously.

"Of course it won't, you twit," the mother said.

"Then what do I do? I can't go around looking like this for ever?"

"You'll have to have it dyed black," the mother said. "But wash it first or there won't be any there to dye."

"Right!" the father shouted, springing into action. "Get me an appointment with your hairdresser this instant for a hair-dyeing job! Tell them it's an emergency! They've got to boot someone else off their list! I'm going upstairs to wash it now!" With that the man dashed out of the room and Mrs Wormwood, sighing deeply, went to the telephone to call the beauty parlour.

"He does do some pretty silly things now and again, doesn't he, mummy?" Matilda said.

The mother, dialling the number on the phone, said, "I'm afraid men are not always quite as clever as they think they are. You will learn that when you get a bit older, my girl."

Miss Honey

Matilda was a little late in starting school. Most children begin Primary School at five or even just before, but Matilda's parents, who weren't very concerned one way or another about their daughter's education, had forgotten to make the proper arrangements in advance. She was five and a half when she entered school for the first time.

The village school for younger children was a bleak brick building called Crunchem Hall Primary School. It had about two hundred and fifty pupils aged from five to just under twelve years old. The head teacher, the boss, the supreme commander of this establishment was a formidable middle-aged lady whose name was Miss Trunchbull.

Naturally Matilda was put in the bottom class, where there were eighteen other small boys and girls about the same age as her. Their teacher was called Miss Honey, and she could not have been more than twenty-three or twenty-four. She had a lovely pale oval madonna face with blue eyes and her hair was light-brown. Her body was so slim and fragile one got the feeling that if she fell over she would smash into a thousand pieces, like a porcelain figure.

Miss Jennifer Honey was a mild and quiet person who never raised her voice and was seldom seen to smile, but there is no doubt she possessed that rare gift for being adored by every small child under her care. She seemed to understand totally the bewilderment and fear that so often overwhelms young children who for the first time in their lives are herded into a classroom and told to obey orders. Some curious warmth that was almost tangible shone out of Miss Honey's face when she spoke to a confused and homesick newcomer to the class.

Miss Trunchbull, the Headmistress, was something else altogether. She was a gigantic holy terror, a fierce tyrannical monster who frightened the life out of the pupils and teachers alike. There was an aura of menace about her even at a distance, and when she came up close you could almost feel the dangerous heat radiating from her as from a red-hot rod of metal. When she marched – Miss Trunchbull never walked, she always marched like a storm trooper with long strides and arms aswinging – when she marched along a corridor you could actually hear her snorting as she went, and if a group of children happened to be in her path, she ploughed right on through them like a tank, with small people bouncing off her to left and right. Thank goodness we don't meet many people like her in this world, although they do exist and all of us are likely to come across at least one of them in a lifetime. If you ever do, you should behave as you would if you met an enraged rhinoceros out in the bush – climb up the nearest tree and stay there until it has gone away. This woman, in all her eccentricities and in her appearance, is almost impossible to describe, but I shall make some attempt to do so a little later on. Let us leave her for the moment and go back to Matilda and her first day in Miss Honey's class.

After the usual business of going through all the names of the children, Miss Honey handed out a brand-new exercise-book to each pupil.

"You have all brought your own pencils, I hope," she said.

"Yes, Miss Honey," they chanted.

"Good. Now this is the very first day of school for each one of you. It is the beginning of at least eleven long years of schooling that

all of you are going to have to go through. And six of those years will be spent right here at Crunchem Hall where, as you know, your Headmistress is Miss Trunchbull. Let me for your own good tell you something about Miss Trunchbull. She insists upon strict discipline throughout the school, and if you take my advice you will do your very best to behave yourselves in her presence. Never argue with her. Never answer her back. Always do as she says. If you get on the wrong side of Miss Trunchbull she can liquidise you like a carrot in a kitchen blender. It's nothing to laugh about, Lavender. Take that grin off your face. All of you will be wise to remember that Miss Trunchbull deals very very severely with anyone who gets out of line in this school. Have you got the message?"

"Yes, Miss Honey," chirruped eighteen eager little voices.

"I myself," Miss Honey went on, "want to

help you to learn as much as possible while you are in this class. That is because I know it will make things easier for you later on. For example, by the end of this week I shall expect every one of you to know the two-times table by heart. And in a year's time I hope you will know all the multiplication tables up to twelve. It will help you enormously if you do. Now then, do any of you happen to have learnt the two-times table already?"

Matilda put up her hand. She was the only one.

Miss Honey looked carefully at the tiny girl with dark hair and a round serious face sitting in the second row. "Wonderful," she said. "Please stand up and recite as much of it as you can."

Matilda stood up and began to say the two-times table. When she got to twice twelve is twenty-four she didn't stop. She went right on with twice thirteen is twenty-six, twice fourteen is twenty-eight, twice fifteen is thirty, twice sixteen is . . .

"Stop!" Miss Honey said. She had been listening slightly spellbound to this smooth recital, and now she said, "How far can you go?"

"How far?" Matilda said. "Well, I don't really know, Miss Honey. For quite a long way, I think."

Miss Honey took a few moments to let this curious statement sink in. "You mean", she said, "that you could tell me what two times twenty-eight is?"

"Yes, Miss Honey."

"What is it?"

"Fifty-six, Miss Honey."

"What about something much harder, like two times four hundred and eighty-seven?

Could you tell me that?"

"I think so, yes," Matilda said.

"Are you sure?"

"Why yes, Miss Honey, I'm fairly sure."

"What is it then, two times four hundred and eighty-seven?"

"Nine hundred and seventy-four," Matilda said immediately. She spoke quietly and politely and without any sign of showing off.

Miss Honey gazed at Matilda with absolute amazement, but when next she spoke she kept her voice level. "That is really splendid," she said. "But of course multiplying by two is a lot easier than some of the bigger numbers. What about the other multiplication tables? Do you know any of those?"

"I think so, Miss Honey. I think I do."

"Which ones, Matilda? How far have you got?"

"I . . . I don't quite know," Matilda said. "I don't know what you mean."

"What I mean is do you for instance know the three-times table?"

"Yes, Miss Honey."

"And the four-times?"

"Yes, Miss Honey."

"Well, how many *do* you know, Matilda? Do you know all the way up to the twelve-times table?"

"Yes, Miss Honey."

"What are twelve sevens?"

"Eighty-four," Matilda said.

Miss Honey paused and leaned back in her chair behind the plain table that stood in the middle of the floor in front of the class. She was considerably shaken by this exchange but took care not to show it. She had never come across a five-year-old before, or indeed a ten-year-old, who could multiply with such facility.

"I hope the rest of you are listening to this," she said to the class. "Matilda is a very lucky girl. She has wonderful parents who have already taught her to multiply lots of numbers. Was it your mother, Matilda, who taught you?"

"No, Miss Honey, it wasn't."

"You must have a great father then. He must be a brilliant teacher."

"No, Miss Honey," Matilda said quietly. "My father did not teach me."

"You mean you taught yourself?"

"I don't quite know," Matilda said truthfully. "It's just that I don't find it very difficult to multiply one number by another."

Miss Honey took a deep breath and let it out slowly. She looked again at the small girl with bright eyes standing beside her desk so sensible and solemn. "You say you don't find it difficult to multiply one number by another," Miss Honey said. "Could you try to explain that a little bit."

"Oh dear," Matilda said. "I'm not really sure."

Miss Honey waited. The class was silent, all listening.

"For instance," Miss Honey said, "if I asked you to multiply fourteen by nineteen . . . No, that's too difficult . . ."

"It's two hundred and sixty-six," Matilda said softly.

Miss Honey stared at her. Then she picked up a pencil and quickly worked out the sum on a piece of paper. "What did you say it was?" she said, looking up.

"Two hundred and sixty-six," Matilda said.

Miss Honey put down her pencil and removed her spectacles and began to polish the lenses with a piece of tissue. The class remained quiet, watching her and waiting for what was coming next. Matilda was still standing up beside her desk.

"Now tell me, Matilda," Miss Honey said, still polishing, "try to tell me exactly what goes on inside your head when you get a multiplication like that to do. You obviously have to work it out in some way, but you seem able to arrive at the answer almost instantly. Take the one you've just done, fourteen multiplied by nineteen."

"I . . . I . . . I simply put the fourteen down in my head and multiply it by nineteen," Matilda said. "I'm afraid I don't know how else to explain it. I've always said to myself that if a little pocket calculator can do it why shouldn't I?"

"Why not indeed," Miss Honey said. "The human brain is an amazing thing."

"I think it's a lot better than a lump of metal," Matilda said. "That's all a calculator is."

"How right you are," Miss Honey said. "Pocket calculators are not allowed in this school anyway." Miss Honey was feeling quite quivery. There was no doubt in her mind that she had met a truly extraordinary mathematical brain, and words like child-genius and prodigy went flitting through her head. She knew that these sort of wonders do pop up in the world from time to time, but only once or twice in a hundred years. After all, Mozart was only five when he started composing for the piano and look what happened to him.

"It's not fair," Lavender said. "How can she do it and we can't?"

"Don't worry, Lavender, you'll soon catch up," Miss Honey said, lying through her teeth.

At this point Miss Honey could not resist the temptation of exploring still further the mind of this astonishing child. She knew that she ought to be paying some attention to the rest of the class but she was altogether too excited to let the matter rest.

"Well," she said, pretending to address the whole class, "let us leave sums for the moment and see if any of you have begun to learn to spell. Hands up anyone who can spell cat."

Three hands went up. They belonged to Lavender, a small boy called Nigel and to Matilda.

"Spell cat, Nigel."

Nigel spelled it.

Miss Honey now decided to ask a question that normally she would not have dreamed of asking the class on its first day. "I wonder," she said, "whether any of you three who know how to spell cat have learned how to read a whole group of words when they are strung together in a sentence?"

"I have," Nigel said.

"So have I," Lavender said.

Miss Honey went to the blackboard and wrote with her white chalk the sentence, *I have already begun to learn how to read long sentences.* She had purposely made it difficult and she knew that there were precious few five-year-olds around who would be able to manage it.

"Can you tell me what that says, Nigel?" she asked.

"That's too hard," Nigel said.

"Lavender?"

"The first word is I," Lavender said.

"Can any of you read the whole sentence?" Miss Honey asked, waiting for the "yes" that she felt certain was going to come from Matilda.

"Yes," Matilda said.

"Go ahead," Miss Honey said.

Matilda read the sentence without hesitation at all.

"That really is very good indeed," Miss Honey said, making the understatement of her life. "How much *can* you read, Matilda?"

"I think I can read most things, Miss

Honey," Matilda said, "although I'm afraid I can't always understand the meanings."

Miss Honey got to her feet and walked smartly out of the room, but was back in thirty seconds carrying a thick book. She opened it at random and placed it on Matilda's desk. "This is a book of humorous poetry," she said. "See if you can read that one aloud."

Smoothly, without a pause and at a nice speed, Matilda began to read:

"An epicure dining at Crewe
Found a rather large mouse in his stew.
Cried the waiter, "Don't shout
And wave it about
Or the rest will be wanting one too."

Several children saw the funny side of the rhyme and laughed. Miss Honey said, "Do you know what an epicure is, Matilda?"

"It is someone who is dainty with his eating," Matilda said.

"That is correct," Miss Honey said. "And do you happen to know what that particular type of poetry is called?"

"It's called a limerick," Matilda said. "That's a lovely one. It's so funny."

"It's a famous one," Miss Honey said, picking up the book and returning to her table in front of the class. "A witty limerick is very hard to write," she added. "They look easy but they most certainly are not."

"I know," Matilda said. "I've tried quite a few times but mine are never any good."

"You have, have you?" Miss Honey said, more startled than ever. "Well Matilda, I would very much like to hear one of these limericks you say you have written. Could you try to remember one for us?"

"Well," Matilda said, hesitating. "I've actually been trying to make up one about you, Miss Honey, while we've been sitting here."

"About *me*!" Miss Honey cried. "Well, we've certainly got to hear that one, haven't we?"

"I don't think I want to say it, Miss Honey."

"Please tell it," Miss Honey said. "I promise I won't mind."

"I think you will, Miss Honey, because I have to use your first name to make things rhyme and that's why I don't want to say it."

"How do you know my first name?" Miss Honey asked.

"I heard another teacher calling you by it just before we came in," Matilda said. "She called you Jenny."

"I insist upon hearing this limerick," Miss Honey said, smiling one of her rare smiles. "Stand up and recite it."

Reluctantly Matilda stood up and very slowly, very nervously, she recited her limerick:

"The thing we all ask about Jenny
Is, 'Surely there cannot be many
Young girls in the place
With so lovely a face?'
The answer to that is, '*Not any!*' "

The whole of Miss Honey's pale and pleasant face blushed a brilliant scarlet. Then once again she smiled. It was a much broader one this time, a smile of pure pleasure.

"Why, thank you, Matilda," she said, still

smiling. "Although it is not true, it is really a very good limerick. Oh dear, oh dear, I must try to remember that one."

From the third row of desks, Lavender said, "It's good. I like it."

"It's true as well," a small boy called Rupert said.

"Of course it's true," Nigel said.

Already the whole class had begun to warm towards Miss Honey, although as yet she had hardly taken any notice of any of them except Matilda.

"Who taught you to read, Matilda?" Miss Honey asked.

"I just sort of taught myself, Miss Honey."

"And have you read any books all by yourself, any children's books, I mean?"

"I've read all the ones that are in the public library in the High Street, Miss Honey."

"And did you like them?"

"I liked some of them very much indeed,"

Matilda said, "but I thought others were fairly dull."

"Tell me one that you liked."

"I liked *The Lion, the Witch and the Wardrobe*," Matilda said. "I think Mr C. S. Lewis is a very good writer. But he had one failing. There are no funny bits in his books."

"You are right there," Miss Honey said.

"There aren't many funny bits in Mr Tolkien either," Matilda said.

"Do you think that all children's books ought to have funny bits in them?" Miss Honey asked.

"I do," Matilda said. "Children are not so serious as grown-ups and they love to laugh."

Miss Honey was astounded by the wisdom of this tiny girl. She said, "And what are you going to do now that you've read all the children's books?"

"I am reading other books," Matilda said. "I borrow them from the library. Mrs Phelps is very kind to me. She helps me to choose them."

Miss Honey was leaning far forward over her work-table and gazing in wonder at the child. She had completely forgotten now about the rest of the class. "What other books?"

she murmured.

"I am very fond of Charles Dickens," Matilda said. "He makes me laugh a lot. Especially Mr Pickwick."

At that moment the bell in the corridor sounded for the end of class.

The Trunchbull

In the interval, Miss Honey left the classroom and headed straight for the Headmistress's study. She felt wildly excited. She had just met a small girl who possessed, or so it seemed to her, quite extraordinary qualities of brilliance. There had not been time yet to find out exactly how brilliant the child was, but Miss Honey had learned enough to realise that something had to be done about it as soon as possible. It would be ridiculous to leave a child like that stuck in the bottom form.

Normally Miss Honey was terrified of the Headmistress and kept well away from her, but at this moment she felt ready to take on anybody. She knocked on the door of the dreaded private study. "Enter!" boomed the deep and dangerous voice of Miss Trunchbull. Miss Honey went in.

Now most head teachers are chosen because they possess a number of fine qualities. They understand children and they have the children's best interests at heart. They are sympathetic. They are fair and they are deeply interested in education. Miss Trunchbull possessed none of these qualities and how she ever got her present job was a mystery.

She was above all a most formidable female. She had once been a famous athlete, and even now the muscles were still clearly in evidence. You could see them in the bull-neck, in the big shoulders, in the thick arms, in the sinewy wrists and in the powerful legs. Looking at her, you got the feeling that this was someone who could bend iron bars and tear telephone directories in half. Her face, I'm afraid, was neither a thing of beauty nor a joy for ever. She had an obstinate chin, a cruel mouth and small arrogant eyes. And as for her clothes . . . they were, to say the least, extremely odd. She always had on a brown cotton smock which was pinched in around the waist with a wide leather belt. The belt was fastened in front with an enormous silver buckle. The massive thighs which emerged from out of the smock were encased in a pair of extraordinary breeches, bottle-green in colour and made of coarse twill. These breeches reached to just below the knees and from there on down she sported green stockings with turn-up tops, which displayed her calf muscles to perfection. On her feet she wore flat-heeled brown brogues with leather flaps. She looked, in short, more like a rather eccentric and bloodthirsty follower of the stag-hounds than the headmistress of a nice school for children.

When Miss Honey entered the study, Miss Trunchbull was standing beside her huge desk with a look of scowling impatience on her face. "Yes, Miss Honey," she said. "What is it you want? You're looking very flushed and flustered this morning. What's the matter with you? Have those little stinkers been flicking spitballs at you?"

"No, Headmistress. Nothing like that."

"Well, what is it then? Get on with it. I'm a busy woman." As she spoke, she reached out and poured herself a glass of water from a jug that was always on her desk.

"There is a little girl in my class called Matilda Wormwood . . ." Miss Honey began.

"That's the daughter of the man who owns Wormwood Motors in the village," Miss Trunchbull barked. She hardly ever spoke in a normal voice. She either barked or shouted. "An excellent person, Wormwood," she went on. "I was in there only yesterday. He sold me a car. Almost new. Only done ten thousand miles. Previous owner was an old lady who

took it out once a year at the most. A terrific bargain. Yes, I liked Wormwood. A real pillar of society. He told me the daughter was a bad lot though. He said to watch her. He said if anything bad ever happened in the school, it was certain to be his daughter who did it. I haven't met the little brat yet, but she'll know about it when I do. Her father said she's a real wart."

"Oh no, Headmistress, that can't be right!" Miss Honey cried.

"Oh yes, Miss Honey, it darn well is right! In fact, now I come to think of it, I'll bet it was she who put that stink-bomb under my desk here first thing this morning. The place stank like a sewer! Of course it was her! I shall have her for that, you see if I don't! What's she look like? Nasty little worm, I'll be bound. I have discovered, Miss Honey, during my long career as a teacher that a bad girl is a far more dangerous creature than a bad boy. What's more, they're much harder to squash. Squashing a bad girl is like trying to squash a bluebottle. You bang down on it and the darn thing isn't there. Nasty dirty things, little girls are. Glad I never was one."

"Oh, but you must have been a little girl

once, Headmistress. Surely you were."

"Not for long anyway," Miss Trunchbull barked, grinning. "I became a woman very quickly."

She's completely off her rocker, Miss Honey told herself. She's barmy as a bedbug. Miss Honey stood resolutely before the Headmistress. For once she was not going to be browbeaten. "I must tell you, Headmistress," she said, "that you are completely mistaken about Matilda putting a stink-bomb under your desk."

"I am never mistaken, Miss Honey!"

"But Headmistress, the child only arrived in school this morning and came straight to the classroom . . ."

"Don't argue with me, for heaven's sake, woman! This little brute Matilda or whatever her name is has stink-bombed my study! There's no doubt about it! Thank you for suggesting it."

"But I didn't suggest it, Headmistress."

"Of course you did! Now what is it you want, Miss Honey? Why are you wasting my time?"

"I came to you to talk about Matilda, Headmistress. I have extraordinary things to report about the child. May I please tell you what happened in class just now?"

"I suppose she set fire to your skirt and scorched your knickers!" Miss Trunchbull snorted.

"No, no!" Miss Honey cried out. "Matilda is a genius."

At the mention of this word, Miss Trunchbull's face turned purple and her whole body seemed to swell up like a bullfrog's. "A *genius*!" she shouted. "What piffle is this you are talking, madam? You must be out of your mind! I have her father's word for it that the child is a gangster!"

"Her father is wrong, Headmistress."

"Don't be a twerp, Miss Honey! You have met the little beast for only half an hour and her father has known her all her life!"

But Miss Honey was determined to have her say and she now began to describe some of the amazing things Matilda had done with arithmetic.

"So she's learnt a few tables by heart, has she?" Miss Trunchbull barked. "My dear woman, that doesn't make her a genius! It makes her a parrot!"

"But Headmistress she can *read*."

"So can I," Miss Trunchbull snapped.

"It is my opinion," Miss Honey said, "that Matilda should be taken out of my form and placed immediately in the top form with the eleven-year-olds."

"Ha!" snorted Miss Trunchbull. "So you want to get rid of her, do you? So you can't handle her? So now you want to unload her on to the wretched Miss Plimsoll in the top form where she will cause even more chaos?"

"No, no!" cried Miss Honey. "That is not my reason at all!"

"Oh, yes it is!" shouted Miss Trunchbull. "I can see right through your little plot, madam! And my answer is no! Matilda stays where she is and it is up to you to see that she behaves herself."

"But Headmistress, please . . ."

"Not another word!" shouted Miss Trunchbull. "And in any case, I have a rule in this school that all children remain in their own age groups regardless of ability. Great Scott, I'm not having a little five-year-old brigand sitting with the senior girls and boys in the top form. Whoever heard of such a thing!"

Miss Honey stood there helpless before this great red-necked giant. There was a lot more she would like to have said but she knew it was useless. She said softly, "Very well, then. It's up to you, Headmistress."

"You're darn right it's up to me!" Miss Trunchbull bellowed. "And don't forget, madam, that we are dealing here with a little viper who put a stink-bomb under my desk . . ."

"She did *not* do that, Headmistress!"

"Of course she did it," Miss Trunchbull boomed. "And I'll tell you what. I wish to heavens I was still allowed to use the birch and belt as I did in the good old days! I'd have roasted Matilda's bottom for her so she couldn't sit down for a month!"

Miss Honey turned and walked out of the study feeling depressed but by no means defeated. I am going to do something about this child, she told herself. I don't know what it will be, but I shall find a way to help her in the end.

The Parents

When Miss Honey emerged from the Headmistress's study, most of the children were outside in the playground. Her first move was to go round to the various teachers who taught the senior class and borrow from them a number of text-books, books on algebra, geometry, French, English Literature and the like. Then she sought out Matilda and called her into the classroom.

"There is no point," she said, "in you sitting in class doing nothing while I am teaching the rest of the form the two-times table and how to spell cat and rat and mouse. So during each lesson I shall give you one of these text-books to study. At the end of the lesson you can come up to me with your questions if you have any and I shall try to help you. How does that sound?"

"Thank you, Miss Honey," Matilda said. "That sounds fine."

"I am sure," Miss Honey said, "that we'll be able to get you moved into a much higher form later on, but for the moment the Headmistress wishes you to stay where you are."

"Very well, Miss Honey," Matilda said. "Thank you so much for getting those books for me."

What a nice child she is, Miss Honey thought. I don't care what her father said about her, she seems very quiet and gentle to me. And not a bit stuck up in spite of her brilliance. In fact she hardly seems aware of it.

So when the class reassembled, Matilda went to her desk and began to study a text-book on geometry which Miss Honey had given her. The teacher kept half an eye on her all the time and noticed that the child very soon became deeply absorbed in the book. She never glanced up once during the entire lesson.

Miss Honey, meanwhile, was making another decision. She was deciding that she would go herself and have a secret talk with Matilda's mother and father as soon as possible. She simply refused to let the matter rest where it was. The whole thing was ridiculous. She couldn't believe that the parents were totally unaware of their daughter's remarkable talents. After all, Mr Wormwood was a successful motor-car dealer so she presumed that he was a fairly intelligent man himself. In any event, parents never *underestimated* the abilities of their own children. Quite the reverse. Sometimes it was well nigh impossible for a teacher to convince the proud father or mother that their beloved offspring was a complete nitwit. Miss Honey felt confident that she would have no difficulty in convincing Mr and Mrs Wormwood that Matilda was something very special indeed. The trouble was going to be to stop them from getting over-enthusiastic.

And now Miss Honey's hopes began to expand even further. She started wondering whether permission might not be sought from the parents for her to give private tuition to Matilda after school. The prospect of coaching a child as bright as this appealed enormously to her professional instinct as a teacher. And suddenly she decided that she would go and call on Mr and Mrs Wormwood that very evening. She would go fairly late, between nine and ten o'clock, when Matilda was sure to be in bed.

And that is precisely what she did. Having got the address from the school records, Miss Honey set out to walk from her own home to the Wormwood's house shortly after nine. She found the house in a pleasant street where each smallish building was separated from its neighbours by a bit of garden. It was a modern brick house that could not have been cheap to buy and the name on the gate said COSY NOOK. Nosey cook might have been better, Miss Honey thought. She was given to playing with words in that way. She walked up the path and rang the bell, and while she stood waiting she could hear the television blaring inside.

The door was opened by a small ratty-looking man with a thin ratty moustache who was wearing a sports-coat that had an orange and red stripe in the material. "Yes?" he said, peering out at Miss Honey. "If you're selling raffle tickets I don't want any."

"I'm not," Miss Honey said. "And please forgive me for butting in on you like this. I am Matilda's teacher at school and it is important I have a word with you and your wife."

"Got into trouble already, has she?" Mr Wormwood said, blocking the doorway. "Well, she's your responsibility from now on. You'll have to deal with her."

"She is in no trouble at all," Miss Honey said. "I have come with good news about her.

Quite startling news, Mr Wormwood. Do you think I might come in for a few minutes and talk to you about Matilda?"

"We are right in the middle of watching one

of our favourite programmes," Mr Wormwood said. "This is most inconvenient. Why don't you come back some other time."

Miss Honey began to lose patience. "Mr Wormwood," she said, "if you think some rotten TV programme is more important than your daughter's future, then you ought not to be a parent! Why don't you switch the darn thing off and listen to me!"

That shook Mr Wormwood. He was not used to being spoken to in this way. He peered carefully at the slim frail woman who stood so resolutely out on the porch. "Oh very well then," he snapped. "Come on in and let's get it over with." Miss Honey stepped briskly inside.

"Mrs Wormwood isn't going to thank you for this," the man said as he led her into the sitting-room where a large platinum-blonde woman was gazing rapturously at the TV screen.

"Who is it?" the woman said, not looking round.

"Some school teacher," Mr Wormwood said. "She says she's got to talk to us about Matilda." He crossed to the TV set and turned down the sound but left the picture on the screen.

"Don't do that, Harry!" Mrs Wormwood cried out. "Willard is just about to propose to Angelica!"

"You can still watch it while we're talking," Mr Wormwood said. "This is Matilda's teacher. She says she's got some sort of news to give us."

"My name is Jennifer Honey," Miss Honey said. "How do you do, Mrs Wormwood."

Mrs Wormwood glared at her and said, "What's the trouble then?"

Nobody invited Miss Honey to sit down so she chose a chair and sat down anyway. "This," she said, "was your daughter's first day at school."

"We know that," Mrs Wormwood said, ratty about missing her programme. "Is that all you came to tell us?"

Miss Honey stared hard into the other woman's wet grey eyes, and she allowed the silence to hang in the air until Mrs Wormwood became uncomfortable. "Do you wish me to explain why I came?" she said.

"Get on with it then," Mrs Wormwood said.

"I'm sure you know," Miss Honey said, "that children in the bottom class at school are not expected to be able to read or spell or juggle

with numbers when they first arrive. Five-year-olds cannot do that. But Matilda can do it all. And if I am to believe her . . ."

"I wouldn't," Mrs Wormwood said. She was still ratty at losing the sound on the TV.

"Was she lying, then," Miss Honey said, "when she told me that nobody taught her to multiply or to read? Did either of you teach her?"

"Teach her what?" Mr Wormwood said.

"To read. To read books," Miss Honey said. "Perhaps you *did* teach her. Perhaps she *was* lying. Perhaps you have shelves full of books all over the house. I wouldn't know. Perhaps you are both great readers."

"Of course we read," Mr Wormwood said. "Don't be so daft. I read the *Autocar* and the *Motor* from cover to cover every week."

"This child has already read an astonishing number of books," Miss Honey said. "I was simply trying to find out if she came from a family that loved good literature."

"We don't hold with book-reading," Mr Wormwood said. "You can't make a living from sitting on your fanny and reading story-books. We don't keep them in the house."

"I see," Miss Honey said. "Well, all I came to tell you was that Matilda has a brilliant mind. But I expect you knew that already."

"Of course I knew she could read," the mother said. "She spends her life up in her room buried in some silly book."

"But does it not intrigue you", Miss Honey said, "that a little five-year-old child is reading long adult novels by Dickens and Hemingway? Doesn't that make you jump up and down with excitement?"

"Not particularly," the mother said. "I'm not in favour of blue-stocking girls. A girl should

think about making herself look attractive so she can get a good husband later on. Looks is more important than books, Miss Hunky . . ."

"The name is Honey," Miss Honey said.

"Now look at *me*," Mrs Wormwood said. "Then look at *you*. You chose books. I chose looks."

Miss Honey looked at the plain plump person with the smug suet-pudding face who was sitting across the room. "What did you say?" she asked.

"I said you chose books and I chose looks," Mrs Wormwood said. "And who's finished up the better off? Me, of course. I'm sitting pretty in a nice house with a successful businessman

and you're left slaving away teaching a lot of nasty little children the ABC."

"Quite right, sugar-plum," Mr Wormwood said, casting a look of such simpering sloppiness at his wife it would have made a cat sick.

Miss Honey decided that if she was going to get anywhere with these people she must not lose her temper. "I haven't told you all of it yet," she said. "Matilda, so far as I can gather at this early stage, is also a kind of mathematical genius. She can multiply complicated figures in her head like lightning."

"What's the point of that when you can buy a calculator?" Mr Wormwood said.

"A girl doesn't get a man by being brainy," Mrs Wormwood said. "Look at that film-star for instance," she added, pointing at the silent TV screen where a bosomy female was being embraced by a craggy actor in the moonlight. "You don't think she got him to do that by multiplying figures at him, do you? Not likely. And now he's going to marry her, you see if he doesn't, and she's going to live in a mansion with a butler and lots of maids."

Miss Honey could hardly believe what she was hearing. She had heard that parents like this existed all over the place and that their children turned out to be delinquents and drop-outs, but it was still a shock to meet a pair of them in the flesh.

"Matilda's trouble," she said, trying once again, "is that she is so far ahead of everyone else around her that it might be worth thinking about some extra kind of private tuition. I seriously believe that she could be brought up to university standard in two or three years with the proper coaching."

"University?" Mr Wormwood shouted, bouncing up in his chair. "Who wants to go to university for heaven's sake! All they learn there is bad habits!"

"That is not true," Miss Honey said. "If you had a heart attack this minute and had to call a doctor, that doctor would be a university graduate. If you got sued for selling someone a rotten second-hand car, you'd have to get a lawyer and he'd be a university graduate, too. Do not despise clever people, Mr Wormwood. But I can see we're not going to agree. I'm sorry I burst in on you like this." Miss Honey rose from her chair and walked out of the room.

Mr Wormwood followed her to the front-door and said, "Good of you to come, Miss Hawkes, or is it Miss Harris?"

"It's neither," Miss Honey said, "but let it go." And away she went.

Throwing the Hammer

The nice thing about Matilda was that if you had met her casually and talked to her you would have thought she was a perfectly normal five-and-a-half-year-old child. She displayed almost no outward signs of her brilliance and she never showed off. "This is a very sensible and quiet little girl," you would have said to yourself. And unless for some reason you had started a discussion with her about literature or mathematics, you would never have known the extent of her brain-power.

It was therefore easy for Matilda to make friends with other children. All those in her class liked her. They knew of course that she was "clever" because they had heard her being questioned by Miss Honey on the first day of term. And they knew also that she was allowed to sit quietly with a book during lessons and not pay attention to the teacher. But children of their age do not search deeply for reasons. They are far too wrapped up in their own small struggles to worry overmuch about what others are doing and why.

Among Matilda's new-found friends was the

girl called Lavender. Right from the first day of term the two of them started wandering round together during the morning-break and in the lunch-hour. Lavender was exceptionally small for her age, a skinny little nymph with deep-brown eyes and with dark hair that was cut in a fringe across her forehead. Matilda liked her because she was gutsy and adventurous. She liked Matilda for exactly the same reasons.

Before the first week of term was up, awesome tales about the Headmistress, Miss Trunchbull, began to filter through to the newcomers. Matilda and Lavender, standing in a corner of the playground during a morning-break on the third day, were approached by a rugged ten-year-old with a boil on her nose, called Hortensia. "New scum, I suppose," Hortensia said to them, looking down from her great height. She was eating from an extra large bag of potato crisps and digging the stuff out in handfuls. "Welcome to borstal," she added, spraying bits of crisp out of her mouth like snowflakes.

The two tiny ones, confronted by this giant, kept a watchful silence.

"Have you met the Trunchbull yet?" Hortensia asked.

"We've seen her at prayers," Lavender said, "but we haven't met her."

"You've got a treat coming to you," Hortensia said. "She hates very small children. She therefore loathes the bottom class and everyone in it. She thinks five-year-olds are grubs that haven't yet hatched out." In went another fistful of crisps and when she spoke again, out sprayed the crumbs. "If you survive your first year you may just manage to live through the rest of your time here. But many don't survive. They get carried out on stretchers screaming. I've seen it often." Hortensia paused to observe the effect these remarks were having on the two titchy ones. Not very much. They seemed pretty cool. So the large one decided to regale them with further information.

"I suppose you know the Trunchbull has a lock-up cupboard in her private quarters called The Chokey? Have you heard about The Chokey?"

Matilda and Lavender shook their heads and continued to gaze up at the giant. Being very small, they were inclined to mistrust any creature that was larger than they were, especially senior girls.

"The Chokey," Hortensia went on, "is a very tall but very narrow cupboard. The floor is only ten inches square so you can't sit down or squat in it. You have to stand. And three of the walls are made of cement with bits of broken glass sticking out all over, so you can't lean against them. You have to stand more or less at attention all the time when you get locked up in there. It's terrible."

"Can't you lean against the door?"

Matilda asked.

"Don't be daft," Hortensia said. "The door's got thousands of sharp spikey nails sticking out of it. They've been hammered through from the outside, probably by the Trunchbull herself."

"Have you ever been in there?" Lavender asked.

"My first term I was in there six times," Hortensia said. "Twice for a whole day and the other times for two hours each. But two hours is quite bad enough. It's pitch dark and you have to stand up dead straight and if you wobble at all you get spiked either by the glass on the walls or the nails on the door."

"Why were you put in?" Matilda asked. "What had you done?"

"The first time," Hortensia said, "I poured half a tin of Golden Syrup on to the seat of the chair the Trunchbull was going to sit on at prayers. It was wonderful. When she lowered herself into the chair, there was a loud squelching noise similar to that made by a hippopotamus when lowering its foot into the mud on the banks of the Limpopo River. But you're too small and stupid to have read the *Just So Stories*, aren't you?"

"I've read them," Matilda said.

"You're a liar," Hortensia said amiably. "You can't even read yet. But no matter. So when the Trunchbull sat down on the Golden Syrup, the squelch was beautiful. And when she jumped up again, the chair sort of stuck to the seat of those awful green breeches she wears and came up with her for a few seconds until the thick syrup slowly came unstuck. Then she clasped her hands to the seat of her breeches and both hands got covered in the muck. You should have heard her bellow."

"But how did she know it was you?" Lavender asked.

"A little squirt called Ollie Bogwhistle sneaked on me," Hortensia said. "I knocked his front teeth out."

"And the Trunchbull put you in The Chokey for a whole day?" Matilda asked, gulping.

"All day long," Hortensia said. "I was off my rocker when she let me out. I was babbling like an idiot."

"What were the other things you did to get put in The Chokey?" Lavender asked.

"Oh I can't remember them all now," Hortensia said. She spoke with the air of an old warrior who has been in so many battles that bravery has become commonplace. "It's all so long ago," she added, stuffing more crisps into her mouth. "Ah yes, I can remember one. Here's what happened. I chose a time when I knew the Trunchbull was out of the way teaching the sixth-formers, and I put up my hand and asked to go to the bogs. But instead of going *there*, I sneaked into the Trunchbull's room. And after a speedy search I found the drawer where she kept all her gym knickers."

"Go on," Matilda said, spellbound. "What happened next?"

"I had sent away by post, you see, for this very powerful itching-powder," Hortensia said. "It cost 50p a packet and was called The Skin-Scorcher. The label said it was made from the powdered teeth of deadly snakes, and it was guaranteed to raise welts the size of walnuts on your skin. So I sprinkled this stuff inside every pair of knickers in the drawer and then folded them all up again carefully." Hortensia paused to cram more crisps into her mouth.

"Did it work?" Lavender asked.

"Well," Hortensia said, "a few days later, during prayers, the Trunchbull suddenly started scratching herself like mad down below. A-ha,

I said to myself. Here we go. She's changed for gym already. It was pretty wonderful to be sitting there watching it all and knowing that I was the only person in the whole school who realised exactly what was going on inside the Trunchbull's pants. And I felt safe, too. I knew I couldn't be caught. Then the scratching got worse. She couldn't stop. She must have thought she had a wasp's nest down there. And then, right in the middle of the Lord's Prayer, she leapt up and grabbed her bottom and

rushed out of the room."

Both Matilda and Lavender were enthralled. It was quite clear to them that they were at this moment standing in the presence of a master. Here was somebody who had brought the art of skulduggery to the highest point of perfection, somebody, moreover, who was willing to risk life and limb in pursuit of her calling. They gazed in wonder at this goddess, and suddenly even the boil on her nose was no longer a blemish but a badge of courage.

"But how *did* she catch you that time?" Lavender asked, breathless with wonder.

"She didn't," Hortensia said. "But I got a day in The Chokey just the same."

"Why?" they both asked.

"The Trunchbull," Hortensia said, "has a nasty habit of guessing. When she doesn't know who the culprit is, she makes a guess at it, and the trouble is she's often right. I was the prime suspect this time because of the Golden Syrup job, and although I knew she didn't have any proof, nothing I said made any difference. I kept shouting, 'How could I have done it, Miss Trunchbull? I didn't even know you kept any spare knickers at school! I don't even know what itching-powder is! I've never heard of it!'

But the lying didn't help me in spite of the great performance I put on. The Trunchbull simply grabbed me by one ear and rushed me to The Chokey at the double and threw me inside and locked the door. That was my second all-day stretch. It was absolute torture. I was spiked and cut all over when I came out."

"It's like a war," Matilda said, overawed.

"You're darn right it's like a war," Hortensia cried. "And the casualties are terrific. *We* are the crusaders, the gallant army fighting for our lives with hardly any weapons at all and the Trunchbull is the Prince of Darkness, the Foul Serpent, the Fiery Dragon with all the weapons at her command. It's a tough life. We all try to support each other."

"You can rely on us," Lavender said, making her height of three feet two inches stretch as tall as possible.

"No, I can't," Hortensia said. "You're only shrimps. But you never know. We may find a use for you one day in some undercover job."

"Tell us just a little bit more about what she does," Matilda said. "Please do."

"I mustn't frighten you before you've been here a week," Hortensia said.

"You won't," Lavender said. "We may be

small but we're quite tough."

"Listen to this then," Hortensia said. "Only yesterday the Trunchbull caught a boy called Julius Rottwinkle eating Liquorice Allsorts during the scripture lesson and she simply picked him up by one arm and flung him clear out of the open classroom window. Our classroom is one floor up and we saw Julius Rottwinkle go sailing out over the garden like a Frisbee and landing with a thump in the middle of the lettuces. Then the Trunchbull turned to us and said, "From now on, anybody caught eating in class goes straight out the window."

"Did this Julius Rottwinkle break any bones?" Lavender asked.

"Only a few," Hortensia said. "You've got to remember that the Trunchbull once threw the hammer for Britain in the Olympics so she's very proud of her right arm."

"What's throwing the hammer?" Lavender asked.

"The hammer," Hortensia said, "is actually a ruddy great cannon-ball on the end of a long bit of wire, and the thrower whisks it round and round his or her head faster and faster and then lets it go. You have to be terrifically

strong. The Trunchbull will throw anything around just to keep her arm in, especially children."

"Good heavens," Lavender said.

"I once heard her say," Hortensia went on, "that a large boy is about the same weight as an Olympic hammer and therefore he's very useful for practising with."

At that point something strange happened. The playground, which up to then had been filled with shrieks and the shouting of children at play, all at once became silent as the grave. "Watch out," Hortensia whispered. Matilda and Lavender glanced round and saw the gigantic figure of Miss Trunchbull advancing through the crowd of boys and girls with menacing strides. The children drew back hastily to let her through and her progress across the asphalt was like that of Moses going through the Red Sea when the waters parted. A formidable figure she was too, in her belted smock and green breeches. Below the knees her calf muscles stood out like grapefruits inside her stockings. "Amanda Thripp!" she was shouting. "You, Amanda Thripp, come here!"

"Hold your hats," Hortensia whispered.

"What's going to happen?" Lavender whispered back.

"That idiot Amanda," Hortensia said, "has let her long hair grow even longer during the hols and her mother has plaited it into pigtails. Silly thing to do."

"Why silly?" Matilda asked.

"If there's one thing the Trunchbull can't stand it's pigtails," Hortensia said.

Matilda and Lavender saw the giant in green breeches advancing upon a girl of about ten who had a pair of plaited golden pigtails hanging over her shoulders. Each pigtail had a blue satin bow at the end of it and it all looked very pretty. The girl wearing the pigtails, Amanda Thripp, stood quite still, watching the advancing giant, and the expression on her face was one that you might find on the face of a person who is trapped in a small field with an enraged bull which is charging flat-out towards her. The girl was glued to the spot, terror-struck, pop-eyed, quivering, knowing for certain that the Day of Judgment had come for her at last.

Miss Trunchbull had now reached the victim and stood towering over her. "I want those filthy pigtails off before you come back

to school tomorrow!" she barked. "Chop 'em off and throw 'em in the dustbin, you understand?"

Amanda, paralysed with fright, managed to stutter, "My m-m-mummy likes them. She pp-plaits them for me every morning."

"Your mummy's a twit!" the Trunchbull bellowed. She pointed a finger the size of a salami at the child's head and shouted, "You look like a rat with a tail coming out of its head!"

"My m-m-mummy thinks I look lovely, Miss T-T-Trunchbull," Amanda stuttered, shaking like a blancmange.

"I don't give a tinker's toot what your mummy thinks!" the Trunchbull yelled, and with that she lunged forward and grabbed hold of Amanda's pigtails in her right fist and lifted the girl clear off the ground. Then she started swinging her round and round her head, faster and faster and Amanda was screaming blue murder and the Trunchbull was yelling, "I'll give you pigtails, you little rat!"

"Shades of the Olympics," Hortensia murmured. "She's getting up speed now just like she does with the hammer. Ten to one she's going to throw her."

And now the Trunchbull was leaning back against the weight of the whirling girl and pivoting expertly on her toes, spinning round and round, and soon Amanda Thripp was travelling so fast she became a blur, and

suddenly, with a mighty grunt, the Trunchbull let go of the pigtails and Amanda went sailing like a rocket right over the wire fence of the playground and high up into the sky.

"Well thrown, sir!" someone shouted from across the playground, and Matilda, who was mesmerised by the whole crazy affair, saw Amanda Thripp descending in a long graceful parabola on to the playing-field beyond. She landed on the grass and bounced three times and finally came to rest. Then, amazingly, she sat up. She looked a trifle dazed and who could blame her, but after a minute or so she was on her feet again and tottering back towards the playground.

The Trunchbull stood in the playground dusting off her hands. "Not bad," she said, "considering I'm not in strict training. Not bad at all." Then she strode away.

"She's mad," Hortensia said.

"But don't the parents complain?" Matilda asked.

"Would yours?" Hortensia asked. "I know mine wouldn't. She treats the mothers and fathers just the same as the children and they're all scared to death of her. I'll be seeing you some time, you two." And with that she sauntered away.

Bruce Bogtrotter and the Cake

"How can she get *away* with it?" Lavender said to Matilda. "Surely the children go home and tell their mothers and fathers. I know my father would raise a terrific stink if I told him the Headmistress had grabbed me by the hair and slung me over the playground fence."

"No, he wouldn't," Matilda said, "and I'll tell you why. He simply wouldn't believe you."

"Of course he would."

"He wouldn't," Matilda said. "And the reason is obvious. Your story would sound too ridiculous to be believed. And that is the Trunchbull's great secret."

"What is?" Lavender asked.

Matilda said, "Never do anything by halves if you want to get away with it. Be outrageous. Go the whole hog. Make sure everything you do is so completely crazy it's unbelievable. No parent is going to believe this pigtail story, not in a million years. Mine wouldn't. They'd call me a liar."

"In that case," Lavender said, "Amanda's mother isn't going to cut her pigtails off."

"No, she isn't," Matilda said. "Amanda will

do it herself. You see if she doesn't."

"Do you think she's mad?" Lavender asked.

"Who?"

"The Trunchbull."

"No, I don't think she's mad," Matilda said. "But she's very dangerous. Being in this school is like being in a cage with a cobra. You have to be very fast on your feet."

They got another example of how dangerous the Headmistress could be on the very next day. During lunch an announcement was made that the whole school should go into the Assembly Hall and be seated as soon as the meal was over.

When all the two hundred and fifty or so boys and girls were settled down in Assembly, the Trunchbull marched on to the platform. None of the other teachers came in with her. She was carrying a riding-crop in her right hand. She stood up there on centre stage in her green breeches with legs apart and riding-crop in hand, glaring at the sea of upturned faces before her.

"What's going to happen?" Lavender whispered.

"I don't know," Matilda whispered back.

The whole school waited for what was

coming next.

"Bruce Bogtrotter!" the Trunchbull barked suddenly. "Where is Bruce Bogtrotter?"

A hand shot up among the seated children.

"Come up here!" the Trunchbull shouted.

"And look smart about it!"

An eleven-year-old boy who was decidedly large and round stood up and waddled briskly forward. He climbed up on to the platform.

"Stand over there!" the Trunchbull ordered, pointing. The boy stood to one side. He looked nervous. He knew very well he wasn't up there to be presented with a prize. He was watching the Headmistress with an exceedingly wary eye and he kept edging farther and farther away from her with little shuffles of his feet, rather as a rat might edge away from a terrier that is watching it from across the room. His plump flabby face had turned grey with fearful apprehension. His stockings hung about his ankles.

"This *clot*," boomed the Headmistress, pointing the riding-crop at him like a rapier, "this *blackhead*, this *foul carbuncle*, this *poisonous pustule* that you see before you is none other than a disgusting criminal, a denizen of the underworld, a member of the Mafia!"

"Who, me?" Bruce Bogtrotter said, looking genuinely puzzled.

"A thief!" the Trunchbull screamed. "A crook! A pirate! A brigand! A rustler!"

"Steady on," the boy said. "I mean, dash it

all, Headmistress."

"Do you deny it, you miserable little gumboil? Do you plead not guilty?"

"I don't know what you're talking about," the boy said, more puzzled than ever.

"I'll tell you what I'm talking about, you suppurating little blister!" the Trunchbull shouted. "Yesterday morning, during break, you sneaked like a serpent into the kitchen and stole a slice of my private chocolate cake from my tea-tray! That tray had just been prepared for me personally by the cook! It was my morning snack! And as for the cake, it was my own private stock! That was not boy's cake! You don't think for one minute I'm going to eat the filth I give to you? That cake was made from real butter and real cream! And he, that robber-bandit, that safe-cracker, that highwayman standing over there with his socks around his ankles stole it and ate it!"

"I never did," the boy exclaimed, turning from grey to white.

"Don't lie to me, Bogtrotter!" barked the Trunchbull. "The cook saw you! What's more, she saw you eating it!"

The Trunchbull paused to wipe a fleck of froth from her lips.

When she spoke again her voice was suddenly softer, quieter, more friendly, and she leaned towards the boy, smiling. "You like my special chocolate cake, don't you, Bogtrotter? It's rich and delicious, isn't it, Bogtrotter?"

"Very good," the boy mumbled. The words were out before he could stop himself.

"You're right," the Trunchbull said. "It *is* very good. Therefore I think you should congratulate the cook. When a gentleman has

had a particularly good meal, Bogtrotter, he always sends his compliments to the chef. You didn't know that, did you, Bogtrotter? But those who inhabit the criminal underworld are not noted for their good manners."

The boy remained silent.

"Cook!" the Trunchbull shouted, turning

her head towards the door. "Come here, cook! Bogtrotter wishes to tell you how good your chocolate cake is!"

The cook, a tall shrivelled female who looked as though all of her body-juices had been dried out of her long ago in a hot oven, walked on to the platform wearing a dirty white apron. Her entrance had clearly been arranged beforehand by the Headmistress.

"Now then, Bogtrotter," the Trunchbull boomed. "Tell cook what you think of her chocolate cake."

"Very good," the boy mumbled. You could see he was now beginning to wonder what all this was leading up to. The only thing he knew for certain was that the law forbade the Trunchbull to hit him with the riding-crop that she kept smacking against her thigh. That was some comfort, but not much because the Trunchbull was totally unpredictable. One never knew what she was going to do next.

"There you are, cook," the Trunchbull cried. "Bogtrotter likes your cake. He adores your cake. Do you have any more of your cake you could give him?"

"I do indeed," the cook said. She seemed to have learnt her lines by heart.

"Then go and get it. And bring a knife to cut it with."

The cook disappeared. Almost at once she was back again staggering under the weight of an enormous round chocolate cake on a china platter. The cake was fully eighteen inches in

diameter and it was covered with dark-brown chocolate icing. "Put it on the table," the Trunchbull said.

There was a small table centre stage with a chair behind it. The cook placed the cake carefully on the table. "Sit down, Bogtrotter," the Trunchbull said. "Sit there."

The boy moved cautiously to the table and sat down. He stared at the gigantic cake.

"There you are, Bogtrotter," the Trunchbull said, and once again her voice became soft, persuasive, even gentle. "It's all for you, every bit of it. As you enjoyed that slice you had yesterday so very much, I ordered cook to bake you an extra large one all for yourself."

"Well, thank you," the boy said, totally bemused.

"Thank cook, not me," the Trunchbull said.

"Thank you, cook," the boy said.

The cook stood there like a shrivelled bootlace, tight-lipped, implacable, disapproving. She looked as though her mouth was full of lemon juice.

"Come on then," the Trunchbull said. "Why don't you cut yourself a nice thick slice and try it?"

"What? Now?" the boy said, cautious. He

knew there was a catch in this somewhere, but he wasn't sure where. "Can't I take it home instead?" he asked.

"That would be impolite," the Trunchbull said, with a crafty grin. "You must show cookie here how grateful you are for all the trouble she's taken."

The boy didn't move.

"Go on, get on with it," the Trunchbull said. "Cut a slice and taste it. We haven't got all day."

The boy picked up the knife and was about to cut into the cake when he stopped. He stared at the cake. Then he looked up at the Trunchbull, then at the tall stringy cook with her lemon-juice mouth. All the children in the hall were watching tensely, waiting for something to happen. They felt certain it must. The Trunchbull was not a person who would give someone a whole chocolate cake to eat just out of kindness. Many were guessing that it had been filled with pepper or castor-oil or some other foul-tasting substance that would make the boy violently sick. It might even be arsenic and he would be dead in ten seconds flat. Or perhaps it was a booby-trapped cake and the whole thing would blow up the moment it was cut, taking Bruce Bogtrotter

with it. No one in the school put it past the Trunchbull to do any of these things.

"I don't want to eat it," the boy said.

"Taste it, you little brat," the Trunchbull said. "You're insulting the cook."

Very gingerly the boy began to cut a thin slice of the vast cake. Then he levered the slice out. Then he put down the knife and took the sticky thing in his fingers and started very slowly to eat it.

"It's good, isn't it?" the Trunchbull asked.

"Very good," the boy said, chewing and swallowing. He finished the slice.

"Have another," the Trunchbull said.

"That's enough, thank you," the boy murmured.

"I said have another," the Trunchbull said, and now there was an altogether sharper edge to her voice. "Eat another slice! Do as you are told!"

"I don't want another slice," the boy said.

Suddenly the Trunchbull exploded. "Eat!" she shouted, banging her thigh with the riding-crop. "If I tell you to eat, you will eat! You wanted cake! You stole cake! And now you've got cake! What's more, you're going to eat it! You do not leave this platform and nobody leaves this hall until you have eaten the entire cake that is sitting there in front of you! Do I make myself clear, Bogtrotter? Do you get my meaning?"

The boy looked at the Trunchbull. Then he looked down at the enormous cake.

"Eat! Eat! Eat!" the Trunchbull was yelling.

Very slowly the boy cut himself another slice and began to eat it.

Matilda was fascinated. "Do you think he can do it?" she whispered to Lavender.

"No," Lavender whispered back. "It's impossible. He'd be sick before he was halfway through."

The boy kept going. When he had finished the second slice, he looked at the Trunchbull, hesitating.

"Eat!" she shouted. "Greedy little thieves who like to eat cake must have cake! Eat faster boy! Eat faster! We don't want to be here all day! And don't stop like you're doing now! Next time you stop before it's all finished you'll go straight into The Chokey and I shall lock the door and throw the key down the well!"

The boy cut a third slice and started to eat it. He finished this one quicker than the other two and when that was done he immediately picked up the knife and cut the next slice. In some peculiar way he seemed to be getting into his stride.

Matilda, watching closely, saw no signs of distress in the boy yet. If anything, he seemed to be gathering confidence as he went along. "He's doing well," she whispered to Lavender.

"He'll be sick soon," Lavender whispered

back. "It's going to be horrid."

When Bruce Bogtrotter had eaten his way through half of the entire enormous cake, he paused for just a couple of seconds and took several deep breaths.

The Trunchbull stood with hands on hips, glaring at him. "Get on with it!" she shouted. "Eat it up!"

Suddenly the boy let out a gigantic belch which rolled around the Assembly Hall like thunder. Many of the audience began to giggle.

"Silence!" shouted the Trunchbull.

The boy cut himself another thick slice and started eating it fast. There were still no signs of flagging or giving up. He certainly did not look as though he was about to stop and cry out, "I can't, I can't eat any more! I'm going to be sick!" He was still in there running.

And now a subtle change was coming over the two hundred and fifty watching children in the audience. Earlier on, they had sensed impending disaster. They had prepared themselves for an unpleasant scene in which the wretched boy, stuffed to the gills with chocolate cake, would have to surrender and beg for mercy and then they would have watched the triumphant Trunchbull forcing more and still more cake into the mouth of the gasping boy.

Not a bit of it. Bruce Bogtrotter was three-quarters of the way through and still going strong. One sensed that he was almost beginning to enjoy himself. He had a mountain to climb and he was jolly well going to reach the top or die in the attempt. What is more, he had now become very conscious of his audience and of how they were all silently rooting for him. This was nothing less than a battle between him and the mighty Trunchbull.

Suddenly someone shouted, "Come on Brucie! You can make it!"

The Trunchbull wheeled round and yelled, "Silence!" The audience watched intently. They were thoroughly caught up in the contest. They were longing to start cheering but they didn't dare.

"I think he's going to make it," Matilda whispered.

"I think so too," Lavender whispered back. "I wouldn't have believed anyone in the world could eat the whole of a cake that size."

"The Trunchbull doesn't believe it either," Matilda whispered. "Look at her. She's turning redder and redder. She's going to kill him if he wins."

The boy was slowing down now. There was no doubt about that. But he kept pushing the stuff into his mouth with the dogged perseverance of a long-distance runner who has sighted the finishing-line and knows he must keep going. As the very last mouthful disappeared, a tremendous cheer rose up from the audience and children were leaping on their chairs and yelling and clapping and shouting, "Well done, Brucie! Good for you,

Brucie! You've won a gold medal, Brucie!"

The Trunchbull stood motionless on the platform. Her great horsy face had turned the colour of molten lava and her eyes were glittering with fury. She glared at Bruce Bogtrotter who was sitting on his chair like some huge overstuffed grub, replete, comatose, unable to move or to speak. A fine sweat was beading his forehead but there was a grin of triumph on his face.

Suddenly the Trunchbull lunged forward and grabbed the large empty china platter on which the cake had rested. She raised it high in the air and brought it down with a crash right on the top of the wretched Bruce Bogtrotter's head and pieces flew all over the platform.

The boy was by now so full of cake he was

like a sackful of wet cement and you couldn't have hurt him with a sledge-hammer. He simply shook his head a few times and went on grinning.

"Go to blazes!" screamed the Trunchbull and she marched off the platform followed closely by the cook.

Lavender

In the middle of the first week of Matilda's first term, Miss Honey said to the class, "I have some important news for you, so listen carefully. You too, Matilda. Put that book down for a moment and pay attention."

Small eager faces looked up and listened.

"It is the Headmistress's custom," Miss Honey went on, "to take over the class for one period each week. She does this with every class in the school and each class has a fixed day and a fixed time. Ours is always two o'clock on Thursday afternoons, immediately after lunch. So tomorrow at two o'clock Miss Trunchbull will be taking over from me for one lesson. I shall be here as well, of course, but only as a silent witness. Is that understood?"

"Yes, Miss Honey," they chirruped.

"A word of warning to you all," Miss Honey said. "The Headmistress is very strict about everything. Make sure your clothes are clean, your faces are clean and your hands are clean. Speak only when spoken to. When she asks you a question, stand up at once before you answer it. Never argue with her. Never answer back. Never try to be funny. If you do, you will make her angry, and when the Headmistress gets angry you had better watch out."

"You can say that again," Lavender murmured.

"I am quite sure," Miss Honey said, "that she will be testing you on what you are meant to have learnt this week, which is your two-times table. So I strongly advise you to swot it up when you get home tonight. Get your mother or father to hear you on it."

"What else will she test us on?" someone asked.

"Spelling," Miss Honey said. "Try to remember everything you have learned these last few days. And one more thing. A jug of water and a glass must always be on the table here when the Headmistress comes in. She never takes a lesson without that. Now who will be responsible for seeing that it's there?"

"I will," Lavender said at once.

"Very well, Lavender," Miss Honey said. "It will be your job to go to the kitchen and get the jug and fill it with water and put it on the table here with a clean empty glass just before the lesson starts."

"What if the jug's not in the kitchen?"

Lavender asked.

"There are a dozen Headmistress's jugs and glasses in the kitchen," Miss Honey said. "They are used all over the school."

"I won't forget," Lavender said. "I promise I won't."

Already Lavender's scheming mind was going over the possibilities that this water-jug job had opened up for her. She longed to do something truly heroic. She admired the older girl Hortensia to distraction for the daring

deeds she had performed in the school. She also admired Matilda who had sworn her to secrecy about the parrot job she had brought off at home, and also the great hair-oil switch which had bleached her father's hair. It was *her* turn now to become a heroine if only she could come up with a brilliant plot.

On the way home from school that afternoon she began to mull over the various possibilities, and when at last the germ of a brilliant idea hit her, she began to expand on it and lay her plans with the same kind of care the Duke of Wellington had done before the Battle of Waterloo. Admittedly the enemy on this occasion was not Napoleon. But you would never have got anyone at Crunchem Hall to admit that the Headmistress was a less formidable foe than the famous Frenchman. Great skill would have to be exercised, Lavender told herself, and great secrecy observed if she was to come out of this exploit alive.

There was a muddy pond at the bottom of Lavender's garden and this was the home of a colony of newts. The newt, although fairly common in English ponds, is not often seen by ordinary people because it is a shy and murky creature. It is an incredibly ugly gruesome-looking animal, rather like a baby crocodile but with a shorter head. It is quite harmless but doesn't look it. It is about six inches long and very slimy, with a greenish-grey skin on top and an orange-coloured belly underneath. It is, in fact, an amphibian, which can live in or out of water.

That evening Lavender went to the bottom of the garden determined to catch a newt. They are swiftly-moving animals and not easy to get hold of. She lay on the bank for a long time waiting patiently until she spotted a whopper. Then, using her school hat as a net, she swooped and caught it. She had lined her pencil-box with pond-weed ready to receive the creature, but she discovered that it was not easy to get the newt out of the hat and into the pencil-box. It wriggled and squirmed like quicksilver and, apart from that, the box was only just long enough to take it. When she did get it in at last, she had to be careful not to trap its tail in the lid when she slid it closed. A boy next door called Rupert Entwistle had told her that if you chopped off a newt's tail, the tail stayed alive and grew into another newt ten times bigger than the first one. It could be the

size of an alligator. Lavender didn't quite believe that, but she was not prepared to risk it happening.

Eventually she managed to slide the lid of the pencil-box right home and the newt was hers. Then, on second thoughts, she opened the lid just the tiniest fraction so that the creature could breathe.

The next day she carried her secret weapon to school in her satchel. She was tingling with excitement. She was longing to tell Matilda about her plan of battle. In fact, she wanted to tell the whole class. But she finally decided to tell nobody. It was better that way because then no one, even when put under the most severe torture, would be able to name her as the culprit.

Lunchtime came. Today it was sausages and baked beans, Lavender's favourite, but she couldn't eat it.

"Are you feeling all right, Lavender?" Miss Honey asked from the head of the table.

"I had such a huge breakfast," Lavender said, "I really couldn't eat a thing."

Immediately after lunch, she dashed off to the kitchen and found one of the Trunchbull's famous jugs. It was a large bulging thing made of blue-glazed pottery. Lavender filled it half-full of water and carried it, together with a glass, into the classroom and set it on the teacher's table. The classroom was still empty. Quick as a flash, Lavender got her pencil box from her satchel and slid open the lid just a tiny bit. The newt was lying quite still. With great care, she held the box over the neck of the jug and pulled the lid fully open and tipped the newt in. There was a plop as it landed in the water, then it thrashed around wildly for a few seconds before settling down. And now, to make the newt feel more at home, Lavender decided to give it all the pond-weed from the pencil-box as well.

The deed was done. All was ready. Lavender put her pencils back into the rather damp pencil-box and returned it to its correct place on her own desk. Then she went out and joined the others in the playground until it was time for the lesson to begin.

The Weekly Test

At two o'clock sharp the class assembled, including Miss Honey who noted that the jug of water and the glass were in the proper place. Then she took up a position standing right at the back. Everyone waited. Suddenly in marched the gigantic figure of the Headmistress in her belted smock and green breeches.

"Good afternoon, children," she barked.

"Good afternoon, Miss Trunchbull," they chirruped.

The Headmistress stood before the class, legs apart, hands on hips, glaring at the small boys and girls who sat nervously at their desks in front of her.

"*Not* a very pretty sight," she said. Her expression was one of utter distaste, as though she were looking at something a dog had done in the middle of the floor. "What a bunch of nauseating little warts you are."

Everyone had the sense to stay silent.

"It makes me vomit," she went on, "to think that I am going to have to put up with a load of garbage like you in my school for the next six years. I can see that I'm going to have to expel as many of you as possible as soon as possible to save myself from going round the bend." She paused and snorted several times. It was a curious noise. You can hear the same sort of thing if you walk through a riding-stable when the horses are being fed. "I suppose," she went on, "your mothers and fathers tell you you're wonderful. Well, I am here to tell you the opposite, and you'd better believe me. Stand up everybody!"

They all got quickly to their feet.

"Now put your hands out in front of you. And as I walk past I want you to turn them over so I can see if they are clean on both sides."

The Trunchbull began a slow march along the rows of desks inspecting the hands. All went well until she came to a small boy in the second row. "What's your name?" she barked.

"Nigel," the boy said.

"Nigel what?"

"Nigel Hicks," the boy said.

"Nigel Hicks what?" the Trunchbull bellowed. She bellowed so loud she nearly blew the little chap out of the window.

"That's it," Nigel said. "Unless you want my

middle names as well." He was a brave little fellow and one could see that he was trying not to be scared by the Gorgon who towered above him.

"I do *not* want your middle names, you blister!" the Gorgon bellowed. "What is *my* name?"

"Miss Trunchbull," Nigel said.

"Then use it when you address me! Now then, let's try again. What is your name?"

"Nigel Hicks, Miss Trunchbull," Nigel said.

"That's better," the Trunchbull said. "Your hands are filthy, Nigel! When did you last wash them?"

"Well, let me think," Nigel said. "That's rather difficult to remember exactly. It could have been yesterday or it could have been the day before."

The Trunchbull's whole body and face seemed to swell up as though she were being inflated by a bicycle-pump.

"I knew it!" she bellowed. "I knew as soon as I saw you that you were nothing but a piece of filth! What is your father's job, a sewage-worker?"

"He's a doctor," Nigel said. "And a jolly good one. He says we're all so covered with bugs anyway that a bit of extra dirt never hurts anyone."

"I'm glad he's not *my* doctor," the Trunchbull said. "And why, might I ask, is there a baked bean on the front of your shirt?"

"We had them for lunch, Miss Trunchbull."

"And do you usually put your lunch on the

front of your shirt, Nigel? Is that what this famous doctor father of yours has taught you to do?"

"Baked beans are hard to eat, Miss Trunchbull. They keep falling off my fork."

"You are disgusting!" the Trunchbull bellowed. "You are a walking germ-factory! I don't wish to see any more of you today! Go and stand in the corner on one leg with your face to the wall!"

"But Miss Trunchbull . . ."

"Don't argue with me, boy, or I'll make you stand on your head! Now do as you're told!"

Nigel went.

"Now stay where you are, boy, while I test you on your spelling to see if you've learnt anything at all this past week. And don't turn round when you talk to me. Keep your nasty little face to the wall. Now then, spell 'write'."

"Which one?" Nigel asked. "The thing you do with a pen or the one that means the opposite of wrong?" He happened to be an unusually bright child and his mother had worked hard with him at home on spelling and reading.

"The one with the pen, you little fool."

Nigel spelled it correctly which surprised

the Trunchbull. She thought she had given him a very tricky word, one that he wouldn't yet have learned, and she was peeved that he had succeeded.

Then Nigel said, still balancing on one leg and facing the wall, "Miss Honey taught us how to spell a new very long word yesterday."

"And what word was that?" the Trunchbull asked softly. The softer her voice became, the greater the danger, but Nigel wasn't to know this.

"'Difficulty'," Nigel said. "Everyone in the class can spell 'difficulty' now."

"What nonsense," the Trunchbull said. "You are not supposed to learn long words like that until you are at least eight or nine. And don't try to tell me *everybody* in the class can spell that word. You are lying to me, Nigel."

"Test someone," Nigel said, taking an awful chance. "Test anyone you like."

The Trunchbull's dangerous glittering eyes roved around the classroom. "You," she said, pointing at a tiny and rather daft little girl called Prudence, "Spell 'difficulty'."

Amazingly, Prudence spelled it correctly and without a moment's hesitation.

The Trunchbull was properly taken aback. "Humph!" she snorted. "And I suppose Miss Honey wasted the whole of one lesson teaching you to spell that one single word?"

"Oh no, she didn't," piped Nigel. "Miss

Honey taught it to us in three minutes so we'll never forget it. She teaches us lots of words in three minutes."

"And what exactly is this magic method, Miss Honey?" asked the Headmistress.

"I'll show you," piped up the brave Nigel again, coming to Miss Honey's rescue. "Can I put my other foot down and turn round, please, while I show you?"

"You may do neither!" snapped the Trunchbull. "Stay as you are and show me just the same!"

"All right," said Nigel, wobbling crazily on his one leg. "Miss Honey gives us a little song about each word and we all sing it together and we learn to spell it in no time. Would you like to hear the song about 'difficulty'?"

"I should be fascinated," the Trunchbull said in a voice dripping with sarcasm.

"Here it is," Nigel said.

"Mrs D, Mrs I, Mrs FFI
Mrs C, Mrs U, Mrs LTY.

That spells difficulty."

"How perfectly ridiculous!" snorted the Trunchbull. "Why are all these women married? And anyway you're not meant to teach poetry when you're teaching spelling. Cut it out in future, Miss Honey."

"But it does teach them some of the harder words wonderfully well," Miss Honey murmured.

"Don't argue with me, Miss Honey!" the Headmistress thundered. "Just do as you're told! I shall now test the class on the multiplication tables to see if Miss Honey has taught you anything at all in that direction." The Trunchbull had returned to her place in front of the class, and her diabolical gaze was moving slowly along the rows of tiny pupils. "You!" she barked, pointing at a small boy called Rupert in the front row. "What is two sevens?"

"Sixteen," Rupert answered with foolish abandon.

The Trunchbull started advancing slow and soft-footed upon Rupert in the manner of a tigress stalking a small deer. Rupert suddenly became aware of the danger signals and quickly tried again. "It's eighteen!" he cried. "Two sevens are eighteen, not sixteen!"

"You ignorant little slug!" the Trunchbull bellowed. "You witless weed! You empty-headed hamster! You stupid glob of glue!" She had now stationed herself directly behind Rupert, and suddenly she extended a hand the size of a tennis racquet and grabbed all the hair on Rupert's head in her fist. Rupert had a lot of golden-coloured hair. His mother thought it was beautiful to behold and took a delight in allowing it to grow extra long. The Trunchbull had as great a dislike for long hair on boys as she had for plaits and pigtails on girls and she was about to show it. She took a firm grip on Rupert's long golden tresses with her giant hand and then, by raising her muscular right arm, she lifted the helpless boy clean out of his chair and held him aloft.

Rupert yelled. He twisted and squirmed and kicked the air and went on yelling like a stuck pig, and Miss Trunchbull bellowed, "Two sevens are fourteen! Two sevens are fourteen! I am not letting you go till you say it!"

From the back of the class, Miss Honey cried out, "Miss Trunchbull! Please let him down! You're hurting him! All his hair might come out!"

"And well it might if he doesn't stop wriggling!" snorted the Trunchbull. "Keep still, you squirming worm!"

It really was a quite extraordinary sight to see this giant Headmistress dangling the small boy high in the air and the boy spinning and twisting like something on the end of a string and shrieking his head off.

"Say it!" bellowed the Trunchbull. "Say two sevens are fourteen! Hurry up or I'll start jerking you up and down and then your hair really will come out and we'll have enough of it to stuff a sofa! Get on with it boy! Say two sevens are fourteen and I'll let you go!"

"T-t-two s-sevens are f-f-fourteen," gasped Rupert, whereupon the Trunchbull, true to her word, opened her hand and quite literally let him go. He was a long way off the ground when she released him and he plummeted to earth and hit the floor and bounced like a football.

"Get up and stop whimpering," the Trunchbull barked.

Rupert got up and went back to his desk massaging his scalp with both hands. The Trunchbull returned to the front of the class. The children sat there hypnotised. None of them had seen anything quite like this before. It was splendid entertainment. It was better than a pantomime, but with one big difference. In this room there was an enormous human bomb in front of them which was liable to explode and blow someone to bits any moment. The children's eyes were riveted on the Headmistress. "I don't like small people," she was saying. "Small people should never be seen by anybody. They should be kept out of sight in boxes like hairpins and buttons. I cannot for the life of me see why children have to take so long to grow up. I think they do it on purpose."

Another extremely brave little boy in the front row spoke up and said, "But surely *you* were a small person once, Miss Trunchbull, weren't you?"

"I was *never* a small person," she snapped. "I have been large all my life and I don't see why others can't be the same way."

"But you must have started out as a baby," the boy said.

"*Me!* A baby!" shouted the Trunchbull. "How dare you suggest such a thing! What cheek! What infernal insolence! What's your name, boy? And stand up when you speak to me!"

The boy stood up. "My name is Eric Ink, Miss Trunchbull," he said.

"Eric *what*?" the Trunchbull shouted.

"Ink," the boy said.

"Don't be an ass, boy! There's no such name!"

"Look in the phone book," Eric said. "You'll

see my father there under Ink."

"Very well, then," the Trunchbull said, "You may be Ink, young man, but let me tell you something. You're not indelible. I'll very soon rub you out if you try getting clever with me. Spell what."

"I don't understand," Eric said. "What do you want me to spell?"

"Spell what, you idiot! Spell the word 'what'!"

"W . . . O . . . T," Eric said, answering too quickly.

There was a nasty silence.

"I'll give you one more chance," the Trunchbull said, not moving.

"Ah yes, I know," Eric said. "It's got an H in it. W . . . H . . . O . . . T. It's easy."

In two large strides the Trunchbull was behind Eric's desk, and there she stood, a pillar of doom towering over the helpless boy. Eric glanced fearfully back over his shoulder at the monster. "I *was* right, wasn't I?" he murmured nervously.

"You were *wrong*!" the Trunchbull barked. "In fact you strike me as the sort of poisonous little pockmark that will *always* be wrong! You sit wrong! You look wrong! You speak wrong!

You are wrong all round! I will give you one more chance to be right! Spell 'what'!"

Eric hesitated. Then he said very slowly, "It's not W . . . O . . . T, and it's not W . . . H . . . O . . . T. Ah, I know. It must be W . . . H . . . O . . . T . . . T."

Standing behind Eric, the Trunchbull reached out and took hold of the boy's two ears, one with each hand, pinching them between forefinger and thumb.

"Ow!" Eric cried. "Ow! You're hurting me!"

"I haven't started yet," the Trunchbull said briskly. And now, taking a firm grip on his two ears, she lifted him bodily out of his seat and held him aloft.

Like Rupert before him, Eric squealed the house down.

From the back of the classroom Miss Honey cried out, "Miss Trunchbull! Don't! Please let him go! His ears might come off!"

"They'll never come off," the Trunchbull shouted back. "I have discovered through long experience, Miss Honey, that the ears of small boys are stuck very firmly to their heads."

"Let him go, Miss Trunchbull, please," begged Miss Honey. "You could damage him, you really could! You could wrench them right off!"

"Ears never come off!" the Trunchbull shouted. "They stretch most marvellously, like these are doing now, but I can assure you they never come off!"

Eric was squealing louder than ever and pedalling the air with his legs.

Matilda had never before seen a boy, or anyone else for that matter, held aloft by his ears alone. Like Miss Honey, she felt sure both ears were going to come off at any moment with all the weight that was on them.

The Trunchbull was shouting, "The word 'what' is spelled W . . . H . . . A . . . T. Now spell it, you little wart!"

Eric didn't hesitate. He had learned from watching Rupert a few minutes before that the quicker you answered the quicker you were released. "W . . . H . . . A . . . T", he squealed, "spells what!"

Still holding him by the ears, the Trunchbull lowered him back into his chair behind his desk. Then she marched back to the front of the class, dusting off her hands one against the other like someone who has been handling something rather grimy.

"That's the way to make them learn, Miss Honey," she said. "You take it from me, it's no good just *telling* them. You've got to *hammer* it into them. There's nothing like a little twisting and twiddling to encourage them to remember things. It concentrates their minds wonderfully."

"You could do them permanent damage, Miss Trunchbull," Miss Honey cried out.

"Oh, I have, I'm quite sure I have," the Trunchbull answered, grinning. "Eric's ears will have stretched quite considerably in the last couple of minutes! They'll be much longer now than they were before. There's nothing wrong with that, Miss Honey. It'll give him an interesting pixie look for the rest of his life."

"But Miss Trunchbull . . ."

"Oh, do shut up, Miss Honey! You're as wet as any of them. If you can't cope in here then you can go and find a job in some cotton-wool private school for rich brats. When you have been teaching for as long as I have you'll realise that it's no good at all being kind to children. Read *Nicholas Nickleby*, Miss Honey, by Mr Dickens. Read about Mr Wackford Squeers, the admirable headmaster of Dotheboys Hall. *He* knew how to handle the little brutes, didn't he! He knew how to use the birch, didn't he! He kept their backsides so warm you could have fried eggs and bacon on them! A fine book, that. But I don't suppose this bunch of morons we've got here will ever read it because by the look of them they are never going to learn to read anything!"

"I've read it," Matilda said quietly.

The Trunchbull flicked her head round and looked carefully at the small girl with dark hair and deep brown eyes sitting in the second row. "What did you say?" she asked sharply.

"I said I've read it, Miss Trunchbull."

"Read what?"

"*Nicholas Nickleby*, Miss Trunchbull."

"You are lying to me, madam!" the Trunchbull shouted, glaring at Matilda. "I doubt there is a single child in the entire school who has read that book, and here you are, an unhatched shrimp sitting in the lowest form there is, trying to tell me a whopping great lie like that! Why do you do it? You must take me for a fool! Do you take me for a fool, child?"

"Well . . ." Matilda said, then she hesitated. She would like to have said, "Yes, I jolly well do," but that would have been suicide. "Well . . ." she said again, still hesitating, still refusing to say "No".

The Trunchbull sensed what the child was thinking and she didn't like it. "Stand up when you speak to me!" she snapped. "What is your name?"

Matilda stood up and said, "My name is Matilda Wormwood, Miss Trunchbull."

"Wormwood, is it?" the Trunchbull said. "In that case you must be the daughter of that man who owns Wormwood Motors?"

"Yes, Miss Trunchbull."

"He's a crook!" the Trunchbull shouted. "A week ago he sold me a second-hand car that he said was almost new. I thought he was a splendid fellow then. But this morning, while I was driving that car through the village, the entire engine fell out on to the road! The whole thing was filled with sawdust! The man's a thief and a robber! I'll have his skin for sausages, you see if I don't!"

"He's clever at his business," Matilda said.

"Clever my foot!" the Trunchbull shouted. "Miss Honey tells me that *you* are meant to be clever, too! Well madam, I don't like clever people! They are all crooked! *You* are most certainly crooked! Before I fell out with your father, he told me some very nasty stories about the way you behaved at home! But you'd better not try anything in this school, young lady. I shall be keeping a very careful eye on you from now on. Sit down and keep quiet."

The First Miracle

Matilda sat down again at her desk. The Trunchbull seated herself behind the teacher's table. It was the first time she had sat down during the lesson. Then she reached out a hand and took hold of her water-jug. Still holding the jug by the handle but not lifting it yet, she said, "I have never been able to understand why small children are so disgusting. They are the bane of my life. They are like insects. They should be got rid of as early as possible. We get rid of flies with fly-spray and by hanging up fly-paper. I have often thought of inventing a spray for getting rid of small children. How splendid it would be to walk into this classroom with a gigantic spray-gun in my hands and start pumping it. Or better still, some huge strips of sticky paper. I would hang them all round the school and you'd all get stuck to them and that would be the end of it. Wouldn't that be a good idea, Miss Honey?"

"If it's meant to be a joke, Headmistress, I don't think it's a very funny one," Miss Honey said from the back of the class.

"You wouldn't, would you, Miss Honey," the Trunchbull said. "And it's *not* meant to be a joke. My idea of a perfect school, Miss Honey, is one that has no children in it at all. One of these days I shall start up a school like that. I think it will be very successful."

The woman's mad, Miss Honey was telling herself. She's round the twist. She's the one who ought to be got rid of.

The Trunchbull now lifted the large blue porcelain water-jug and poured some water into her glass. And suddenly, with the water, out came the long slimy newt straight into the glass, *plop*!

The Trunchbull let out a yell and leapt off her chair as though a firecracker had gone off underneath her. And now the children also saw the long thin slimy yellow-bellied lizard-like creature twisting and turning in the glass, and they squirmed and jumped about as well, shouting, "What is it? Oh, it's disgusting! It's a snake! It's a baby crocodile! It's an alligator!"

"Look out, Miss Trunchbull!" cried Lavender. "I'll bet it bites!"

The Trunchbull, this mighty female giant, stood there in her green breeches, quivering like a blancmange. She was especially furious that someone had succeeded in making her jump and yell like that because she prided herself on her toughness. She stared at the creature twisting and wriggling in the glass. Curiously enough, she had never seen a newt before. Natural history was not her strong point. She hadn't the faintest idea what this thing was. It certainly looked extremely

unpleasant. Slowly she sat down again in her chair. She looked at this moment more terrifying than ever before. The fires of fury and hatred were smouldering in her small black eyes.

"Matilda!" she barked. "Stand up!"

"Who, me?" Matilda said. "What have *I* done?"

"Stand up, you disgusting little cockroach!"

"I haven't done anything, Miss Trunchbull, honestly I haven't. I've never seen that slimy thing before!"

"Stand up at once, you filthy little maggot!"

Reluctantly, Matilda got to her feet. She was in the second row. Lavender was in the row behind her, feeling a bit guilty. She hadn't intended to get her friend into trouble. On the other hand, she was certainly not about to own up.

"You are a vile, repulsive, repellent, malicious little brute!" the Trunchbull was shouting. "You are not fit to be in this school! You ought to be behind bars, that's where you ought to be! I shall have you drummed out of this establishment in utter disgrace! I shall have the prefects chase you down the corridor and out of the front-door with hockey-sticks! I shall have the staff escort you home under armed guard! And then I shall make absolutely sure you are sent to a reformatory for delinquent girls for the minimum of forty years!"

The Trunchbull was in such a rage that her face had taken on a boiled colour and little flecks of froth were gathering at the corners of her mouth. But she was not the only one who was losing her cool. Matilda was also beginning to see red. She didn't in the least mind being accused of having done something she had actually done. She could see the justice of that. It was, however, a totally new experience for her to be accused of a crime that she definitely had not committed. She had had absolutely nothing to do with that beastly creature in the glass. By golly, she thought, that rotten Trunchbull isn't going to pin this one on me!

"I did not do it!" she screamed.

"Oh yes, you did!" the Trunchbull roared back. "Nobody else could have thought up a trick like that!

Your father was right to warn me about you!" The woman seemed to have lost control of herself completely. She was ranting like a maniac. "You are finished in this school, young lady!" she shouted. "You are finished everywhere. I shall personally see to it that you are put away in a place where not even the crows can land their droppings on you! You will probably never see the light of day again!"

"I'm telling you I did not do it!" Matilda screamed. "I've never even seen a creature like that in my life!"

"You have put a . . . a . . . a crocodile in my drinking water!" the Trunchbull yelled back. "There is no worse crime in the world against a Headmistress! Now sit down and don't say a word! Go on, sit down at once!"

"But I'm telling you . . ." Matilda shouted, refusing to sit down.

"I am telling you to shut up!" the Trunchbull roared. "If you don't shut up at once and sit down I shall remove my belt and let you have it with the end that has the buckle!"

Slowly Matilda sat down. Oh, the rottenness of it all! The unfairness! How dare they expel her for something she hadn't done!

Matilda felt herself getting angrier . . . and angrier . . . and angrier . . . so unbearably angry that something was bound to explode inside her very soon.

The newt was still squirming in the tall glass of water. It looked horribly uncomfortable. The glass was not big enough for it. Matilda glared at the Trunchbull. How she hated her. She glared at the glass with the newt in it. She longed to march up and grab the glass and tip the contents, newt and all, over the Trunchbull's head. She trembled to think what the Trunchbull would do to her if she did that.

The Trunchbull was sitting behind the teacher's table staring with a mixture of horror and fascination at the newt wriggling in the glass. Matilda's eyes were also riveted on the glass. And now, quite slowly, there began to creep over Matilda a most extraordinary and peculiar feeling. The feeling was mostly in the eyes. A kind of electricity seemed to be gathering inside them. A sense of power was brewing in those eyes of hers, a feeling of great strength was settling itself deep inside her eyes. But there was also another feeling which was something else altogether, and which she could not understand. It was like flashes of lightning. Little waves of lightning seemed to be flashing out of her eyes. Her eyeballs were beginning to get hot, as though vast energy was building up somewhere inside them. It was an amazing sensation. She kept her eyes steadily on the glass, and now the power was concentrating itself in one small part of each eye and growing stronger and stronger and it felt as though millions of tiny little invisible arms with hands on them were shooting out of her eyes towards the glass she was staring at.

"Tip it!" Matilda whispered. *"Tip it over!"*

She saw the glass wobble. It actually tilted backwards a fraction of an inch, then righted itself again. She kept pushing at it with all those millions of invisible little arms and hands that were reaching out from her eyes, feeling the power that was flashing straight from the two little black dots in the very centres of her eyeballs.

"Tip it!" she whispered again. *"Tip it over!"*

Once more the glass wobbled. She pushed harder still, willing her eyes to shoot out more power. And then, very very slowly, so slowly she could hardly see it happening, the glass began to lean backwards, farther and farther backwards until it was balancing on just one edge of its base. And there it teetered for a few seconds before finally toppling over and falling with a sharp tinkle on to the desk-top. The water in it and the squirming newt splashed out all over Miss Trunchbull's enormous bosom. The headmistress let out a yell that must have rattled every window-pane in the building and for the second time in the last five minutes she shot out of her chair like a rocket. The newt clutched desperately at the cotton smock where it covered the great chest and there it clung with its little claw-like feet.

The Trunchbull looked down and saw it and she bellowed even louder and with a swipe of her hand she sent the creature flying across the classroom. It landed on the floor beside Lavender's desk and very quickly she ducked down and picked it up and put it into her pencil-box for another time. A newt, she decided, was a useful thing to have around.

The Trunchbull, her face more like a boiled ham than ever, was standing before the class quivering with fury. Her massive bosom was heaving in and out and the splash of water down the front of it made a dark wet patch that had probably soaked right through to her skin.

"Who did it?" she roared. *"Come on! Own up! Step forward! You won't escape this time! Who is responsible for this dirty job? Who pushed over this glass?"*

Nobody answered. The whole room remained silent as a tomb.

"Matilda!" she roared. "It was you! I know it was you!"

Matilda, in the second row, sat very still and said nothing. A strange feeling of serenity and confidence was sweeping over her and all of a sudden she found that she was frightened by nobody in the world. With the power in her eyes alone she had compelled a glass of water to tip and spill its contents over the horrible Headmistress, and anybody who could do that could do anything.

"Speak up, you clotted carbuncle!" roared the Trunchbull. "Admit that you did it!"

Matilda looked right back into the flashing eyes of this infuriated female giant and said with total calmness, "I have not moved away from my desk, Miss Trunchbull, since the lesson began. I can say no more."

Suddenly the entire class seemed to rise up against the Headmistress. "She didn't move!"

they cried out. "Matilda didn't move! Nobody moved! You must have knocked it over yourself!"

"I most certainly did not knock it over myself!" roared the Trunchbull. "How dare you suggest a thing like that! Speak up, Miss Honey! You must have seen something! Who knocked over my glass?"

"None of the children did, Miss Trunchbull," Miss Honey answered. "I can vouch for it that nobody has moved from his or her desk all the time you've been here, except for Nigel and he has not moved from his corner."

Miss Trunchbull glared at Miss Honey. Miss Honey met her gaze without flinching. "I am telling you the truth, Headmistress," she said. "You must have knocked it over without knowing it. That sort of thing is easy to do."

"I am fed up with you useless bunch of midgets!" roared the Trunchbull. "I refuse to waste any more of my precious time in here!" And with that she marched out of the classroom, slamming the door behind her.

In the stunned silence that followed, Miss Honey walked up to the front of the class and stood behind her table. “Phew!” she said. “I think we’ve had enough school for one day, don’t you? The class is dismissed. You may all go out into the playground and wait for your parents to come and take you home.”

The Second Miracle

Matilda did not join the rush to get out of the classroom. After the other children had all disappeared, she remained at her desk, quiet and thoughtful. She knew she had to tell somebody about what had happened with the glass. She couldn't possibly keep a gigantic secret like that bottled up inside her. What she needed was just one person, one wise and sympathetic grown-up who could help her to understand the meaning of this extraordinary happening.

Neither her mother nor her father would be of any use at all. If they believed her story, and it was doubtful they would, they almost certainly would fail to realise what an astounding event it was that had taken place in the classroom that afternoon. On the spur of the moment, Matilda decided that the one person she would like to confide in was Miss Honey.

Matilda and Miss Honey were now the only two left in the classroom. Miss Honey had seated herself at her table and was riffling through some papers. She looked up and said,

"Well, Matilda, aren't you going outside with the others?"

Matilda said, "Please may I talk to you for a moment?"

"Of course you may. What's troubling you?"

"Something very peculiar has happened to me, Miss Honey."

Miss Honey became instantly alert. Ever since the two disastrous meetings she had had recently about Matilda, the first with the Headmistress and the second with the dreadful Mr and Mrs Wormwood, Miss Honey had been thinking a great deal about this child and wondering how she could help her. And now, here was Matilda sitting in the classroom with a curiously exalted look on her face and asking if she could have a private talk. Miss Honey had never seen her looking so wide-eyed and peculiar before.

"Yes, Matilda," she said. "Tell me what has happened to you that is so peculiar."

"Miss Trunchbull isn't going to expel me, is she?" Matilda asked. "Because it wasn't me who put that creature in her jug of water. I promise you it wasn't."

"I know it wasn't," Miss Honey said.

"Am I going to be expelled?"

"I think not," Miss Honey said. "The Headmistress simply got a little over-excited, that's all."

"Good," Matilda said. "But that isn't what I want to talk to you about."

"What do you want to talk to me about, Matilda?"

"I want to talk to you about the glass of water with the creature in it," Matilda said. "You saw it spilling all over Miss Trunchbull, didn't you?"

"I did indeed."

"Well, Miss Honey, I didn't touch it. I never went near it."

"I know you didn't," Miss Honey said. "You heard me telling the Headmistress that it couldn't possibly have been you."

"Ah, but it *was* me, Miss Honey," Matilda said. "That's exactly what I want to talk to you about."

Miss Honey paused and looked carefully at the child. "I don't think I quite follow you," she said.

"I got so angry at being accused of something I hadn't done that I made it happen."

"You made what happen, Matilda?"

"I made the glass tip over."

"I still don't quite understand what you mean," Miss Honey said gently.

"I did it with my eyes," Matilda said. "I was staring at it and wishing it to tip and then my eyes went all hot and funny and some sort of power came out of them and the glass just toppled over."

Miss Honey continued to look steadily at Matilda through her steel-rimmed spectacles and Matilda looked back at her just as steadily.

"I am still not following you," Miss Honey said. "Do you mean you actually willed the glass to tip over?"

"Yes," Matilda said. "With my eyes."

Miss Honey was silent for a moment. She did not think Matilda was meaning to tell a lie. It was more likely that she was simply allowing her vivid imagination to run away with her. "You mean you were sitting where you are now and you told the glass to topple over and it did?"

"Something like that, Miss Honey, yes."

"If you did that, then it is just about the greatest miracle a person has ever performed since the time of Jesus."

"I did it, Miss Honey."

It is extraordinary, thought Miss Honey, how often small children have flights of fancy like this. She decided to put an end to it as gently as possible. "Could you do it again?" she asked, not unkindly.

"I don't know," Matilda said, "but I think I might be able to."

Miss Honey moved the now empty glass to the middle of the table. "Should I put water in it?" she asked, smiling a little.

"I don't think it matters," Matilda said.

"Very well, then. Go ahead and tip it over."

"It may take some time."

"Take all the time you want," Miss Honey said. "I'm in no hurry."

Matilda, sitting in the second row about ten feet away from Miss Honey, put her elbows on the desk and cupped her face in her hands, and this time she gave the order right at the beginning. *"Tip glass, tip!"* she ordered, but her lips didn't move and she made no sound. She simply shouted the words inside her head.

And now she concentrated the whole of her mind and her brain and her will up into her eyes and once again but much more quickly than before she felt the electricity gathering and the power was beginning to surge and the hotness was coming into the eyeballs, and then the millions of tiny invisible arms with hands on them were shooting out towards the glass, and without making any sound at all she kept on shouting inside her head for the glass to go over. She saw it wobble, then it tilted, then it toppled right over and fell with a tinkle on to the table-top not twelve inches from Miss Honey's folded arms.

Miss Honey's mouth dropped open and her eyes stretched so wide you could see the whites all round. She didn't say a word. She couldn't. The shock of seeing the miracle performed had struck her dumb. She gaped at the glass, leaning well away from it now as

though it might be a dangerous thing. Then slowly she lifted her head and looked at Matilda. She saw the child white in the face, as white as paper, trembling all over, the eyes glazed, staring straight ahead and seeing nothing. The whole face was transfigured, the eyes round and bright and she was sitting there speechless, quite beautiful in a blaze of silence.

Miss Honey waited, trembling a little herself and watching the child as she slowly stirred herself back into consciousness. And then suddenly, *click* went her face into a look of almost seraphic calm. "I'm all right," she said and smiled. "I'm quite all right, Miss Honey, so don't be alarmed."

"You seemed so far away," Miss Honey whispered, awestruck.

"Oh, I was. I was flying past the stars on silver wings," Matilda said. "It was wonderful."

Miss Honey was still gazing at the child in absolute wonderment, as though she were The Creation, The Beginning Of The World, The First Morning.

"It went much quicker this time," Matilda said quietly.

"It's not possible!" Miss Honey was gasping. "I don't believe it! I simply don't believe it!"

She closed her eyes and kept them closed for quite a while, and when she opened them again it seemed as though she had gathered herself together. "Would you like to come back and have tea at my cottage?" she asked.

"Oh, I'd love to," Matilda said.

"Good. Gather up your things and I'll meet you outside in a couple of minutes."

"You won't tell anyone about this . . . this thing that I did, will you, Miss Honey?"

"I wouldn't dream of it," Miss Honey said.

Miss Honey's Cottage

Miss Honey joined Matilda outside the school gates and the two of them walked in silence through the village High Street. They passed the greengrocer with his window full of apples and oranges, and the butcher with bloody lumps of meat on display and naked chickens hanging up, and the small bank, and the grocery store and the electrical shop, and then they came out at the other side of the village on to the narrow country road where there were no people any more and very few motor-cars.

And now suddenly that they were alone, Matilda all of a sudden became wildly animated. It seemed as though a valve had burst inside her and a great gush of energy was being released. She trotted beside Miss Honey with wild little hops and her fingers flew as if she would scatter them to the four winds and her words went off like fireworks, with terrific speed. It was Miss Honey this and Miss Honey that and Miss Honey I do honestly feel I could move almost anything in the world, not just tipping over glasses and little things like

that . . . I feel I could topple tables and chairs, Miss Honey . . . Even when people are sitting in the chairs I think I could push them over, and bigger things too, much bigger things than chairs and tables . . . I only have to take a moment to get my eyes strong and then I can push it out, this strongness, at anything at all so long as I am staring at it hard enough . . . I have to stare at it very hard, Miss Honey, very very hard, and then I can feel it all happening behind my eyes, and my eyes get hot just as though they were burning but I don't mind that in the least, and Miss Honey . . .

"Calm yourself down, child, calm yourself down," Miss Honey said. "Let us not get ourselves too worked up so early in the proceedings."

"But you do think it is *interesting*, don't you, Miss Honey?"

"Oh, it is *interesting* all right," Miss Honey said. "It is *more* than interesting. But we must tread very carefully from now on, Matilda."

"Why must we tread carefully, Miss Honey?"

"Because we are playing with mysterious forces, my child, that we know nothing about. I do not think they are evil. They may be good.

They may even be divine. But whether they are or not, let us handle them carefully."

These were wise words from a wise old bird, but Matilda was too steamed up to see it that way. "I don't see why we have to be so careful?" she said, still hopping about.

"I am trying to explain to you," Miss Honey said patiently, "that we are dealing with the unknown. It is an unexplainable thing. The right word for it is a phenomenon. It is a phenomenon."

"Am I a phenomenon?" Matilda asked.

"It is quite possible that you are," Miss Honey said. "But I'd rather you didn't think about yourself as anything in particular at the moment. What I thought we might do is to explore this phenomenon a little further, just the two of us together, but making sure we take things very carefully all the time."

"You want me to do some more of it then, Miss Honey?"

"That is what I am tempted to suggest," Miss Honey said cautiously.

"Goody-good," Matilda said.

"I myself," Miss Honey said, "am probably far more bowled over by what you did than you are, and I am trying to find some reasonable explanation."

"Such as what?" Matilda asked.

"Such as whether or not it's got something to do with the fact that you are quite exceptionally precocious."

"What exactly does that word mean?" Matilda said.

"A precocious child," Miss Honey said, "is one that shows amazing intelligence early on. You are an unbelievably precocious child."

"Am I really?" Matilda asked.

"Of course you are. You must be aware of that. Look at your reading. Look at your mathematics."

"I suppose you're right," Matilda said.

Miss Honey marvelled at the child's lack of conceit and self-consciousness.

"I can't help wondering," she said, "whether this sudden ability that has come to you, of being able to move an object without touching it, whether it might not have something to do with your brainpower."

"You mean there might not be room in my head for all those brains so something has to push out?"

"That's not quite what I mean," Miss Honey said, smiling. "But whatever happens, and I say it again, we must tread carefully from now on. I have not forgotten that strange and distant glimmer on your face after you tipped over the last glass."

"Do you think doing it could actually hurt me? Is that what you're thinking, Miss Honey?"

"It made you feel pretty peculiar, didn't it?"

"It made me feel lovely," Matilda said. "For a moment or two I was flying past the stars on silver wings. I told you that. And shall I tell you something else, Miss Honey? It was easier the second time, much much easier. I think it's like anything else, the more you practise it, the easier it gets."

Miss Honey was walking slowly so that the small child could keep up with her without trotting too fast, and it was very peaceful out there on the narrow road now that the village was behind them. It was one of those golden autumn afternoons and there were blackberries and splashes of old man's beard in the hedges, and the hawthorn berries were ripening scarlet for the birds when the cold winter came along. There were tall trees here and there on either side, oak and sycamore and ash and occasionally a sweet chestnut. Miss

Honey, wishing to change the subject for the moment, gave the names of all these to Matilda and taught her how to recognise them by the shape of their leaves and the pattern of the bark on their trunks. Matilda took all this in and stored the knowledge away carefully in her mind.

They came finally to a gap in the hedge on the left-hand side of the road where there was a five-barred gate. "This way," Miss Honey said, and she opened the gate and led Matilda through and closed it again. They were now walking along a narrow lane that was no more than a rutted cart-track. There was a high hedge of hazel on either side and you could see clusters of ripe brown nuts in their green jackets. The squirrels would be collecting them all very soon, Miss Honey said, and storing them away carefully for the bleak months ahead.

"You mean you *live* down here?" Matilda asked.

"I do," Miss Honey replied, but she said no more.

Matilda had never once stopped to think about where Miss Honey might be living. She had always regarded her purely as a teacher, a person who turned up out of nowhere and taught at school and then went away again. Do any of us children, she wondered, ever stop to ask ourselves where our teachers go when school is over for the day? Do we wonder if they live alone, or if there is a mother at home or a sister or a husband? "Do you live all by yourself, Miss Honey?" she asked.

"Yes," Miss Honey said. "Very much so."

They were walking over the deep sun-baked mud-tracks of the lane and you had to watch where you put your feet if you didn't want to twist your ankle. There were a few small birds around in the hazel branches but that was all.

"It's just a farm-labourer's cottage," Miss Honey said. "You mustn't expect too much of it. We're nearly there."

They came to a small green gate half-buried

in the hedge on the right and almost hidden by the overhanging hazel branches. Miss Honey paused with one hand on the gate and said, "There it is. That's where I live."

Matilda saw a narrow dirt-path leading to a tiny red-brick cottage. The cottage was so small it looked more like a doll's house than a human dwelling. The bricks it was built of were old and crumbly and very pale red. It had a grey slate roof and one small chimney, and there were two little windows at the front. Each window was no larger than a sheet of tabloid newspaper and there was clearly no upstairs to the place. On either side of the path there was a wilderness of nettles and blackberry thorns and long brown grass. An enormous oak tree stood overshadowing the cottage. Its massive spreading branches seemed to be enfolding and embracing the tiny building, and perhaps hiding it as well from the rest of the world.

Miss Honey, with one hand on the gate which she had not yet opened, turned to Matilda and said, "A poet called Dylan Thomas once wrote some lines that I think of every time I walk up this path."

Matilda waited, and Miss Honey, in a rather wonderful slow voice, began reciting the poem:

"Never and never, my girl riding far and near
In the land of the hearthstone tales, and spelled
  asleep,
Fear or believe that the wolf in the sheepwhite
  hood
Loping and bleating roughly and blithely shall
  leap, my dear, my dear,
Out of a lair in the flocked leaves in the dew
  dipped year
To eat your heart in the house in the rosy
  wood."

There was a moment of silence, and Matilda, who had never before heard great romantic poetry spoken aloud, was profoundly moved. "It's like music," she whispered.

"It is music," Miss Honey said. And then, as though embarrassed at having revealed such a secret part of herself, she quickly pushed open the gate and walked up the path. Matilda hung back. She was a bit frightened of this place now. It seemed so unreal and remote and fantastic and so totally away from this earth. It was like an illustration in Grimm or Hans Andersen. It was the house where the poor woodcutter lived with Hansel and Gretel and where Red Riding Hood's grandmother lived and it was also the house of The Seven Dwarfs and The Three Bears and all the rest of them. It was straight out of a fairy-tale.

"Come along, my dear," Miss Honey called back, and Matilda followed her up the path.

The front-door was covered with flaky green paint and there was no keyhole. Miss Honey simply lifted the latch and pushed open the door and went in. Although she was not a tall woman, she had to stoop low to get through the doorway. Matilda went after her and found herself in what seemed to be a dark narrow tunnel.

"You can come through to the kitchen and help me make the tea," Miss Honey said, and she led the way along the tunnel into the kitchen – that is if you could call it a kitchen. It was not much bigger than a good-sized clothes cupboard and there was one small window in the back wall with a sink under the window, but there were no taps over the sink. Against another wall there was a shelf, presumably for preparing food, and there was a single cupboard above the shelf. On the shelf itself there stood a Primus stove, a saucepan and a half-full bottle of milk. A

Primus is a little camping-stove that you fill with paraffin and you light it at the top and then you pump it to get pressure for the flame.

"You can get me some water while I light the Primus," Miss Honey said. "The well is out at the back. Take the bucket. Here it is. You'll find a rope in the well. Just hook the bucket on to the end of the rope and lower it down, but don't fall in yourself." Matilda, more bemused than ever now, took the bucket and carried it out into the back garden. The well had a little wooden roof over it and a simple winding device and there was the rope dangling down into a dark bottomless hole. Matilda pulled up the rope and hooked the handle of the bucket on to the end of it. Then she lowered it until she heard a splash and the rope went slack. She pulled it up again and lo and behold, there was water in the bucket.

"Is this enough?" she asked, carrying it in.

"Just about," Miss Honey said. "I don't suppose you've ever done that before?"

"Never," Matilda said. "It's fun. How do you get enough water for your bath?"

"I don't take a bath," Miss Honey said. "I wash standing up. I get a bucketful of water and I heat it on this little stove and I strip and wash myself all over."

"Do you honestly do that?" Matilda said.

"Of course I do," Miss Honey said. "Every poor person in England used to wash that way until not so very long ago. And *they* didn't have a Primus. They had to heat the water over the fire in the hearth."

"Are *you* poor, Miss Honey?"

"Yes," Miss Honey said. "Very. It's a good little stove, isn't it?" The Primus was roaring away with a powerful blue flame and already the water in the saucepan was beginning to bubble. Miss Honey got a teapot from the cupboard and put some tea leaves into it. She also found half a small loaf of brown bread. She cut two thin slices and then, from a plastic container, she took some margarine and spread it on the bread.

Margarine, Matilda thought. She really must be poor.

Miss Honey found a tray and on it she put two mugs, the teapot, the half bottle of milk and a plate with the two slices of bread. "I'm afraid I don't have any sugar," she said. "I never use it."

"That's all right," Matilda said. In her wisdom she seemed to be aware of the delicacy of the situation and she was taking great care not to say anything to embarrass her companion.

"Let's have it in the sitting-room," Miss Honey said, picking up the tray and leading the way out of the kitchen and down the dark little tunnel into the room at the front. Matilda followed her, but just inside the doorway of the so-called sitting-room she stopped and stared around her in absolute amazement. The room was as small and square and bare as a prison cell. The pale daylight that entered came from a single tiny window in the front wall, but there were no curtains. The only objects in the entire room were two upturned wooden boxes to serve as chairs and a third box between them for a table. That was all. There were no pictures on the walls, no carpet on the floor, only rough unpolished wooden planks, and there were gaps between the planks where dust

and bits of grime had gathered. The ceiling was so low that with a jump Matilda could nearly touch it with her finger-tips. The walls were white but the whiteness didn't look like paint. Matilda rubbed her palm against it and a white powder came off on to her skin. It was whitewash, the cheap stuff that is used in cowsheds and stables and hen-houses.

Matilda was appalled. Was this really where

her neat and trimly-dressed school teacher lived? Was this all she had to come back to after a day's work? It was unbelievable. And what was the reason for it? There was something very strange going on around here, surely.

Miss Honey put the tray on one of the upturned boxes. "Sit down, my dear, sit down," she said, "and we'll have a nice hot cup of tea. Help yourself to bread. Both slices are for you. I never eat anything when I get home. I have a good old tuck-in at the school lunch and that keeps me going until the next morning."

Matilda perched herself carefully on an upturned box and more out of politeness than anything else she took a slice of bread and margarine and started to eat it. At home she would have been having buttered toast and strawberry jam and probably a piece of sponge-cake to round it off. And yet this was somehow far more fun. There was a mystery here in this house, a great mystery, there was no doubt about that, and Matilda was longing to find out what it was.

Miss Honey poured the tea and added a little milk to both cups. She appeared to be not in the least ill at ease sitting on an upturned box in a bare room and drinking tea out of a mug that she balanced on her knee.

"You know," she said, "I've been thinking very hard about what you did with that glass. It is a great power you have been given, my child, you know that."

"Yes, Miss Honey, I do," Matilda said, chewing her bread and margarine.

"So far as I know," Miss Honey went on, "nobody else in the history of the world has been able to compel an object to move without touching it or blowing on it or using any outside help at all."

Matilda nodded but said nothing.

"The fascinating thing," Miss Honey said, "would be to find out the real limit of this power of yours. Oh, I know you think you can move just about anything there is, but I have my doubts about that."

"I'd love to try something really huge," Matilda said.

"What about distance?" Miss Honey asked. "Would you always have to be close to the thing you were pushing?"

"I simply don't know," Matilda said. "But it would be fun to find out."

Miss Honey's Story

"We mustn't hurry this," Miss Honey said, "so let's have another cup of tea. And do eat that other slice of bread. You must be hungry."

Matilda took the second slice and started eating it slowly. The margarine wasn't at all bad. She doubted whether she could have told the difference if she hadn't known. "Miss Honey," she said suddenly, "do they pay you very badly at our school?"

Miss Honey looked up sharply. "Not too badly," she said. "I get about the same as the others."

"But it must still be very little if you are so dreadfully poor," Matilda said. "Do all the teachers live like this, with no furniture and no kitchen stove and no bathroom?"

"No, they don't," Miss Honey said rather stiffly. "I just happen to be the exception."

"I expect you just happen to like living in a very simple way," Matilda said, probing a little further. "It must make house cleaning an awful lot easier and you don't have furniture to polish or any of those silly little ornaments lying around that have to be dusted every day.

And I suppose if you don't have a fridge you don't have to go out and buy all sorts of junky things like eggs and mayonnaise and ice-cream to fill it up with. It must save a terrific lot of shopping."

At this point Matilda noticed that Miss Honey's face had gone all tight and peculiar-looking. Her whole body had become rigid. Her shoulders were hunched up high and her lips were pressed together tight and she sat there gripping her mug of tea in both hands and staring down into it as though searching for a way to answer these not-quite-so-innocent questions.

There followed a rather long and embarrassing silence. In the space of thirty seconds the atmosphere in the tiny room had changed completely and now it was vibrating with awkwardness and secrets. Matilda said, "I am very sorry I asked you those questions, Miss Honey. It is not any of my business."

At this, Miss Honey seemed to rouse herself. She gave a shake of her shoulders and then very carefully she placed her mug on the tray.

"Why shouldn't you ask?" she said. "You were bound to ask in the end. You are much too bright not to have wondered. Perhaps I even *wanted* you to ask. Maybe that is why I invited you here after all. As a matter of fact you are the first visitor to come to the cottage since I moved in two years ago."

Matilda said nothing. She could feel the tension growing and growing in the room.

"You are so much wiser than your years, my dear," Miss Honey went on, "that it quite staggers me. Although you look like a child, you are not really a child at all because your mind and your powers of reasoning seem to be fully grown-up. So I suppose we might call you a grown-up child, if you see what I mean."

Matilda still did not say anything. She was

waiting for what was coming next.

"Up to now," Miss Honey went on, "I have found it impossible to talk to anyone about my problems. I couldn't face the embarrassment, and anyway I lack the courage. Any courage I had was knocked out of me when I was young. But now, all of a sudden I have a sort of desperate wish to tell everything to somebody. I know you are only a tiny little girl, but there is some kind of magic in you somewhere. I've seen it with my own eyes."

Matilda became very alert. The voice she was hearing was surely crying out for help. It must be. It had to be.

Then the voice spoke again. "Have some more tea," it said. "I think there's still a drop left."

Matilda nodded.

Miss Honey poured tea into both mugs and added milk. Again she cupped her own mug in both hands and sat there sipping.

There was quite a long silence before she said, "May I tell you a story?"

"Of course," Matilda said.

"I am twenty-three years old," Miss Honey said, "and when I was born my father was a doctor in this village. We had a nice old house, quite large, red-brick. It's tucked away in the woods behind the hills. I don't think you'd know it."

Matilda kept silent.

"I was born there," Miss Honey said. "And then came the first tragedy. My mother died when I was two. My father, a busy doctor, had to have someone to run the house and to look after me. So he invited my mother's unmarried sister, my aunt, to come and live with us. She agreed and she came."

Matilda was listening intently. "How old was the aunt when she moved in?" she asked.

"Not very old," Miss Honey said. "I should say about thirty. But I hated her right from the start. I missed my mother terribly. And the aunt was not a kind person. My father didn't know that because he was hardly ever around but when he did put in an appearance, the aunt behaved differently."

Miss Honey paused and sipped her tea. "I can't think why I am telling you all this," she said, embarrassed.

"Go on," Matilda said. "Please."

"Well," Miss Honey said, "then came the second tragedy. When I was five, my father died very suddenly. One day he was there and the next day he was gone. And so I was left to live alone with my aunt. She became my legal guardian. She had all the powers of a parent over me. And in some way or another, she became the actual owner of the house."

"How did your father die?" Matilda asked.

"It is interesting you should ask that," Miss Honey said. "I myself was much too young to question it at the time, but I found out later that there was a good deal of mystery surrounding his death."

"Didn't they know how he died?" Matilda asked.

"Well, not exactly," Miss Honey said, hesitating. "You see, no one could believe that he would ever have done it. He was such a very sane and sensible man."

"Done what?" Matilda asked.

"*Killed* himself."

Matilda was stunned.

"Did he?" she gasped.

"That's what it *looked* like," Miss Honey said. "But who knows?" She shrugged and turned away and stared out of the tiny window.

"I know what you're thinking," Matilda said. "You're thinking that the aunt killed him and made it look as though he'd done it himself."

"I am not thinking anything," Miss Honey said. "One must never think things like that without proof."

The little room became quiet. Matilda noticed that the hands clasping the mug were trembling slightly. "What happened after that?" she asked. "What happened when you were left all alone with the aunt? Wasn't she nice to you?"

"Nice?" Miss Honey said. "She was a demon. As soon as my father was out of the way she became a holy terror. My life was a nightmare."

"What did she do to you?" Matilda asked.

"I don't want to talk about it," Miss Honey said. "It's too horrible. But in the end I became so frightened of her I used to start shaking when she came into the room. You must understand I was never a strong character like you. I was always shy and retiring."

"Didn't you have any other relations?" Matilda asked. "Any uncles or aunts or grannies who would come and see you?"

"None that I knew about," Miss Honey said. "They were all either dead or they'd gone to Australia. And that's still the way it is now, I'm afraid."

"So you grew up in that house alone with your aunt," Matilda said. "But you must have gone to school."

"Of course," Miss Honey said. "I went to the same school you're going to now. But I lived at home." Miss Honey paused and stared down into her empty tea-mug. "I think what I am trying to explain to you," she said, "is that over the years I became so completely cowed and dominated by this monster of an aunt that when she gave me an order, no matter what it was, I obeyed it instantly. That can happen, you know. And by the time I was ten, I had become her slave. I did all the housework. I made her bed. I washed and ironed for her. I did all the cooking. I learned how to do everything."

"But surely you could have complained to *somebody*?" Matilda said.

"To whom?" Miss Honey said. "And anyway, I was far too terrified to complain. I told you, I was her slave."

"Did she beat you?"

"Let's not go into details," Miss Honey said.

"How simply *awful*," Matilda said. "Did you cry nearly all the time?"

"Only when I was alone," Miss Honey said. "I wasn't allowed to cry in front of her. But I lived in fear."

"What happened when you left school?" Matilda asked.

"I was a bright pupil," Miss Honey said. "I could easily have got into university. But there was no question of that."

"Why not, Miss Honey?"

"Because I was needed at home to do the work."

"Then how did you become a teacher?" Matilda asked.

"There is a Teacher's Training College in Reading," Miss Honey said. "That's only forty minutes' bus-ride away from here. I was allowed to go there on condition I came straight home again every afternoon to do the washing and ironing and to clean the house and cook the supper."

"How old were you then?" Matilda asked.

"When I went into Teacher's Training I was eighteen," Miss Honey said.

"You could have just packed up and walked away," Matilda said.

"Not until I got a job," Miss Honey said. "And don't forget, I was by then dominated by my aunt to such an extent that I wouldn't have dared. You can't imagine what it's like to be completely controlled like that by a very strong personality. It turns you to jelly. So that's it. That's the sad story of my life. Now I've talked enough."

"Please don't stop," Matilda said. "You haven't finished yet. How did you manage to get away from her in the end and come and live in this funny little house?"

"Ah, that was something," Miss Honey said. "I was proud of that."

"Tell me," Matilda said.

"Well," Miss Honey said, "when I got my teacher's job, the aunt told me I owed her a lot of money. I asked her why. She said, 'Because I've been feeding you for all these years and buying your shoes and your clothes!' She told me it added up to thousands and I had to pay her back by giving her my salary for the next ten years. 'I'll give you one pound a week pocket-money,' she said. 'But that's all you're going to get.' She even arranged with the school authorities to have my salary paid directly into her own bank. She made me sign the paper."

"You shouldn't have done that," Matilda said. "Your salary was your chance of freedom."

"I know, I know," Miss Honey said. "But by then I had been her slave nearly all my life and I hadn't the courage or the guts to say no. I was still petrified of her. She could still hurt me badly."

"So how did you manage to escape?" Matilda asked.

"Ah," Miss Honey said, smiling for the first time, "that was two years ago. It was my greatest triumph."

"Please tell me," Matilda said.

"I used to get up very early and go for walks while my aunt was still asleep," Miss Honey said. "And one day I came across this tiny cottage. It was empty. I found out who owned it. It was a farmer. I went to see him. Farmers also get up very early. He was milking his cows. I asked him if I could rent his cottage. 'You can't live there!' he cried. 'It's got no conveniences, no running water, no nothing!'"

" 'I want to live there,' I said. 'I'm a romantic. I've fallen in love with it. Please rent it to me.'

" 'You're mad,' he said. 'But if you insist, you're welcome to it. The rent will be ten pence a week.'

" 'Here's one month's rent in advance,' I said, giving him 40p. 'And thank you so much!'"

"How super!" Matilda cried. "So suddenly you had a house all of your own! But how did you pluck up the courage to tell the aunt?"

"That was tough," Miss Honey said. "But I steeled myself to do it. One night, after I had cooked her supper, I went upstairs and packed the few things I possessed in a cardboard box and came downstairs and announced I was leaving. 'I've rented a house,' I said.

"My aunt exploded. 'Rented a house!' she shouted. 'How can you rent a house when you have only one pound a week in the world?'

" 'I've done it,' I said.

" 'And how are you going to buy food for yourself?'

" 'I'll manage,' I mumbled and rushed out of the front door."

"Oh, well done you!" Matilda cried. "So you were free at last!"

"I was free at last," Miss Honey said. "I can't tell you how wonderful it was."

"But have you really managed to live here on one pound a week for two years?" Matilda asked.

"I most certainly have," Miss Honey said. "I pay ten pence rent, and the rest just about buys me paraffin for my stove and for my lamp, and a little milk and tea and bread and margarine. That's all I need really. As I told you, I have a jolly good tuck-in at the school lunch."

Matilda stared at her. What a marvellously brave thing Miss Honey had done. Suddenly she was a heroine in Matilda's eyes. "Isn't it awfully cold in the winter?" she asked.

"I've got a little paraffin stove," Miss Honey said. "You'd be surprised how snug I can make it in here."

"Do you have a bed, Miss Honey?"

"Well not exactly," Miss Honey said, smiling again. "But they say it's very healthy to sleep on a hard surface."

All at once Matilda was able to see the whole situation with absolute clarity. Miss Honey needed help. There was no way she could go on existing like this indefinitely. "You would be a lot better off, Miss Honey," she said, "if you gave up your job and drew unemployment money."

"I would never do that," Miss Honey said. "I love teaching."

"This awful aunt," Matilda said, "I suppose

she is still living in your lovely old house?"

"Very much so," Miss Honey said. "She's still only about fifty. She'll be around for a long time yet."

"And do you think your father really meant her to own the house for ever?"

"I'm quite sure he didn't," Miss Honey said. "Parents will often give a guardian the right to occupy the house for a certain length of time, but it is nearly always left in trust for the child. It then becomes the child's property when he or she grows up."

"Then surely it is your house?" Matilda said.

"My father's will was never found," Miss Honey said. "It looks as though somebody destroyed it."

"No prizes for guessing who," Matilda said.

"No prizes," Miss Honey said.

"But if there is no will, Miss Honey, then surely the house goes automatically to you. You are the next of kin."

"I know I am," Miss Honey said. "But my aunt produced a piece of paper supposedly written by my father saying that he leaves the house to his sister-in-law in return for her kindness in looking after me. I am certain it's a forgery. But no one can prove it."

"Couldn't you try?" Matilda said. "Couldn't you hire a good lawyer and make a fight of it."

"I don't have the money to do that," Miss Honey said. "And you must remember that this aunt of mine is a much respected figure in the community. She has a lot of influence."

"Who is she?" Matilda asked.

Miss Honey hesitated a moment. Then she said softly, "Miss Trunchbull."

The Names

"Miss Trunchbull!" Matilda cried, jumping about a foot in the air. "You mean *she* is your aunt? *She* brought you up?"

"Yes," Miss Honey said.

"No *wonder* you were terrified!" Matilda cried. "The other day we saw her grab a girl by the pigtails and throw her over the playground fence!"

"You haven't seen anything," Miss Honey said. "After my father died, when I was five and a half, she used to make me bath myself all alone. And if she came up and thought I hadn't washed properly she would push my head under the water and hold it there. But don't get me started on what she used to do. That won't help us at all."

"No," Matilda said, "it won't."

"We came here," Miss Honey said, "to talk about *you* and I've been talking about nothing but myself the whole time. I feel like a fool. I am much more interested in just how much you can do with those amazing eyes of yours."

"I can move things," Matilda said. "I know I can. I can push things over."

"How would you like it," Miss Honey said, "if we made some very cautious experiments to see just how much you can move and push?"

Quite surprisingly, Matilda said, "If you don't mind, Miss Honey, I think I would rather not. I want to go home now and think and think about all the things I've heard this afternoon."

Miss Honey stood up at once. "Of course," she said. "I have kept you here far too long. Your mother will be starting to worry."

"She never does that," Matilda said, smiling. "But I would like to go home now please, if you don't mind."

"Come along then," Miss Honey said. "I'm sorry I gave you such a rotten tea."

"You didn't at all," Matilda said. "I loved it."

The two of them walked all the way to Matilda's house in complete silence. Miss Honey sensed that Matilda wanted it that way. The child seemed so lost in thought she hardly looked where she was walking, and when they reached the gate of Matilda's home, Miss Honey said, "You had better forget everything I told you this afternoon."

"I won't promise to do that," Matilda said,

"but I will promise not to talk about it to anyone any more, not even to you."

"I think that would be wise," Miss Honey said.

"I won't promise to stop thinking about it, though, Miss Honey," Matilda said. "I've been thinking about it all the way back from your cottage and I believe I've got just a tiny little bit of an idea."

"You mustn't," Miss Honey said. "Please forget it."

"I would like to ask you three last things before I stop talking about it," Matilda said. "Please will you answer them, Miss Honey?"

Miss Honey smiled. It was extraordinary, she told herself, how this little snippet of a girl seemed suddenly to be taking charge of her problems, and with such authority, too. "Well," she said, "that depends on what the questions are."

"The first thing is this," Matilda said. "What did Miss Trunchbull call *your father* when they were around the house at home?"

"I'm sure she called him Magnus," Miss Honey said. "That was his first name."

"And what did your father call Miss Trunchbull?"

"Her name is Agatha," Miss Honey said. "That's what he would have called her."

"And lastly," Matilda said, "what did your father and Miss Trunchbull call *you* around the house?"

"They called me Jenny," Miss Honey said.

Matilda pondered these answers very carefully. "Let me make sure I've got them right," she said. "In the house at home, your father was Magnus, Miss Trunchbull was Agatha and you were Jenny. Am I right?"

"That is correct," Miss Honey said.

"Thank you," Matilda said. "And now I won't mention the subject any more."

Miss Honey wondered what on earth was going on in the mind of this child. "Don't do anything silly," she said.

Matilda laughed and turned away and ran up the path to her front-door, calling out as she went, "Good-bye, Miss Honey! Thank you so much for the tea."

The Practice

Matilda found the house empty as usual. Her father was not yet back from work, her mother was not yet back from bingo and her brother might be anywhere. She went straight into the living room and opened the drawer of the sideboard where she knew her father kept a box of cigars. She took one out and carried it up to her bedroom and shut herself in.

Now for the practice, she told herself. It's going to be tough but I'm determined to do it.

Her plan for helping Miss Honey was beginning to form beautifully in her mind. She had it now in almost every detail, but in the end it all depended upon her being able to do one very special thing with her eye-power. She knew she wouldn't manage it right away, but she felt fairly confident that with a great deal of practice and effort, she would succeed in the end. The cigar was essential. It was perhaps a bit thicker than she would have liked, but the weight was about right. It would be fine for practising with.

There was a small dressing-table in Matilda's bedroom with her hairbrush and comb on it

and two library books. She cleared these things to one side and laid the cigar down in the middle of the dressing-table. Then she walked away and sat on the end of her bed. She was now about ten feet from the cigar.

She settled herself and began to concentrate, and very quickly this time she felt the electricity beginning to flow inside her head, gathering itself behind the eyes, and the eyes

became hot and millions of tiny invisible hands began pushing out little sparks towards the cigar. "Move!" she whispered, and to her intense surprise, almost at once, the cigar with its little red and gold paper band around its middle rolled away across the top of the dressing-table and fell on to the carpet.

Matilda had enjoyed that. It was lovely doing it. It had felt as though sparks were going round and round inside her head and flashing out of her eyes. It had given her a sense of power that was almost ethereal. And how quick it had been this time! How simple!

She crossed the bedroom and picked up the cigar and put it back on the table.

Now for the difficult one, she thought. But if I have the power to *push*, then surely I also have the power to *lift*? It is *vital* I learn how to lift it. I *must* learn how to lift it right up into the air and keep it there. It is not a very heavy thing, a cigar.

She sat on the end of the bed and started again. It was easy now to summon up the power behind her eyes. It was like pushing a trigger in the brain. *"Lift!"* she whispered. *"Lift! Lift!"*

At first the cigar started to roll away. But then, with Matilda concentrating fiercely, one end of it slowly lifted up about an inch off the table-top. With a colossal effort, she managed to hold it there for about ten seconds. Then it fell back again.

"Phew!" she gasped. "I'm getting it! I'm starting to do it!"

For the next hour, Matilda kept practising, and in the end she had managed, by the sheer power of her eyes, to lift the whole cigar clear off the table about six inches into the air and hold it there for about a minute. Then suddenly she was so exhausted she fell back on the bed and went to sleep.

That was how her mother found her later in the evening.

"What's the matter with you?" the mother said, waking her up. "Are you ill?"

"Oh gosh," Matilda said, sitting up and looking around. "No. I'm all right. I was a bit

tired, that's all."

From then on, every day after school, Matilda shut herself in her room and practised with the cigar. And soon it all began to come together in the most wonderful way. Six days later, by the following Wednesday evening, she was able not only to lift the cigar up into the air but also to move it around exactly as she wished. It was beautiful. "I can do it!" she cried. "I can really do it! I can pick the cigar up just with my eye-power and push it and pull it in the air any way I want!"

All she had to do now was to put her great plan into action.

The Third Miracle

The next day was Thursday, and that, as the whole of Miss Honey's class knew, was the day on which the Headmistress would take charge of the first lesson after lunch.

In the morning Miss Honey said to them, "One or two of you did not particularly enjoy the last occasion when the Headmistress took the class, so let us all try to be especially careful and clever today. How are your ears, Eric, after your last encounter with Miss Trunchbull?"

"She stretched them," Eric said. "My mother said she's positive they are bigger than they were."

"And Rupert," Miss Honey said, "I am glad to see you didn't lose any of your hair after last Thursday."

"My head was jolly sore afterwards," Rupert said.

"And you, Nigel," Miss Honey said, "do please try not to be smart-aleck with the Headmistress today. You were really quite cheeky to her last week."

"I hate her," Nigel said.

"Try not to make it so obvious," Miss Honey said. "It doesn't pay. She's a very strong woman. She has muscles like steel ropes."

"I wish I was grown up," Nigel said. "I'd knock her flat."

"I doubt you would," Miss Honey said. "No one has ever got the better of her yet."

"What will she be testing us on this afternoon?" a small girl asked.

"Almost certainly the three-times table," Miss Honey said. "That's what you are all meant to have learnt this past week. Make sure you know it."

Lunch came and went.

After lunch, the class reassembled. Miss Honey stood at one side of the room. They all sat silent, apprehensive, waiting. And then, like some giant of doom, the enormous Trunchbull strode into the room in her green breeches and cotton smock. She went straight to her jug of water and lifted it up by the handle and peered inside.

"I am glad to see," she said, "that there are no slimy creatures in my drinking-water this time. If there had been, then something exceptionally unpleasant would have happened to every single member of this class. And that includes you, Miss Honey."

The class remained silent and very tense. They had learnt a bit about this tigress by now and nobody was about to take any chances.

"Very well," boomed the Trunchbull. "Let us see how well you know your three-times table. Or to put it another way, let us see how badly Miss Honey has taught you the three-times table." The Trunchbull was standing in front of the class, legs apart, hands on hips, scowling at Miss Honey who stood silent to one side.

Matilda, sitting motionless at her desk in the second row, was watching things very closely.

"You!" the Trunchbull shouted, pointing a finger the size of a rolling-pin at a boy called Wilfred. Wilfred was on the extreme right of the front row. "Stand up, you!" she shouted at him.

Wilfred stood up.

"Recite the three-times table backwards!" the Trunchbull said.

"Backwards?" stammered Wilfred. "But I haven't learnt it backwards."

"There you are!" cried the Trunchbull, triumphant. "She's taught you nothing! Miss Honey, why have you taught them absolutely nothing at all in the last week?"

"That is not true, Headmistress," Miss Honey said. "They have all learnt their three-times table. But I see no point in teaching it to them backwards. There is little point in teaching anything backwards. The whole object of life, Headmistress, is to go forwards. I venture to ask whether even you, for example, can spell a simple word like *wrong* backwards straight away. I very much doubt it."

"Don't you get impertinent with me, Miss Honey!" the Trunchbull snapped, then she turned back to the unfortunate Wilfred. "Very well, boy," she said. "Answer me this. I have seven apples, seven oranges and seven bananas. How many pieces of fruit do I have altogether? Hurry up! Get on with it! Give me the answer!"

"That's *adding up*!" Wilfred cried. "That isn't the three-times table!"

"You blithering idiot!" shouted the Trunchbull. "You festering gumboil! You fleabitten fungus! That *is* the three-times table! You have three separate lots of fruit and each lot has seven pieces. Three sevens are twenty-one. Can't you see that, you stagnant cesspool! I'll give you one more chance. I have eight coconuts, eight monkey-nuts and eight nutty little idiots like you. How many nuts do I have altogether? Answer me quickly."

Poor Wilfred was properly flustered. "Wait!" he cried. "Please wait! I've got to add up eight coconuts and eight monkey-nuts . . ." He started counting on his fingers.

"You bursting blister!" yelled the Trunchbull. "You moth-eaten maggot! This is *not* adding up! This is multiplication! The answer is three eights! Or is it eight threes? What is the difference between three eights and eight threes? Tell me that, you mangled little wurzel and look sharp about it!"

By now Wilfred was far too frightened and bewildered even to speak.

In two strides the Trunchbull was beside him, and by some amazing gymnastic trick, it may have been judo or karate, she flipped the back of Wilfred's legs with one of her feet so that the boy shot off the ground and turned a somersault in the air. But halfway through the somersault she caught him by an ankle and held him dangling upside-down like a plucked chicken in a shop-window.

"Eight threes," the Trunchbull shouted, swinging Wilfred from side to side by his ankle, "eight threes is the same as three eights and

three eights are twenty-four! Repeat that!"

At exactly that moment Nigel, at the other end of the room, jumped to his feet and started pointing excitedly at the blackboard and screaming, "The chalk! The chalk! Look at the chalk! It's moving all on its own!"

So hysterical and shrill was Nigel's scream that everyone in the place, including the Trunchbull, looked up at the blackboard. And there, sure enough, a brand-new piece of chalk was hovering near the grey-black writing surface of the blackboard.

"It's writing something!" screamed Nigel. *"The chalk is writing something!"*

And indeed it was.

"What the blazes is this?" yelled the Trunchbull. It had shaken her to see her own first name being written like that by an invisible hand. She dropped Wilfred on to the floor. Then she yelled at nobody in particular, "Who's *doing* this? Who's *writing* it?"

The chalk continued to write.

Everyone in the place heard the gasp that came from the Trunchbull's throat. "No!" she cried, "It can't be! It can't be Magnus!"

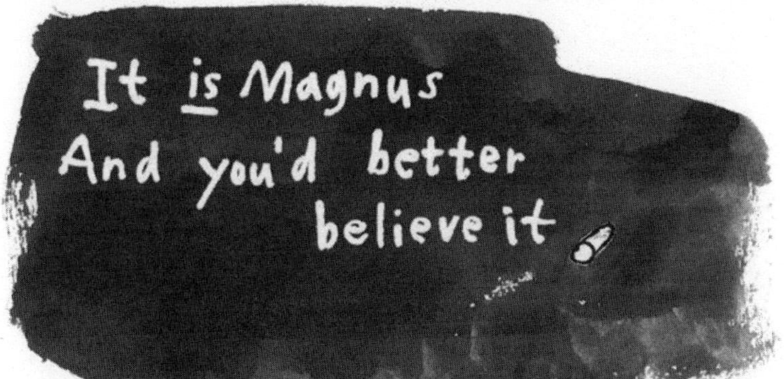

Miss Honey, at the side of the room glanced swiftly at Matilda. The child was sitting very straight at her desk, the head held high, the mouth compressed, the eyes glittering like two stars.

For some reason everyone now looked at the Trunchbull. The woman's face had turned white as snow and her mouth was opening and shutting like a halibut out of water and giving out a series of strangled gasps.

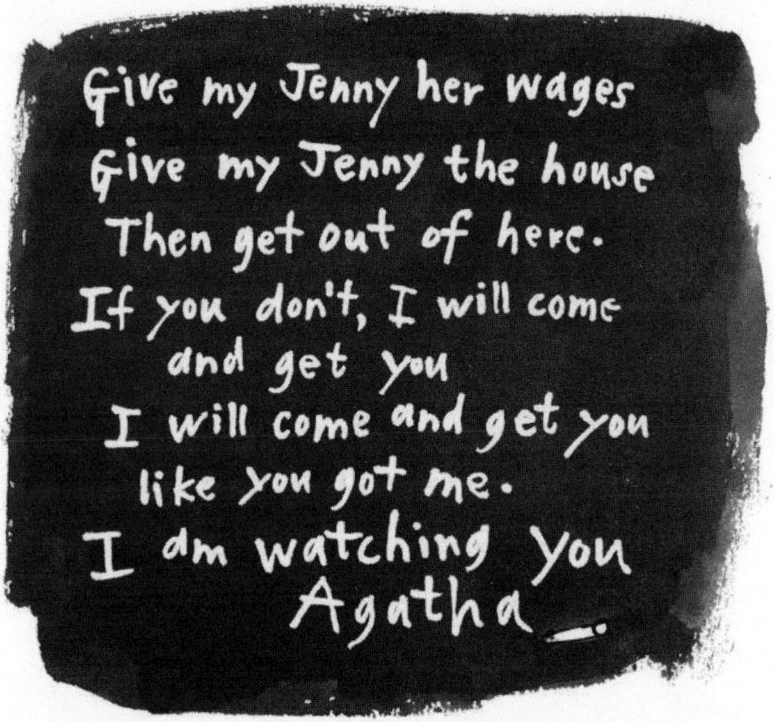

The chalk stopped writing. It hovered for a few moments, then suddenly it dropped to the floor with a tinkle and broke in two.

Wilfred, who had managed to resume his seat in the front row, screamed, "Miss Trunchbull has fallen down! Miss Trunchbull is on the floor!"

This was the most sensational bit of news of all and the entire class jumped up out of their seats to have a really good look. And there she

was, the huge figure of the Headmistress, stretched full-length on her back across the floor, out for the count.

Miss Honey ran forward and knelt beside the prostrate giant. "She's fainted!" she cried. "She's out cold! Someone go and fetch the

matron at once." Three children ran out of the room.

Nigel, always ready for action, leapt up and seized the big jug of water. "My father says cold water is the best way to wake up someone who's fainted," he said, and with that he tipped the entire contents of the jug over the Trunchbull's head. No one, not even Miss Honey, protested.

As for Matilda, she continued to sit motionless at her desk. She was feeling curiously elated. She felt as though she had touched something that was not quite of this world, the highest point of the heavens, the farthest star. She had felt most wonderfully the power surging up behind her eyes, gushing like a warm fluid inside her skull, and her eyes had become scorching hot, hotter than ever before, and things had come bursting out of her eye-sockets and then the piece of chalk had lifted itself up and had begun to write. It seemed as though she had hardly done anything, it had all been so simple.

The school matron, followed by five teachers, three women and two men, came rushing into the room.

"By golly, somebody's floored her at last!" cried one of the men, grinning. "Congratulations, Miss Honey!"

"Who threw the water over her?" asked the matron.

"I did," said Nigel proudly.

"Good for you," another teacher said. "Shall

we get some more?"

"Stop that," the matron said. "We must carry her up to the sick-room."

It took all five teachers and the matron to lift the enormous woman and stagger with her out of the room.

Miss Honey said to the class, "I think you'd all better go out to the playground and amuse yourselves until the next lesson." Then she turned and walked over to the blackboard and carefully wiped out all the chalk writing.

The children began filing out of the classroom. Matilda started to go with them, but as she passed Miss Honey she paused and her twinkling eyes met the teacher's eyes and Miss Honey ran forward and gave the tiny child a great big hug and a kiss.

A New Home

Later that day, the news began to spread that the Headmistress had recovered from her fainting-fit and had then marched out of the school building tight-lipped and white in the face.

The next morning she did not turn up at school. At lunchtime, Mr Trilby, the Deputy Head, telephoned her house to enquire if she was feeling unwell. There was no answer to the phone.

When school was over, Mr Trilby decided to investigate further, so he walked to the house where Miss Trunchbull lived on the edge of the village, the lovely small red-brick Georgian building known as The Red House, tucked away in the woods behind the hills.

He rang the bell. No answer.

He knocked loudly. No answer.

He called out, "Is anybody at home?" No answer.

He tried the door and to his surprise found it unlocked. He went in.

The house was silent and there was no one in it, and yet all the furniture was still in place.

Mr Trilby went upstairs to the main bedroom. Here also everything seemed to be normal until he started opening drawers and looking into cupboards. There were no clothes or underclothes or shoes anywhere. They had all gone.

She's done a bunk, Mr Trilby said to himself and he went away to inform the School Governors that the Headmistress had apparently vanished.

On the second morning, Miss Honey received by registered post a letter from a firm of local solicitors informing her that the last will and testament of her late father, Dr Honey, had suddenly and mysteriously turned up. This document revealed that ever since her father's death, Miss Honey had in fact been the rightful owner of a property on the edge of the village known as The Red House, which until recently had been occupied by a Miss Agatha Trunchbull. The will also showed that her father's lifetime savings, which fortunately were still safely in the bank, had also been left to her. The solicitor's letter added that if Miss Honey would kindly call in to the office as soon as possible, then the property and the money could be transferred into her name very rapidly.

Miss Honey did just that, and within a couple of weeks she had moved into The Red House, the very place in which she had been brought up and where luckily all the family furniture and pictures were still around. From then on, Matilda was a welcome visitor to The Red House every single evening after school, and a very close friendship began to develop between the teacher and the small child.

Back at school, great changes were also taking place. As soon as it became clear that Miss Trunchbull had completely disappeared from the scene, the excellent Mr Trilby was appointed Head Teacher in her place. And very soon after that, Matilda was moved up into the top form where Miss Plimsoll quickly discovered that this amazing child was every bit as bright as Miss Honey had said.

One evening a few weeks later, Matilda was having tea with Miss Honey in the kitchen of The Red House after school as they always did, when Matilda said suddenly, "Something strange has happened to me, Miss Honey."

"Tell me about it," Miss Honey said.

"This morning," Matilda said, "just for fun I tried to push something over with my eyes and

I couldn't do it. Nothing moved. I didn't even feel the hotness building up behind my eyeballs. The power had gone. I think I've lost it completely."

Miss Honey carefully buttered a slice of brown bread and put a little strawberry jam on it. "I've been expecting something like that to happen," she said.

"You have? Why?" Matilda asked.

"Well," Miss Honey said, "it's only a guess, but here's what I think. While you were in my class you had nothing to do, nothing to make you struggle. Your fairly enormous brain was going crazy with frustration. It was bubbling and boiling away like mad inside your head. There was tremendous energy bottled up in there with nowhere to go, and somehow or other you were able to shoot that energy out through your eyes and make objects move. But now things are different. You are in the top form competing against children more than twice your age and all that mental energy is being used up in class. Your brain is for the first time having to struggle and strive to keep really busy, which is great. That's only a theory, mind you, and it may be a silly one, but I don't think it's far off the mark."

"I'm glad it's happened," Matilda said. "I wouldn't want to go through life as a miracle-worker."

"You've done enough," Miss Honey said. "I can still hardly believe you made all this happen for me."

Matilda, who was perched on a tall stool at the kitchen table, ate her bread and jam slowly. She did so love these afternoons with

Miss Honey. She felt completely comfortable in her presence, and the two of them talked to each other more or less as equals.

"Did you know," Matilda said suddenly, "that the heart of a mouse beats at the rate of *six hundred and fifty times a minute*?"

"I did not," Miss Honey said smiling. "How absolutely fascinating. Where did you read that?"

"In a book from the library," Matilda said. "And that means it goes so fast you can't even hear the separate beats. It must sound just like a buzz."

"It must," Miss Honey said.

"And how fast do you think a hedgehog's heart beats?" Matilda asked.

"Tell me," Miss Honey said, smiling again.

"It's not as fast as a mouse," Matilda said. "It's three hundred times a minute. But even so, you wouldn't have thought it went as fast as that in a creature that moves so slowly, would you, Miss Honey?"

"I certainly wouldn't," Miss Honey said. "Tell me one more."

"A horse," Matilda said. "That's really slow. It's only forty times a minute."

This child, Miss Honey told herself, seems

to be interested in everything. When one is with her it is impossible to be bored. I love it.

The two of them stayed sitting and talking in the kitchen for an hour or so longer, and then, at about six o'clock, Matilda said goodnight and set out to walk home to her parents' house, which was about an eight-minute journey away. When she arrived at her own gate, she saw a large black Mercedes motor-car parked outside. She didn't take too much notice of that. There were often strange cars parked outside her father's place. But when she entered the house, she was confronted by a scene of utter chaos. Her mother and father were both in the hall frantically stuffing clothing and various objects into suitcases.

"What on earth's going on?" she cried. "What's happening, daddy?"

"We're off," Mr Wormwood said, not looking up. "We're leaving for the airport in half an hour so you'd better get packed. Your brother's upstairs all ready to go. Get a move on, girl! Get going!"

"Off?" Matilda cried out. "Where to?"

"Spain," the father said. "It's a better climate than this lousy country."

"Spain!" Matilda cried. "I don't want to go to Spain! I love it here and I love my school!"

"Just do as you're told and stop arguing," the father snapped. "I've got enough troubles without messing about with you!"

"But daddy . . ." Matilda began.

"Shut up!" the father shouted. "We're

leaving in thirty minutes! I'm not missing that plane!"

"But how long for, daddy?" Matilda cried. "When are we coming back?"

"We aren't," the father said. "Now beat it! I'm busy!"

Matilda turned away from him and walked out through the open front-door. As soon as she was on the road she began to run. She headed straight back towards Miss Honey's house and she reached it in less than four minutes. She flew up the drive and suddenly she saw Miss Honey in the front garden, standing in the middle of a bed of roses doing something with a pair of clippers. Miss Honey heard the sound of Matilda's feet racing over the gravel and now she straightened up and turned and stepped out of the rose-bed as the child came running up.

"My, my!" she said. "What in the world is the matter?"

Matilda stood before her, panting, out of breath, her small face flushed crimson all over.

"They're *leaving*!" she cried. "They've all gone mad and they're filling their suitcases and they're leaving for Spain in about thirty minutes!"

"Who is?" Miss Honey asked quietly.

"Mummy and daddy and my brother Mike and they say I've got to go with them!"

"You mean for a holiday?" Miss Honey asked.

"For *ever*!" Matilda cried. "Daddy said we were *never* coming back!"

There was a brief silence, then Miss Honey said, "Actually I'm not very surprised."

"You mean you *knew* they were going?" Matilda cried. "Why didn't you tell me?"

"No, darling," Miss Honey said. "I did not know they were going. But the news still doesn't surprise me."

"Why?" Matilda cried. "Please tell me why." She was still out of breath from the running and from the shock of it all.

"Because your father," Miss Honey said, "is in with a bunch of crooks. Everyone in the village knows that. My guess is that he is a receiver of stolen cars from all over the country. He's in it deep."

Matilda stared at her open-mouthed.

Miss Honey went on, "People brought stolen cars to your father's workshop where he changed the number-plates and resprayed the bodies a different colour and all the rest of it.

And now somebody's probably tipped him off that the police are on to him and he's doing what they all do, running off to Spain where they can't get him. He'll have been sending his money out there for years, all ready and waiting for him to arrive."

They were standing on the lawn in front of the lovely red-brick house with its weathered old red tiles and its tall chimneys, and Miss Honey still had the pair of garden clippers in one hand. It was a warm golden evening and a blackbird was singing somewhere near by.

"I don't want to go with them!" Matilda shouted suddenly. "I won't go with them."

"I'm afraid you must," Miss Honey said.

"I want to live here with you," Matilda cried out. "Please let me live here with you!"

"I only wish you could," Miss Honey said. "But I'm afraid it's not possible. You cannot leave your parents just because you want to. They have a right to take you with them."

"But what if they agreed?" Matilda cried eagerly. "What if they said yes, I can stay with you? Would you let me stay with you then?"

Miss Honey said softly, "Yes, that would be heaven."

"Well, I think they might!" Matilda cried. "I

honestly think they might! They don't actually care tuppence about me!"

"Not so fast," Miss Honey said.

"We've got to be fast!" Matilda cried. "They're leaving any moment! Come on!" she shouted, grasping Miss Honey's hand. "Please come with me and ask them! But we'll have to hurry! We'll have to run!"

The next moment the two of them were running down the drive together and then out on to the road, and Matilda was ahead, pulling Miss Honey after her by her wrist, and it was a wild and wonderful dash they made along the country lane and through the village to the house where Matilda's parents lived. The big black Mercedes was still outside and now its boot and all its doors were open and Mr and Mrs Wormwood and the brother were scurrying around it like ants, piling in the suitcases, as Matilda and Miss Honey came dashing up.

"Daddy and mummy!" Matilda burst out, gasping for breath. "I don't want to go with you! I want to stay here and live with Miss Honey and she says that I can but only if you give me permission! Please say yes! Go on, daddy, say yes! Say yes, mummy!"

The father turned and looked at Miss Honey. "You're that teacher woman who once came here to see me, aren't you?" he said. Then he went back to stowing the suitcases into the car.

His wife said to him, "This one'll have to go on the back seat. There's no more room in the boot."

"I would love to have Matilda," Miss Honey said. "I would look after her with loving care, Mr Wormwood, and I would pay for everything. She wouldn't cost you a penny. But it was not my idea. It was Matilda's. And I will not agree to take her without your full and willing consent."

"Come on, Harry," the mother said, pushing a suitcase into the back seat. "Why don't we let

her go if that's what she wants. It'll be one less to look after."

"I'm in a hurry," the father said. "I've got a plane to catch. If she wants to stay, let her stay. It's fine with me."

Matilda leapt into Miss Honey's arms and hugged her, and Miss Honey hugged her back, and then the mother and father and brother were inside the car and the car was pulling away with the tyres screaming. The brother gave a wave through the rear window, but the other two didn't even look back. Miss Honey was still hugging the tiny girl in her arms and neither of them said a word as they stood there watching the big black car tearing round the corner at the end of the road and disappearing for ever into the distance.

The Witches

Contents

A Note about Witches	411
My Grandmother	417
How to Recognise a Witch	432
The Grand High Witch	444
Summer Holidays	460
The Meeting	477
Frizzled Like a Fritter	482
Formula 86 Delayed Action Mouse-Maker	496
The Recipe	510
Bruno Jenkins Disappears	520
The Ancient Ones	531
Metamorphosis	538
Bruno	545
Hello Grandmamma	552
The Mouse-Burglar	568
Mr and Mrs Jenkins Meet Bruno	580
The Plan	588
In the Kitchen	593
Mr Jenkins and His Son	617
The Triumph	623
The Heart of a Mouse	631
It's Off to Work We Go!	639

A Note about Witches

In fairy-tales, witches always wear silly black hats and black cloaks, and they ride on broomsticks.

But this is not a fairy-tale. This is about REAL WITCHES.

The most important thing you should know about REAL WITCHES is this. Listen very carefully. Never forget what is coming next.

REAL WITCHES dress in ordinary clothes and look very much like ordinary women. They live in ordinary houses and they work in ORDINARY JOBS.

That is why they are so hard to catch.

A REAL WITCH hates children with a red-hot sizzling hatred that is more sizzling and red-hot than any hatred you could possibly imagine.

A REAL WITCH spends all her time plotting to get rid of the children in her particular territory. Her passion is to do away with them, one by one. It is all she thinks about the whole day long. Even if she is working as a cashier in a supermarket or typing letters for a businessman or driving around in a fancy car (and she could be doing any of these things), her mind will always be plotting and scheming and churning and burning and whizzing and phizzing with murderous bloodthirsty thoughts.

"Which child," she says to herself all day long, "exactly which child shall I choose for my next squelching?"

A REAL WITCH gets the same pleasure from squelching a child as *you* get from eating a plateful of strawberries and thick cream.

She reckons on doing away with one child a week. Anything less than that and she becomes grumpy.

One child a week is fifty-two a year.

Squish them and squiggle them and make them disappear.

That is the motto of all witches.

Very carefully a victim is chosen. Then the witch stalks the wretched child like a hunter stalking a little bird in the forest. She treads softly. She moves quietly. She gets closer and closer. Then at last, when everything is ready . . . *phwisst!* . . . and she swoops! Sparks fly. Flames leap. Oil boils. Rats howl. Skin shrivels. And the child disappears.

A witch, you understand, does not knock children on the head or stick knives into them or shoot at them with a pistol. People who do those things get caught by the police.

A witch never gets caught. Don't forget that she has magic in her fingers and devilry dancing in her blood. She can make stones jump about like frogs and she can make tongues of flame go flickering across the surface of the water.

These magic powers are very frightening.

Luckily, there are not a great number of REAL WITCHES in the world today. But there are still quite enough to make you nervous. In England, there are probably about one hundred of them altogether. Some countries have more, others have not quite so many. No country in the world is completely free from WITCHES.

A witch is always a woman.

I do not wish to speak badly about women. Most women are lovely. But the fact remains that all witches *are* women. There is no such thing as a male witch.

On the other hand, a ghoul is always a male. So indeed is a barghest. Both are dangerous. But neither of them is half as dangerous as a REAL WITCH.

As far as children are concerned, a REAL WITCH is easily the most dangerous of all the living creatures on earth. What makes her doubly dangerous is the fact that she doesn't *look* dangerous. Even when you know all the secrets (you will hear about those in a minute), you can still never be quite sure whether it is a witch you are gazing at or just a kind lady. If a tiger were able to make himself look like a large dog with a waggy tail, you would probably go up and pat him on the head. And that would be the end of you. It is the same with witches. They all look like nice ladies.

Kindly examine the picture opposite. Which

lady is the witch? That is a difficult question, but it is one that every child must try to answer.

For all you know, a witch might be living next door to you right now.

Or she might be the woman with the bright eyes who sat opposite you on the bus this morning.

She might be the lady with the dazzling smile who offered you a sweet from a white paper bag in the street before lunch.

She might even – and this will make you jump – she might even be your lovely schoolteacher who is reading these words to you at this very moment. Look carefully at that teacher. Perhaps she is smiling at the absurdity of such a suggestion. Don't let that put you off. It could be part of her cleverness.

I am not, of course, telling you for one second that your teacher actually is a witch. All I am saying is that she *might* be one. It is most unlikely. But – and here comes the big "but" – *it is not impossible.*

Oh, if only there were a way of telling for sure whether a woman was a witch or not, then we could round them all up and put them in the meat-grinder. Unhappily, there is no such way. But there *are* a number of little signals you can look out for, little quirky habits that all witches have in common, and if you know about these, if you remember them always, then you might just possibly manage to escape from being squelched before you are very much older.

My Grandmother

I myself had two separate encounters with witches before I was eight years old. From the first I escaped unharmed, but on the second occasion I was not so lucky. Things happened to me that will probably make you scream when you read about them. That can't be helped. The truth must be told. The fact that I am still here and able to speak to you (however peculiar I may look) is due entirely to my wonderful grandmother.

My grandmother was Norwegian. The Norwegians know all about witches, for Norway, with its black forests and icy mountains, is where the first witches came from. My father and my mother were also Norwegian, but because my father had a business in England, I had been born there and had lived there and had started going to an English school. Twice a year, at Christmas and in the summer, we went back to Norway to visit my grandmother. This old lady, as far as I could gather, was just about the only surviving relative we had on either side of our family. She was my mother's mother and I absolutely adored her. When she and I were together we spoke in either Norwegian or in English. It didn't matter which. We were equally fluent in both languages, and I have to admit that I felt closer to her than to my mother.

Soon after my seventh birthday, my parents took me as usual to spend Christmas with my grandmother in Norway. And it was over there, while my father and mother and I were driving in icy weather just north of Oslo, that our car skidded off the road and went tumbling down into a rocky ravine. My parents were killed. I was firmly strapped into the back seat and received only a cut on the forehead.

I won't go into the horrors of that terrible afternoon. I still get the shivers when I think about it. I finished up, of course, back in my grandmother's house with her arms around me tight and both of us crying the whole night long.

"What are we going to do now?" I asked her through the tears.

"You will stay here with me," she said, "and I will look after you."

"Aren't I going back to England?"

"No," she said. "I could never do that. Heaven shall take my soul, but Norway shall keep my bones."

The very next day, in order that we might both try to forget our great sadness, my grandmother started telling me stories. She was a wonderful story-teller and I was enthralled by everything she told me. But I didn't become really excited until she got on to the subject of witches. She was apparently a great expert on these creatures and she made it very clear to me that her witch stories, unlike most of the others, were not imaginary tales. They were all true. They were the *gospel* truth. They were history. Everything she was telling me about witches had actually happened and I had better believe it. What was worse, what was far, far worse, was that witches were still with us. They were all around us and I had better believe that, too.

"Are you *really* being truthful, Grandmamma? *Really* and *truly* truthful?"

"My darling," she said, "you won't last long in this world if you don't know how to spot a witch when you see one."

"But you told me that witches look like ordinary women, Grandmamma. So how can I spot them?"

"You must listen to me," my grandmother said. "You must remember everything I tell you. After that, all you can do is cross your heart and pray to heaven and hope for the best."

We were in the big living-room of her house in Oslo and I was ready for bed. The curtains were never drawn in that house, and through the windows I could see huge snowflakes falling slowly on to an outside world that was black as tar. My grandmother was tremendously old and wrinkled, with a massive wide body which was smothered in grey lace. She sat there majestic in her armchair, filling every inch of it. Not even a mouse could have squeezed in to sit beside her. I myself, just seven years old, was crouched on the floor at her feet, wearing pyjamas, dressing-gown and slippers.

"You swear you aren't pulling my leg?" I kept saying to her. "You swear you aren't just pretending?"

"Listen," she said. "I have known no less than five children who have simply vanished off the face of this earth, never to be seen again. The witches took them."

"I still think you're just trying to frighten me," I said.

"I am trying to make sure you don't go the same way," she said. "I love you and I want you to stay with me."

"Tell me about the children who disappeared," I said.

My grandmother was the only grandmother I ever met who smoked cigars. She lit one now, a long black cigar that smelt of burning rubber. "The first child I knew who disappeared", she said, "was called Ranghild Hansen. Ranghild was about eight at the time, and she was playing with her little sister on the lawn. Their mother, who was baking bread in the kitchen, came outside for a breath of air. 'Where's Ranghild?' she asked.

"'She went away with the tall lady,' the little sister said.

"'What tall lady?' the mother said.

"'The tall lady in white gloves,' the little sister said. 'She took Ranghild by the hand and led her away.' No one", my grandmother said, "ever saw Ranghild again."

"Didn't they search for her?" I asked.

"They searched for miles around. Everyone in the town helped, but they never found her."

"What happened to the other four children?" I asked.

"They vanished just as Ranghild did."

"How, Grandmamma? How did they just vanish?"

"In every case a strange lady was seen outside the house, just before it happened."

"But how did they vanish?" I asked.

"The second one was very peculiar," my grandmother said. "There was a family called Christiansen. They lived up on Holmenkollen, and they had an old oil-painting in the living-room which they were very proud of. The painting showed some ducks in the yard

outside a farmhouse. There were no people in the painting, just a flock of ducks on a grassy farmyard and the farmhouse in the background. It was a large painting and rather pretty. Well, one day their daughter Solveg came home from school eating an apple. She said a nice lady had given it to her on the street. The next morning little Solveg was not in her bed. The parents searched everywhere but they couldn't find her. Then all of a sudden her father shouted, 'There she is! That's Solveg feeding the ducks!' He was pointing at the oil-painting, and sure enough Solveg was in it. She was standing in the farmyard in the act of throwing bread to the ducks out of a basket. The father rushed up to the painting and touched her. But that didn't help. She was simply part of the painting, just a picture painted on the canvas."

"Did *you* ever see that painting, Grandmamma, with the little girl in it?"

"Many times," my grandmother said. "And the peculiar thing was that little Solveg kept changing her position in the picture. One day she would actually be inside the farmhouse and you could see her face looking out of the window. Another day she would be far over to the left with a duck in her arms."

"Did you ever see her moving in the picture, Grandmamma?"

"Nobody did. Wherever she was, whether outside feeding the ducks or inside looking out of the window, she was always motionless, just a figure painted in oils. It was all very odd," my grandmother said. "Very odd indeed. And what was most odd of all was that as the years went by, she kept growing older in the picture. In ten years, the small girl had become a young woman. In thirty years, she was middle-aged. Then all at once, fifty-four years after it all happened, she disappeared from the picture altogether."

"You mean she died?" I said.

"Who knows?" my grandmother said. "Some very mysterious things go on in the world of witches."

"That's two you've told me about," I said. "What happened to the third one?"

"The third one was little Birgit Svenson," my grandmother said. "She lived just across the road from us. One day she started growing feathers all over her body. Within a month, she had turned into a large white chicken. Her parents kept her for years in a pen in the garden. She even laid eggs."

"What colour eggs?"

"Brown ones," my grandmother said. "Biggest eggs I've ever seen in my life. Her mother made omelettes out of them. Delicious they were."

I gazed up at my grandmother who sat there like some ancient queen on her throne. Her eyes were misty-grey and they seemed to be looking at something many miles away. The cigar was the only real thing about her at that moment, and the smoke it made billowed round her head in blue clouds.

"But the little girl who became a chicken didn't disappear?"

"No, not Birgit. She lived on for many years laying her brown eggs."

"You said all of them disappeared."

"I made a mistake," my grandmother said. "I am getting old. I can't remember everything."

"What happened to the fourth child?" I asked.

"The fourth was a boy called Harald," my grandmother said. "One morning his skin went all greyish-yellow. Then it became hard and crackly, like the shell of a nut. By evening, the boy had turned to stone."

"Stone?" I said. "You mean real stone?"

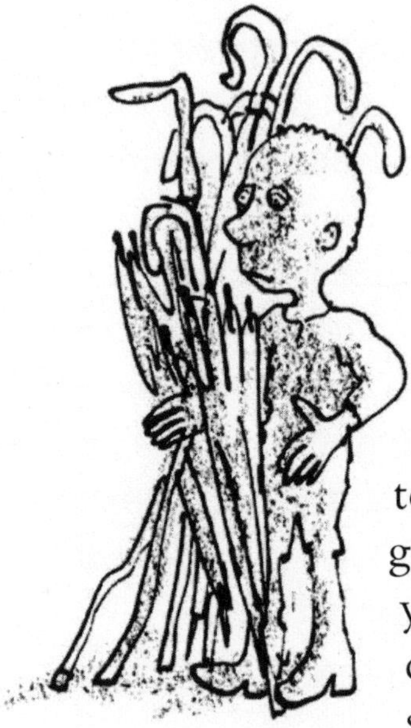

"Granite," she said. "I'll take you to see him if you like. They still keep him in the house. He stands in the hall, a little stone statue. Visitors lean their umbrellas up against him."

Although I was very young, I was not prepared to believe everything my grandmother told me. And yet she spoke with such conviction, with such utter seriousness, and with never a smile on her face or a twinkle in her eye, that I found myself beginning to wonder.

"Go on, Grandmamma," I said. "You told me there were five altogether. What happened to the last one?"

"Would you like a puff of my cigar?" she said.

"I'm only seven, Grandmamma."

"I don't care what age you are," she said. "You'll never catch a cold if you smoke cigars."

"What about number five, Grandmamma?"

"Number five," she said, chewing the end of her cigar as though it were a delicious asparagus, "was rather an interesting case. A nine-year-old boy called Leif was summer-holidaying with his family on the fjord, and the whole family was picnicking and swimming off some rocks on one of those little islands. Young Leif dived into the water and his father, who was watching him, noticed that he stayed under for an unusually long time. When he came to the surface at last, he wasn't Leif any more."

"What was he, Grandmamma?"

"He was a porpoise."

"He wasn't! He couldn't have been!"

"He was a lovely young porpoise," she said. "And as friendly as could be."

"Grandmamma," I said.

"Yes, my darling?"

"Did he really and truly turn into a porpoise?"

"Absolutely," she said. "I knew his mother well. She told me all about it. She told me how Leif the Porpoise stayed with them all that afternoon giving his brothers and sisters rides on his back, they had a wonderful time. Then he waved a flipper at them and swam away, never to be seen again."

"But Grandmamma," I said, "how did they know that the porpoise was actually Leif?"

"He talked to them," my grandmother said. "He laughed and joked with them all the time he was giving them rides."

"But wasn't there a most tremendous fuss when this happened?"

"Not much," my grandmother said. "You must remember that here in Norway we are used to that sort of thing. There are witches everywhere. There's probably one living in our street this very moment. It's time you went to bed."

"A witch wouldn't come in through my

window in the night, would she?" I asked, quaking a little.

"No," my grandmother said. "A witch will never do silly things like climbing up drainpipes or breaking into people's houses. You'll be quite safe in your bed. Come along. I'll tuck you in."

How to Recognise a Witch

The next evening, after my grandmother had given me my bath, she took me once again into the living-room for another story.

"Tonight," the old woman said, "I am going to tell you how to recognise a witch when you see one."

"Can you always be sure?" I asked.

"No," she said, "you can't. And that's the trouble. But you can make a pretty good guess."

She was dropping cigar ash all over her lap, and I hoped she wasn't going to catch on fire before she'd told me how to recognise a witch.

"In the first place," she said, "a REAL WITCH is certain always to be wearing gloves when you meet her."

"Surely not *always*," I said. "What about in the summer when it's hot?"

"Even in the summer," my grandmother said. "She has to. Do you want to know why?"

"Why?" I said.

"Because she doesn't have finger-nails. Instead of finger-nails, she has thin curvy claws, like a cat, and she wears the gloves to hide them. Mind you, lots of very respectable women wear gloves, especially in winter, so this doesn't help you very much."

"Mamma used to wear gloves," I said.

"Not in the house," my grandmother said. "Witches wear gloves even in the house. They only take them off when they go to bed."

"How do you know all this, Grandmamma?"

"Don't interrupt," she said. "Just take it all in. The second thing to remember is that a REAL WITCH is always bald."

"*Bald?*" I said.

"Bald as a boiled egg," my grandmother said.

I was shocked. There was something indecent about a bald woman. "Why are they bald, Grandmamma?"

"Don't ask me why," she snapped. "But you can take it from me that not a single hair grows on a witch's head."

"How horrid."

"Disgusting," my grandmother said.

"If she's bald, she'll be easy to spot," I said.

"Not at all," my grandmother said. "A REAL WITCH always wears a wig to hide her baldness. She wears a first-class wig. And it is almost impossible to tell a really first-class wig from ordinary hair unless you give it a pull to see if it comes off."

"Then that's what I'll have to do," I said.

"Don't be foolish," my grandmother said. "You can't go round pulling at the hair of every lady you meet, even if she *is* wearing gloves. Just you try it and see what happens."

"So that doesn't help much either," I said.

"None of these things is any good on its own," my grandmother said. "It's only when you put them all together that they begin to make a little sense. Mind you," my grandmother went on, "these wigs do cause a rather serious problem for witches."

"What problem, Grandmamma?"

"They make the scalp itch most terribly," she said. "You see, when an actress wears a wig, or if you or I were to wear a wig, we would be putting it on over our own hair, but a witch has to put it straight on to her naked scalp. And the underneath of a wig is always very rough and scratchy. It sets up a frightful itch on the bald scalp. It causes nasty sores on the head. Wig-rash, the witches call it. And it doesn't half itch."

"What other things must I look for to recognise a witch?" I asked.

"Look for the nose-holes," my grandmother said. "Witches have slightly larger nose-holes than ordinary people. The rim of each nose-hole is pink and curvy, like the rim of a certain kind of sea-shell."

"Why do they have such big nose-holes?" I asked.

"For smelling with," my grandmother said. "A REAL WITCH has the most amazing powers of smell. She can actually smell out a child who is standing on the other side of the street on a pitch-black night."

"She couldn't smell me," I said. "I've just had a bath."

"Oh yes she could," my grandmother said. "The cleaner you happen to be, the more smelly you are to a witch."

"That can't be true," I said.

"An absolutely clean child gives off the most ghastly stench to a witch," my grandmother said. "The dirtier you are, the less you smell."

"But that doesn't make sense, Grandmamma."

"Oh yes it does," my grandmother said. "It isn't the *dirt* that the witch is smelling. It is *you*. The smell that drives a witch mad actually comes right out of your own skin. It comes oozing out of your skin in waves, and these waves, stink-waves the witches call them, go floating through the air and hit the witch right smack in her nostrils. They send her reeling."

"Now wait a minute, Grandmamma . . ."

"Don't interrupt," she said. "The point is this. When you haven't washed for a week and your skin is all covered over with dirt, then quite obviously the stink-waves cannot come oozing out nearly so strongly."

"I shall never have a bath again," I said.

"Just don't have one too often," my grandmother said. "Once a month is quite enough for a sensible child."

It was at moments like these that I loved my grandmother more than ever.

"Grandmamma," I said, "if it's a dark night, how can a witch smell the difference between a child and a grown-up?"

"Because grown-ups don't give out stink-waves," she said. "Only children do that."

"But I don't *really* give out stink-waves, do I?" I said. "I'm not giving them out at this very moment, am I?"

"Not to me you aren't," my grandmother said. "To me you are smelling like raspberries and cream. But to a witch you would be smelling absolutely disgusting."

"What would I be smelling of?" I asked.

"Dogs' droppings," my grandmother said.

I reeled. I was stunned. "*Dogs' droppings!*" I cried. "I am *not* smelling of dogs' droppings! I don't believe it! I *won't* believe it!"

"What's more," my grandmother said, speaking with a touch of relish, "to a witch you'd be smelling of *fresh* dogs' droppings."

"That simply is not true!" I cried. "I know I am not smelling of dogs' droppings, stale or fresh!"

"There's no point in arguing about it," my grandmother said. "It's a fact of life."

I was outraged. I simply couldn't bring myself to believe what my grandmother was telling me.

"So if you see a woman holding her nose as she passes you in the street," she went on, "that woman could easily be a witch."

I decided to change the subject. "Tell me what else to look for in a witch," I said.

"The eyes," my grandmother said. "Look carefully at the eyes, because the eyes of a REAL WITCH are different from yours and mine. Look in the middle of each eye where there is normally a little black dot. If she is a witch, the black dot will keep changing colour, and you will see fire and you will see ice dancing right in the very centre of the coloured dot. It will send shivers running all over your skin."

My grandmother leant back in her chair and sucked away contentedly at her foul black cigar. I squatted on the floor, staring up at her, fascinated. She was not smiling. She looked deadly serious.

"Are there other things?" I asked her.

"Of course there are other things," my grandmother said. "You don't seem to understand that witches are not actually women at all. They *look* like women. They talk like women. And they are able to act like women. But in actual fact, they are totally different animals. They are demons in human shape. That is why they have claws and bald heads and queer noses and peculiar eyes, all of which they have to conceal as best they can from the rest of the world."

"What else is different about them, Grandmamma?"

"The feet," she said. "Witches never have toes."

"No toes!" I cried. "Then what do they have?"

"They just have feet," my grandmother said. "The feet have square ends with no toes on them at all."

"Does that make it difficult to walk?" I asked.

"Not at all," my grandmother said. "But it does give them a problem with their shoes. All ladies like to wear small rather pointed shoes, but a witch, whose feet are rather wide and square at the ends, has the most awful job squeezing her feet into those neat little pointed shoes."

"Why doesn't she wear wide comfy shoes with square ends?" I asked.

"She dare not," my grandmother said. "Just as she hides her baldness with a wig, she must also hide her ugly witch's feet by squeezing them into pretty shoes."

"Isn't that terribly uncomfortable?' I said.

"Extremely uncomfortable," my grandmother said. "But she has to put up with it."

"If she's wearing ordinary shoes, it won't help me to recognise her, will it, Grandmamma?"

"I'm afraid it won't," my grandmother said. "You might possibly see her limping very slightly, but only if you were watching closely."

"Are those the only differences then, Grandmamma?"

"There's one more," my grandmother said.

"Just one more."

"What is it, Grandmamma?"

"Their spit is blue."

"Blue!" I cried. "Not blue! Their spit can't be *blue*!"

"Blue as a bilberry," she said.

"You don't mean it, Grandmamma! Nobody can have blue spit!"

"Witches can," she said.

"Is it like ink?" I asked.

"Exactly," she said. "They even use it to write with. They use those old-fashioned pens that have nibs and they simply lick the nib."

"Can you *notice* the blue spit, Grandmamma? If a witch was talking to me, would I be able to notice it?"

"Only if you looked carefully," my grandmother said.

"If you looked very carefully you would probably see a slight blueish tinge on her teeth.

But it doesn't show much."

"It would if she spat," I said.

"Witches never spit," my grandmother said. "They daren't."

I couldn't believe my grandmother would be lying to me. She went to church every morning of the week and she said grace before every meal, and somebody who did that would never tell lies. I was beginning to believe every word she spoke.

"So there you are," my grandmother said. "That's about all I can tell you. None of it is very helpful. You can still never be absolutely sure whether a woman is a witch or not just by looking at her. But if she is wearing the gloves, if she has the large nose-holes, the queer eyes and the hair that looks as though it might be a wig, and if she has a bluish tinge on her teeth – if she has all of these things, then you run like mad."

"Grandmamma," I said, "when you were a little girl, did *you* ever meet a witch?"

"Once," my grandmother said. "Only once."

"What happened?"

"I'm not going to tell you," she said. "It would frighten you out of your skin and give you bad dreams."

"Please tell me," I begged.

"No," she said. "Certain things are too horrible to talk about."

"Does it have something to do with your missing thumb?" I asked.

Suddenly, her old wrinkled lips shut tight as a pair of tongs and the hand that held the cigar (which had no thumb on it) began to quiver very slightly.

I waited. She didn't look at me. She didn't speak. All of a sudden she had shut herself off completely. The conversation was finished.

"Goodnight, Grandmamma," I said, rising from the floor and kissing her on the cheek.

She didn't move. I crept out of the room and went to my bedroom.

The Grand High Witch

The next day, a man in a black suit arrived at the house carrying a brief-case, and he held a long conversation with my grandmother in the living-room. I was not allowed in while he was there, but when at last he went away, my grandmother came in to me, walking very slowly and looking very sad.

"That man was reading me your father's will," she said.

"What is a will?" I asked her.

"It is something you write before you die," she said. "And in it you say who is going to have your money and your property. But most important of all, it says who is going to look after your child if both the mother and father are dead."

A fearful panic took hold of me. "It did say you, Grandmamma?" I cried. "I don't have to go to somebody else, do I?"

"No," she said. "Your father would never have done that. He has asked me to take care of you for as long as I live, but he has also asked that I take you back to your own house in England. He wants us to stay there."

"But why?" I said. "Why can't we stay here in Norway? You would hate to live anywhere else! You told me you would!"

"I know," she said. "But there are a lot of complications with money and with the house that you wouldn't understand. Also, it said in the will that although all your family is Norwegian, you were born in England and you have started your education there and he wants you to continue going to English schools."

"Oh Grandmamma!" I cried. "*You* don't want to go and live in our English house, I know you don't!"

"Of course I don't," she said. "But I am afraid I must. The will said that your mother felt the same way about it, and it is important to respect the wishes of the parents."

There was no way out of it. We had to go to England, and my grandmother started making arrangements at once. "Your next school term begins in a few days," she said, "so we don't have any time to waste."

On the evening before we left for England, my grandmother got on to her favourite subject once again. "There are not as many witches in England as there are in Norway," she said.

"I'm sure I won't meet one," I said.

"I sincerely hope you won't," she said, "because those English witches are probably the most vicious in the whole world."

As she sat there smoking her foul cigar and talking away, I kept looking at the hand with the missing thumb. I couldn't help it. I was fascinated by it and I kept wondering what awful thing had happened that time when she had met a witch. It must have been something absolutely appalling and gruesome otherwise she would have told me about it. Maybe the thumb had been twisted off. Or perhaps she had been forced to jam her thumb down the spout of a boiling kettle until it was steamed away. Or did someone pull it out of her hand like a tooth? I couldn't help trying to guess.

"Tell me what those English witches do, Grandmamma," I said.

"Well," she said, sucking away at her stinking cigar, "their favourite ruse is to mix up a powder that will turn a child into some creature or other that all grown-ups hate."

"What sort of creature, Grandmamma?"

"Often it's a slug," she said. "A slug is one of their favourites. Then the grown-ups step on the slug and squash it without knowing it's a child."

"That's perfectly beastly!" I cried.

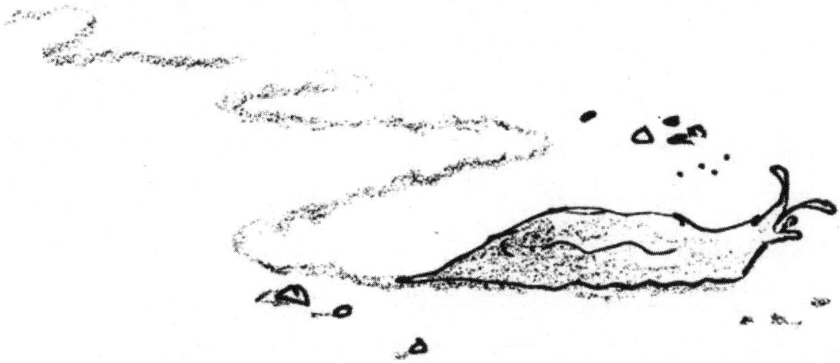

"Or it might be a flea," my grandmother said. "They might turn you into a flea, and without realising what she was doing your own mother would get out the flea-powder and then it's goodbye you."

"You're making me nervous, Grandmamma. I don't think I want to go back to England."

"I've known English witches," she went on, "who have turned children into pheasants and then sneaked the pheasants up into the woods the very day before the pheasant-shooting season opened."

"Owch," I said. "So they get shot?"

"Of course they get shot," she said. "And then they get plucked and roasted and eaten for supper."

I pictured myself as a pheasant flying frantically over the men with the guns, swerving and dipping as the guns exploded below me.

"Yes," my grandmother said, "it gives the English witches great pleasure to stand back and watch the grown-ups doing away with their own children."

"I really don't want to go to England, Grandmamma."

"Of course you don't," she said. "Nor do I. But I'm afraid we've got to."

"Are witches different in every country?" I asked.

"Completely different," my grandmother said. "But I don't know much about the other countries."

"Don't you even know about America?" I asked.

"Not really," she answered. "Although I have heard it said that over there the witches are able to make the grown-ups eat their own children."

"Never!" I cried. "Oh no, Grandmamma! That couldn't be true!"

"I don't know whether it's true or not," she said. "It's only a rumour I've heard."

"But how could they possibly make them eat their own children?" I asked.

"By turning them into hot-dogs," she said. "That wouldn't be too difficult for a clever witch."

"Does every single country in the world have its witches?" I asked.

"Wherever you find people, you find witches," my grandmother said. "There is a Secret Society of Witches in every country."

"And do they all know one another, Grandmamma?"

"They do not," she said. "A witch only knows the witches in her own country. She is strictly forbidden to communicate with any foreign witches. But an English witch, for example, will know all the other witches in England. They are all friends. They ring each other up. They swap deadly recipes. Goodness knows what else they talk about. I hate to think."

I sat on the floor, watching my grandmother. She put her cigar stub in the ashtray and folded her hands across her stomach. "Once a year," she went on, "the witches of each separate country hold their own secret meeting. They all get together in one place to receive a lecture from The Grand High Witch Of All The World."

"From *who*?" I cried.

"She is the ruler of them all," my grandmother said. "She is all-powerful. She is without mercy. All other witches are petrified of her. They see her only once a year at their Annual Meeting. She goes there to whip up excitement and enthusiasm, and to give orders. The Grand High Witch travels from country to country attending these Annual Meetings."

"Where do they have these meetings, Grandmamma?"

"There are all sorts of rumours," my grandmother answered. "I have heard it said that they just book into an hotel like any other group of women who are holding a meeting. I have also heard it said that some very peculiar things go on in the hotels they stay in. It is rumoured that the beds are never slept in, that there are burn marks on the bedroom carpets, that toads are discovered in the bathtubs, and that down in the kitchen the cook once found a baby crocodile swimming in his saucepan of soup."

My grandmother picked up her cigar and took another puff, inhaling the foul smoke deeply into her lungs.

"Where does The Grand High Witch live when she's at home?" I asked.

"Nobody knows," my grandmother said. "If we knew that, then she could be rooted out and destroyed. Witchophiles all over the world have spent their lives trying to discover the secret Headquarters of The Grand High Witch."

"What is a witchophile, Grandmamma?"

"A person who studies witches and knows a lot about them," my grandmother said.

"Are you a witchophile, Grandmamma?"

"I am a retired witchophile," she said. "I am too old to be active any longer. But when I was younger, I travelled all over the globe trying to track down The Grand High Witch. I never came even close to succeeding."

"Is she rich?" I asked.

"She's rolling," my grandmother said. "Simply rolling in money. Rumour has it that there is a machine in her headquarters which is exactly like the machine the government uses to print the bank-notes you and I use. After all, bank-notes are only bits of paper with special designs and pictures on them. Anyone can make them who has the right machine and the right paper. My guess is that The Grand High Witch makes all the money she wants and she dishes it out to witches everywhere."

"What about foreign money?" I asked.

"Those machines can make *Chinese* money

if you want them to," my grandmother said. "It's only a question of pressing the right button."

"But Grandmamma," I said, "if nobody has ever seen The Grand High Witch, how can you be so sure she exists?"

My grandmother gave me a long and very severe look. "Nobody has ever seen the Devil," she said, "but we know he exists."

The next morning, we sailed for England and soon I was back in the old family house in Kent, but this time with only my grandmother to look after me. Then the Easter Term began and every weekday I went to school and everything seemed to have come back to normal again.

Now at the bottom of our garden there was an enormous conker tree, and high up in its branches Timmy (my best friend) and I had started to build a magnificent tree-house. We were able to work on it only at weekends, but we were getting along fine. We had begun with the floor, which we built by laying wide planks between two quite far-apart branches and nailing them down. Within a month, we had finished the floor. Then we constructed a wooden railing around the floor and that left

only the roof to be built. The roof was the difficult bit.

One Saturday afternoon when Timmy was in bed with 'flu, I decided to make a start on the roof all by myself. It was lovely being high up there in that conker tree, all alone with the pale young leaves coming out everywhere around me. It was like being in a big green cavern. And the height made it extra exciting. My grandmother had told me that if I fell I would break a leg, and every time I looked down, I got a tingle along my spine.

I worked away, nailing the first plank on the roof. Then suddenly, out of the corner of my eye, I caught sight of a woman standing immediately below me. She was looking up at me and smiling in the most peculiar way. When most people smile, their lips go out sideways. This woman's lips went upwards and downwards, showing all her front teeth and gums. The gums were like raw meat.

It is always a shock to discover that you are being watched when you think you are alone.

And what was this strange woman doing in our garden anyway?

I noticed that she was wearing a small black hat and she had black gloves on her hands and

the gloves came nearly up to her elbows.

Gloves! She was wearing *gloves*!

I froze all over.

"I have a present for you," she said, still staring at me, still smiling, still showing her teeth and gums.

I didn't answer.

"Come down out of that tree, little boy," she

said, "and I will give you the most exciting present you've ever had." Her voice had a curious rasping quality. It made a sort of metallic sound, as though her throat was full of drawing-pins.

Without taking her eyes from my face, she very slowly put one of those gloved hands into her purse and drew out a small green snake. She held it up for me to see.

"It's tame," she said.

The snake began to coil itself around her forearm. It was brilliant green.

"If you come down here, I shall give him to you," she said.

Oh, Grandmamma, I thought, come and help me!

Then I panicked. I dropped the hammer and shot up that enormous tree like a monkey. I didn't stop until I was as high as I could possibly go, and there I stayed, quivering with fear. I couldn't see the woman now. There were layers and layers of leaves between her and me.

I stayed up there for hours and I kept very still. It began to grow dark. At last, I heard my grandmother calling my name.

"I'm up here," I shouted back.

"Come down at once!" she called out. "It's

past your suppertime."

"Grandmamma!" I shouted. "Has that woman gone?"

"What woman?" my grandmother called back.

"The woman in the black gloves!"

There was silence from below. It was the silence of somebody who was too stunned to speak.

"Grandmamma!" I shouted again. "*Has she gone?*"

"Yes," my grandmother answered at last. "She's gone. I'm here, my darling. I'll look after you. You can come down now."

I climbed down. I was trembling. My grandmother enfolded me in her arms. "I've seen a witch," I said.

"Come inside," she said. "You'll be all right with me."

She led me into the house and gave me a cup of hot cocoa with lots of sugar in it. "Tell me everything," she said.

I told her.

By the time I had finished, it was my grandmother who was trembling. Her face was ashy grey and I saw her glance down at that hand of hers that didn't have a thumb. "You know what this means," she said. "It means that there is one of them in our district. From now on I'm not letting you walk alone to school."

"Do you think she could be after me specially?" I asked.

"No," she said. "I doubt that. One child is as good as any other to those creatures."

It is hardly surprising that after that I became a very witch-conscious little boy. If I happened to be alone on the road and saw a woman approaching who was wearing gloves, I would quickly skip across to the other side. And as the weather remained pretty cold during the whole of that month, nearly *everybody* was wearing gloves. Curiously enough, though, I never saw the woman with the green snake again.

That was my first witch. But it wasn't my last.

Summer Holidays

The Easter holidays came and went, and the Summer Term began at school. My grandmother and I had already planned to take our summer holiday in Norway and we talked about almost nothing else every evening. She had booked a cabin for each of us on the boat from Newcastle to Oslo at the earliest possible moment after my school broke up, and from Oslo she was going to take me to a place she knew down on the south coast near Arendal where she had spent her own summer holidays as a child nearly eighty years ago.

"All day long," she said, "my brother and I were out in the rowing-boat. The whole coast is dotted with tiny islands and there's nobody on them. We used to explore them and dive into the sea off the lovely smooth granite rocks, and sometimes on the way out we would drop the anchor and fish for cod and whiting, and if we caught anything we would build a fire on an island and fry the fish in a pan for our lunch. There is no finer fish in the world than absolutely fresh cod."

"What did you use for bait, Grandmamma,

when you went fishing?"

"Mussels," she said. "Everyone uses mussels for bait in Norway. And if we didn't catch any fish, we would boil the mussels in a saucepan and eat those."

"Were they good?"

"Delicious," she said. "Cook them in sea-water and they are tender and salty."

"What else did you do, Grandmamma?"

"We used to row out and wave to the shrimp-boats on their way home, and they would stop and give us a handful of shrimps each. The shrimps were still warm from having been just cooked, and we would sit in the rowing-boat peeling them and gobbling them up. The head was the best part."

"The head?" I said.

"You squeeze the head between your teeth and suck out the inside. It's marvellous. You and I will do all those things this summer, my darling," she said.

"Grandmamma," I said, "I can't wait. I simply can't wait to go."

"Nor can I," she said.

When there were only three weeks of the Summer Term left, an awful thing happened. My grandmother got pneumonia. She became very ill, and a trained nurse moved into the house to look after her. The doctor explained to me that pneumonia is not normally a dangerous illness nowadays because of penicillin, but when a person is more than eighty years old, as my grandmother was, then it is very dangerous indeed. He said he didn't even dare to move her to hospital in her condition, so she stayed in her bedroom and I hung about outside the door while oxygen cylinders and all sorts of other frightening things were taken in to her.

"Can I go in and see her?" I asked.

"No, dear," the nurse said. "Not at the moment."

A fat and jolly lady called Mrs Spring, who used to come and clean our house every day, also moved in and slept in the house. Mrs Spring looked after me and cooked my meals. I liked her very much, but she wasn't a patch on my grandmother for telling stories.

One evening, about ten days later, the doctor came downstairs and said to me, "You can go in and see her now, but only for a short time. She's been asking for you."

I flew up the stairs and burst into my grandmother's room and threw myself into her arms.

"Hey there," the nurse said. "Be careful with her."

"Will you be all right now, Grandmamma?" I asked.

"The worst is over," she said. "I'll soon be up again."

"Will she?" I said to the nurse.

"Oh yes," the nurse answered, smiling. "She told us she simply had to get better because she had to look after you."

I gave her another hug.

"They won't let me have a cigar," she said. "But you wait till they're gone."

"She's a tough old bird," the nurse said. "We'll have her up in another week."

The nurse was right. Within a week, my grandmother was thumping around the house with her gold-topped cane and interfering with Mrs Spring's cooking. "I thank you for all your help, Mrs Spring," she said, "but you can go home now."

"Oh, no I can't," Mrs Spring said. "Doctor told me to see that you take it very easy for the next few days."

The doctor said more than that. He dropped a bombshell on my grandmother and me by telling us that on no account were we to risk the journey to Norway this summer.

"Rubbish!" my grandmother cried. "I've promised him we'll go!"

"It's too far," the doctor said. "It would be very dangerous. But I'll tell you what you *can* do. You can take your grandson to a nice hotel on the south coast of England instead. The sea air is just what you need."

"Oh no!" I said.

"Do you want your grandmother to die?"

the doctor asked me.

"Never!" I said.

"Then don't let her go on a long journey this summer. She's not yet strong enough. And stop her smoking those vile black cigars."

In the end, the doctor had his way about the holiday, but not about the cigars. Rooms were booked for us in a place called the Hotel Magnificent in the famous seaside town of Bournemouth. Bournemouth, my grandmother told me, was full of old people like herself. They retired there by the thousand because the air was so bracing and healthy it kept them, so they believed, alive for a few extra years.

"Does it?" I asked.

"Of course not," she said. "It's tommyrot. But just for once I think we've got to obey the doctor."

Soon after that, my grandmother and I took the train to Bournemouth and settled into the Hotel Magnificent. It was an enormous white building on the sea-front and it looked to me like a pretty boring place to spend a summer holiday in. I had my own separate bedroom, but there was a door connecting my room with my grandmother's room so that we could visit each other without going into the corridor.

Just before we left for Bournemouth, my grandmother had given me, as consolation, a present of two white mice in a little cage and of course I took them with me. They were terrific fun, those mice. I called them William and Mary, and in the hotel I set out right away teaching them to do tricks. The first trick I taught them was to creep up the sleeve of my jacket and come out by my neck. Then I taught them to climb up the back of my neck on to the top of my head. I did this by putting cake crumbs in my hair.

On the very first morning after our arrival, the chambermaid was making my bed when one of my mice poked its head out from under the sheets. The maid let out a shriek that brought a dozen people running to see who was being murdered. I was reported to the Manager. There followed an unpleasant scene in the

Manager's office with the Manager, my grandmother and me.

The Manager, whose name was Mr Stringer, was a bristly man in a black tail-coat. "I cannot permit mice in my hotel, madam," he said to my grandmother.

"How dare you say that when your rotten hotel is full of rats anyway!" my grandmother cried.

"Rats!" cried Mr Stringer, going mauve in the face. "There are no rats in this hotel!"

"I saw one this very morning," my grandmother said. "It was running down the corridor into the kitchen!"

"That is not true!" cried Mr Stringer.

"You had better get the rat-catcher in at once," my grandmother said, "before I report you to the Public Health Authorities. I expect there's rats scuttling all over the kitchen floor and stealing the food off the shelves and jumping in and out of the soup!"

"Never!" cried Mr Stringer.

"No wonder my breakfast toast was all nibbled round the edges this morning," my grandmother went on relentlessly. "No wonder it had a nasty ratty taste. If you're not careful, the Health people will be ordering the entire hotel to be closed before everyone gets typhoid fever."

"You are not being serious, madam," Mr Stringer said.

"I was never more serious in my life," my grandmother said. "Are you or are you not going to allow my grandson to keep his white mice in his room?"

The Manager knew when he was beaten. "May I suggest a compromise, madam?" he said. "I will permit him to keep them in his

room as long as they are never allowed out of the cage. How's that?"

"That will suit us very well," my grandmother said, and she stood up and marched out of the room with me behind her.

There was no way you can train mice inside a cage. Yet I dared not let them out because the chambermaid was spying on me all the time. She had a key to my door and she kept bursting in at all hours, trying to catch me with the mice out of the cage. She told me that the first mouse to break the rules would be drowned in a bucket of water by the hall-porter.

I decided to seek a safer place where I could carry on with the training. There must surely be an empty room in this enormous hotel. I put one mouse into each trouser-pocket and wandered downstairs in search of a secret spot.

The ground floor of the hotel was a maze of public rooms, all of them named in gold letters on the doors. I wandered through "The Lounge" and "The Smoking-Room" and "The Card-Room" and "The Reading-Room" and "The Drawing-Room". None of them was empty. I went down a long wide corridor and at the end of it I came to "The Ballroom".

There were double-doors leading into it, and in front of the doors there was a large notice-board on a stand. The notice on the board said,

RSPCC MEETING

STRICTLY PRIVATE
THIS ROOM IS RESERVED
FOR THE
ANNUAL MEETING
OF
THE ROYAL SOCIETY
FOR THE PREVENTION
OF CRUELTY TO CHILDREN

The double-doors into the room were open. I peeped in. It was a colossal room. There were rows and rows of chairs, all facing a platform. The chairs were painted gold and they had little red cushions on the seats. But there was not a soul in sight.

I sidled cautiously into the room. What a lovely secret silent place it was. The meeting of the Royal Society for the Prevention of Cruelty to Children must have taken place earlier in the day, and now they had all gone home. Even if they hadn't, even if they *did*

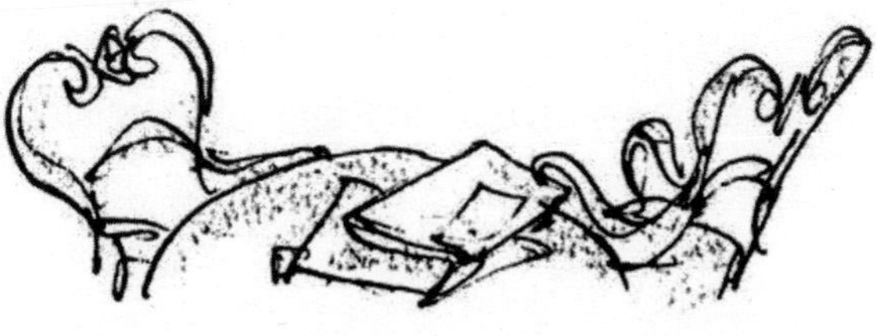

suddenly come pouring in, they would be wonderful kind people who would look with favour upon a young mouse-trainer going about his business.

At the back of the room there was a large folding screen with Chinese dragons painted on it. I decided, just to be on the safe side, to go behind this screen and do my training there. I wasn't a bit frightened of the Prevention of Cruelty to Children people, but there was always a chance that Mr Stringer, the Manager, might pop his head round the door. If he did and if he saw the mice, the poor things would be in the hall-porter's bucket of water before I could shout stop.

I tiptoed to the back of the room and settled myself on the thick green carpet behind the big screen. What a splendid place this was! Ideal for mouse-training! I took William and Mary out of my trouser-pockets. They sat beside me on the carpet, quiet and well-behaved.

The trick I was going to teach them today was tight-rope walking. It is not all that difficult to train an intelligent mouse to be an expert tight-rope walker provided you know exactly how to go about it. First, you must have a piece of string. I had that. Then you must have some good cake. A fine currant cake is the favourite food of white mice. They are dotty about it. I had brought with me a rock cake which I had pocketed while having tea with Grandmamma the day before.

Now here's what you have to do. You stretch the string tight between your two hands, but you start by keeping it very short, only about three inches. You put the mouse on your right hand and a little piece of cake on your left hand. The mouse is therefore only three inches away from the cake. He can see it and he can smell it. His whiskers twitch with excitement. He can almost reach the cake by leaning forward, but not quite. He only has to take two steps along the string to reach this tasty morsel. He ventures forward, one paw on the string, then the other. If the mouse has a good sense of balance, and most of them have, he will get across easily. I started with William. He walked the string without a moment's hesitation. I let him have a quick nibble of the cake just to whet his appetite. Then I put him back on my right hand.

This time I lengthened the string. I made it about six inches long. William knew what to do now. With superb balance, he walked step by step along the string until he reached the cake. He was rewarded with another nibble.

Quite soon, William was walking a twenty-four-inch tight-rope (or rather tight-string) from one hand to the other to reach the cake. It was wonderful to watch him. He was enjoying himself tremendously. I was careful to hold the string near the carpet so that if he did lose his balance, he wouldn't have far to fall.

But he never fell. William was obviously a natural acrobat, a great tight-rope-walking mouse.

Now it was Mary's turn. I put William on the carpet beside me and rewarded him with some extra crumbs and a currant. Then I started going through the same routine all over again with Mary. My blinding ambition, you see, my dream of dreams, was to become one day the owner of a White Mouse Circus. I would have a small stage with red curtains in front of it, and when the curtains were drawn apart, the audience would see my world-famous performing mice walking on tight-ropes, swinging from trapezes, turning somersaults in the air, bouncing on trampolines and all the rest of it. I would have white mice riding on white rats, and the rats would gallop furiously round and round the stage. I was beginning to picture myself travelling first-class all over the globe with my Famous White Mouse Circus, and performing before all the crowned heads of Europe.

I was about halfway through Mary's training when suddenly I heard voices outside the Ballroom door. The sound grew louder. It swelled into a great babble of speech from many throats. I recognised the voice of the awful Hotel Manager, Mr Stringer.

Help, I thought.

But thank heavens for the huge screen.

I crouched behind it and peered through the crack between two of the folding sections. I could see the entire length and width of the Ballroom without anyone seeing me.

"Well, ladies, I am sure you will be quite comfortable in here," Mr Stringer's voice was saying. Then in through the double-doors he marched, black tail-coat and all, spreading his arms wide as he ushered in a great flock of ladies. "If there is anything we can do for you, do not hesitate to let me know," he went on. "Tea will be served for all of you on the Sunshine Terrace after you have concluded your meeting." With that, he bowed and scraped himself out of the room as a vast herd of ladies from the Royal Society for the Prevention of Cruelty to Children came streaming in. They wore pretty clothes and all of them had hats on their heads.

The Meeting

Now that the Manager had gone, I was not particularly alarmed. What better than to be imprisoned in a room full of these splendid ladies? If I ever got talking to them, I might even suggest that they come and do a bit of cruelty-to-children preventing at my school. We could certainly use them there.

In they came, talking their heads off. They began milling round and choosing their seats, and there was a whole lot of stuff like, "Come and sit next to me, Millie dear," and "Oh, hel-*lo* Beatrice! I haven't seen you since the last meeting! What an adorable dress you have on."

I decided to stay where I was and let them get on with their meeting while I got on with my mouse-training, but I watched them for a while longer through the crack in the screen, waiting for them to settle down. How many were there? I guessed about two hundred. The back rows filled up first. They all seemed to want to sit as far back from the platform as possible.

There was a lady wearing a tiny green hat

in the middle of the back row who kept scratching the nape of her neck. She couldn't leave it alone. It fascinated me the way her fingers kept scratching away at the hair on the back of her neck. Had she known somebody was watching her from behind, I'm sure she would have been embarrassed. I wondered if she had dandruff. All of a sudden, I noticed that the lady next to her was doing the same thing!

And the next one!

And the next!

The whole lot of them were doing it. They were all scratching away like mad at the hair on the backs of their necks!

Did they have fleas in their hats?

More likely it was nits.

A boy at school called Ashton had had nits in his hair last term and the matron had made him dip his whole head in turpentine. It killed the nits all right, but it nearly killed Ashton as well. Half the skin came away from his scalp.

I began to be fascinated by these hair-scratching ladies. It is always funny when you catch someone doing something coarse and she thinks no one is looking. Nose-picking, for example, or scratching her bottom. Hair-scratching is very nearly as unattractive, especially if it goes on and on.

I decided it had to be nits.

Then the most astonishing thing happened. I saw one lady pushing her fingers up *underneath* the hair on her head, and the hair, *the entire head of hair* lifted upwards all in one piece, and the hand slid underneath the hair and went on scratching!

She was wearing a wig! She was also wearing

gloves! I glanced swiftly around the rest of the now seated audience. *Every one of them was wearing gloves!*

My blood turned to ice. I began to shake all over. I glanced frantically behind me for a back door to escape through. There wasn't one.

Should I leap out from behind the screen and make a dash for the double-doors?

Those double-doors were already closed and I could see a woman standing in front of them. She was bending forward and fixing some sort of a metal chain round the two door-handles.

Keep still, I told myself. No one has seen you yet. There's no reason in the world why they should come and look behind the screen. But one false move, one cough, one sneeze, one nose-blow, one little sound of any sort and it won't just be one witch that gets you. It'll be two hundred!

At that point, I think I fainted. The whole thing was altogether too much for a small boy to cope with. But I don't believe I was out for more than a few seconds, and when I came to, I was lying on the carpet and I was still, thank heavens, behind the screen. There was absolute silence all around me.

Rather shakily, I got to my knees and peered once again through the crack in the screen.

Frizzled Like a Fritter

All the women, or rather the witches, were now sitting motionless in their chairs and staring as though hypnotised at somebody who had suddenly appeared on the platform. That somebody was another woman.

The first thing I noticed about this woman was her size. She was tiny, probably no more than four and a half feet. She looked quite young, I guessed about twenty-five or six, and she was very pretty. She had on a rather stylish long black dress that reached right to the ground and she wore black gloves that came up to her elbows. Unlike the others, she wasn't wearing a hat.

She didn't look to me like a witch at all, but she couldn't

possibly *not* be one, otherwise what on earth was she doing up there on the platform? And why, for heaven's sake, were all the other witches gazing at her with such a mixture of adoration, awe and fear?

Very slowly, the young lady on the platform raised her hands to her face. I saw her gloved fingers unhooking something behind her ears, and then . . . then she caught hold of her cheeks and lifted her face clean away! The whole of that pretty face came away in her hands!

It was a mask!

As she took off the mask, she turned sideways and placed it carefully upon a small table near by, and when she turned round again and faced us, I very nearly screamed out loud.

That face of hers was the most frightful and frightening thing I have ever seen. Just looking at it gave me the shakes all over. It was so crumpled and wizened, so shrunken and shrivelled, it looked as though it had been pickled in vinegar. It was a fearsome and ghastly sight. There was something terribly wrong with it, something foul and putrid and decayed. It seemed quite literally to be rotting away at the edges, and in the middle of the face, around the mouth and cheeks, I could see the skin all cankered and worm-eaten, as though maggots were working away in there.

There are times when something is so frightful you become mesmerised by it and can't look away. I was like that now. I was transfixed. I was numbed. I was magnetised by the sheer horror of this woman's features. But there was more to it than that. There was a

look of serpents in those eyes of hers as they flashed around the audience.

I knew immediately, of course, that this was none other than The Grand High Witch herself. I knew also why she had worn a mask. She could never have moved around in public, let alone book in at an hotel, with her real face. Everyone who saw her would have run away screaming.

"The doors," shouted The Grand High Witch in a voice that filled the room and bounced around the walls. "Are they chained and bolted?"

"The doors are chained and bolted, Your Grandness," answered a voice in the audience.

The brilliant snake's eyes that were set so deep in that dreadful rotting worm-eaten face glared unblinkingly at the witches who sat facing her. "You may rrree-moof your gloves!" she shouted. Her voice, I noticed, had that same hard metallic quality as the voice of the witch I had met under the conker tree, only it was far louder and much much harsher. It grated. It snarled. It scraped. It shrieked. And it growled.

Everyone in the room was peeling off her gloves. I was watching the hands of those in the back row. I wanted very much to see what

their fingers looked like and whether my grandmother had been right. Ah! . . . Yes! . . . I could see several of them now! I could see the brown claws curving over the tips of the fingers! They were about two inches long, those claws, and sharp at the ends!

"You may rrree-moof your shoes!" barked The Grand High Witch.

I heard a sigh of relief going up from all the witches in the room as they kicked off their narrow high-heeled shoes, and then I got a glimpse under the chairs of several pairs of stockinged feet, square and completely toeless.

Revolting they were, as though the toes had been sliced away from the feet with a carving-knife.

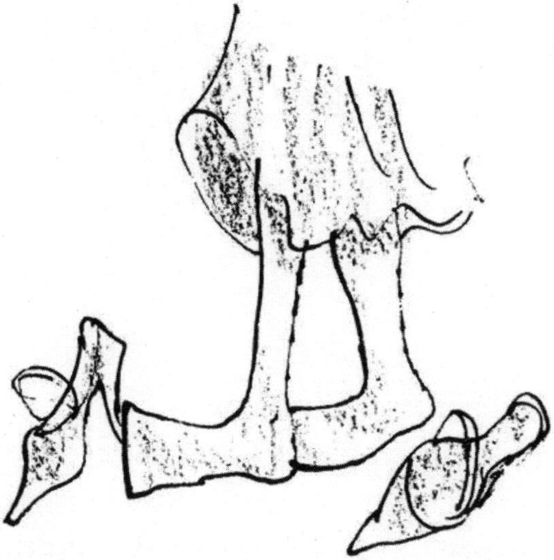

"You may rrree-moof your vigs!" snarled The Grand High Witch. She had a peculiar way of speaking. There was some sort of foreign accent there, something harsh and guttural, and she seemed to have trouble pronouncing the letter w. As well as that, she did something funny with her letter r. She would roll it round and round her mouth like a piece of hot pork-crackling before spitting it out. "Rrree-moof your vigs and get some fresh air into your spotty scalps!" she shouted, and another sigh of relief arose from the audience as all the hands went

up to the heads and all the wigs (with the hats still on them) were lifted away.

There now appeared in front of me row upon row of bald female heads, a sea of naked scalps, every one of them red and itchy-looking from being rubbed by the linings of the wigs. I simply cannot tell you how awful they were, and somehow the whole sight was made more grotesque because underneath those frightful scabby bald heads, the bodies were dressed in fashionable and rather pretty clothes. It was monstrous. It was unnatural.

Oh heavens, I thought. Oh help! Oh Lord have mercy on me! These foul bald-headed females are child-killers every one of them, and here I am imprisoned in the same room and I can't escape!

At that point, a new and doubly horrifying thought struck me. My grandmother had said that with their special nose-holes they could smell out a child on a pitch-black night from right across the other side of the road. Up to now, my grandmother had been right every time. It seemed a certainty therefore that one of the witches in the back row was going to sniff me out at any moment and then the yell of "Dogs' droppings!" would go up all over the room and I would be cornered like a rat.

I knelt on the carpet behind the screen, hardly daring to breathe.

Then suddenly I remembered another very important thing my grandmother had told me. "The dirtier you are," she had said, "the harder it is for a witch to smell you out."

How long since I had last had a bath?

Not for ages. I had my own room in the hotel and my grandmother never bothered with silly things like that. Come to think of it, I don't believe I'd had a bath since we arrived.

When had I last washed my hands or face?

Certainly not this morning.

Not yesterday either.

I glanced down at my hands. They were covered with smudge and mud and goodness knows what else besides.

So perhaps I had a chance after all. The stink-waves couldn't possibly get out through all that dirt.

"Vitches of Inkland!" shouted The Grand High Witch. She herself I noticed had not taken off either her wig or her gloves or her shoes. "Vitches of Inkland!" she yelled.

The audience stirred uneasily and sat up straighter in their chairs.

"Miserrrable vitches!" she yelled. "Useless lazy vitches! Feeble frrribbling vitches! You are a heap of idle good-for-nothing vurms!"

A shudder went through the audience. The Grand High Witch was clearly in an ugly mood and they knew it. I had a feeling that something awful was going to happen soon.

"I am having my breakfast this morning," cried The Grand High Witch, "and I am looking out of the vindow at the beach, and vot am I seeing? I am asking you, *vot am I seeing?* I am seeing a rrree-volting sight! I am seeing hundreds, I am seeing *thousands* of rrrotten rrree-pulsive little children playing on the sand! It is putting me rrright off my food! *Vye have you not got rrrid of them?*" she screamed. "Vye have you not rrrubbed them all out, these filthy smelly children?"

With each word she spoke, flecks of pale-blue phlegm shot from her mouth like little bullets.

"I am asking you *vye*!" she screamed.

Nobody answered her question.

"Children smell!" she screamed. "They stink out the vurld! Vee do not vont these children around here!"

The bald heads in the audience all nodded vigorously.

"Vun child a veek is no good to me!" The Grand High Witch cried out. "Is that the best you can do?"

"We will do better," murmured the audience. "We will do much better."

"Better is no good either!" shrieked The

Grand High Witch. "I demand maximum rrree-sults! So here are my orders! My orders are that every single child in this country shall be rrrubbed out, sqvashed, sqvirted, sqvittered and frrrittered before I come here again in vun year's time! Do I make myself clear?"

A great gasp went up from the audience. I saw the witches all looking at one another with deeply troubled expressions. And I heard one witch at the end of the front row saying aloud, "*All* of them! We can't possibly wipe out *all* of them!"

The Grand High Witch whipped round as though someone had stuck a skewer into her bottom. "Who said that?" she snapped. "Who dares to argue vith me? It vos you, vos it not?" She pointed a gloved finger as sharp as a needle at the witch who had spoken.

"I didn't mean it, Your Grandness!" the witch cried out. "I didn't mean to argue! I was just talking to myself!"

"You dared to argue vith me!" screamed The Grand High Witch.

"I was just talking to myself!" cried the wretched witch. "I swear it, Your Grandness!" She began to shake with fear.

The Grand High Witch took a quick step forward, and when she spoke again, it was in a voice that made my blood run cold.

"A stupid vitch who answers back
Must burn until her bones are black!" she screamed.

"No, no!" begged the witch in the front row. The Grand High Witch went on,

"A foolish vitch vithout a brain
Must sizzle in the fiery flame!"

"Save me!" cried the wretched witch in the front row. The Grand High Witch took no notice of her. She spoke again.

"An idiotic vitch like you
Must rrroast upon the barbecue!"

"Forgive me, O Your Grandness!" cried the miserable culprit. "I didn't mean it!" But The Grand High Witch continued with her terrible recital.

"A vitch who dares to say I'm wrrrong
Vill not be vith us very long!"

A moment later, a stream of sparks that looked like tiny white-hot metal-filings came shooting out of The Grand High Witch's eyes and flew straight towards the one who had dared to speak. I saw the sparks striking against her and burrowing into her and she screamed a horrible howling scream and a puff of smoke rose up around her. A smell of burning meat filled the room.

Nobody moved. Like me, they were all watching the smoke, and when it had cleared away, the chair was empty. I caught a glimpse of something wispy-white, like a little cloud, fluttering upwards and disappearing out of the window.

A great sigh rose up from the audience.

The Grand High Witch glared around the room. "I hope nobody else is going to make me cross today," she remarked.

There was a deathly silence.

"Frrrizzled like a frrritter," said The Grand High Witch. "Cooked like a carrot. You vill never see *her* again. Now vee can get down to business."

Formula 86 Delayed Action Mouse-Maker

"Children are rrree-volting!" screamed The Grand High Witch. "Vee vill vipe them all avay! Vee vill scrrrub them off the face of the earth! Vee vill flush them down the drain!"

"Yes, yes!" chanted the audience. "Wipe them away! Scrub them off the earth! Flush them down the drain!"

"Children are foul and filthy!" thundered The Grand High Witch.

"They are! They are!" chorused the English witches. "They are foul and filthy!"

"Children are dirty and stinky!" screamed The Grand High Witch.

"Dirty and stinky!" cried the audience, getting more and more worked up.

"Children are smelling of *dogs' drrroppings*!" screeched The Grand High Witch.

"Pooooooo!" cried the audience. "Pooooooo! Pooooooo! Pooooooo!"

"They are vurse than dogs' drrroppings!" screeched The Grand High Witch. "Dogs' drrroppings is smelling like violets and prrrimroses compared with children!"

"Violets and primroses!" chanted the audience. They were clapping and cheering almost every word spoken from the platform. The speaker seemed to have them completely under her spell.

"To talk about children is making me sick!" screamed The Grand High Witch. "I am feeling sick even *thinking* about them! Fetch me a basin!"

The Grand High Witch paused and glared at the mass of eager faces in the audience. They waited, wanting more.

"So now!" barked The Grand High Witch. "So now I am having a plan! I am having a giganticus plan for getting rrrid of every single child in the whole of Inkland!"

The witches gasped. They gaped. They turned and gave each other ghoulish grins of excitement.

"Yes!" thundered The Grand High Witch. "Vee shall svish them and svollop them and vee shall make to disappear every single little brrrat in Inkland in vun strrroke!"

"Whoopee!" cried the witches, clapping their hands. "You are brilliant, O Your

Grandness! You are fantabulous!"

"Shut up and listen!" snapped The Grand High Witch. "Listen very carefully and let us not be having any muck-ups!"

The audience leaned forward, eager to learn how this magic was going to be performed.

"Each and every vun of you," thundered The Grand High Witch, "is to go back to your home towns immediately and rrree-sign from your jobs. Rrree-sign! Give notice! Rrree-tire!"

"We will!" they cried. "We will resign from our jobs!"

"And after you have rrree-signed from your jobs," The Grand High Witch went on, "each and every vun of you vill be going out and you will be buying . . ." She paused.

"What will we be buying?" they cried. "Tell us, O Brilliant One, what is it we shall be buying?"

"Sveet-shops!" shouted The Grand High Witch.

"Sweet-shops!" they cried. "We are going to buy sweet-shops! What a frumptious wheeze!"

"Each of you vill be buying for herself a

sveet-shop. You vill be buying the very best and most rrree-spectable sveet-shops in Inkland."

"We will! We will!" they answered. Their dreadful voices were like a chorus of dentists' drills all grinding away together.

"I am vonting no tuppenny-ha'penny crrrummy little tobacco-selling-newspaper-sveet-shops!" shouted The Grand High Witch. "I am vonting you to get only the very best shops filled up high vith piles and piles of luscious sveets and tasty chocs!"

"The best!" they cried. "We shall buy the best sweet-shops in town!"

"You vill be having no trouble in getting vot you vont," shouted The Grand High Witch, "because you vill be offering four times as much as a shop is vurth and nobody is rrree-fusing an offer like that! Money is not a prrroblem to us vitches as you know very well. I have brrrought vith me six trrrunks stuffed full of Inklish bank-notes, all new and crrrisp. And all of them," she added with a fiendish leer, "all of them home-made."

The witches in the audience grinned, appreciating this joke.

At that point, one foolish witch got so excited at the possibilities presented by owning a sweet-shop that she leapt to her stockinged feet and shouted, "The children will come flocking to my shop and I will feed them poisoned sweets and poisoned chocs and wipe them all out like weasels!"

The room became suddenly silent. And I saw the tiny body of The Grand High Witch stiffen and then go rigid with rage. "Who spoke?" she shrieked. "It vos *you*! You over there!"

The culprit sat down fast and covered her

face with her clawed hands.

"You blithering bumpkin!" screeched The Grand High Witch. "You brrrainless bogvumper! Are you not rrree-alising that if you are going rrround poisoning little children you vill be caught in five minutes flat? Never in my life am I hearing such a boshvolloping suggestion coming from a vitch!"

The entire audience cowered and shook. I'm quite sure they all thought, as I did, that the terrible white-hot sparks were about to start flying again.

Curiously enough, they didn't.

"If such a tomfiddling idea is all you can be coming up with," thundered The Grand High Witch, "then it is no vunder Inkland is still svorming vith rrrotten little children!"

There was another silence. The Grand High Witch glared at the witches in the audience. "Do you not know," she shouted at them, "that vee vitches are vurrrking only with magic?"

"We know, Your Grandness!" they all answered. "Of course we know."

The Grand High Witch grated her bony gloved hands against each other and cried out, "So each of you is owning a magnificent sveet-shop! The next move is that each of you vill be announcing in the vindow of your shop that on a certain day you vill be having a Great Gala Opening with frree sveets and chocs for every child!"

"That will bring them in, the greedy little brutes!" cried the audience. "They'll be fighting to get through the doors!"

"Next," continued The Grand High Witch, "you vill prepare yourselves for this Great Gala Opening by filling every choc and every sveet in your shop vith my very latest and grrreatest magic formula! This is known as FORMULA 86 DELAYED ACTION MOUSE-MAKER!"

"Delayed Action Mouse-Maker!" they chanted. "She's done it again! Her Grandness has concocted yet another of her wondrous magic child-killers! How do we make it, O Brilliant One?"

"Exercise patience," answered The Grand High Witch. "First, I am explaining to you how my Formula 86 Delayed Action Mouse-Maker is vurrrking. Listen carefully."

"We are listening!" cried the audience who were now jumping up and down in their chairs with excitement.

"Delayed Action Mouse-Maker is a green liqvid," explained The Grand High Witch, "and vun droplet in each choc or sveet vill be qvite enough. So here is vot happens:

"Child eats choc vich has in it Delayed Action Mouse-Maker liqvid . . .

"Child goes home feeling fine . . .

"Child goes to bed, still feeling fine . . .

"Child vakes up in the morning still okay . . .

"Child goes to school still feeling fine . . .

"Formula, you understand, is *delayed action*, and is not vurrrking yet."

"We understand, O Brainy One!" cried the audience. "But when does it start working?"

"It is starting to vurrrk at exactly nine o'clock, vhen the child is arriving at school!" shouted The Grand High Witch triumphantly. "Child arrives at school. Delayed Action Mouse-Maker immediately starts to vurrrk. Child starts to shrrrink. Child is starting to grow fur. Child is starting to grow tail. All is happening in prrree-cisely tventy-six seconds. After tventy-six seconds, child is not a child any longer. It is a mouse!"

"A mouse!" cried the witches. "What a frumptious thought!"

"Classrooms vill be svorming vith mice!" shouted The Grand High Witch. "Chaos and pandemonium vill be rrreigning in every school in Inkland! Teachers vill be hopping up and down! Vimmen teachers vill be standing on desks and holding up skirts and yelling, 'Help, help, help!'"

"They will! They will!" cried the audience.

"And vot", shouted The Grand High Witch, "is happening next in every school?"

"Tell us!" they cried. "Tell us, O Brainy One!"

The Grand High Witch stretched her stringy neck forward and grinned at the audience, showing two rows of pointed teeth, slightly blue. She raised her voice louder than ever and shouted, "*Mouse-trrraps is coming out!*"

"Mouse-traps!" cried the witches.

"And cheese!" shouted The Grand High Witch. "Teachers is all rrrushing and rrrunning out and getting mouse-trrraps and baiting them vith cheese and putting them down all over school! Mice is nibbling cheese! Mouse-trrraps is going off! All over school, mouse-trrraps is going *snappety-snap* and mouse-heads is rrrolling across the floors like marbles! All over Inkland, in everrry school in Inkland, noise of snapping mouse-trrraps vill be heard!"

At this point, the disgusting old Grand High Witch began to do a sort of witch's dance up and down the platform, stamping her feet and clapping her hands. The entire audience joined in the clapping and foot-stamping. They were making such a tremendous racket that I thought surely Mr Stringer would hear it and come banging at the door. But he didn't.

Then, above all the noise, I heard the voice of The Grand High Witch screaming out some sort of an awful gloating song,

"Down vith children! Do them in!
Boil their bones and fry their skin!
Bish them, sqvish them, bash them, mash them!
Brrreak them, shake them, slash them, smash them!
Offer chocs vith magic powder!
Say 'Eat up!' then say it louder.
Crrram them full of sticky eats,
Send them home still guzzling sveets.
And in the morning little fools
Go marching off to separate schools.
A girl feels sick and goes all pale.
She yells, 'Hey look! I've grrrown a tail!'

A boy who's standing next to her
Screams, 'Help! I think I'm grrrowing fur!'
Another shouts, 'Vee look like frrreaks!
There's viskers growing on our cheeks!'
A boy who vos extremely tall
Cries out, 'Vot's wrong? I'm grrrowing
small!'
Four tiny legs begin to sprrrout
From everybody rrround about.
And all at vunce, all in a trrrice,
There are no children! Only MICE!
In every school is mice galore
All rrrunning rrround the school-rrroom
floor!
And all the poor demented teachers
Is yelling, 'Hey, who are these crrreatures?'
They stand upon the desks and shout,
'Get out, you filthy mice! Get out!
Vill someone fetch some mouse-trrraps
please!
And don't forget to bring the cheese!'
Now mouse-trrraps come and every trrrap
Goes *snippy-snip* and *snappy-snap.*
The mouse-trrraps have a powerful spring,
The springs go *crack* and *snap* and *ping*!
Is lovely noise for us to hear!
Is music to a vitch's ear!

Dead mice is every place arrround,
Piled two feet deep upon the grrround,
Vith teachers searching left and rrright,
But not a single child in sight!
The teachers cry, 'Vot's going on?
Oh vhere have all the children gone?
Is half-past nine and as a rrrule
They're never late as this for school!'

Poor teachers don't know vot to do.
Some sit and rrread, and just a few
Amuse themselves throughout the day
By sveeping all the mice avay.
AND ALL US VITCHES SHOUT HOORAY!"

The Recipe

I hope you haven't forgotten that while all this was going on I was still stuck behind the screen on my hands and knees with one eye glued to the crack. I don't know how long I had been there but it seemed like for ever. The worst part of it was not being allowed to cough or make a sound, and knowing that if I did, I was as good as dead. And all the way through I was living in constant terror that one of the witches in the back row was going to get a whiff of my presence through those special nose-holes of hers.

My only hope, as I saw it, was the fact that I hadn't washed for days. That and the never-ending excitement and clapping and shouting that was going on in the room. The witches were thinking of nothing except The Grand High Witch up there on the platform and her great plan for wiping out all the children of England. They certainly weren't sniffing around for a child in the room. In their wildest dreams (if witches have dreams), that would never have occurred to any of them. I kept still and prayed.

The Grand High Witch's dreadful gloating song was over now, and the audience was clapping madly and shouting, "Brilliant! Sensational! Marvellous! You are a genius, O Brainy One! It is a thrilling invention, this Delayed Action Mouse-Maker! It is a winner! And the beauty of it is that the teachers will be the ones who bump off the stinking little children! It won't be us doing it! We shall never be caught!"

"Vitches are never caught!" snapped The Grand High Witch. "Attention now! I vont everybody's attention for I am about to be telling you vot you must do to prepare Formula 86 Delayed Action Mouse-Maker!"

Suddenly there came a great gasp from the audience. This was followed by a hubbub of shrieking and yelling, and I saw many of the witches leaping to their feet and pointing at the platform and crying out, "Mice! Mice! Mice! She's done it to show us! The Brainy One has turned two children into mice and there they are!"

I looked toward the platform. The mice were there all right, two of them, running around near The Grand High Witch's skirts.

But these were not field mice or house

mice or wood mice or harvest mice. They were *white mice*! I recognised them immediately as being my own little William and Mary.

"Mice!" shouted the audience. "Our leader has made mice to appear out of nowhere! Get the mouse-traps! Fetch the cheese!"

I saw The Grand High Witch peering down at the floor and staring with obvious puzzlement down at William and Mary. She bent lower to get a closer look. Then she straightened up and shouted, "Qviet!"

The audience became silent and sat down.

"These mice are nothing to do vith me!" she shouted. "These mice are *pet* mice! These mice are quite obviously belonging to some rrree-pellant little child in the hotel! A boy it vill be for a certainty because girls are not keeping pet mice!"

"A boy!" cried the witches. "A filthy smelly little boy! We'll swipe him! We'll swizzle him! We'll have his tripes for breakfast!"

"Silence!" shouted The Grand High Witch, raising her hands. "You know perrrfectly vell you must do nothing to drrraw attention to yourselves vhile you are living in the hotel! Let us by all means get rrrid of this evil-smelling little sqvirt, but vee must do it as qvietly as possible, for are vee not all of us the most rrree-spectable ladies of the Rrroyal Society for the Prrree-vention of Crrruelty to Children?"

"What do you suggest then, O Brainy One?" they cried out. "How shall we dispose of this small pile of filth?"

They're talking about me, I thought. These females are actually talking about how to kill me. I began to sweat.

"Whoever he is, he is not important," announced The Grand High Witch. "Leave him to me. I shall smell him out and turn him into a mackerel and have him dished up for supper."

"Bravo!" cried the witches. "Cut off his head and chop off his tail and fry him in hot butter!"

You can imagine that none of this was making me feel very comfortable. William and Mary were still running around on the platform, and I saw The Grand High Witch aim a swift running kick at William. She caught him right on the point of her toe and sent him flying. She did the same to Mary. Her aim was extraordinary. She would have made a great football player. Both mice crashed against the wall, and for a few moments they lay stunned. Then they got to their feet and scampered away.

"Attention again!" The Grand High Witch was shouting. "I vill now give you the rrrecipe for concocting Formula 86 Delayed Action Mouse-Maker! Get out pencils and paper."

Handbags were opened all over the room and notebooks were fished out.

"Give us the recipe, O Brainy One!" cried the audience impatiently. "Tell us the secret."

"First," said The Grand High Witch, "I had to find something that vould cause the children to become very small very qvickly."

"And what was that?" cried the audience.

"That part vos simple," said The Grand High Witch. "All you have to do if you are wishing to make a child very small is to look at him through the wrrrong end of a telescope."

"She's a wonder!" cried the audience. "Who else would have thought of a thing like that?"

"So you take the wrrrong end of telescope," continued The Grand High Witch, "and you boil it until it gets soft."

"How long does it take?" they asked her.

"Tventy-vun hours of boiling," answered The Grand High Witch. "And while this is going on, you take exactly forty-five brrrown mice and you chop off their tails vith a

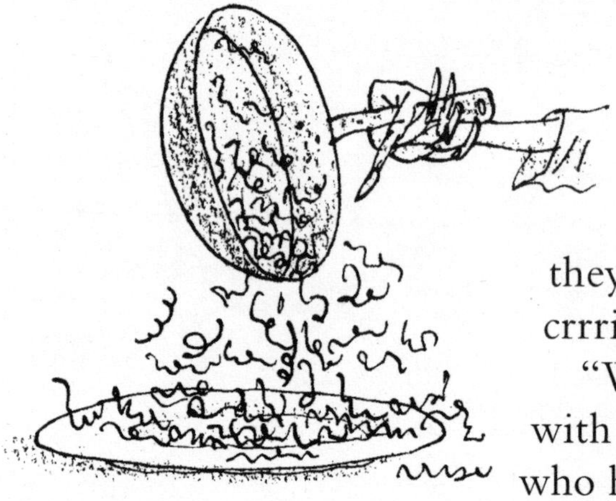

carving-knife and you fry the tails in hair-oil until they are nice and crrrisp."

"What do we do with all those mice who have had their tails chopped off?" asked the audience.

"You simmer them in frog-juice for vun hour," came the answer. "But listen to me. So far I have only given you the easy part of the rrrecipe. The rrreally difficult problem is to put in something that vill have a genuine delayed action rrree-sult, something that can be eaten by children on a certain day but vhich vill not start vurrrking on them until nine o'clock the next morning vhen they arrive at school."

"What did you come up with, O Brainy One?" they called out. "Tell us the great secret!"

"The secret," announced The Grand High Witch triumphantly, "is an *alarm-clock*!"

"An alarm-clock!" they cried. "It's a stroke of genius!"

"Of course it is," said The Grand High Witch. "You can set a tventy-four-hour alarm-clock today and at exactly nine o'clock tomorrow it will go off."

"But we will need five million alarm-clocks!" cried the audience. "We will need one for each child!"

"Idiots!" shouted The Grand High Witch. "If you are vonting a steak, you do not cook the whole cow! It is the same with alarm-clocks, vun clock will make enough for a thousand children. Here is vhat you do. You set your alarm-clock to go off at nine o'clock tomorrow morning. Then you rrroast it in the oven until it is crrrisp and tender. Are you wrrriting this down?"

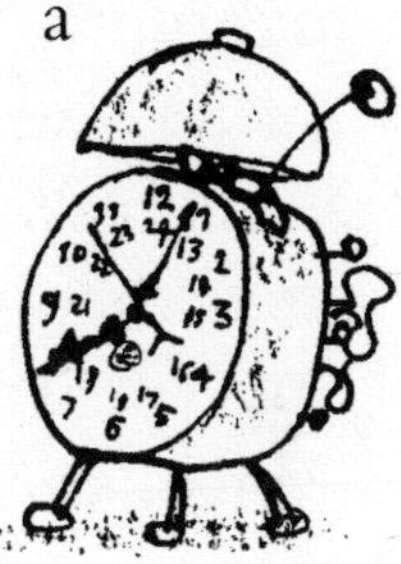

"We are, Your Grandness, we are!" they cried.

"Next," said The Grand High Witch, "you take your boiled telescope and your frrried

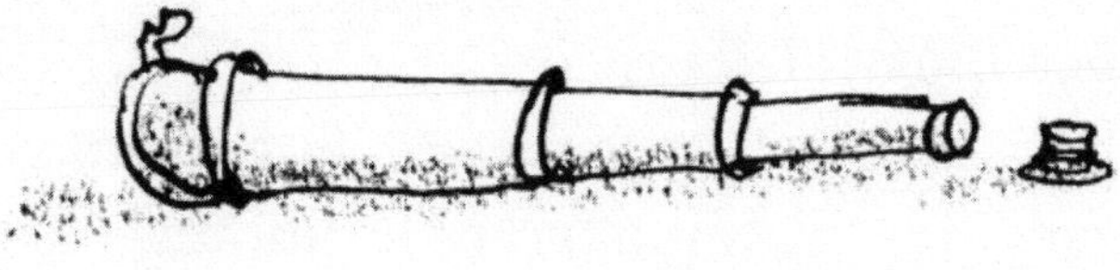

mouse-tails and your cooked mice and your rrroasted alarm-clock and all together you put them into the mixer. Then you mix them at full speed. This vill give you a nice thick paste. Vhile the mixer is still mixing you must add to it the yolk of vun grrruntle's egg."

"A gruntle's egg!" cried the audience. "We shall do that!" Underneath all the clamour that was going on I heard one witch in the back row saying to her neighbour, "I'm getting a bit old to go bird's nesting. Those ruddy gruntles always nest very high up."

"So you mix in the egg," The Grand High Witch went on, "and vun after the other you also mix in the following items: the claw of a

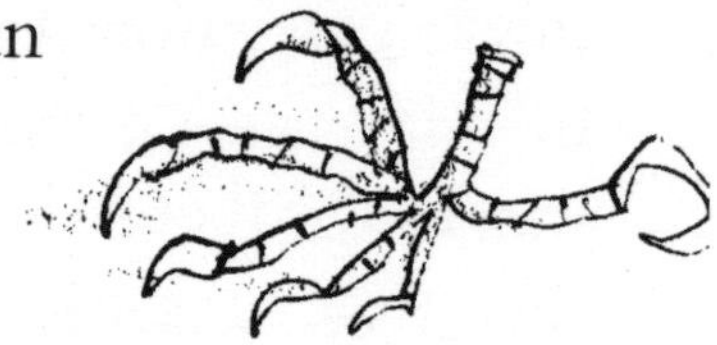

crrrabcrrruncher, the beak of a blabbersnitch, the snout of a grrrobblesqvirt

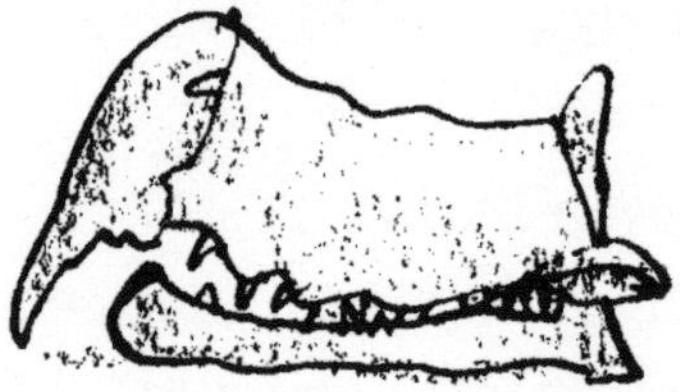

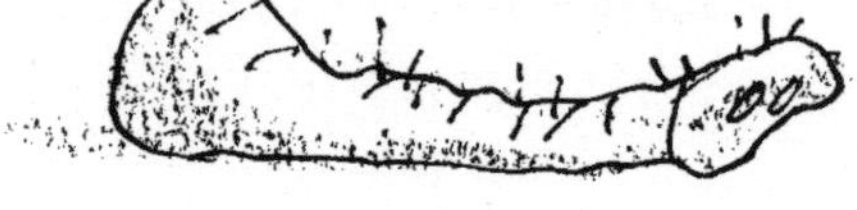

and the tongue of a catsprrringer. I trust

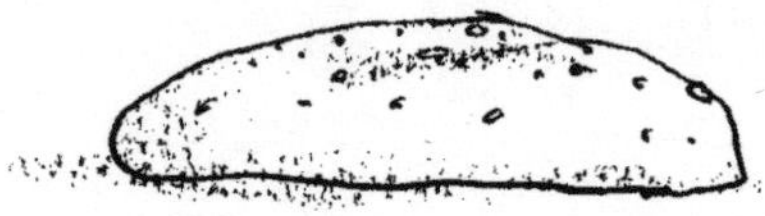

you are not having any trrrouble finding those."

"None at all!" they cried out. "We will spear the blabbersnitch and trap the crabcruncher and shoot the grobblesquirt and catch the catspringer in his burrow!"

"Excellent!" said The Grand High Witch. "Vhen you have mixed everything together in the mixer, you vill have a most marvellous-looking grrreen liqvid. Put vun drop, just vun titchy droplet of this liqvid into a chocolate or a sveet, and *at nine o'clock the next morning* the child who ate it vill turn into a mouse in tventy-six seconds! But vun vurd of vorning. Never increase the dose! Never put more than vun drrrop into each sveet or chocolate. And never give more than vun sweet or chocolate to each child. An overdose of Delayed Action Mouse-Maker vill mess up the timing of the alarm-clock and cause the child to turn into a mouse too early. A large overdose might even have an instant effect, and you vouldn't vont that, vould you? You vouldn't vont the children turning into mice rrright there in your sveet-shops. That vould give the game away. So be very carrreful! Do not overdose!"

Bruno Jenkins Disappears

The Grand High Witch was starting to talk again. "I am now going to prrrove to you," she said, "that this rrrecipe is vurrrking to perrrfection. You understand, of course, that you can set the alarm-clock to go off at any time you like. It does not *have* to be nine o'clock. So yesterday I am personally prrree-paring a small quantity of the magic formula in order to give you a public demonstration. But I am making vun small change in the rrrecipe. Before I am rrroasting the alarm-clock, I am setting it to go off, not at nine o'clock the next morning, but at half-past thrrree the next afternoon. Vhich means half-past thrrree *this* afternoon. And that," she said, glancing at her wrist-watch, "is in prrree-cisely seven minutes' time!"

The audience of witches was listening intently, sensing that something dramatic was about to happen.

"So vot am I doing yesterday vith this magic liqvid?" asked The Grand High Witch. "I vill tell you vot I am doing. I am putting vun drrroplet of it into a very sqvishy chocolate bar and I am giving this bar to a rrree-pulsive smelly little boy who is hanging rrround the lobby of the hotel."

The Grand High Witch paused. The audience remained silent, waiting for her to go on.

"I votched this rrree-pulsive little brrrute gobbling up the sqvishy bar of chocolate and vhen he had finished, I said to him, 'Vos that good?' He said it vos great. So I said to him, 'Vould you like some more?' And he said, 'Yes.' So I said, 'I vill give you *six* more chocolate bars like that if you vill meet me in the Ballroom of this hotel at tventy-past thrrree tomorrow afternoon.' 'Six bars!' cried this greedy little svine. 'I'll be there! You bet I'll be there!'

"So the stage is set!" shouted The Grand High Witch. "The prrroof of the pudding is about to begin! Do not forget that before I am rrroasting the alarm-clock yesterday, I am setting it for half-past thrrree today. It is now" – she glanced again at her watch – "it is now exactly tventy-five minutes past thrrree and the nasty little stinker who vill be turning into a mouse in five minutes' time should at this very moment be standing outside the doors!"

And by gum, she was absolutely right. The boy, whoever he might be, was already rattling the door-handle and banging on the doors with his fist.

"Qvick!" shrieked The Grand High Witch. "Put on your vigs! Put on your gloves! Put on your shoes!"

There was a great rustle and bustle of putting on wigs and gloves and shoes, and I saw The Grand High Witch herself reach for her face-mask and put it on over that revolting face of hers. It was astonishing how that mask transformed her. All of a sudden she became once again a rather pretty young lady.

"Let me in!" came the boy's voice from behind the doors. "Where are those chocolate bars you promised me? I'm here to collect! Dish them out!"

"He is not only smelling, he is also greedy," said The Grand High Witch. "Rrree-moof the chains from the doors and let him come in." The extraordinary thing about the mask was that its lips moved quite naturally when she spoke. You really couldn't see it was a mask at all.

One of the witches leapt to her feet and unfastened the chains. She opened the two huge doors. Then I heard her saying, "Why *hello*, little man. How lovely to see you. You have come for your chocolate bars, have you not? They are all ready for you. Do come in."

A small boy wearing a white tee-shirt and grey shorts and gymshoes entered the room. I recognised him at once. He was called Bruno Jenkins and he was staying in the hotel with his parents. I didn't care for him. He was one of those boys who is always eating something whenever you meet him. Meet him in the hotel lobby and he is stuffing sponge cake into his mouth. Pass him in the corridor and he is fishing potato crisps out of a bag by the fistful. Catch sight of him in the hotel garden and he is wolfing a Dairy Milk Bar and has two more sticking out of his trouser-pocket. What's more, Bruno never stopped boasting about how his father made more money than my father and that they owned three cars. But worse than that, yesterday morning I had found him kneeling on the flagstones of the hotel terrace with a magnifying-glass in his hand. There was a column of ants marching across one of the flagstones and Bruno Jenkins was focusing the sun through his magnifying-glass and roasting the ants one by one. "I like watching them burn," he said. "That's horrible!" I cried. "Stop doing it!" "Let's see you stop me," he said. At that point I had pushed him with all my might and he had crashed sideways on to the flagstones. His magnifying-glass had splintered into many pieces and he had leapt up shrieking, "My father is going to get you for this!" Then he had run off, presumably to find his wealthy dad. That was the last time I had seen Bruno Jenkins until now. I doubted very much that he was to be turned into a mouse, although I must confess that I was secretly hoping it might happen. Either way, I didn't envy him being up there in front of all those witches.

"Darling boy," cooed The Grand High Witch from up on the platform. "I have your chocolates all rrready for you. Do come up here firrrst and say hello to all these lovely ladies." Her voice was quite different now. It was soft and gentle and absolutely dripping with syrup.

Bruno was looking a bit bewildered, but he allowed himself to be led up on to the platform, where he stood beside The Grand High Witch and said, "Okay, where are my six bars of chocolate?"

I saw the witch who had let him in quietly putting the chain back on the door-handles. Bruno didn't notice this. He was too busy asking for his chocolate.

"The time is now vun minute before half-past thrrree!" announced The Grand High Witch.

"What the heck's going on?" Bruno asked.

He wasn't frightened, but he wasn't looking exactly comfortable either. "What *is* this?" he said. "Gimme my chocolate!"

"Thirty seconds to go!" cried The Grand High Witch, gripping Bruno by the arm. Bruno shook himself clear and stared at her. She stared back at him, smiling with the lips of her mask. Every witch in the audience was staring at Bruno.

"Tventy seconds!" cried The Grand High Witch.

"Gimme the chocolate!" shouted Bruno, becoming suddenly suspicious. "Gimme the chocolate and let me out of here!"

"Fifteen seconds!" cried The Grand High Witch.

"Will one of you crazy punks kindly tell me what all this is about?" shouted Bruno.

"Ten seconds!" cried The Grand High Witch. "Nine . . . eight . . . seven . . . six . . . five . . . four . . . thrrree . . . two . . . vun . . . zero! Vee have ignition!"

I could have sworn I heard an alarm-clock ringing. I saw Bruno jump. He jumped as though someone had stuck a hatpin deep into his bottom and he yelled, "Ow!" He jumped so high that he landed on a small table up there on the stage, and he started hopping about on the top of this table, waving his arms and yelling his head off. Then suddenly he became silent. His whole body stiffened.

"The alarm has gone off!" shrieked The Grand High Witch. "The Mouse-Maker is beginning to vurrrk!" She started hopping about on the platform and clapping her gloved hands together and then she shouted out,

"This smelly brrrat, this filthy scum
This horrid little louse
Vill very very soon become
A lovely little MOUSE!"

Bruno was getting smaller by the second. I could see him shrinking . . .

Now his clothes seemed to be disappearing and brown fur was growing all over his body . . .

Suddenly he had a tail . . .

And then he had whiskers . . .

Now he had four feet . . .

It was all happening so quickly . . .

It was a matter of seconds only . . .

And all at once he wasn't there any more . . .

A small brown mouse was running around on the table top . . .

"Bravo!" yelled the audience. "She's done it! It works! It's fantastic! It's colossal! It's the greatest yet! You are a miracle, O Brainy One!" They were all standing up and clapping and cheering and The Grand High Witch produced a mouse-trap from the folds of her dress and started to set it.

Oh no! I thought. I don't want to see this!

Bruno Jenkins may have been a bit of a stinker but I'm dashed if I want to watch him having his head chopped off!

"Vhere is he?" snapped The Grand High Witch, searching the platform. "Vhere has that mouse got to?"

She couldn't find him. Clever Bruno must have jumped down off the table and scampered off into some corner or even down a small hole. Thank heavens for that.

"It matters not!" shouted The Grand High Witch. "Silence and sit down!"

The Ancient Ones

The Grand High Witch stood on the very centre of the platform, and those dangerous eyes of hers travelled slowly around the audience of witches who were sitting so meekly before her. "All those over seventy put up your hands!" she barked suddenly.

Seven or eight hands went up in the air.

"It comes to me," said The Grand High Witch, "that you ancient vuns vill not be able to climb high trrrees in search of grrruntles' eggs."

"We won't, Your Grandness! We are afraid we won't!" chanted the ancient ones.

"Nor vill you be able to catch the crrrabcrrruncher, who lives high up on the rrrocky cliffs," The Grand High Witch went on. "I can't exactly see you sprrrinting after the speedy catsprrringer either, or diving into deep vorters to spear the blabbersnitch, or striding the bleak moors vith a gun under your arm to shoot the grrrobblesqvirt. You are too old and feeble for those things."

"We are," chanted the ancient ones. "We are! We are!"

"You ancient vuns have served me vell over many years," said The Grand High Witch, "and I do not vish to deny you the pleasure of bumping off a few thousand children each just because you have become old and feeble. I have therefore prepared personally vith my own hands a limited qvanity of Delayed Action Mouse-Maker vhich I vill distrrribute to the ancient vuns before you leave the hotel."

"Oh, thank you, thank you!" cried the old witches. "You are far too good to us, Your Grandness! You are so kind and thoughtful!"

"Here is a sample of vot I am giving you," shouted The Grand High Witch. She fished around in a pocket of her dress and brought out a very small bottle. She held it up and shouted, "In this tiny bottle is five hundred doses of Mouse-Maker! Is enough to turrrn five hundred children into mice!" I could see that the bottle was made of dark-blue glass and that it was very small, about the same size as the ones you can buy at the chemist with nose-drops in them. "Each of you ancient vuns vill get two of these bottles!" she shouted.

"Thank you, thank you, O Most Generous and Thoughtful One!" chorused the ancient witches. "Not one drop will be wasted! Each

of us will promise to squish and squallop and squiggle one thousand children!"

"Our meeting is over!" announced The Grand High Witch. "Here is the time-table for the rrree-mainder of your stay in this hotel.

"Rrright now, vee must all go out on to the Sunshine Terrace and have tea vith that rrridiculous Manager.

"Next, at six o'clock tonight, those vitches who are too old to climb trees after grrruntles' eggs vill rrree-port to my rrroom to rrree-ceive two bottles each of Mouse-Maker. My rrroom number is 454. Do not forget it.

"Then, at eight o'clock, all of you vill assemble in the Dining-Rrroom for supper. Vee are the lovely ladies of the RSPCC and they are setting up two long tables specially for us. But do not forget to put the cotton plugs up your noses. That Dining-Rrroom vill be full of filthy little children and vithout the nose-plugs the stink vill be unbearrrable. Apart from that, rrree-member to behave normally at all times. Is everything clear? Any qvestions?"

"I have one question, Your Grandness," said a voice in the audience. "What happens if one of the chocolates we are giving away in our shops gets eaten by a grown-up?"

"That's just too bad for the grrrown-up," said The Grand High Witch. "This meeting is over!" she shouted. "Out you go!"

The witches stood up and began gathering their things together. I was watching them through the crack and hoping to heaven they would hurry up and leave so that I might be safe at last.

"*Wait!*" shrieked one of the witches in the back row. "*Hold everything!*" Her shrieking voice echoed through the Ballroom like a trumpet. All the witches suddenly stopped and turned and looked towards the speaker. She was one of the taller witches and I could see her standing there with her head tilted back and her nose in the air and she was sucking in great long breaths of air through those curvy

pink sea-shelly nostrils of hers.

"*Wait!*" she shouted again.

"What is it?" the others cried out.

"Dogs' droppings!" she yelled. "Just then I got a whiff of dogs' droppings!"

"Surely not!" the others shouted. "There couldn't be!"

"Yes yes!" shouted the first witch. "There it is again! It's not strong! But it's there! I mean it's here! It's definitely somewhere not too far away!"

"Vot's going on down there?" shouted The Grand High Witch, glaring down from the platform.

"Mildred's just got a whiff of dogs' droppings, Your Grandness!" someone called back to her.

"Vot rrrubbish is this?" shouted The Grand High Witch. "She has dogs' drrroppings on the brain! There are no children in this rrroom!"

"Hang on!" cried the witch called Mildred. "Hang on everybody! Don't move! I'm getting it again!" Her huge curvy nose-holes were waving in and out like a pair of fish-tails. "It's getting stronger! It's hitting me harder now! Can't the rest of you smell it?"

All the noses of all the witches in that room

went up in the air, and all the nostrils began to suck and sniff.

"She's right!" cried another voice. "She's absolutely right! Dogs' droppings it is, strong and foul!"

In a matter of seconds, the entire assembly of witches had taken up the dreaded cry of dogs' droppings. "Dogs' droppings!" they shouted. "The room is full of it! Poo! Poo-oo-oo-oo-oo-oo-ooo! Why did we not smell it before? It stinks like a sewer! Some little swine must be hiding not so very far away from here!"

"Find it!" screamed The Grand High Witch. "Trrrack it down! Rrrrootle it out! Follow your noses till you get it!"

The hairs on my head were standing up like the bristles of a nail-brush and a cold sweat was breaking out all over me.

"Rrrootle it out, this small lump of dung!" screeched The Grand High Witch. "Don't let it escape! If it is in here it has observed the most secret things! It must be exterrrminated immediately!"

Metamorphosis

I remember thinking to myself, *There is no escape for me now! Even if I make a run for it and manage to dodge the lot of them, I still won't get out because the doors are chained and locked! I'm finished! I'm done for! Oh Grandmamma, what are they going to do to me?*

I looked round and I saw a hideous painted and powdered witch's face staring down at me, and the face opened its mouth and yelled triumphantly, "It's here! It's behind the screen! Come and get it!" The witch reached out a gloved hand and grabbed me by the hair but I twisted free and jumped away. I ran, oh how I ran! The sheer terror of it all put wings on my feet! I flew around the outside of the great Ballroom and not one of them had a chance of catching me. As I came level with the doors, I paused and tried to open them but the big chain was on them and they didn't even rattle.

The witches were not bothering to chase me. They simply stood there in small groups, watching me and knowing for certain that there was no way I could escape. Several of them were holding their noses with gloved fingers and there were cries of, "Poo! What a stink! We can't stand this much longer!"

"Catch it then, you idiots!" screamed The Grand High Witch from up on the platform. "Sprrread out in a line across the room and close in on it and grab it! Corner this filthy little gumboil and seize it and bring it up here to me!"

The witches spread out as they were told. They advanced towards me, some from one end, some from the other, and some came down the middle between the rows of empty chairs. They were bound to get me now. They had me cornered.

From sheer and absolute terror, I began to scream. "*Help!*" I screamed, turning my head towards the doors in the hope that somebody outside might hear me. "Help! Help! Hel-l-l-lp!"

"Get it!" shouted The Grand High Witch. "Grrrab hold of it! Stop it yelling!"

They rushed at me then, and about five of them grabbed me by the arms and legs and lifted me clear off the ground. I went on screaming, but one of them clapped a gloved hand over my mouth and that stopped me.

"Brrring it here!" shouted The Grand High

Witch. "Brrring the spying little vurm up here to me!"

I was carried on to the platform with my arms and legs held tight by many hands, and I lay there suspended in the air, facing the ceiling. I saw The Grand High Witch standing over me, grinning at me in the most horrible way. She held up the small blue bottle of Mouse-Maker and she said, "Now for a little medicine! Hold his nose to make him open his mouth!"

Strong fingers pinched my nose. I kept my mouth closed tight and held my breath. But I couldn't do it for long. My chest was bursting. I opened my mouth to get one big breath of air and as I did so, The Grand High Witch poured the entire contents of the little bottle down my throat!

Oh, the pain and the fire! It felt as though a kettleful of boiling water had been poured into my mouth. My throat was going up in flames! Then very quickly the frightful burning searing scorching feeling started spreading down into my chest and into my tummy and on and on into my arms and legs and all over my body! I screamed and screamed but once again the gloved hand was clapped over my lips. The next thing I felt was my skin beginning to tighten. How else can I describe it? It was quite literally a tightening and a shrinking of the skin all over my body from the top of my head to the tips of my fingers to the ends of my toes! I felt as though I was a balloon and somebody was twisting the top of the balloon and twisting and twisting and the balloon was getting smaller and smaller and the skin was getting tighter and tighter and soon it was going to burst.

Then the *squeezing* began. This time I was inside a suit of iron and somebody was turning a screw, and with each turn of the screw the iron suit became smaller and smaller so that I was squeezed like an orange into a pulpy mess with the juice running out of my sides.

After that there came a fierce prickling sensation all over my skin (or what was left of my skin) as though tiny needles were forcing their way out through the surface of the skin from the inside, and this, I realise now, was the growing of the mouse-fur.

Far away in the distance, I heard the voice of The Grand High Witch yelling, "Five hundred doses! This stinking little carbuncle has had five hundred doses and the alarm-clock has been smashed and now vee are having *instantaneous action*!" I heard clapping and cheering and I remember thinking: *I am not myself any longer! I have gone clear out of my own skin!*

I noticed that the floor was only an inch from my nose.

I noticed also a pair of little furry front paws resting on the floor. I was able to move those paws. They were mine!

At that moment, I realised that I was not a little boy any longer. I was a MOUSE.

"Now for the mouse-trrrap!" I heard The Grand High Witch yelling. "I've got it right here! And here's a piece of cheese!"

But I wasn't going to wait for *that*. I was off across the platform like a streak of lightning! I was astonished at my own speed! I leapt over witches' feet right and left, and in no time at all I was down the steps and on to the floor of the

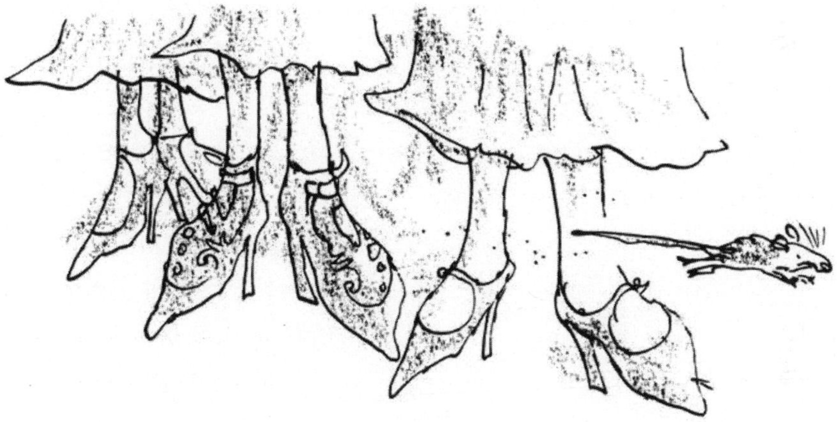

Ballroom itself and skittering off among the rows of chairs. What I especially liked was the fact that I made no sound at all as I ran. I was a swift and silent mover. And quite amazingly, the pain had all gone now. I was feeling quite remarkably well. *It is not a bad thing after all*, I thought to myself, *to be tiny as well as speedy when there is a bunch of dangerous females after*

your blood. I selected the back leg of a chair and squeezed up against it and kept very still.

In the distance, The Grand High Witch was shouting, "Leave the little stinkpot alone! It is not vurth bothering about! It is only a mouse now! Somebody else vill soon catch it! Let us get out of here! The meeting is over! Unlock the doors and shove off to the Sunshine Terrace to have tea vith that idiotic Manager!"

Bruno

I peeped round the leg of the chair and watched the hundreds of witches' feet walking out through the doors of the Ballroom. When they had all gone and the place was absolutely silent, I began to move cautiously about on the floor. Suddenly I remembered Bruno. He must surely be around here somewhere, too. "Bruno!" I called out.

I wasn't seriously expecting that I would be able to speak at all now that I had become a mouse, so I got the shock of my life when I heard my own voice, my own perfectly normal rather loud voice, coming out of my tiny mouth.

It was wonderful. I was thrilled. I tried it again. "Bruno Jenkins, where are you?" I called out. "If you can hear me, give a shout!"

My voice was exactly the same and just as loud as it had been when I was a boy. "Hey there, Bruno Jenkins!" I called. "Where are you?"

There was no answer.

I pottered about between the seat-legs trying to get used to being so close to the ground. I decided I rather liked it. You are probably wondering why I wasn't depressed at all. I found myself thinking, *What's so wonderful about being a little boy anyway? Why is that necessarily any better than being a mouse? I know that mice get hunted and they sometimes get poisoned or caught in traps. But little boys sometimes get killed, too. Little boys can be run over by motor-cars or they can die of some awful illness. Little boys have to go to school. Mice don't. Mice don't have to pass exams. Mice don't have to worry about money. Mice, as far as I can see, have only two enemies, humans and cats. My grandmother is a human, but I know for certain that she will always love me whoever I am. And she never, thank goodness, keeps a cat. When mice grow up, they don't ever have to go to war and fight against other mice. Mice,* I felt pretty certain, *all like each other. People don't.*

Yes, I told myself, *I don't think it is at all a bad thing to be a mouse.*

I was wandering around the Ballroom floor thinking about all this when I spotted another mouse. It was crouching on the floor holding a piece of bread in its front paws and nibbling away at it with great gusto.

It had to be Bruno. "Hello, Bruno," I said.

He glanced up at me for about two seconds,

then went right on guzzling.

"What have you found?" I asked him.

"One of them dropped it," he answered. "It's a fish-paste sandwich. Pretty good."

He too spoke with a perfectly normal voice. One would have expected that a mouse (if it was going to talk at all) would do so with the smallest and squeakiest voice you could imagine. It was terrifically funny to hear the voice of the rather loud-mouthed Bruno coming out of that tiny mouse's throat.

"Listen, Bruno," I said. "Now that we are both mice, I think we ought to start thinking a bit about the future."

He stopped eating and stared at me with small black eyes. "What do you mean *we*?" he said. "The fact that you're a mouse has nothing to do with me."

"But you're a mouse, too, Bruno."

"Don't be a fool," he said. "I'm not a mouse."

"I'm afraid you are, Bruno."

"I most certainly am not!" he shouted. "Why are you insulting me? I haven't been rude to you! Why do you call *me* a mouse?"

"Don't you know what's happened to you?" I said.

"What on earth are you talking about?" Bruno said.

"I have to inform you," I said, "that not very long ago the witches turned you into a mouse. Then they did the same to me."

"You're lying!" he cried. "I'm not a mouse!"

"If you hadn't been so busy guzzling that sandwich," I said, "you would have noticed your hairy paws. Take a look at them."

Bruno looked down at his paws. He jumped. "Good grief!" he cried. "I *am* a mouse! You wait till my father hears about this!"

"He may think it's an improvement," I said.

"I don't want to be a mouse!" Bruno shouted, jumping up and down. "I refuse to be a mouse! I'm Bruno Jenkins!"

"There are worse things than being a mouse," I said. "You can live in a hole."

"I don't want to live in a hole!" Bruno shouted.

"And you can creep into the larder at night," I said, "and nibble through all the packets of raisins and cornflakes and chocolate biscuits and everything else you can find. You can stay there all night eating yourself silly. That's what mice do."

"Now that's a thought," Bruno said, perking up a bit. "But how am I going to open the door of the fridge to get at the cold chicken and all the leftovers? That's something I do every evening at home."

"Maybe your rich father will get you a special little mouse-fridge all to yourself," I said. "One that you can open."

"You say a witch did this to me?" Bruno said. "Which witch?"

"The one who gave you the chocolate bar in the hotel lobby yesterday," I told him. "Don't you remember?"

"The filthy old cow!" he shouted. "I'll get her for this! Where is she? Who is she?"

"Forget it," I said. "You don't have a hope. Your biggest problem at the moment is your parents. How are they going to take this? Will they treat you with sympathy and kindness?"

Bruno considered this for a moment. "I think," he said, "that my father is going to be a bit put out."

"And your mother?"

"She's terrified of mice," Bruno said.

"Then you've got a problem, haven't you?"

"Why only me?" he said. "What about you?"

"My grandmother will understand perfectly," I said. "She knows all about witches."

Bruno took another bite of his sandwich. "What do you suggest?" he said.

"I suggest we both go first of all and consult my grandmother," I said. "She'll know exactly what to do."

I moved towards the doors which were standing open. Bruno, still grasping part of the sandwich in one paw, followed after me.

"When we get out into the corridor," I said, "we're going to run like mad. Stick close to the wall all the way and follow me. Do not talk and do not let anyone see you. Don't forget that just about anyone who catches sight of you will try to kill you."

I snatched the sandwich out of his paw and threw it away. "Here goes," I said. "Keep behind me."

Hello Grandmamma

As soon as I was out of the Ballroom, I took off like a flash. I streaked down the corridor, went through the Lounge and the Reading-Room and the Library and the Drawing-Room and came to the stairs. Up the stairs I went, jumping quite easily from one to the other, keeping well in against the wall all the time. "Are you with me, Bruno?" I whispered.

"Right here," he said.

My grandmother's room and my own were on the fifth floor. It was quite a climb, but we made it without meeting a single person on the way because everyone was using the lift. On the fifth floor, I raced along the corridor to the door of my grandmother's room. A pair of her shoes was standing outside the door to be cleaned. Bruno was alongside me. "What do we do now?" he said.

Suddenly, I caught sight of a chambermaid coming along the corridor towards us. I saw at once that she was the one who had reported me to the manager for keeping white mice. Not, therefore, the sort of person I wanted to meet in my present condition. "Quick!" I said to Bruno. "Hide in one of those shoes!" I hopped into one shoe and Bruno hopped into the other. I waited for the maid to walk past us. She didn't. When she came to the shoes, she bent down and picked them up. In doing this, she put her hand inside the one I was hiding in. When one of her fingers touched me, I bit it. It was a silly thing to do, but I did it instinctively, without thinking. The maid let out a scream that must have been heard by ships far out in the English Channel, and she dropped the shoes and ran like the wind down the corridor.

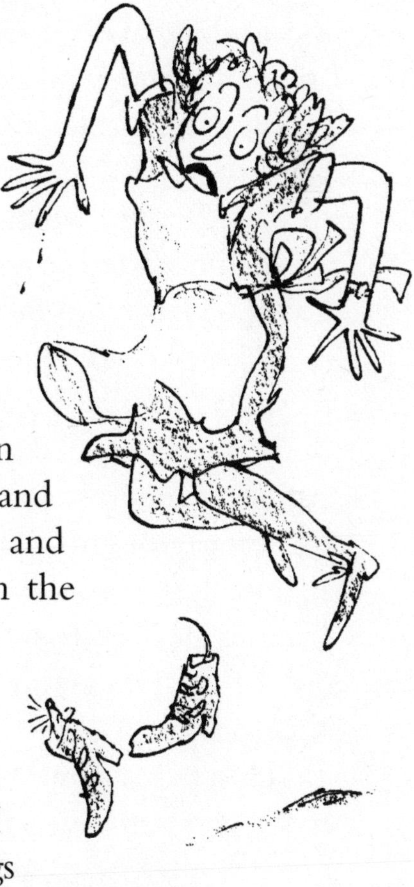

My grandmother's door opened. "What on earth is going on out here?" she said. I darted between her legs into her room and Bruno followed me.

"Close the door, Grandmamma!" I cried.

"Please hurry!"

She looked around and saw two small brown mice on the carpet.

"Please close it," I said, and this time she actually saw me talking and recognised my voice. She froze and became absolutely motionless. Every part of her body, her fingers and hands and arms and head became suddenly as stiff as a marble statue. Her face turned even paler than marble and her eyes were stretched so wide I could see the whites all around them. Then she started to tremble. I thought she was going to faint and fall over.

"Please close the door quickly, Grandmamma," I said. "That awful maid might come in."

She somehow managed to gather herself together enough to close the door. She leaned against it, staring down at me white-faced and shaking all over. I saw tears beginning to come out of her eyes and go dribbling down her cheeks.

"Don't cry, Grandmamma," I said. "Things could be a lot worse. I did get away from them. I'm still alive. So is Bruno."

Very slowly, she bent down and picked me up with one hand. Then she picked Bruno up with the other hand and put us both on the table. There was a bowl of bananas in the centre of the table and Bruno jumped straight into it and began tearing away with his teeth at one of the banana skins to get at the fruit inside.

My grandmother grasped the arm of her chair to steady herself, but her eyes never left me.

"Sit down, dear Grandmamma," I said.

She collapsed into her chair.

"Oh, my darling," she murmured and now the tears were really streaming down her cheeks. "Oh, my poor sweet darling. What *have* they done to you?"

"I know what they've done, Grandmamma, and I know what I am, but the funny thing is that I don't honestly feel especially bad about it. I don't even feel angry. In fact, I feel rather good. I know I'm not a boy any longer and I never will be again, but I'll be quite all right as long as there's always you to look after me." I was not just trying to console her, I was being absolutely honest about the way I felt. You may think it odd that I wasn't weeping myself. It *was* odd. I simply can't explain it.

"Of course I'll look after you," my grandmother murmured. "Who is the other one?"

"That was a boy called Bruno Jenkins," I told her. "They got him first."

My grandmother took a new long black cigar out of a case in her handbag and put it in her mouth. Then she got out a box of matches. She struck a match but her fingers were shaking so much that the flame kept missing the end of the cigar. When she got it lit at last, she took a long pull and sucked in the smoke. That seemed to calm her down a bit.

"Where did it happen?" she whispered. "Where is the witch now? Is she in the hotel?"

"Grandmamma," I said. "It wasn't just one. It was *hundreds*! They're all over the place! They're right here in the hotel this very moment!"

She leant forward and stared at me. "You don't mean . . . you don't actually mean . . . you don't mean to tell me they're holding the Annual Meeting right here in the hotel?"

"They've held it, Grandmamma! It's finished! I heard it all! And all of them including The Grand High Witch herself are downstairs now! They're pretending they're the Royal Society for the Prevention of Cruelty to Children! They're all having tea with the Manager!"

"And they caught you?"

"They smelt me out," I said.

"Dogs' droppings, was it?" she said, sighing.

"I'm afraid so. But it wasn't strong. They very nearly didn't smell me because I hadn't had a bath for ages."

"Children should *never* have baths," my grandmother said. "It's a dangerous habit."

"I agree, Grandmamma."

She paused, sucking at her cigar.

"Do you *really* mean to tell me that they are now all downstairs having tea?" she said.

"I'm certain of it, Grandmamma."

There was another pause. I could see the old glint of excitement slowly coming back into my grandmother's eyes, and all of a sudden she sat up very straight in her chair and said sharply, "Tell me everything, right from the beginning. And please hurry."

I took a deep breath and began to talk. I told about going to the Ballroom and hiding behind the screen to do my mouse-training. I told about the notice saying Royal Society for the Prevention of Cruelty to Children. I told her all about the women coming in and sitting down and about the small woman who appeared on the stage and took off her mask. But when it came to describing what her face looked like underneath the mask, I simply couldn't find the right words. "It was horrible, Grandmamma!" I said. "Oh, it was so horrible! It was . . . it was like something that was going rotten!"

"Go on," my grandmother said. "Don't stop."

Then I told her about all the others taking off their wigs and their gloves and their shoes, and how I saw before me a sea of bald pimply heads and how the women's fingers had little claws and how their feet had no toes.

My grandmother had come forward now in her armchair so that she was sitting right on the edge of it. Both her hands were cupped over the gold knob of the stick that she always used when walking, and she was staring at me with eyes as bright as two stars.

Then I told her how The Grand High Witch had shot out the fiery white-hot sparks and how they had turned one of the other witches into a puff of smoke.

"I've heard about that!" my grandmother cried out excitedly. "But I never quite believed it! You are the first non-witch ever to see it happening! It is The Grand High Witch's most famous punishment! It is known as 'getting fried', and all the other witches are petrified of having it done to them! I am told that The Grand High Witch makes it a rule to fry at least one witch at each Annual Meeting. She does it in order to keep the rest of them on their toes."

"But they don't *have* any toes, Grandmamma."

"I *know* they don't, my darling, but please go on."

So then I told my grandmother about the Delayed Action Mouse-Maker and when I came to the bit about turning all the children of England into mice, she actually leapt out of her chair shouting, "I knew it! I knew they were brewing up something tremendous!"

"We've got to stop them," I said.

She turned and stared at me. "You can't stop witches," she said. "Just look at the power that terrible Grand High Witch has in her eyes alone! She could kill any of us at any time with those white-hot sparks of hers! You saw it yourself!"

"Even so, Grandmamma, we've still got to

stop her from turning all the children of England into mice."

"You haven't quite finished," she said. "Tell me about Bruno. How did they get *him*?"

So I described how Bruno Jenkins had come in and how I had actually seen him with my own eyes being shrunk into a mouse. My grandmother looked at Bruno who was guzzling away in the bowl of bananas.

"Does he never stop eating?" she asked.

"Never," I said. "Can you explain something to me, Grandmamma?"

"I'll try," she said. She reached out and lifted me off the table and put me on her lap. Very gently, she began stroking the soft fur along my back. It felt nice. "What is it you want to ask me, my darling?" she said.

"The thing I don't understand," I said, "is how Bruno and I are still able to talk and think just like we did before."

"It's quite simple," my grandmother said. "All they've done is to shrink you and give you four legs and a furry coat, but they haven't been able to change you into a one hundred per cent mouse. You are still yourself in everything except your appearance. You've still got your own mind and your own brain and your own voice, and thank goodness for that."

"So I'm not really an *ordinary* mouse at all," I said. "I'm a sort of mouse-person."

"Quite right," she said. "You are a human in mouse's clothing. You are very special."

We sat there in silence for a few moments while my grandmother went on stroking me very gently with one finger and puffing her cigar with the other hand. The only sound in the room was made by Bruno as he attacked the bananas in the bowl. But I wasn't doing nothing as I lay there on her lap. I was thinking like mad. My brain was whizzing as it had never whizzed before.

"Grandmamma," I said. "I may have a bit of an idea."

"Yes, my darling. What is it?"

"The Grand High Witch told them her room was number 454. Right?"

"Right," she said.

"Well, *my* room is number 554. Mine, 554, is on the fifth floor, so hers, 454, will be on the fourth floor."

"That is correct," my grandmother said.

"Then don't you think it's possible that room 454 is directly underneath room 554?"

"That's more than likely," she said. "These

modern hotels are all built like boxes of bricks. But what if it is?"

"Would you please take me out on to my balcony so I can look down," I said.

All the rooms in the Hotel Magnificent had small private balconies. My grandmother carried me through into my own bedroom and out on to my balcony. We both peered down to the balcony immediately below.

"Now if that *is* her room," I said, "then I'll bet I could climb down there somehow and get in."

"And get caught all over again," my grandmother said. "I won't allow it."

"At this moment," I said, "all the witches are down on the Sunshine Terrace having tea with the Manager. The Grand High Witch probably won't be back until six o'clock or just before. That's when she's going to dish out supplies of that foul formula to the ancient ones who are too old to climb trees after gruntles' eggs."

"And what if you did manage to get into her room?" my grandmother said. "What then?"

"Then I should try to find the place where she keeps her supply of Delayed Action Mouse-Maker, and if I succeeded then I would steal one bottle of it and bring it back here."

"Could you carry it?"

"I think so," I said. "It's a very small bottle."

"I'm frightened of that stuff," my grandmother said. "What would you do with it if you did manage to get it?"

"One bottle is enough for five hundred people," I said. "That would give each and every witch down there a double dose at least. We could turn them all into mice."

My grandmother jumped about an inch in the air. We were out on my balcony and there was a drop of about a million feet below us and I very nearly bounced out of her hand over the railings when she jumped.

"Be careful with me, Grandmamma," I said.

"What an idea!" she cried. "It's fantastic! It's tremendous! You're a genius, my darling!"

"Wouldn't it be something?" I said. "Wouldn't that really be something?"

"We'd get rid of every witch in England in one swoop!" she cried. "*And* The Grand High Witch into the bargain!"

"We've got to try it," I said.

"Listen," she said, nearly dropping me over the balcony once again in her excitement. "If we brought this off, it would be the greatest triumph in the whole history of witchery!"

"There's a lot of work to do," I said.

"Of course there's a lot of work to do," she said. "Just for a start, supposing you did manage to get hold of one of those bottles, how would you get it into their food?"

"We'll work that out later," I said. "Let's try to get the stuff first. How can we find out for sure if that's her room just below us?"

"We shall check it out immediately!" my grandmother cried. "Come along! There's not a second to waste!" Carrying me in one hand, she went bustling out of the bedroom and along the corridor, banging her stick on the carpet with each step she took. We went down the

stairs one flight to the fourth floor. The bedrooms on either side of the corridor had their numbers painted on the doors in gold.

"Here it is!" my grandmother cried. "Number 454." She tried the door. It was locked of course. She looked up and down the long empty hotel corridor. "I do believe you're right," she said. "This room is almost certainly directly below yours." She marched back along the corridor, counting the number of doors from The Grand High Witch's room to the staircase. There were six.

She climbed back up to the fifth floor and repeated the exercise.

"She *is* directly below you!" my grandmother cried out. "Her room is right below yours!"

She carried me back into my own bedroom and went out once again on to the balcony. "That's her balcony down there," she said. "And what's more, the door from her balcony into her bedroom is wide open! How are you going to climb down?"

"I don't know," I said. Our rooms were in the front of the hotel and they looked down on to the beach and the sea. Immediately below my balcony thousands of feet below, I could see a fence of spiked railings. If I fell, I'd be a gonner.

"I've got it!" my grandmother cried. With me in her hand, she rushed back into her own room and began rummaging in the chest-of-drawers. She came out with a ball of blue knitting-wool. One end was attached to some needles and a half-finished sock she had been knitting for me. "This is perfect," she said. "I shall put you in the sock and lower you down on to The Grand High Witch's balcony. But we *must* hurry! Any moment now that monster will be returning to her room!"

The Mouse-Burglar

My grandmother hustled me back into my own bedroom and out on to the balcony. "Are you ready?" she asked. "I'm going to put you in the sock now."

"I hope I can manage this," I said. "I'm only a little mouse."

"You'll manage," she said. "Good luck, my darling." She popped me into the sock and started lowering me over the balcony. I crouched inside the sock and held my breath. Through the stitches I could see out quite clearly. Miles below me, the children playing on the beach were the size of beetles. The sock started swinging in the breeze. I looked up and saw my grandmother's head sticking out over the railings of the balcony above. "You're nearly there!" she called out. "Here we go! Gently does it. You're down!"

I felt a slight bump. "In you go!" my grandmother was shouting. "Hurry, hurry, hurry! Search the room!"

I jumped out of the sock and ran into The Grand High Witch's bedroom. There was the same musty smell about the place that I had

noticed in the Ballroom. It was the stench of witches. It reminded me of the smell inside the men's public lavatory at our local railway-station.

As far as I could see, the room was tidy enough. There was no sign anywhere that it was inhabited by anyone but an ordinary person. But then there wouldn't be, would there? No witch would be stupid enough to leave anything suspicious lying around for the hotel maid to see.

Suddenly I saw a frog jumping across the carpet and disappearing under the bed. I jumped myself.

"*Hurry up*!" came my grandmother's voice from somewhere high up outside. "Grab the stuff and *get out*!"

I started skittering round and trying to search the room. It wasn't so easy. I couldn't, for example, open any of the drawers. I couldn't open the doors of the big wardrobe either. I stopped skittering about: I sat in the middle of the floor and had a think. If The Grand High Witch wanted to hide something top secret, where would she put it? Certainly not in any ordinary drawer. Not in the wardrobe either. It was too obvious. I jumped up on to the bed to get a better view of the room. *Hey, I thought,* what about under the *mattress*? Very carefully, I lowered myself over the edge of the bed and wormed my way underneath the mattress. I had to push forward hard to make any headway, but I kept at it. I couldn't see a thing. I was scrabbling about

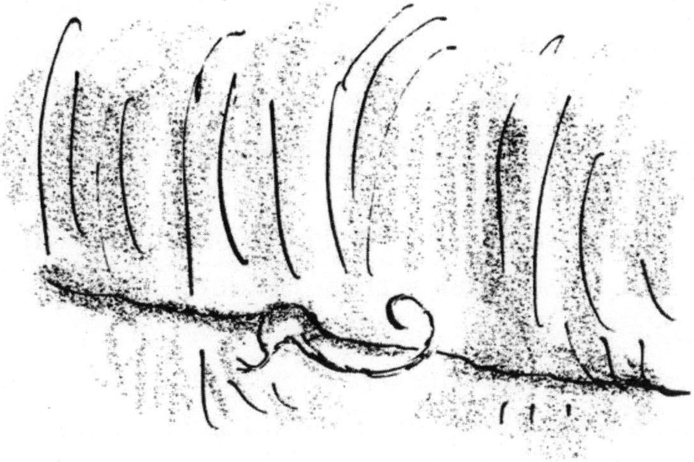

under the mattress when my head suddenly bumped against something hard *inside* the mattress above me. I reached up and felt it with my paw. Could it be a little bottle? It *was* a little bottle! I could trace the shape of it through the cloth of the mattress. And right alongside it, I felt another hard lump, and another and another. The Grand High Witch must have slit open the mattress and put all the bottles inside and then sewn it all up again. I began tearing away frantically at the mattress cloth above my head with my teeth. My front teeth were extremely sharp and it didn't take me long to make a small hole. I climbed into the hole and grabbed a bottle by the neck. I pushed it down through the hole in the mattress and climbed out after it.

Walking backwards and dragging the bottle behind me, I managed to reach the edge of the mattress. I rolled the bottle off the bed on to the carpet. It bounced but it didn't break. I jumped down off the bed. I examined the bottle. It was identical to the one The Grand High Witch had had in the Ballroom. There was a label on this one. FORMULA 86, it said. DELAYED ACTION MOUSE-MAKER. Then it said, *This bottle contains five hundred doses.* Eureka! I felt tremendously pleased with myself.

Three frogs came hopping out from under the bed. They crouched on the carpet, staring at me with large black eyes. I stared back at them. Those huge eyes were the saddest things I had ever seen. It suddenly occurred to me that almost certainly once upon a time they

had been children, those frogs, before The Grand High Witch had got hold of them. I stood there clutching the bottle and staring at the frogs. "Who are you?" I asked them.

At that exact moment, I heard a key turning in the lock of the door and the door burst open and The Grand High Witch swept into the room. The frogs jumped underneath the bed again in one quick hop. I darted after them, still clutching the bottle, and I ran back against the wall and squeezed in behind one of the bedposts. I heard feet walking on the carpet. I peeped round the bedpost. The three frogs were clustered together under the middle of the bed. Frogs cannot hide like mice. They cannot run like mice, either. All they can do, poor things, is to hop about rather clumsily.

Suddenly The Grand High Witch's face came into view, peering under the bed. I popped my head back behind the bedpost. "So there you are, my little frrroggies," I heard her saying. "You can stay vhere you are until I go to bed tonight, then I shall thrrrow you out of the vindow and the seagulls can have you for supper."

Suddenly very loud and clear there came the sound of my grandmother's voice through the

open balcony door. "Hurry up, my darling!" it shouted. "Do hurry up! You'd better come out quickly!"

"Who is calling?" snapped The Grand High Witch. I peeped round the bedpost again and saw her walking across the carpet to the balcony door. "Who is this on my balcony?" she muttered. "Who is it? Who dares to trrrespass on my balcony?" She went through the door on to the balcony itself.

"Vot is this knitting-vool hanging down here?" I heard her saying.

"Oh, hello," came my grandmother's voice. "I just dropped my knitting over the balcony by mistake. But it's all right. I've got hold of one end of it. I can pull it up by myself, thank you all the same." I marvelled at the coolness of her voice.

"Who vur you talking to just now?" snapped The Grand High Witch. "Who vur you telling to hurry up and come out qvickly?"

"I was talking to my little grandson," I heard my grandmother saying. "He's been in the bathroom for hours and it's time he came out. He sits in there reading books and he forgets completely where he is! Do *you* have any children, my dear?"

"I do not!" shouted The Grand High Witch, and she came quickly back into the bedroom, *slamming the balcony door behind her.*

I was cooked. My escape route was closed. I was shut up in the room with The Grand High Witch and three terrified frogs. I was just as terrified as the frogs. I was quite sure that if I was spotted, I would be caught and thrown out over the balcony for the seagulls.

There came a knock on the bedroom door. "Vot is it this time?" shouted The Grand High Witch.

"It is we ancient ones," said a meek voice from behind the door. "It is six o'clock and we have come to collect the bottles that you promised us, O Your Grandness."

I saw her crossing the carpet towards the door. The door was opened and then I saw a whole lot of feet and shoes beginning to enter the room. They were coming in slowly and hesitantly, as though the owners of those shoes were frightened of entering. "Come in! Come in!" snapped The Grand High Witch. "Do not stand out there dithering in the corrri-dor! I don't have all night!"

I saw my chance. I jumped out from behind the bedpost and ran like lightning towards the open door. I jumped over several pairs of shoes on the way and in three seconds I was out in the corridor, still clutching the precious bottle to my chest. No one had seen me. There were no shouts of *Mouse! Mouse!* All I could hear were the voices of the ancient witches burbling their silly sentences about "How kind Your Grandness is" and all the rest of it. I went scampering down the corridor to the stairs and up one flight. I went to the fifth floor and then along the corridor again until I came to the door of my own bedroom. Thank goodness there was no one in sight. Using the bottom of the little bottle, I began tap-tap-tapping on the door. *Tap tap tap tap*, I went. *Tap tap tap . . . tap tap tap . . .* Would my grandmother hear me? I thought that she must. The bottle made quite a loud tap each time it struck. *Tap tap tap . . . tap tap tap . . .* Just so long as nobody came along the corridor.

But the door didn't open. I decided to take a risk. "Grandmamma!" I shouted as loudly as I possibly could. "Grandmamma! It's me! Let me in!"

I heard her feet coming across the carpet and the door opened. I went in like an arrow. "I've done it!" I cried, jumping up and down. "I've got it, Grandmamma! Look, here it is! I've got a whole bottle of it!"

She closed the door. She bent down and picked me up and hugged me. "Oh my darling!" she cried. "Thank heavens you're safe!" She took the little bottle from me and read the label aloud. "'Formula 86 Delayed Action Mouse-Maker!'" she read. "'This bottle contains five hundred doses!' You brilliant darling boy! You're a wonder! You're a marvel! How on earth did you get out of her room?"

"I nipped out when the ancient witches were coming in," I told her. "It was all a bit hairy, Grandmamma. I wouldn't want to do it again."

"I saw her too!" my grandmother said.

"I know you did, Grandmamma. I heard you talking to each other. Didn't you think she was absolutely foul?"

"She's a murderer," my grandmother said.

"She's the most evil woman in the entire world!"

"Did you see her mask?" I asked.

"It's amazing," my grandmother said. "It looks just like a real face. Even though I knew it was a mask, I still couldn't tell. Oh, my darling!" she cried, giving me a hug. "I thought I'd never see you again! I'm so happy you got away."

Mr and Mrs Jenkins Meet Bruno

My grandmother carried me back into her own bedroom and put me on the table. She set the precious bottle down beside me. "What time are those witches having supper in the Dining-Room?" she asked.

"Eight o'clock," I said.

She looked at her watch. "It is now ten-past six," she said. "We've got until eight o'clock to work out our next move." Suddenly, her eye fell upon Bruno. He was still in the banana bowl on the table. He had eaten three bananas and was now attacking a fourth. He had become immensely fat.

"That's quite enough," my grandmother said, lifting him out of the bowl and putting him on the table-top. "I think it's time we returned this little fellow to the bosom of his family. Don't you agree, Bruno?"

Bruno scowled at her. I had never seen a mouse scowl before, but he managed it. "My parents let me eat as much as I want," he said. "I'd rather be with them than with you."

"Of course you would," my grandmother said. "Do you know where your parents might be at this moment?"

"They were in the Lounge not long ago," I said. "I saw them sitting there as we dashed through on our way up here."

"Right," my grandmother said. "Let's go and see if they are still there. Do you want to come along?" she added, looking at me.

"Yes, please," I said.

"I shall put you both in my handbag," she said. "Keep quiet and stay out of sight. If you must peep out now and again, don't show more than your nose."

Her handbag was a large bulky black-leather affair with a tortoise-shell clasp. She picked up Bruno and me and popped us into it. "I shall leave the clasp undone," she said. "But be sure to keep out of sight."

I had no intention of keeping out of sight. I wanted to see everything. I seated myself in a little side-pocket inside the bag, near the clasp, and from there I was able to poke my head out whenever I wanted to.

"Hey!" Bruno called out. "Give me the rest of that banana I was eating."

"Oh all right," my grandmother said. "Anything to keep you quiet." She dropped the half-eaten banana into the bag, then slung the bag over her arm and marched out of the room and went thumping along the corridor with her walking-stick.

We went down in the lift to the ground floor and made our way through the Reading-Room to the Lounge. And there, sure enough, sat Mr and Mrs Jenkins in a couple of armchairs with a low round glass-covered table between them. There were several other groups in there as well, but the Jenkinses were the only couple sitting alone. Mr Jenkins was reading a newspaper. Mrs Jenkins was knitting something large and mustard-coloured. Only my nose and eyes were above the clasp of my grandmother's handbag, but I had a super view. I could see everything.

My grandmother, dressed in black lace, went thumping across the floor of the Lounge and halted in front of the Jenkins's table. "Are you

Mr and Mrs Jenkins?" she asked.

Mr Jenkins looked at her over the top of his newspaper and frowned. "Yes," he said. "I am Mr Jenkins. What can I do for you, madam?"

"I'm afraid I have some rather alarming news for you," she said. "It's about your son, Bruno."

"What about Bruno?" Mr Jenkins said.

Mrs Jenkins looked up but went on knitting. "What's the little blighter been up to now?" Mr Jenkins asked. "Raiding the kitchen, I suppose."

"It's a bit worse than that," my grandmother said. "Do you think we might go somewhere more private while I tell you about it?"

"Private?" Mr Jenkins said. "Why do we have to be private?"

"This is not an easy thing for me to explain," my grandmother said. "I'd much rather we all went up to your room and sat down before I tell you any more."

Mr Jenkins lowered his paper. Mrs Jenkins stopped knitting. "I don't *want* to go up to my room, madam," Mr Jenkins said. "I'm quite comfortable here, thank you very much." He was a large coarse man and he wasn't used to being pushed around by anybody. "Kindly state

your business and then leave us alone," he added. He spoke as though he was addressing someone who was trying to sell him a vacuum-cleaner at the back door.

My poor grandmother, who had been doing her best to be as kind to them as possible, now began to bristle a bit. "We really can't talk in here," she said. "There are too many people.

This is a rather delicate and personal matter."

"I'll talk where I dashed well want to, madam," Mr Jenkins said. "Come on now, out with it! If Bruno has broken a window or smashed your spectacles, then I'll pay for the damage, but I'm not budging out of this seat!"

One or two other groups in the room were beginning to stare at us now.

"Where *is* Bruno anyway?" Mr Jenkins said. "Tell him to come here and see me."

"He's here already," my grandmother said. "He's in my handbag." She patted the big floppy leather bag with her walking-stick.

"What the heck d'you mean he's in your handbag?" Mr Jenkins shouted.

"Are you trying to be funny?" Mrs Jenkins said, very prim.

"There's nothing funny about this," my grandmother said. "Your son has suffered a rather unfortunate mishap."

"He's always suffering mishaps," Mr Jenkins said. "He suffers from overeating and then he suffers from wind. You should hear him after supper. He sounds like a brass band! But a good dose of castor-oil soon puts him right again. Where *is* the little beggar?"

"I've already told you," my grandmother

said. "He's in my handbag. But I do think it might be better if we went somewhere private before you meet him in his present state."

"This woman's mad," Mrs Jenkins said. "Tell her to go away."

"The plain fact is", my grandmother said, "that your son Bruno has been rather drastically altered."

"*Altered!*" shouted Mr Jenkins. "What the devil d'you mean *altered*?"

"Go away!" Mrs Jenkins said. "You're a silly old woman!"

"I am trying to tell you as gently as I possibly can that Bruno really is in my handbag," my grandmother said. "My own grandson actually saw them doing it to him."

"Saw *who* doing *what* to him, for heaven's sake?" shouted Mr Jenkins. He had a black moustache which jumped up and down when he shouted.

"Saw the witches turning him into a mouse," my grandmother said.

"Call the Manager, dear," Mrs Jenkins said to her husband. "Have this mad woman thrown out of the hotel."

At this point, my grandmother's patience came to an end. She fished around in her handbag and found Bruno. She lifted him out and dumped him on the glass-topped table. Mrs Jenkins took one look at the fat little brown mouse who was still chewing a bit of banana and she let out a shriek that rattled the crystals on the chandelier. She sprang out of her chair yelling, "It's a mouse! Take it away! I can't stand the things!"

"It's Bruno," my grandmother said.

"You nasty cheeky old woman!" shouted Mr Jenkins. He started flapping his newspaper at Bruno, trying to sweep him off the table. My grandmother rushed forward and managed to grab hold of him before he was swept away. Mrs Jenkins was still screaming her head off and Mr Jenkins was towering over us and shouting, "Get out of here! How dare you frighten my wife like that! Take your filthy mouse away this instant!"

"Help!" screamed Mrs Jenkins. Her face had gone the colour of the underside of a fish.

"Well, I did my best," my grandmother said, and with that she turned and sailed out of the room, carrying Bruno with her.

The Plan

When we got back to the bedroom, my grandmother took both me and Bruno out of her handbag and put us on the table. "Why on earth didn't you speak up and tell your father who you were?" she said to Bruno.

"Because I had my mouth full," Bruno said. He jumped straight back into the bowl of bananas and went on with his eating.

"What a disagreeable little boy you are," my grandmother said to him.

"Not boy," I said. "Mouse."

"Quite right, my darling. But we don't have time to worry about him at this moment. We have plans to make. In about an hour and a half's time, all the witches will be going down to supper in the Dining-Room. Right?"

"Right," I said.

"And every one of them has got to be given a dose of Mouse-Maker," she said. "How on earth are we going to do that?"

"Grandmamma," I said. "I think you are forgetting that a mouse can go places where human beings can't."

"That's quite right," she said. "But even a

mouse can't go creeping around on the table-top carrying a bottle and sprinkling Mouse-Maker all over the witches' roast beef without being spotted."

"I wasn't thinking of doing it in the Dining-Room," I said.

"Then where?" she asked.

"In the kitchen," I said, "while their food is being got ready."

My grandmother stared at me. "My darling child," she said slowly, "I do believe that turning you into a mouse has doubled your brain-power!"

"A little mouse", I said, "can go scuttling round the kitchen among the pots and pans, and if he's very careful no one will ever see him."

"Brilliant!" my grandmother cried out. "By golly, I think you've got it!"

"The only thing is," I said, "how will I know which food is theirs? I don't want to put it in the wrong saucepan. It would be disastrous if I turned all the other guests into mice by mistake, and especially you, Grandmamma."

"Then you'll just have to creep into the kitchen and find a good hiding-place and wait . . . and listen. Just lie there in some dark cranny listening and listening to what the cooks are saying . . . and then, with a bit of luck, somebody's going to give you a clue. Whenever they have a very big party to cook for, the food is always prepared separately."

"Right," I said. "That's what I'll have to do. I shall wait there and I shall listen and I shall hope for a bit of luck."

"It's going to be very dangerous," my grandmother said. "Nobody welcomes a mouse in the kitchen. If they see you, they'll squash you to death."

"I won't let them see me," I said.

"Don't forget you'll be carrying the bottle," she said, "so you won't be nearly so quick and nippy."

"I can run quite fast standing up with the bottle in my arms," I said. "I did it just now, don't you remember? I came all the way up from The Grand High Witch's room carrying it."

"What about unscrewing the top?" she said. "That might be difficult for you."

"Let me try," I said. I took hold of the little bottle and using both my front paws, I found I was able to unscrew the cap quite easily.

"That's great," my grandmother said. "You really are a very clever mouse." She glanced at her watch. "At half-past seven," she said, "I shall go down to the Dining-Room for supper with you in my handbag. I shall then release you under the table together with

the precious bottle and from then on you'll be on your own. You will have to work your way unseen across the Dining-Room to the door that leads into the kitchen. There will be waiters going in and out of that door all the time. You will have to choose the right moment and nip in behind one of them, but for heaven's sake be sure that you don't get trodden on or squeezed in the door."

"I'll try not to," I said.

"And whatever happens, you mustn't let them catch you."

"Don't go on about it, Grandmamma. You're making me nervous."

"You're a brave little fellow," she said. "I do love you."

"What shall we do with Bruno?" I asked her.

Bruno looked up. "I'm coming with you," he said, speaking with his mouth full of banana. "I'm not going to miss my supper!"

My grandmother considered this for a moment. "I'll take you along," she said, "if you promise to stay in my bag and keep absolutely silent."

"Will you pass food down to me from the table?" Bruno asked.

"Yes," she said, "if you promise to behave yourself. Would *you* like something to eat, my darling?" she said to me.

"No, thank you," I said. "I'm too excited to eat. And I've got to keep fit and frisky for the big job ahead."

"It's a big job all right," my grandmother said. "You'll never do a bigger one."

In the Kitchen

"The time has come!" my grandmother said. "The great moment has arrived! Are you ready, my darling?"

It was exactly half-past seven. Bruno was in the bowl finishing that fourth banana. "Hang on," he said. "Just a few more bites."

"No!" my grandmother said. "We've got to go!" She picked him up and held him tight in her hand. She was very tense and nervous. I had never seen her like that before. "I'm going to put you both in my handbag now," she said, "but I shall leave the clasp undone." She popped Bruno into it first. I waited, clutching the little bottle to my chest. "Now *you*," she said. She picked me up and gave me a kiss on the nose. "Good luck, my darling. Oh, by the way, you do realise you've got a tail, don't you?"

"A what?" I said.

"A tail. A long curly tail."

"I must say that never occurred to me," I said. "Good gracious me, so I have! I can see it now! I can actually move it! It *is* rather grand, isn't it?"

"I mention it only because it might come in

useful when you're climbing about in the kitchen," my grandmother said. "You can curl it around and you can hook it on to things and you can swing from it and lower yourself to the ground from high places."

"I wish I'd known this before," I said. "I could have practised using it."

"Too late now," my grandmother said. "We've got to go." She popped me into her handbag with Bruno, and at once I took up my usual perch in the small side-pocket so that I could poke my head out and see what was going on.

My grandmother picked up her walking-stick and out she went into the corridor to the lift. She pressed the button and the lift came up and she got in. There was no one in there with us.

"Listen," she said. "I won't be able to talk to you much once we're in the Dining-Room. If I do, people will think I'm dotty and talking to myself."

The lift reached the ground floor and stopped with a jerk. My grandmother walked out of it and crossed the lobby of the hotel and entered the Dining-Room. It was a huge room with gold decorations on the ceiling and big mirrors around the walls. The regular guests always had their tables reserved for them and most of them were already in their places and starting to eat their suppers. Waiters were buzzing about all over the place, carrying plates and dishes. Our table was a small one beside the right-hand wall about halfway down the room. My grandmother made her way to it and sat down.

Peeping out of the handbag, I could see in the very centre of the room two long tables that were not yet occupied. Each of them carried a notice fixed on to a sort of silver stick and the notices said, RESERVED FOR MEMBERS OF THE RSPCC.

My grandmother looked towards the long tables but said nothing. She unfolded her napkin and spread it over the handbag on her lap. Her hand slid under the napkin and took hold of me gently. With the napkin covering me, she lifted me up close to her face and whispered, "I am about to put you on the floor under the table. The table-cloth reaches almost to the ground so no one will see you. Have you got hold of the bottle?"

"Yes," I whispered back. "I'm ready, Grandmamma."

Just then, a waiter in a black suit came and stood by our table. I could see his legs from under the napkin and as soon as I heard his voice, I knew who he was. His name was William. "Good evening, madam," he said to my grandmother. "Where is the little gentleman tonight?"

"He's not feeling very well," my grandmother said. "He's staying in his room."

"I'm sorry to hear that," William said. "Today there is green-pea soup to start with, and for the main course you have a choice of either grilled fillet of sole or roast lamb."

"Pea soup and lamb for me, please," my grandmother said. "But don't hurry it, William. I'm in no rush tonight. In fact, you can bring me a glass of dry sherry first."

"Of course, madam," William said, and he went away.

My grandmother pretended she had dropped something, and as she bent down, she slid me out from under the napkin on to the floor under the table. "Go, darling, go!" she whispered, then she straightened up again.

I was on my own now. I stood clasping the little bottle. I knew exactly where the door into the kitchen was. I had to go about halfway

round the enormous Dining-Room to reach it. Here goes, I thought, and like a flash I skittled out from under the table and made for the wall. I had no intention of going across the Dining-Room floor. It was far too risky. My plan was to cling to the skirting of the wall all the way round until I reached the kitchen door.

I ran. Oh, how I ran. I don't think anyone saw me. They were all too busy eating. But to reach the door leading to the kitchen I had to

cross the main entrance to the Dining-Room. I was just about to do this when in poured a great flood of females. I pressed myself against the wall clutching the bottle. At first I saw only the shoes and ankles of these women who were surging in through the door, but when I glanced up a bit higher I knew at once who they were. They were the witches coming in to dinner!

I waited until they had all passed me by, then I dashed on towards the kitchen door. A waiter opened it to go in. I nipped in after him and hid behind a big garbage-bin on the floor. I stayed there for several minutes, just listening to all the talk and the racket. By golly, what a place that kitchen was! The noise! And the steam! And the clatter of pots and pans! And the cooks all shouting! And the waiters all rushing in and out of from the Dining-Room yelling the food orders to the cooks! "Four soups and two lambs and two fish for table twenty-eight! Three apple-pies and two strawberry ice-creams for number seventeen!" Stuff like that going on all the time.

Not far above my head there was a handle sticking out from the side of the garbage-bin. Still clutching the bottle, I gave a leap, turned

a somersault in the air, and caught hold of the handle with the end of my tail. Suddenly there I was swinging to and fro upside down. It was terrific. I loved it. *This*, I told myself, *is how a trapeze artist in a circus must feel as he goes swishing through the air high up in the circus tent.* The only difference was that his trapeze could only swing backwards and forwards. My trapeze (my tail) could swing me in any direction I wanted. Perhaps I would become a circus mouse after all.

Just then, a waiter came in with a plate in his hand and I heard him saying, "The old hag on table fourteen says this meat is too tough! She wants another portion!" One of the cooks said, "Gimme her plate!" I dropped to the floor and peeped round the garbage-bin. I saw the cook scrape the meat off the plate and slap another bit on. Then he said, "Come on boys, give her some gravy!" He carried the plate round to everyone in the kitchen and do you know what they did? Every one of those cooks and kitchen-boys spat on to the old lady's plate! "See how she likes it now!" said the cook, handing the plate back to the waiter.

Quite soon another waiter came in and he shouted, "Everyone in the big RSPCC party wants the soup!" That's when I started sitting up and taking notice. I was all ears now. I edged a bit farther round the garbage-bin so that I could see everything that was going on in the kitchen. A man with a tall white hat who must have been the head chef shouted, "Put the soup for the big party in the larger silver soup-tureen!"

I saw the head chef place a huge silver basin on to the wooden side-bench that ran along the whole length of the kitchen against the opposite wall. *Into that silver basin is where the soup is going,* I told myself. *So that's where the stuff in my little bottle must go as well.*

I noticed that high up near the ceiling, above the side-bench, there was a long shelf crammed with saucepans and frying-pans. *If I can somehow clamber up on to that shelf,* I thought, *then I've got it made. I shall be directly above the silver basin.*

But first I must somehow get across to the other side of the kitchen and then up on to the middle shelf. A great idea came to me! Once again, I jumped up and hooked my tail around the handle of the garbage-bin. Then, hanging upside down, I began to swing. Higher and higher I swung. I was remembering the trapeze artist in the circus I had seen last Easter and the way he had got the trapeze swinging higher and higher and higher and had then let go and gone

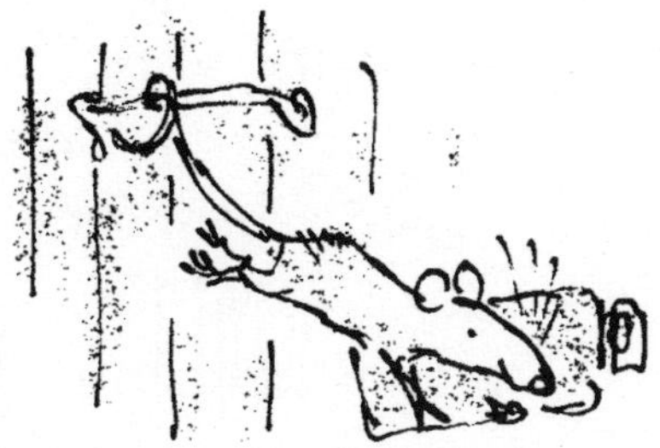

flying through the air. So just at the right moment, at the top of my swing, I let go with my tail and went soaring clear across the kitchen and made a perfect landing on the middle shelf!

By golly, I thought, what marvellous things a mouse can do! And I'm only a beginner!

No one had seen me. They were all far too busy with their pots and pans. From the middle shelf I somehow managed to shinny up a little water-pipe in the corner, and in no time at all I was up on the very top shelf just under the ceiling, among all the saucepans and the frying-pans. I knew that no one could possibly see me

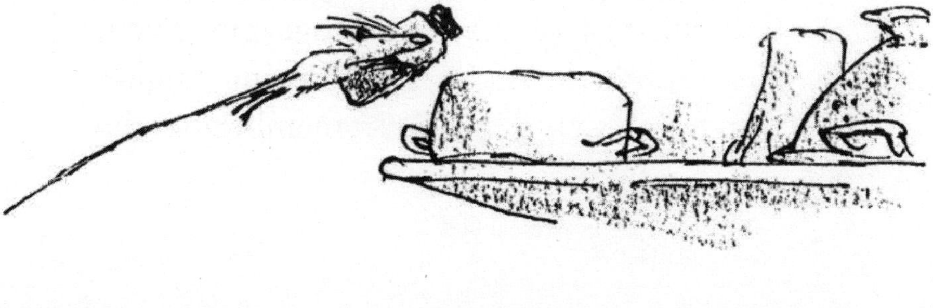

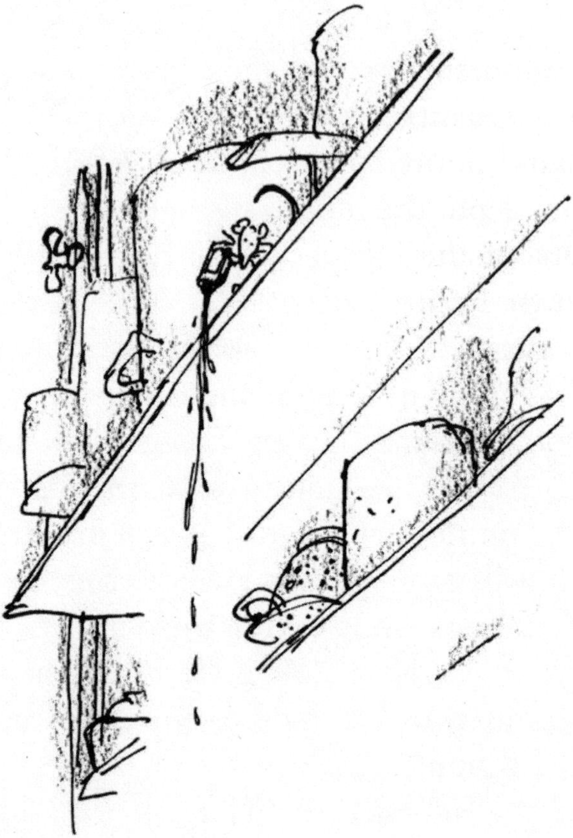

up there. It was a super position, and I began working my way along the shelf until I was directly above the big empty silver basin they were going to pour the soup into. I put down my bottle. I unscrewed the top and crept to the edge of the shelf and quickly poured what was in it straight into the silver basin below. The

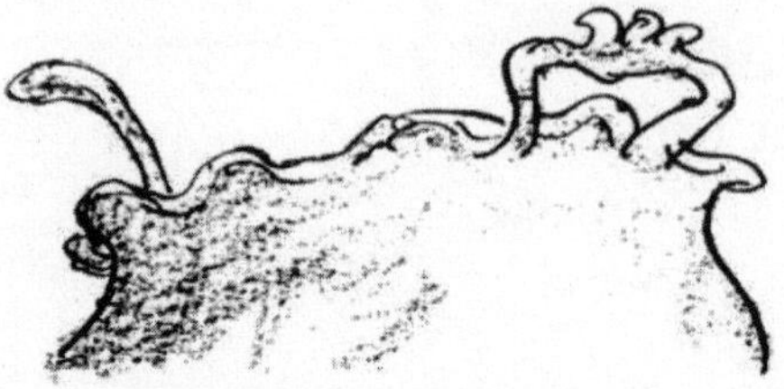

next moment, one of the cooks came along with a gigantic saucepan of steaming green soup and poured the whole lot into the silver basin. He put the lid on the basin and shouted, "Soup for the big party all ready to go out!" Then the waiter arrived and carried the silver basin away.

I had done it! Even if I never got back alive to my grandmother, the witches were still going to get the Mouse-Maker! I left the empty bottle behind a large saucepan and began working my way back along the top shelf. It was much easier to move about

without the bottle. I began using my tail more and more. I swung from the handle of one saucepan to the handle of another all the way along that top shelf, while far below me cooks and waiters were all bustling about and kettles were steaming and pans were spluttering and pots were boiling and I thought to myself, *Oh, boy, this is the life! What fun it is to be a mouse doing an exciting job like this!* I kept right on swinging. I swung most marvellously from handle to handle, and I was enjoying myself so much that I completely forgot I was in full view of anyone in the kitchen who might happen to glance upwards. What came next happened so quickly I had no time to save myself. I heard a man's voice yelling, "A mouse! Look at that dirty little mouse!" and I caught a glimpse below me of a white-coated figure in a tall white hat and then there was a flash of steel as the carving-knife whizzed through the air and there was a shoot of pain in the end of my tail and suddenly I was falling and falling head-first towards the floor.

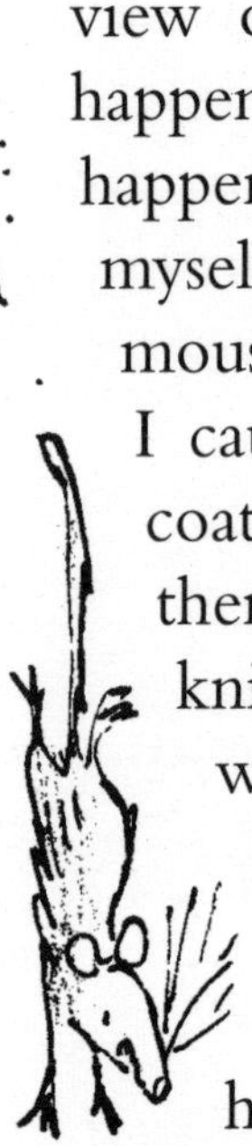

Even as I fell, I knew just what had happened. I knew that the tip of my tail had been cut off and that I was about to crash on to the floor and everyone in the kitchen would be after me. "A mouse!" they were shouting. "A mouse! A mouse! Catch it quick!" I hit the floor and jumped up and ran for my life. All around me there were big black boots going *stamp stamp stamp*, and I dodged around them and ran and ran and ran, twisting and turning, and dodging and swerving across the kitchen floor. "Get it!" they were shouting. "Kill it! Stamp on it!" The whole floor seemed to be full of black boots stamping away at me and I dodged and swerved and twisted and turned and then in sheer desperation, hardly knowing what I was doing, wanting only a place to hide, I ran up the trouser-leg of one of the cooks and clung to his sock!

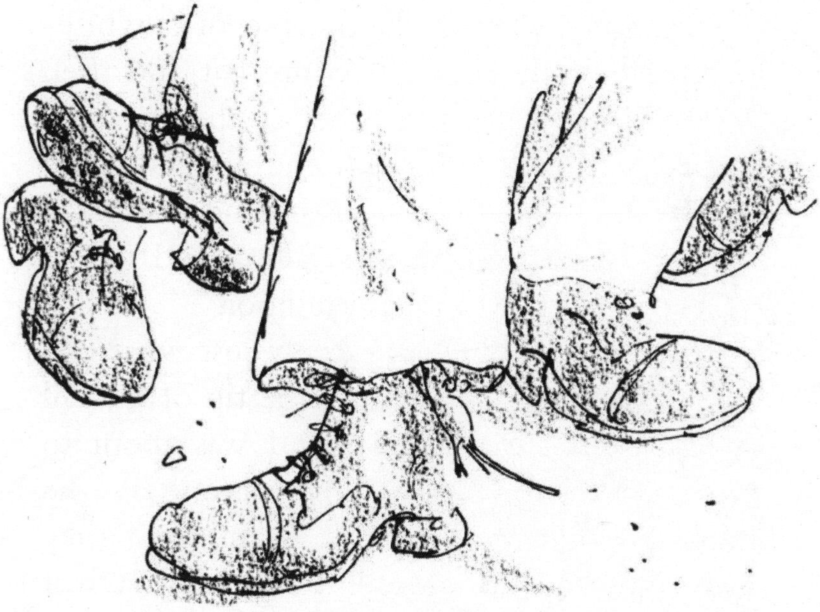

"Hey!" the cook shouted. "Jeepers creepers! He's gone up my trouser! Hold on, boys! I'll get him this time!"

The man's hands began slap-slapping at the trouser-leg and now I really *was* going to get smashed if I didn't move quickly. There was only one way to go and that was up. I dug my little claws into the hairy skin of the man's leg and scuttled upwards, higher and higher, past the calf and past the knee and on to the thigh.

"Holy smoke!" the man was yelling. "It's going all the way up! It's going right up my

leg!" I heard shrieks of laughter coming from the other cooks but I can promise you I wasn't laughing myself. I was running for my life. The man's hands were slap-slap-slapping all around me and he was jumping up and down as though he was standing on hot bricks, and I kept climbing and I kept dodging and very soon I reached the very top of the trouser-leg and there was nowhere else to go.

"Help! Help! Help!" the man was screaming. "It's in my knickers! It's running round in my flaming knickers! Get it out! Someone help me to get it out!"

"Take off your trousers, you silly slob!" someone else shouted. "Pull down your pants and we'll soon catch him!"

I was in the middle of the man's trousers now, in the place where the two trouser-legs meet and zip begins. It was dark and awfully hot in there. I knew I had to keep going. I dashed onward and found the top of the other trouser-leg. I went down it like greased lightning and came out at the bottom of it and once again I was on the floor. I heard the stupid cook still shouting, "It's in my trousers! Get it out! Will somebody *please* help me to get it out before it bites me!" I caught a flashing glimpse of the entire kitchen staff crowding round him and laughing their heads off and nobody saw the little brown mouse as it flew across the floor and dived into a sack of potatoes.

I burrowed down in among the dirty potatoes and held my breath.

The cook must have started taking his trousers right off because now they were shouting, "It's not in there! There's no mice in

there, you silly twerp!"

"There was! I swear there was!" the man was shouting back. "You've never *had* a mouse in your trousers! You don't know what it feels like!"

The fact that a tiny creature like me had caused such a commotion among a bunch of grown-men gave me a happy feeling. I couldn't help smiling in spite of the pain in my tail.

I stayed where I was until I was sure they had forgotten about me. Then I crept out of the potatoes and cautiously poked my tiny head over the edge of the sack. Once again the kitchen was all of a bustle with cooks and waiters rushing about everywhere. I saw the waiter who had come in earlier with the complaint about tough meat coming in again. "Hey boys!" he shouted. "I asked the old hag if the new bit of meat was any better and she said it was perfectly delicious! She said it was really tasty!"

I had to get out of that kitchen and back to my grandmother. There was only one way to do this. I must make a dash clear across the floor and out through the door behind one of the waiters. I stayed quite still, watching for my chance. My tail was hurting terribly. I curled it round so as to have a look at it. About two inches of it were missing and it was bleeding quite a lot. There was a waiter loading up with a batch of plates full of pink ice-cream. He had a plate in each hand and two more balanced on each arm. He went towards the door. He pushed it open with his shoulder. I leapt out of the sack of potatoes and went across that kitchen floor and into the Dining-Room like a streak of light, and I didn't stop running until I was underneath my grandmother's table.

It was lovely to see my grandmother's feet again in those old-fashioned black shoes with their straps and buttons. I shinnied up one of her legs and landed on her lap. "Hello, Grandmamma!" I whispered. "I'm back! I did it! I poured it all into their soup!"

Her hand came down and caressed me. "Well *done*, my darling!" she whispered back. "Well done you! They are at this very moment eating that soup!" Suddenly, she withdrew her hand. "You're bleeding!" she whispered. "My darling, what's happened to you?"

"One of the cooks cut off my tail with a carving-knife," I whispered back. "It hurts like billy-o."

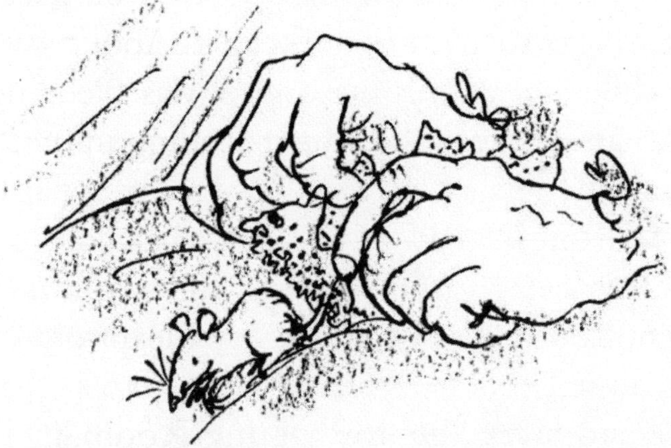

"Let me look at it," she said. She bent her head and examined my tail. "You poor little thing," she whispered. "I'm going to bandage it up with my handkerchief. That will stop the bleeding."

She fished a small lace-edged handkerchief out of her bag and this she somehow managed to wrap around the end of my tail. "You'll be all right now," she said. "Just try to forget about it. Did you really manage to pour the whole bottle into their soup?"

"Every drop," I said. "Do you think you could put me where I can watch them?"

"Yes," she answered. "My handbag is on your own empty chair beside me. I'm going to pop you in there now and you can peep out as long as you are careful not to be seen. Bruno is there as well, but take no notice of him. I gave him a roll to eat and that's keeping him busy for a while."

Her hand closed around me and I was lifted off her lap and transferred to the handbag. "Hello, Bruno," I said.

"This is a great roll," he said, nibbling away in the bottom of the bag. "But I wish there was butter on it."

I peered over the top of the handbag. I could see the witches quite clearly sitting at their two long tables in the centre of the room. They had finished their soup now, and the waiters were clearing away the plates. My grandmother had lit up one of her disgusting black cigars and was puffing smoke over everything. All around us the summer-holiday guests in this rather grand hotel were babbling away and tucking into their suppers. About half of them were old people with walking-sticks, but there were also plenty of families with a husband, a wife and several children. They were all well-to-do people. You had to be if you wanted to stay in the Hotel Magnificent.

"That's her, Grandmamma!" I whispered. "That's The Grand High Witch!"

"I know!" my grandmother whispered back. "She's the tiny one in black sitting at the head of the nearest table!"

"She could kill you!" I whispered. "She could kill anyone in this room with her white-hot sparks!"

"Look out!" my grandmother whispered. "The waiter's coming!"

I popped down out of sight and I heard William saying, "Your roast lamb, madam. And which vegetable would you like? Peas or carrots?"

"Carrots, please," my grandmother said. "But no potatoes."

I heard the carrots being dished out. There was a pause. Then my grandmother's voice was whispering, "It's all right. He's gone." I popped my head up again. "Surely no one will notice my little head sticking out like this?" I whispered.

"No," she answered. "I don't suppose they will. *My* problem is I've got to talk to you without moving my lips."

"You're doing beautifully," I said.

"I've counted the witches," she said. "There aren't nearly as many as you thought. You were just guessing, weren't you, when you said two hundred?"

"It just *seemed* like two hundred," I said.

"I was wrong, too," my grandmother said. "I thought there were a lot more witches than this in England."

"How many are there?" I asked.

"Eighty-four," she said.

"There *were* eighty-five," I said. "But one of them got fried."

At that moment, I caught sight of Mr Jenkins, Bruno's father, heading straight for our table. "Look out, Grandmamma!" I whispered. "Here comes Bruno's father!"

Mr Jenkins and His Son

Mr Jenkins came striding up to our table with a very purposeful look on his face.

"Where is that grandson of yours?" he said to my grandmother. He spoke rudely and looked very angry.

My grandmother put on her frostiest look, but didn't answer him.

"My guess is that he and my son Bruno are up to some devilment," Mr Jenkins went on. "Bruno hasn't turned up for his supper and it takes a lot to make that boy miss his food!"

"I must admit he has a very healthy appetite," my grandmother said.

"My feeling is that *you're* in on this as well," Mr Jenkins said. "I don't know who the devil you are and I don't much care, but you played a nasty trick on me and my wife this afternoon. You put a dirty little mouse on the table. That makes me think all three of you are up to something. So if you know where Bruno's hiding, kindly tell me at once."

"That was no trick I played on you," my grandmother said. "That mouse I tried to give you was your own little boy, Bruno. I was being kind to you. I was trying to restore him to the bosom of his family. You refused to take him in."

"What the blazes do you mean, madam?" shouted Mr Jenkins. "My son isn't a *mouse*!" His black moustache was jumping up and down like crazy as he spoke. "Come on, woman! Where is he? Out with it!"

The family at the table nearest to us had all stopped eating and were staring at Mr Jenkins. My grandmother sat there puffing away calmly at her black cigar. "I can well understand your anger, Mr Jenkins," she said. "Any other English father would be just as cross as you are. But over in Norway where I come from, we are quite used to these sort of happenings. We have learnt to accept them as part of everyday life."

"You must be mad, woman!" cried Mr Jenkins. "Where is Bruno? If you don't tell me at once I shall summon the police!"

"Bruno is a mouse," my grandmother said, calm as ever.

"He most certainly is *not* a mouse!" shouted Mr Jenkins.

"Oh yes I am!" Bruno said, poking his head up out of the handbag.

Mr Jenkins leapt about three feet into the air.

"Hello, Dad," Bruno said. He had a silly sort of mousy grin on his face.

Mr Jenkins's mouth dropped open so wide I could see the gold fillings in his back teeth.

"Don't worry, Dad," Bruno went on. "It's not as bad as all that. Just so long as the cat doesn't get me."

"B-B-Bruno!" stammered Mr Jenkins.

"No more school!" said Bruno, grinning a broad and asinine mouse-grin. "No more homework! I shall live in the kitchen cupboard and feast on raisins and honey!"

"B-b-but B-B-Bruno!" stammered Mr Jenkins again. "H-how did this happen?" The poor man had no wind left in his sails at all.

"Witches," my grandmother said. "The witches did it."

"I can't have a mouse for a son!" shrieked Mr Jenkins.

"You've got one," my grandmother said. "Be nice to him, Mr Jenkins."

"Mrs Jenkins will go crazy!" yelled Mr Jenkins. "She can't stand the things!"

"She'll just have to get used to him," my grandmother said. "I hope you don't keep a cat in the house."

"We do! We do!" cried Mr Jenkins. "Topsy is my wife's favourite creature!"

"Then you'll just have to get rid of Topsy," my grandmother said. "Your son is more important than your cat."

"He certainly is!" Bruno shouted from inside the handbag. "You tell Mum she's got to get rid of Topsy before I go home!"

By now half the Dining-Room was watching our little group. Knives and forks and spoons had been put down and all over the place heads were turning round to stare at Mr Jenkins as he stood there spluttering and shouting. They couldn't see either Bruno or me and they were wondering what all the fuss was about.

"By the way," my grandmother said, "would you like to know who did this to him?" There was a mischievous little smile on her face and I could see that she was about to get Mr Jenkins into trouble.

"Who?" he cried. "Who did it?"

"That woman over there," my grandmother said. "The small one in a black dress at the head of the long table."

"She's RSPCC!" cried Mr Jenkins. "She's the Chairwoman."

"No, she's not," my grandmother said. "She's The Grand High Witch Of All The World."

"You mean *she* did it, that skinny little woman over there!" shouted Mr Jenkins, pointing at her with a long finger. "By gad, I'll have my lawyers on to her for this! I'll make her pay through the nose!"

"I wouldn't do anything rash," my grandmother said to him. "That woman has magic powers. She might decide to turn *you* into something even sillier than a mouse. A cockroach perhaps."

"Turn *me* into a *cockroach*!" shouted Mr Jenkins, puffing out his chest. "I'd like to see her try!" He swung around and started marching across the Dining-Room towards The Grand High Witch's table. My grandmother and I watched him. Bruno had jumped up on to our table and was also watching his father. Practically everyone in the Dining-Room was watching Mr Jenkins now. I stayed where I was, peeping out of my grandmother's handbag. I thought it might be wiser to stay put.

The Triumph

Mr Jenkins had not gone more than a few paces towards The Grand High Witch's table when a piercing scream rose high above all the other noises in the room, and at the same moment I saw The Grand High Witch go shooting up into the air!

Now she was standing on her chair, still screaming . . .

Now she was on the table-top, waving her arms . . .

"What on earth's happening, Grandmamma?"

"Wait!" my grandmother said. "Keep quiet and watch."

Suddenly all the other witches, more than eighty of them, were beginning to scream and jump up out of their seats as though spikes were being stuck into their bottoms. Some were standing on chairs, some were up on the tables and all of them were wiggling about and waving their arms in the most extraordinary manner.

Then, all at once, they became quiet.

Then they stiffened. Every single witch stood there as stiff and silent as a corpse.

The whole room became deathly still.

"They're shrinking, Grandmamma!" I said. "They're shrinking just like I did!"

"I know they are," my grandmother said.

"It's the Mouse-Maker!" I cried. "Look! Some of them are growing fur on their faces! Why is it working so quickly, Grandmamma?"

"I'll tell you why," my grandmother said. "Because all of them have had massive overdoses, just like you. It's thrown the alarm-clock right out of whack!"

Everyone in the Dining-Room was standing up now to get a better view. People were moving closer. They were beginning to crowd round the two long tables. My grandmother lifted Bruno and me up so that we wouldn't miss any of the fun. In her excitement, she jumped up on to her chair so that she could see over the heads of the crowd.

In another few seconds, all the witches had completely disappeared and the tops of the two long tables were swarming with small brown mice.

All over the Dining-Room women were

screaming and strong men were turning white in the face and shouting, "It's crazy! This can't happen! Let's get the heck out of here quick!" Waiters were attacking the mice with chairs and wine-bottles and anything else that came to hand. I saw a chef in a tall white hat rushing from the kitchen brandishing a frying-pan, and another one just behind *him* was wielding a carving-knife above his head, and everyone was yelling, "Mice! Mice! Mice! We must get rid of the mice!" Only the children in the room were really enjoying it. They all seemed to know instinctively that something good was going on right there in front of them, and they were clapping and cheering and laughing like mad.

"It's time to go," my grandmother said. "Our work is done." She got down off her chair and picked up her handbag and slung it over her arm. She had me in her right hand and Bruno in her left. "Bruno," she said, "the time has come to restore you to the famous bosom of your family."

"My mum's not very crazy about mice," Bruno said.

"So I noticed," my grandmother said. "She'll just have to get used to you, won't she?"

It was not difficult to find Mr and Mrs Jenkins. You could hear Mrs Jenkins's shrill voice all over the room. "Herbert!" it was screaming. "Herbert, get me out of here! There's mice everywhere! They'll go up my skirts!" She had her arms high up around her husband and from where I was she seemed to be swinging from his neck.

My grandmother advanced upon them and thrust Bruno into Mr Jenkins's hand. "Here's your little boy," she said. "He needs to go on a diet."

"Hi, Dad!" Bruno said. "Hi, Mum!"

Mrs Jenkins screamed even louder. My grandmother, with me in her hand, turned and marched out of the room. She went straight across the hotel lobby and out through the front entrance into the open air.

Outside it was a lovely warm evening and I could hear the waves breaking on the beach just across the road from the hotel.

"Is there a taxi here?" my grandmother said to the tall doorman in his green uniform.

"Certainly, madam," he said, and he put two fingers into his mouth and blew a long shrill whistle. I watched him with envy. For weeks I had been trying to whistle like that but I hadn't succeeded once. Now I never would.

The taxi came. The driver was an oldish man with a thick black drooping moustache. The moustache hung over his mouth like the roots of some plant. "Where to, madam?" he asked. Suddenly he caught sight of me, a little mouse, nestling in my grandmother's hand. "Blimey!" he said. "What's that?"

"It's my grandson," my grandmother said. "Drive us to the station, please."

"I always liked mice," the old taxi-driver said. "I used to keep 'undreds of 'em when I was a boy. Mice is the fastest breeders in the world, did you know that, ma'am? So if 'ee's your grandson, then I reckon you'll be having a few *great* grandsons to go with 'im in a couple of weeks' time!"

"Drive us to the station, please," my

grandmother said, looking prim.

"Yes, ma'am," he said. "Right away."

My grandmother got into the back of the taxi and sat down and put me on her lap.

"Are we going home?" I asked her.

"Yes," she answered. "Back to Norway."

"Hooray!" I cried. "Oh, hooray, hooray, hooray!"

"I thought you'd like that," she said.

"But what about our luggage?"

"Who cares about luggage?" she said.

The taxi was driving through the streets of Bournemouth and this was the time of day when the pavements were crowded with holiday-makers all wandering about aimlessly with nothing to do.

"How are you feeling, my darling?" my grandmother said.

"Fine," I said. "Quite marvellous."

She began stroking the fur on the back of my neck with one finger. "We have accomplished great feats today," she said.

"It's been terrific," I said. "Absolutely terrific."

The Heart of a Mouse

It was lovely to be back in Norway once again in my grandmother's fine old house. But now that I was so small, everything looked different and it took me quite a while to find my way around. Mine was a world of carpets and table-legs and chair-legs and the little crannies behind large pieces of furniture. A closed door could not be opened and nothing could be reached that was on a table.

But after a few days, my grandmother began to invent gadgets for me in order to make life a bit easier. She got a carpenter to put together a number of slim tall stepladders and she placed one of these against each table in the house so that I could climb up whenever I wanted to. She herself invented a wonderful door-opening device made out of wires and springs and pulleys, with heavy weights dangling on cords, and soon every door in the house had a door-opener on it. All I had to do was to press my front paws on to a tiny wooden platform and hey presto, a spring would stretch and a weight would drop and the door would swing open.

Next, she rigged up an equally ingenious

system whereby I could switch on the light whenever I entered a room at night. I cannot explain how it worked because I know nothing about electricity, but there was a little button let into the floor near the door in every room in the house, and when I pressed the button gently with one paw, the light would come on. When I pressed it a second time, the light would go off again.

My grandmother made me a tiny toothbrush, using a matchstick for the handle, and into this she stuck little bits of bristle that she had snipped off one of her hairbrushes. "You *must* not get any holes in your teeth," she said. "I can't take a *mouse* to the dentist! He'd think I was crazy!"

"It's funny," I said, "but ever since I became a mouse I've hated the taste of sweets and chocolate. So I don't think I'll get any holes."

"You are still going to brush your teeth after every meal," my grandmother said. And I did.

For a bath-tub she gave me a silver sugar-basin, and I bathed in it every night before going to bed. She allowed no one else into the house, not even a servant or a cook. We kept entirely to ourselves and we were very happy in each other's company.

One evening, as I lay on my grandmother's lap in front of the fire, she said to me, "I wonder what happened to that little Bruno."

"I wouldn't be surprised if his father gave him to the hall-porter to drown in the fire-bucket," I answered.

"I'm afraid you may be right," my grandmother said. "The poor little thing."

We were silent for few minutes, my grandmother puffing away at her black cigar while I dozed comfortably in the warmth.

"Can I ask you something, Grandmamma?" I said.

"Ask me anything you like, my darling."

"How long does a mouse live?"

"Ah," she said. "I've been waiting for you to

ask me that."

There was a silence. She sat there smoking away and gazing at the fire.

"Well," I said. "How long *do* we live, us mice?"

"I have been reading about mice," she said. "I have been trying to find out everything I can about them."

"Go on then, Grandmamma. Why don't you tell me?"

"If you really want to know," she said, "I'm afraid a mouse doesn't live for a very long time."

"How long?" I asked.

"Well, an *ordinary* mouse only lives for about three years," she said. "But you are not an ordinary mouse. You are a mouse-person, and that is a very different matter."

"How different?" I asked. "How long does a a mouse-person live, Grandmamma?"

"Longer," she said. "Much longer."

"How much longer?" I asked.

"A mouse-person will almost certainly live for three times as long as an ordinary mouse," my grandmother said. "About nine years."

"Good!" I cried. "That's great! It's the best news I've ever had!"

"Why do you say that?" she asked, surprised.

"Because I would never want to live longer than you," I said. "I couldn't stand being looked after by anybody else."

There was a short silence. She had a way of fondling me behind the ears with the tip of one finger. It felt lovely.

"How old are *you*, Grandmamma?" I asked.

"I'm eighty-six," she said.

"Will you live another eight or nine years?"

"I might," she said. "With a bit of luck."

"You've got to," I said. "Because by then I'll be a very old mouse and you'll be a very old grandmother and soon after that we'll both die together."

"That would be perfect," she said.

I had a little doze after that. I just shut my eyes and thought of nothing and felt at peace with the world.

"Would you like me to tell you something about yourself that is very interesting?" my grandmother said.

"Yes please, Grandmamma," I said, without opening my eyes.

"I couldn't believe it at first, but apparently it's quite true," she said.

"What is it?" I asked.

"The heart of a mouse," she said, "and that means *your* heart, is beating at the rate of *five hundred times a minute*! Isn't that amazing?"

"That's not possible," I said, opening my eyes wide.

"It's as true as I'm sitting here," she said. "It's a sort of miracle."

"That's nearly nine beats every second!" I cried, working it out in my head.

"Correct," she said. "Your heart is going so fast it's impossible to hear the separate beats. All one hears is a soft humming sound."

She was wearing a lace dress and the lace

kept tickling my nose. I had to rest my head on my front paws.

"Have *you* ever heard my heart humming away, Grandmamma?" I asked her.

"Often," she said. "I hear it when you are lying very close to me on the pillow at night."

The two of us remained silent in front of the fire for a long time after that, thinking about these wonderful things.

"My darling," she said at last, "are you sure you don't mind being a mouse for the rest of your life?"

"I don't mind at all," I said. "It doesn't matter who you are or what you look like so long as somebody loves you."

It's Off to Work We Go!

For supper that evening my grandmother had a plain omelette and one slice of bread. I had a piece of that brown Norwegian goats' milk cheese known as *gjetost* which I had loved even when I was a boy. We ate in front of the fire, my grandmother in her armchair and me on the table with my cheese on a small plate.

"Grandmamma," I said, "now that we have done away with The Grand High Witch, will all the other witches in the world gradually disappear?"

"I'm quite sure they won't," she answered.

I stopped chewing and stared at her. "But they *must*!" I cried. "Surely they must!"

"I'm afraid not," she said.

"But if she's not there any longer how are they going to get all the money they need? And who is going to give them orders and jazz them up at the Annual Meetings and invent all their magic formulas for them?"

"When a queen bee dies, there is always another queen in the hive ready to take her place," my grandmother said. "It's the same with witches. In the great Headquarters where

The Grand High Witch lives, there is always another Grand High Witch waiting in the wings to take over should anything happen."

"Oh no!" I cried. "That means everything we did was for nothing! Have I become a mouse for nothing at all?"

"We saved the children of England," she said. "I don't call that nothing."

"I know, I know!" I cried. "But that's not nearly good enough! I felt sure that all the witches of the world would slowly fade away after we had got rid of their leader! Now you tell me everything is going to go on just the same as before!"

"Not exactly as before," my grandmother said. "For instance, there are no longer any witches in England. That's quite a triumph, isn't it?"

"But what about the rest of the world?" I cried. "What about America and France and Holland and Germany? And what about Norway?"

"You must not think I have been sitting back and doing nothing these last few days," she said. "I have been giving a great deal of thought and time to that particular problem."

I was looking up at her face when she said

this, and all at once I noticed that a little secret smile was beginning to spread slowly around her eyes and the corners of her mouth. "Why are you smiling, Grandmamma?" I asked her.

"I have some rather interesting news for you," she said.

"What news?"

"Shall I tell it to you right from the beginning?"

"Yes please," I said. "I like good news."

She had finished her omelette, and I had had enough of my cheese. She wiped her lips with a napkin and said, "As soon as we arrived back in Norway, I picked up the telephone and made a call to England."

"Who in England, Grandmamma?"

"To the Chief of Police in Bournemouth, my darling. I told him I was the Chief of Police for the whole of Norway and that I was interested in the peculiar happenings that had taken place recently in the Hotel Magnificent."

"Now hang on a sec, Grandmamma," I said. "There's no way an English policeman is going to believe that *you* are the Head of the Norwegian Police."

"I am very good at imitating a man's voice," she said. "Of course he believed me. The policeman in Bournemouth was honoured to get a call from the Chief of Police for the whole of Norway."

"So what did you ask him?"

"I asked him for the name and address of the lady who had been living in Room 454 in the Hotel Magnificent, the one who disappeared."

"You mean The Grand High Witch!" I cried.

"Yes, my darling."

"And did he give it to you?"

"Naturally he gave it to me. One policeman will always help another policeman."

"By golly, you've got a nerve. Grandmamma!"

"I wanted her address," my grandmother said.

"But did he *know* her address?"

"He did indeed. They had found her passport in her room and her address was in it. It was also in the hotel register. Everyone who stays in an hotel has to put a name and address in the book."

"But surely The Grand High Witch wouldn't have put her *real* name and address in the hotel register?" I said.

"Why ever not?" my grandmother said. "Nobody in the world had the faintest idea who she was except the other witches. Wherever she went, people simply knew her as a nice lady. *You*, my darling, and *you alone*, were the only non-witch ever to see her with her mask off. Even in her home district, in the village where she lived, people knew her as a kindly and very wealthy Baroness who gave large sums of money to charity. I have checked up on that."

I was getting excited now. "And that address you got, Grandmamma, that must have been the secret Headquarters of The Grand High Witch."

"It still is," my grandmother said. "And that will be where the new Grand High Witch is certain to be living at this very moment with her retinue of special Assistant Witches. Important rulers are always surrounded by a large retinue of assistants."

"Where is her Headquarters, Grandmamma?" I cried. "Tell me quick where it is!"

"It is a Castle," my grandmother said. "And the fascinating thing is that in that Castle will be all the names and addresses of all the witches in the world! How else could a Grand High Witch run her business? How else could she summon the witches of the various countries to their Annual Meetings?"

"Where is the Castle, Grandmamma?" I cried impatiently. "Which country? Tell me quick!"

"Guess," she said.

"Norway!" I cried.

"Right first time!" she answered. "High up in the mountains above a small village."

This was thrilling news. I did a little dance of excitement on the table-top. My grandmother was getting pretty worked up herself and now she heaved herself out of her chair and began pacing up and down the room,

thumping the carpet with her stick.

"So we have work to do, you and I!" she cried out. "We have a great task ahead of us! Thank heavens you are a mouse! A mouse can go anywhere! All I'll have to do is put you down somewhere near The Grand High Witch's Castle and you will very easily be able to get inside it and creep around looking and listening to your heart's content!"

"I will! I will!" I answered. "No one will ever see me! Moving about in a big Castle will be child's play compared with going into a crowded kitchen full of cooks and waiters!"

"You could spend *days* in there if necessary!" my grandmother cried. In her excitement she was waving her stick all over the place, and suddenly she knocked over a tall and very beautiful vase that went crashing on to the floor and smashed into a million pieces. "Forget it," she said. "It's only Ming. You could spend *weeks* in that Castle if you wanted to and

they'd never know you were there! I myself would get a room in the village and you could sneak out of the Castle and have supper with me every night and tell me what was going on."

"I could! I could!" I cried out. "And inside the Castle I could go snooping around simply everywhere!"

"But your main job, of course," my grandmother said, "would be to destroy every witch in the place. That really *would* be the end of the whole organisation!"

"*Me* destroy *them*?" I cried. "How could I do that?"

"Can't you guess?" she said.

"Tell me," I said.

"Mouse-Maker!" my grandmother shouted. "Formula 86 Delayed Action Mouse-Maker all over again! You will feed it to everyone in the Castle by putting drops of it into their food! You do remember the recipe, don't you?"

"Every bit of it!" I answered. "You mean we're going to make it ourselves?"

"Why not?" she cried. "If *they* can make it, so can we! It's just a question of knowing what goes into it!"

"Who's going to climb up the tall trees to get the gruntles' eggs?" I asked her.

"I will!" she cried. "I'll do it myself! There's plenty of life in this old dog yet!"

"I think I'd better do that part of it, Grandmamma. You might come a cropper."

"Those are just details!" she cried, waving her stick again. "We shall let nothing stand in our way!"

"And what happens after that?" I asked her. "After every new Grand High Witch and everyone else in the Castle have been turned into mice?"

"Then the Castle will be completely empty and I shall come in and join you and . . ."

"Wait!" I cried. "Hold on, Grandmamma! I've just had a nasty thought!"

"What nasty thought?" she said.

"When the Mouse-Maker turned *me* into a mouse," I said, "I didn't become just any old ordinary mouse that you catch with mouse-traps. I became a talking thinking intelligent mouse-person who wouldn't go *near* a mouse-trap!"

My grandmother stopped dead in her tracks. She already knew what was coming next.

"Therefore," I went on, "if we use the Mouse-Maker to turn the new Grand High

Witch and all the other witches in the Castle into mice, the whole place will be swarming with very clever, very nasty, very dangerous talking thinking mouse-witches! They'll all be witches in mouse's clothing. And that", I added, "could be very horrible indeed."

"By golly, you're right!" she cried. "That never occurred to me!"

"I couldn't possibly take on a castleful of mouse-witches," I said.

"Nor could I," she said. "They'd have to be got rid of at once. They'd have to be smashed and bashed and chopped up into little pieces exactly as they were in the Hotel Magnificent."

"I'm not doing that," I said. "I couldn't anyway. I don't think you could either, Grandmamma. And mouse-traps wouldn't be the slightest use. By the way," I added, "The Grand High Witch who did me in was wrong about mouse-traps wasn't she?"

"Yes, yes," my grandmother said impatiently. "But I'm not concerned with *that* Grand High Witch. She's been chopped up long ago by the hotel chef. It's the *new* Grand High Witch we've got to deal with now, the one up in the Castle, and all her assistants. A Grand High

Witch is bad enough when she's disguised as a lady, but just think of what she could do if she were a mouse! She could go anywhere!"

"I've got it!" I shouted, leaping about a foot in the air. "I've got the answer!"

"Tell me!" my grandmother snapped.

"The answer is CATS!" I shouted. "Bring on the cats!"

My grandmother stared at me. Then a great grin spread over her face and she shouted, "It's brilliant! Absolutely brilliant!"

"Shove half-a-dozen cats into that Castle," I cried, "and they'll kill every mouse in the place in five minutes, I don't care how clever they are!"

"You're a magician!" my grandmother shouted, starting to wave her stick about once again.

"Look out for the vases, Grandmamma!"

"To heck with the vases!" she shouted. "I'm so thrilled I don't care if I break the lot!"

"Just one thing," I said. "You've got to make absolutely sure I'm well out of the way myself before you put the cats in."

"That's a promise," she said.

"What will we do after the cats have killed all the mice?" I asked her.

"I'll take all the cats back to the village and

then you and I will have the Castle completely to ourselves."

"And then?" I said.

"Then we shall go through the records and get the names and addresses of all the witches in the whole wide world!"

"And after that?" I said, quivering with excitement.

"After that, my darling, the greatest task of all will begin for you and me! We shall pack our bags and go travelling all over the world! In every country we visit, we shall seek out the houses where the witches are living! We shall find each house, one by one, and having found it, you will creep inside and leave your little drops of deadly Mouse-Maker in the bread, or the cornflakes, or the rice-pudding or whatever food you see lying about. It will be a triumph, my darling! A colossal unbeatable triumph. We shall do it entirely by ourselves, just you and me! That will be our work for the rest of our lives!"

My grandmother picked me up off the table and kissed me on the nose. "Oh, my goodness me, we're going to be busy these next few weeks and months and years!" she cried.

"I think we are," I said. "But what fun and

excitement it's going to be!"

"You can say that again!" my grandmother cried, giving me another kiss. "I can't wait to get started!"

There's more to Roald Dahl than great stories . . .

Did you know that 10% of author royalties* from this book go to help the work of the Roald Dahl charities?

ROALD DAHL'S Marvellous Children's Charity

Roald Dahl's Marvellous Children's Charity aims to raise as much money as possible to make seriously ill children's lives better because it believes that every child has the right to a marvellous life.

This marvellous charity helps thousands of children each year in the UK living with serious conditions of the blood and the brain – causes important to Roald Dahl in his lifetime.

Whether by providing nurses, equipment, carers or toys, the charity helps to care for children with conditions including acquired brain injury, epilepsy and blood disorders such as sickle cell disease. It can be very hard for families to care for a child with one of these serious or life-threatening conditions and the charity believes that helping them is a truly marvellous thing to do.

Can you do something marvellous to help others?
Find out how at **www.marvellouschildrenscharity.org**

* Donated royalties are net of commission

The Roald Dahl Museum and Story Centre, based in Great Missenden just outside London, is in the Buckinghamshire village where Roald Dahl lived and wrote. At the heart of the Museum, intended to inspire a love of reading and writing, is his unique archive of letters and manuscripts. As well as two fun-packed biographical galleries, the Museum boasts an interactive Story Centre. It is a place for the family, teachers and their pupils to explore the exciting world of creativity and literacy.

www.roalddahlmuseum.org